BATTERY LIFE

BATTERY LIFE

Brennan Gilpatrick
& Gregory Lang

**BLACK
STONE**
PUBLISHING

Printed in the United States of America

First edition: 2023
ISBN 979-8-200-81333-9
Fiction / Science Fiction / General

Version 1

Blackstone Publishing
31 Mistletoe Rd.
Ashland, OR 97520

www.BlackstonePublishing.com

BATTERY LIFE

PROLOGUE

A Ruin

A light tremor shook the mound of junk, sending rusty nails and broken glass tumbling in every direction. To the naked eye, the disturbance was random—an effect without a cause. It might have startled onlookers, but there were none present. All eyes in the world were pointed elsewhere.

Gradually, the ruckus settled. The trash heap fell back into its utter stillness, and a deep quiet returned to the courthouse. It used to be called a courthouse, anyway. Now it was a nameless place with a military cargo plane lodged through its ceiling, the contents of which covered the floor in a festering pile. Concrete rubble blocked the windows and doors, sealing the chamber off from its long-dead community. Like many places in the Junkyard, it was silent. It had been that way for centuries.

Until now.

Virgil burst from the mound, scattering shards of scrap metal. He brushed the nails and broken glass from his beard, tore off his gas mask, and lifted the fruits of his dumpster dive to eye level: one box filled with old plasma-rifle components; two bionic hands, slightly rusted but operational; and a motherboard in pristine condition. This was good junk. Damn good junk. When Virgil finished up here, he would drive to the nearest village and trade these gems for whatever supplies he needed.

Virgil was a junkie. That was what junkies did.

To most junkies, finding these treasures would have been cause for celebration. But to *this* junkie, they were mere consolation prizes. Virgil had come to this forgotten place in pursuit of something, and it wasn't here. After four months of searching—an eternity in Junkyard time—he was beginning to think that it wasn't anywhere. He would have spat a disdainful loogie on the courthouse floor just then, but his body lacked the water for such a gesture. This wild-goose chase had all but drained his living supplies, hence the need to dig around for trade goods in the first place.

Virgil satiated his rage by flipping a middle finger to the room around him, then he moved on.

He stuffed the junk into his backpack and clambered up the mound, toward a fracture between the ceiling and the wrecked plane. As he climbed, Virgil caught glimpses of himself mirrored in bits of glass bedazzling the trash heap. He wore combat boots, patchy cargo pants, a brown hooded trench coat, and a steel vest designed to repel laser fire. An array of little bags and pouches hung from his belt, as did a knife holster and a magnum handgun old enough to shoot actual bullets. He grimaced a bit at the sight of his own face, at the toll that time and sickness had taken there, but the disgust was only half genuine. Virgil was not a vain man, and he felt the loss of beauty was no great loss at all. Besides, no one reached his age in the Junkyard with their looks intact. He was lucky to have all his limbs.

Virgil pulled himself through the roof, then onto his feet, leaning on the cargo plane for support. The sun was on its way down, stretching shadows, lighting the polluted sky in a way that reminded him of the Firelands. He could see for miles up here, and in one last desperate attempt to find what he was looking for, he scanned his surroundings.

The junkie found himself at the center of an aircraft graveyard. Something had taken out a whole armada of planes and hovertanks, raining them down upon a small desert township like kamikaze angels. At the edge of town, he could see the sheets of tin hiding his vehicle, gear, and near-empty water jug from sight. He'd gotten damn good at impromptu camouflage over the years, and even from this bird's-eye view, the old jeep and trailer were totally invisible.

He looked beyond, into the sprawling wastes of the Junkyard.

He saw dust devils rollick over toxic plains. Rolling dunes caked in trash, *made* of trash. To the east, he saw the distant patch of gray smog forever hanging between the sky and the megalopolis of Jericho—where they still had skyscrapers, rent-a-cops, and other such luxuries. To the west, slag fields morphed into rocky hills. To the north: more of the same.

Virgil weighed his options. He had come to this place on a false lead, and now his target's trail was cold and dead. Was it finally time to throw in the towel? Was it finally time to go home?

Not quite, cabrón.

The pain came out of nowhere, a sucker punch.

First, waves of nausea. Everything tilted around him, blurring into a shapeless cyclone. Then came the fire, like his organs were burning through his skin. Hazy vision, boiling blood, the works. Virgil collapsed and nearly slid off the rooftop, saved only by the grace of a guardrail. In his sizzling brain, he cursed his own stupid negligence. He should have seen this coming.

The pain wasn't new to him. To survive in the Junkyard, you had to accept a few hard facts. Chief among them: the world was toxic and everyone was sick. Everyone suffered a lifelong reliance on a drug that could halt the effects of radiation poisoning and replace the blood cells their bodies had lost. Temporarily, of course. Everything was temporary in the Junkyard.

Side effects may include loss of taste, respiratory illness, and varying degrees of brain damage.

Junkies had it the worst. They didn't get to live in villages or walled Jericho; they were nomads. Everything, from the wind on their backs to the machine parts in their trucks, pulsed with harmful radiation. All junkies had the Junkyard Blues. It was just another occupational hazard, albeit a chronic one. Like his peers, Virgil didn't view himself as "sick." He was just low. Low on Battery.

Time to recharge.

Blindly, he rummaged through his backpack until he felt the cold aluminum tube of an inhaler. He pulled it out, and even through the

Blues, he could make out the green glow of a liquid Battery capsule lodged within. A good junkie always reloaded their inhaler after each use. A good junkie was a junkie who wasn't dead.

Trembling, Virgil lifted the inhaler to his lips, pressed the eject button, and a rush of medicinal vapor exploded into his lungs. The Battery felt like a million needles scraping down his throat, smelled like formaldehyde, and tasted like acid. He gagged, coughing up puffs of emerald smoke. The dose was still good.

He rolled onto his back, gasping. Sight returned. The pain and nausea faded away; all that was left was a nagging thirst. Funny, how he'd understocked his water but brought more than enough Battery. A junkie's priorities.

Once the inhaler was refilled and packed away, Virgil staggered to a broken plane wing bridging the roof and the ground below. Four months of work and he'd reached a dead end, and Virgil needed water. It was time to cut his losses.

A Village

"Has anyone seen Cassy?" Chief Orro called down to the sweaty workers on the factory floor.

The computer that ran their automated assembly line had broken down weeks ago, and now it was all hands on deck. Their village was built out of a renovated Nutribrik factory, and those little nutrient bars were the community's only export. As of last week, those bars weren't going to cook themselves.

"Cassy? Anyone?" Orro called again. The workers who could hear him over the industrial blenders and pounding hydraulic stampers shook their heads, and Orro rushed back to the factory's corporate complex. The offices here had been converted into family apartments, and he checked for Cassy in each one. No dice.

Orro found only children playing out in the factory yard; all the adults were inside working. He made a mental list of all the places he had looked. Cassy's apartment. The cafeteria. The parking garage. It suddenly occurred to him that she may have left without saying good-bye, and the sadness from that was unbearable. Sure, their argument from the night before had grown heated, but she wouldn't hurt him like that. Would she?

"Fungi house," Otto blurted out, scaring a kid nearby.

A memory from Cassy's childhood suddenly came to him; she used to love sneaking into the fungi house after dark. It smelled as foul to her as it did to anyone, but Cassy always had a fascination with bizarre things. It was her best and most annoying quality.

The fungi house was a tin hovel behind the main factory building. Its seams were taped down with plastic sheets to keep in the moisture. Constructing this hut was easily the proudest moment of Chief Orro's reign. The village no longer relied on fungi farms to provide ingredients; their Nutribriks were 100 percent homemade. That boosted net profits considerably.

Orro entered the humid space, ignoring the brown liquid that dripped from the ceiling onto his tattered blazer. He found Cassy deep in the mushroom jungle, her back turned as she groped and kissed someone in the shadows. Her clothes were still on, thank god.

Orro coughed.

Cassy whipped around with a start, and her partner stepped timidly into the light. It was Kal, the village's only resident cyborg. The steel plating on his head glistened with water beads, and a red light blinked from the processing unit on his left temple.

"Can I get a word with my sister?" Orro asked.

Gaze averted, Kal hurried past the chief. Orro watched him leave, glimpsing the fiber-optic cable running along his spine, just under the skin. Kal was a good kid. Even after he finished paying off his cybersurgery debt, even after the loyalty kill switch had been removed from his skull, he had chosen to stay and help around the factory. Orro didn't mind that Kal had the hots for Cassy. If only Cassy liked him back enough—maybe then she'd stick around too.

"Easily the weirdest place for that," Orro said, once they were alone.

Cassy shrugged, and her oversized hunting jacket rustled around her shoulders. "It's secluded. I don't mind the smell, and Kal can't smell anything anyway."

"He going with you?" Orro asked.

"Not a chance. He loves it here. You're like family to him."

"We're your family too, *chamaca*—" Orro caught himself falling into last night's argument. He pulled his inhaler out of his breast pocket, took a hit of Battery. He didn't feel the Junkyard Blues yet, but the motions gave him time to cool down. Time to find the right words.

"What's your plan?" he asked, coughing up green.

"I'll find Caravan first," Cassy said, "trade some Nutribriks to board. See if I can find a junkie who's taking apprentices."

"Do junkies do that?" Orro asked.

"I'll find out."

Orro approached his kid sister, footsteps muffled in the compost carpet between them. "You don't know what it's like out there. If the roadkillers don't get you, the Peacekeepers will. Or the bugs. Or you'll just run out of water."

Cassy took her brother's hands and pressed them to her cheeks, like she did when they were children. Orro tried to stifle the tears behind his eyes, but it was a fool's errand.

"I hear you," Cassy said. "I understand. But I have to go. Townie life isn't for me. I want to see the Junkyard, as much of it as I can."

Orro exhaled, a shaky hybrid between a sigh and a sob. He was saying goodbye to the only blood family he had left.

Hand in hand, they left the fungi house together.

A Fortress

Unblinking, the Masked Man looked to the north. He studied the noxious red sky, his rocky muscles tense with anticipation. Here was a man who believed in destiny, and destiny had made him a promise one year ago. Today was the day it delivered. Today he would have everything he needed to make the world a better place.

He stood on a railed balcony high above the Heap—the closest thing the anarchistic Junkyard had to a capital city. Jericho was another universe, inaccessible behind its great wall. The Heap was where all the junkies came to deal their goods, where the great mercenary clans chose to call home. When he looked down, the Masked Man could see every corner of the shanty metropolis laid out before him. *His* shanty metropolis, now. He could hear the aftershocks of his conquest echoing from below. Civilian mobs quelled. Order beating chaos into submission. The Masked Man took no pleasure in such violence, but he was an agent of peace. Peace required sacrifice.

He drowned out the screams and plasma gunshots, focusing instead on the sweet musical whispers at the edge of his consciousness. Their singsong messages defined him, and soon, they would redefine the Junkyard entirely.

The Masked Man grinned, still watching the northern sky. The future was coming, and it belonged to him.

A deep moan bellowed from the east.

It was an odd noise, like a thunderclap on a loop. All commotion ceased in the city below, and the Masked Man turned to see a shadow filling the distant clouds. It grew denser, stretched wider in every direction, painting the land beneath in artificial night.

The moan built to a crescendo. The Masked Man held his breath.

A flaming needle punctured the sky, ripping the clouds in two. It seemed to fall in slow motion, and a cascade of twisting metal poured after it. Like a top spinning off its axis, the structure entered the atmosphere in one unfathomable piece, but as it descended, the cone of its body shattered in half, and one of its rings snapped away on its own. Three distinct pieces collided with the Junkyard, launching a sandstorm from the impact.

A powerful tremor shook the earth.

The Masked Man gripped the balcony's rail while some of the

shabbier buildings below crumbled into the streets. More screams, followed by more gunshots. Before the tectonic shift even had time to settle, the Heap's pandemonium resumed in full force.

Behind the Masked Man, an old velvet curtain whipped to the side. Dr. Isaac ran onto the balcony, his dirty lab coat flapping in the wind.

"It's farther east than you predicted," the Masked Man said.

Dr. Isaac gaped at the rising dust and said nothing.

"Send word to Sixty-Seven. It needs to reach the crash site before the junkies pick it clean. Probably a day's journey from where we stationed it, maybe two. Tell it to travel without stopping."

"But what about the bounty on Sixty-Seven's head?" Dr. Isaac asked, rousing from his shock. "We agreed it should only travel at night."

"It needs to move now."

The Masked Man turned around, and Dr. Isaac quickly averted his eyes. Even after all this time, the scientist still couldn't bring himself to look at that mask for too long.

"We can't afford to play it safe now, my friend," the Masked Man said. "All the pieces are in place. Time to save the world."

This was really happening. Their plan, their shared delusion, would truly come to pass.

Dr. Isaac swallowed hard. "As you wish."

When they were back in the factory yard, Chief Orro pulled Cassy aside. "If I really can't stop you from leaving, I want you to have this."

He presented a small cardboard box from his pocket. Inside, Cassy found two thin rolls of yellowing paper, both stuffed with dry brown flakes of . . . something.

"They're cigarettes," Orro explained, "made with tobacco. Real tobacco."

Cassy wrinkled her nose. "But tobacco's been—"

"I thought so too. But I met a guy a few years back. Only junkie on the planet who sells them. Cost me a fortune in Nutribriks."

Cassy held the box to her chest. If what her brother said was true, then it was the most valuable thing she had ever seen. "What do I do with them?"

"Smoke one," Orro said, "sell the other. Should get you started on the right foot."

Cassy hugged her brother tighter than either of them thought possible. But as they both wept over the impending goodbye, night fell too early over the village.

No, not night. The sun wouldn't set for another hour, and not this quickly. The darkness falling over them was unnatural, and it was all-consuming. The yard, the factory, the fungi house, all of it slipped into the shadow's embrace.

Orro and Cassy looked up.

With a demonic roar, the heavens burned away. A blinding fire consumed the night, drenching the village in a guttering nether-blaze. No more clouds. Only metal, stretching as far as the eye could see, dropping down from outer space in a flaming aura. Getting bigger. *Closer.*

Locked in each other's arms, the siblings watched their factory obliterate from the roof down. The fungi house followed.

A scorching heat. A crushing pain. Then nothing. Nothing at all.

"Hot damn!"

Virgil nearly lost his balance. He was surfing down the broken plane wing, halfway to ground level, when a flickering dot more brilliant than the sun fell through the sky. It was a ways off, no bigger than Virgil's palm from this distance, but he knew that to burn that bright from that far away, you had to be pretty damn hot. Pretty damn big. Even after it disappeared, he could still see its afterglow lingering in the air.

That's when a voice crackled from the edge of town, under the tin sheets hiding his vehicle. "*Virgil?*" a tired voice called. "*Virgil, you read?*"

Virgil wasted no time sliding down the wing and running to his jeep. A CB radio was rigged to the central console, tuned to a very specific frequency. He reached under the tin slab, felt for the radio mic, and yanked it up to his mouth.

"I read you, Hobble," he said, his own voice gravelly and winded.

"*I wish you wouldn't call me that,*" Hobble complained.

Virgil frowned. "Everybody calls you that. *You* call you that."

"*Yeah, and I'm sick of it. I've got more going on than a missing leg. I got good eyes. Folks could call me 'Eagle Eyes'*—"

Virgil cut in, "If you got something for me, I'll call you whatever the hell you want."

He heard the agitated *click-whoosh-cough* from Hobble taking a Battery hit, then: "*You see that thing fall from the sky,* culero?"

"Yup," Virgil confirmed.

"*I saw a tribe of Peacekeepers headed right for it. Looked like one of them was wearing a mask. Freakiest thing I ever seen.*"

Virgil almost lost his balance again. *That was it. That was the target.* "I thought they only traveled at night."

"*Guess you were wrong,*" Hobble said. "*You gonna check it out?*"

Virgil paused, leaving white noise to fill the silence. Hobble was stationed far to the north, meaning the Peacekeepers were farther from the glowing whatever-it-was than Virgil. Virgil could beat them there. He knew he could.

"Good work," Virgil said. "I owe ya one, Bird Eye."

"*No, it's Eagle*—"

"Over and out."

Virgil hung up the mic.

CHAPTER 1

One Day Earlier

The quakes were getting worse, and Diane knew it.

She'd timed the last one. It had struck without warning, turning Cabin Three-One-Seven—her broom closet of a living space—upside-down. It tore the pictures off her aseptic chrome walls, throwing a slideshow of mountains, cities, and other long-lost places into a mad flurry. It launched her oatmeal out of its bowl, spraying her with a mushy, flavorless geyser. Diane tried to dive under her bunk, but the quake had other plans. Gravity dissipated midleap, and she joined the photographs and oatmeal in a weightless dance without rhythm or tempo: tossing, spinning, until physics came crashing back, and she found herself pinned to the floor with no hope for movement, no hope to do anything but wait.

After sixty seconds of this horrible cycle, the chaos ended. The gravity field stabilized. The photos came to rest. The oatmeal oozed from the ceiling, over Diane's burgundy jumpsuit, and all through her jet-black hair. There had been three quakes the previous day, roughly thirty over the past month. None of them had made a mess like this. None of them had lasted this long.

Shaking, Diane rinsed off in the sink two feet away from her pillow. As she watched her oatmeal vanish down the vacuum drain, a familiar tone chimed out from a speaker in the ceiling. A familiar voice followed it.

"Good morning, colonists! This is your Caretaker speaking . . ."

Despite the recent trauma, Diane couldn't help but smile. The Caretaker began all of his announcements with a formal introduction, as if she hadn't heard his cheery voice each day for the seventeen orbits she had been alive.

"As I'm sure you noticed, we're experiencing a bit more turbulence this morning. While this sequence of solar flares is lasting longer than anticipated, I want to remind you it's nothing our shields can't handle. Our orbit is unaffected. All systems are online. Cradle *flies on."*

Another chime to punctuate, and the speaker fell silent.

Solar flares? That made no sense. In Diane's experience, solar flares shook *Cradle* with quick, pulsing vibrations. They messed with electronics, made the LED lights flicker and strobe. None of that had happened just now. This felt like a problem with the gravity. It had to be.

But the Caretaker said it was solar flares, and the Caretaker's word was final.

Diane wiped her head with a towel, doing her best to dry up the water and the unwanted feeling that something was terribly wrong. She knew what would happen if this fear received a voice. She knew exactly what everyone would say: the same thing they had been saying since "the accident" one orbit ago. For the sake of time, she delivered a more concise version of that message to herself: "Shut up, Diane. You're being paranoid."

There. That was easy.

Head dry, Diane took one last look around as she made the low-gravity hop toward the cabin's automatic door. The ceiling oatmeal would turn stalactite if she left it uncleaned, but unfortunately it and the downed photographs would have to wait. She was already late for her Session, and tardiness was unacceptable. Hopefully, the quake had put everyone else on *Cradle* behind schedule too. An entire space station fighting against the clock . . . what an image.

The door hissed open, and Diane left Cabin Three-One-Seven behind.

The connecting residence hall was full of people—an echo chamber of laughter, a metal grid of catwalks and ladders ringing with upbeat conversation.

"That was wild!"

"One way to get out of bed!"

"A . . . roller coaster! Is that what they were called?"

Recently, Diane had learned the importance of *reading the room*, and while doing so now in Residential Block Three, she understood that her creeping dread was hers alone. So she put on a smile, took a deep breath of recycled air, and joined the flow of burgundy jumpsuits racing after lost time. Her neighbors ranged from eleven- to twenty-year-olds, from children who had just graduated Block Two all the way to young adults who were an orbit away from Block Four. One hundred souls in total, bounding along like rubber balls. Springy, but not without weight. Care-free, but not without direction. They flew where their schedules tossed them, and they were happy to do it. They had never known any other way.

Once, when she was still new to Cabin Three-One-Seven, Diane had asked a man from Block Five what would happen if *Cradle* ran out of rooms. The question earned her a laugh, a condescending pat on the shoulder, and a brief lesson on population control. That was the day she learned where babies come from: incubation vats.

Block Three poured its occupants into the Residential Junction, a wide foam-padded cylinder linking all six blocks to *Cradle* proper. One hundred bodies became four hundred fifty; the infants in Block One never left their nursery. Moving with the herd, Diane took stock of the various cliques gathering around her. Block Sixers hung in the back, chatting idly. Block Twos scampered after their assigned Nurse droids— black orbs that floated just ahead of the pack, singing their children's names in sweet arpeggiated voices.

Crammed in the middle, Diane spotted three familiar faces: the last three colonists her age willing to pretend her "accident" had never happened. They were the closest thing she had to friends, and as her Sessions made abundantly clear, friends were important to have.

She wiggled her way toward the trio like a rogue blood cell travers- ing a bleach-white vein.

"I'm telling you, there's no other explanation!" Phillip Three-Six-Two was saying to the others. He had green eyes that twinkled when he spoke and front teeth ever-so-slightly crooked. These were the only features distinguishing him from Gareth Three-One-Six, who smiled with perfect teeth as Phillip ranted, watching him with hazel eyes. *Cradle* made a point to keep its genetic combinations as versatile as possible, but occasional overlaps did occur.

"That's so dumb!" laughed Jessica Three-Three-Two, the final member of the trio. She had Diane's hair, but nothing else in common. "Beyond dumb."

"What's dumb?" Diane said as she reached the circle. The others winced a little at the sound of her voice, so quick it was almost imperceptible. They had grown very skilled at hiding this reaction, and Diane had become an expert at ignoring it.

"We're talking about what's *really* wrong with *Cradle*," Gareth said.

Diane's heartbeat quickened. Did others doubt the Caretaker's story too?

"Phillip thinks it's aliens," Gareth continued.

Phillip waved his hands emphatically. "They're hiding in the space junk! They want to eat our brains!"

He burst out laughing, and Diane did her best to not look disappointed. They were joking. Of course they were joking.

Gareth shook his head. "You got to quit watching those old horror movies in Archive. They're rotting your brain."

"Which means I'm safe from the aliens," Phillip sneered.

"What *do* you think's causing the quakes?" Diane asked Gareth. That was her default social strategy. Engage without offending. Ask fun questions. Keep it light.

Gareth mulled the question over for a moment, then brightened. "Easy! The war on Earth."

Jessica rolled her eyes. "Oh, it's *Earth* now!"

"Why not?" Gareth said. "They want to shoot us down, steal *Cradle*'s juicy tech. That's why Mr. Armstrong put those dumb palm-scanner locks on everything."

Gareth looked to Phillip, and the two shared a mock "eureka" moment. Diane giggled with them. It was an old *Cradle* conspiracy theory, like gremlins. Electrical problems? Must be an attack from Earth. Bellyache? Those pesky Earthlings poisoned your food. It never failed to get a laugh. Except with Jessica. She had grown tired of the old gag.

"If there are still people on Earth," she said, "they're throwing sticks and stones."

"Okay, buzzkill," Phillip said. "What's your take?"

Jessica struggled to think of something clever. "I don't know . . . Maybe the Gravity Core's going to explode?"

Diane felt another surge of excitement.

Phillip groaned. "Come on, you can do better—"

"That's what I'm thinking!" Diane said to Jessica. "Or something like that."

Diane opened up to the others, tact forgotten, relieved to be speaking her fears aloud. "I had photographs on my walls, and the turbulence . . . it didn't just knock them off. They were flying all over the place. Light, heavy. Light, heavy. It feels like disruptions in the gravity field, right? And if the Core gives out . . . I mean, even if we don't get dragged down to Earth, there'd be nothing to keep the space junk from tearing us to pieces—"

Diane stopped. She saw the way the others were looking at her, and she immediately realized her mistake. Her error in *reading the room*.

The more she discussed her theory, the more she felt convinced that it was true. But clearly, the idea had never even occurred to the others. They lived in the lighthearted reality of a *Cradle* everlasting, and that left no room for a doomsday scenario. It wasn't just scary; it was utterly insane. Diane had known they might react this way, but she was desperate to get the dread off her chest. She had taken things to a heavy place, and now they were looking at her like she was an alien or a savage from Earth. She knew the look well.

"Um," Jessica said, trying to break the awkwardness, "good thing it's just solar flares."

"But they don't feel like solar flares," Diane said. "Can't you feel that?"

"Then why did the Caretaker tell us they were?" Gareth asked.

There it was. The question Diane had been asking herself all month. The missing piece of an impossible puzzle.

Why would the Caretaker lie?

If something was wrong with the Gravity Core, and *Cradle* was in mortal jeopardy, why wouldn't the Caretaker just tell them? The sooner they knew, the sooner they could make repairs or begin evacuation.

Why would the Caretaker lie? Diane could offer no good answer, so she salvaged her smile and tried to laugh the whole thing off. "I was just kidding. Obviously."

"Sure," Phillip said, but he wasn't convinced. None of them were. Diane could see it in their faces.

At least her social blunder made the walk go by faster. Before she knew it, Diane was stepping out from the Residential Junction, through an archway of blue neon lights, and into the Central Atrium. Here, the burgundy jumpsuits scattered in all directions. The Fours, Fivers, and Sixers drifted off to their morning tasks, passing into corridors labeled "Thermal Control," "Incubation Lab," "Nutrient Recycling," et cetera. Most of the Threes rushed after them, eager to begin another day of hands-on job shadowing.

Meanwhile, Diane froze. She stood on the walkway lining the atrium's second story, gazing ahead. The chamber's opposite wall was made entirely of glass, three stories tall, shatterproof and UV filtered. The other colonists eyed Diane warily as they passed her, but she had forgotten all about them.

She did this every time she saw the Earth.

Through the panoramic window, a nightmare world blotted out the stars. If it harbored any continents still, they were lost beneath a violent maelstrom of thick brown clouds, a polluted atmosphere churning with messy rainbows of atomic energy. An oil slick on the universe. Green lighting flashed between the nimbuses; Diane had spent many nights wondering how its thunder must sound. A deep rumbling? Or maybe shrill and piercing, reminiscent of a scream?

"It's all wrong!"

A cluster of children from Block Two were gathered nearby, and a boy no older than five orbits cried out to his Nurse droid: "I saw Earth on the computer! It's blue!"

"Indeed, the Earth was once blue," the floating orb sang. "But that was before *Cradle*'s exodus. Remember, the Earth has not been blue for centuries."

Like the wide-eyed children, Diane gawked at the hellscape her genetic ancestors once called home. She had received a clear view of the Earth her entire life, but somehow it always managed to unsettle her.

"Diane?"

Startled, she turned to see Phillip, Jessica, and Gareth lingering outside a hall marked "Exterior Maintenance." They had actually noticed her absence for once. How sweet.

"You still got your Sessions?"

Now it was Diane's turn to wince. "Yeah . . . But I should be clear soon." She tried to smile again but could only manage a grimace. "Finally."

"See you later, then." Phillip led the others away.

Diane always felt loneliest in these moments, right after someone who wanted to avoid her had gotten their wish. Her present fears made it all the harder to watch them go. Her friends—not good friends, but the best ones she had—could be in danger, but they didn't believe it, or her. That was the hardest part about the last orbit. Not the social isolation. Not the constant anxiety in seeing what others missed. It was that everything she said was so easily ignored. *Don't mind Diane. She hasn't been the same since the accident.*

It would be enough to drive her out of *Cradle* altogether . . . if only she had somewhere else to go.

But no time to dwell on that. She was late.

Hurrying off down the walkway, Diane passed the Nurse droid as it recited the tale of Mr. Armstrong—a wise twenty-first-century industrialist who had seen war coming—to the children in its flock.

"While the governments and corporations built weapons and shaky allegiances, Mr. Armstrong escaped to the stars. And he took your genetic ancestors with him."

The children were spellbound, but Diane paid the history lesson no mind. She had heard it all before, and she was too busy imagining what her "friends" must be saying about her. Phillip would probably crack a joke at her expense. Gareth and Jessica would laugh their heads off.

They'd still be laughing after they put on their spacesuits, still riffing as they stepped out onto *Cradle*'s exterior, where Fivers and Sixers would teach them all about repairing the hull.

Diane should have been out there too, but she'd had her accident one orbit ago. So instead, she went to her Session.

This Session began like all the others.

Diane sat in a memory-foam chair at the Session Room's center. She liked to imagine this was how all the Nurse droids appeared from the inside: a perfect sphere made entirely of seamless LCD screens. For a while, nothing happened. Diane waited patiently, trying not to catch her reflection in the black mirror above, below, and to all sides. Seeing herself like that, all bulbous and fish-eyed, made her uneasy. Then, in a brilliant flash of white light, the Session began.

The screens all came to life at once, blazed with digital noise, then settled into a calming gradient of blue and black. The Armstrong Technologies logo—a lowercase *a* beside a stylized uppercase *T*—hovered for a moment, then gave way to a simplistic cartoon face: two circles for eyes, a line for its mouth.

"Good morning, Diane Three-One-Seven," the face said.

"Good morning, Nurse," Diane replied.

The artificial intelligence called Nurse influenced more than just the droids outside. She was in the computers, teaching science and history as *Cradle* saw fit to tell it. She was in the residential cabins, offering counsel to colonists in need. And when that need exceeded the occasional evening chat, she was here in the Session Room. If the Caretaker was *Cradle*'s protective father, Nurse was the nurturing mother.

"How are you feeling today?" Nurse asked.

"Fine," Diane said casually. "Normal."

"Are you sure? I detect that your heart rate is elevated to one hundred and nineteen beats per minute, a thirty BPM increase from your typical resting rate of ninety."

Diane pressed a finger beneath her jaw, searching for the pulse. "You can tell that?"

"Yes," Nurse said. "Is there something troubling you, Diane?"

"I . . ." Diane faltered. She remembered the look her friends gave her. How much could she reveal without sounding unwell? Then again, if there was a safe space to speak her mind, this was it. Maybe Nurse knew something the colonists didn't.

"I guess . . . I'm a little nervous about the turbulence," Diane ventured.

The cartoon face smiled. "That is a normal reaction to chaotic circumstances. In the event of future turbulence, remember that *Cradle* has survived many solar flares before now."

"But are we positive they're really solar flares?" Diane asked.

"It is the Caretaker's official announcement—"

"But it doesn't feel like solar flares," Diane interrupted. "Everything about this feels like a gravity disturbance. Maybe the Caretaker's mistaken?"

Nurse did not reply. The digital face remained static. Smiling. Watching.

"Hello?" Diane asked after a few uncomfortable seconds. In all her Sessions, and there had been many, Nurse had never paused.

"Could these suspicions be a result of your incident last orbit?" Nurse asked.

"What? No." Diane shifted awkwardly in her chair. This was the exact question she wanted to avoid.

"Are you positive?" Nurse said. "This accusation—that the Caretaker's assessment is inaccurate—aligns with claims you made during your hysterical period just after the incident."

"I wasn't—" Diane stopped herself. She wasn't going to have this argument again. She always lost. So she pivoted: "This has nothing to do with that. I'm almost better, anyway. You said so yourself. Last Session."

"I did," Nurse said, "and you have shown great progress. But in light of your recent disposition . . . perhaps we should put that progress to the test."

"What do you mean?" Diane asked.

The cartoon face disappeared, and white static filled the once-peaceful screens.

"Commencing Exposure Therapy Protocol," Nurse announced.

Diane's belly went cold, and her elevated heart rate cranked up a few more BPM. Not this, not again. "Wait—"

The static cleared.

Now, the screens projected a video feed from a spacesuit's helmet-mounted camera. There was no audio to accompany the footage, only Diane's heavy breathing. A timecode dated the recording from last orbit.

On-screen, two nylon hands worked to remove a tiny shard of space junk from *Cradle*'s hull. The gravity shield kept the larger chunks at bay, but smaller pieces often snuck between the cracks. Once the iron splinter was removed, a second astronaut gave the camera a thumbs-up and set about sealing the breach with a laser torch. The camera turned and followed its own suit's umbilical tether back toward the airlock. One nylon hand brought the space junk with it, for proper disposal.

"Nurse, I've already watched this," Diane said.

The free hand slid along the tether, using it as a guide rope. The cable was sleeved with unbreakable plastic. The airlock door was in sight.

"Please . . . turn it off."

Suddenly, dark smoke burst from the airlock, followed by a flurry of sparks. The umbilical tether snapped at the root, and a sudden force knocked the camera away from the station. The gravity shield, meant to repel foreign objects, did nothing to anchor it.

Diane squeezed the chair's armrest. She began to sweat.

The camera somersaulted through outer space. *Cradle* spun through the frame—a scintillating conical structure paved with titanium and solar panels, encircled by two great rings. A blur of stars and broken satellites followed, then the Earth. The horrible, toxic planet filled the screen, then spun away with everything else.

Hands flailed. Stars whirled out of control.

Through each rotation, *Cradle* got smaller. The Earth grew bigger. Bigger. *Closer.*

"*Turn it off*!"

The video paused, right as Earth dominated the frame. Diane gasped for air, heart thundering in her chest. She didn't need to see anymore; she knew what happened next. The unlucky astronaut would remember the space junk clutched in her hand. Thinking fast, she would slice a hole in her suit, and the pressure release would send her flying back toward *Cradle*. A team of colonists would pull her inside. They would remove her helmet, find her sobbing. She wouldn't stop sobbing for days.

Nurse's face returned. "The psychological trauma from your one-in-a-million tether malfunction yielded two symptoms: an absolute aversion to further space walks and a pathological obsession with identifying structural deficiencies, real or otherwise."

Diane said nothing.

"The latter symptom yields social consequences—your unfounded mistrust in *Cradle* puts you at odds with the majority—but the former makes you a liability to *Cradle* itself. There are no specialists here. Every colonist must be capable of performing every task. If half the residential cabins lost oxygen, the remaining colonists could pick up operations seamlessly."

"I know," Diane whispered. "I'm trying."

"For *Cradle*'s sake, you must try harder."

Diane nodded. She understood now that she wasn't almost better; her fear was as fresh as it was the day of the accident. Maybe the observational skills she'd spent the last orbit honing, both to protect her body and to navigate her newfound social dissonance, were really just paranoia in disguise. Maybe the only problem on *Cradle* was her.

"Our time is up," Nurse said with default cheeriness. "Thank you for participating—"

Suddenly another quake, just like the one that had left Diane's oatmeal on her ceiling that morning, began.

Her chair tilted and wobbled with the rest of the Session Room, and Diane clung to the seat bottom to keep from falling off. Like before, she felt light as a feather one moment, heavy as a boulder the next. Metal groaned and rattled all around her.

None of this was new to Diane, but what she saw happening to the LCDs definitely was.

During a solar flare, these screens would flicker on and off, struggling to retain power against the electromagnetic disturbance. That's not what happened now. Instead, the screens glitched out of control, intercutting Diane's helmet footage with countless random images: Incubation Lab training videos. Video feeds from security cameras. An old Western movie from Archive. Interspersed between them all: scrolling lines of code, brief glimpses into *Cradle*'s digital nervous system. The text was jumbled, incoherent.

```
c={state:function()]error}cmd=recall.TOWER(if cmd=recall
{override})_error = override invalid (cmd=recall.TOWER)
[override]error(cmd=recall.TOWER)[override]error
```

And so on.

Two whole minutes of this, then the turbulence ended. The chair settled. The screens regained their composure.

". . . participating in this mandatory Psych Health Session," Nurse continued, as though nothing had happened. "Have a lovely day."

Diane left the Session Room without another word.

"How many escape pods does *Cradle* have?"

Diane was elbows deep in a broken Nurse droid when she asked this. After the Session, she had hurried off to her first job shadow of the day: Interior Maintenance. Though every colonist was meant to be a jack-of-all-trades, this task was easily Diane's favorite. It put her "pathological obsession" to good use. Analyze problems, find solutions, all while safely indoors.

Today, the problem was a Nurse droid that had collided with a wall in Block Three during the last quake. Diane searched it for damaged components while under the casual supervision of Ben Five-Zero-Nine—her assigned mentor for all Interior Maintenance training. They both wore tool belts, and they were alone in the residential block.

"Why do you ask?" Ben said. He had Phillip's eyes, green and mischievous, but hazier. Cloudy with age and empathy.

"Just curious," Diane replied. She had spoken her mind twice that day already. The results weren't encouraging.

"Is it the turbulence?" Ben pressed. He was among the colonists who had pulled Diane back inside during the accident, and he had made a point to show her kindness over the last orbit. Maybe that was the real reason she enjoyed Interior Maintenance so much.

"You got nothing to worry about," he said. "I don't think solar flares—"

"But what if it's not flares?" Diane blurted out again.

She saw the alarm on his face, but it was too late to reel herself in. *Solar flares* had become a new trigger phrase.

"I know everyone says it's that," she said, "so it's got to be that. But, just for fun, let's say the obvious gravity issues are real, and the Caretaker messed up, and it's something worse. How many escape pods are there?"

Ben's face softened. Diane knew he wasn't convinced, but he pitied her. That was enough.

"Five hundred and one," he said. "A pod for every colonist, plus one for the Caretaker. We've got a whole evacuation protocol. You remember the drills."

Diane pulled her hands out of the droid. "And if we do evacuate, what happens next? Do we just float around space? We can't go back to Earth."

"Sure we can," Ben said.

Diane must have looked utterly shocked, because Ben laughed.

"Did you forget about the scouts?" he asked.

If the Nurse droid had been operational, it might have chimed in with another history lesson. It would have reminded Diane that ever since Earth fell into a communications blackout, *Cradle* had been sending brave scouts to get a lay of the land. A few volunteers were deployed every fifty orbits, making one-way trips to find safe landing zones for *Cradle*'s hypothetical return. Surgically modified to handle the planet's increased gravity, they communicated directly with the Caretaker. Only with the Caretaker.

"I did. I did forget about the scouts."

"I hear they've got settlements waiting for us," Ben said. "It'd be a harder life, but not impossible."

Diane felt relieved, but only briefly. "But that's assuming everyone makes it to their pod in time. What if we get separated, and I'm stuck alone with the other Block Threes? They're the worst."

Ben chuckled again. "I wouldn't worry too much about it, since *Cradle's fine.*"

But Diane did worry. She didn't want to. She wanted to feel safe and content like everyone else. But every time *Cradle* shook, she felt herself falling without a tether. She felt the Earth growing closer.

Ben recognized this, and he said, "If you see it for yourself, will you relax?"

"See what?" Diane asked.

"Follow me."

Ben hopped off toward the Residential Junction, leaving the Nurse droid unfixed. After a moment's hesitation, Diane followed after him.

They made their way back to the Central Atrium, passing a few colonists who greeted Ben while ignoring Diane, and came to an autodoor marked *Station Security.* The door was fitted with a glass panel emitting light in the shape of a hand.

"You remember the trick?" Ben asked.

Diane glanced nervously around the atrium. Other colonists hustled between the sectors, too focused on their next destination to notice much else.

"What about the guard on duty?" Diane whispered.

"I know the guy on this shift," Ben said. "He's a lazy old Sixer, likes to hang around the mess hall."

That didn't surprise Diane. Security was easily *Cradle's* dullest task. Nurse handled most of the cameras and alerts, and people older than Block Two rarely broke the rules. The addition of a single human guard was merely a precaution. People skipped shifts all the time.

"I'll take the blame if he's in there," Ben said. "Come on, do what I showed you."

Diane took one last look over her shoulder, then she got to work.

During a slow day, Ben had taught Diane all about the palm scanners. *Cradle* stored every colonist's biometric data in its computer system, and the scanners were designed to accept only the palm vein patterns of those scheduled to enter restricted areas during a given shift. Any attempt to deactivate a scanner would alert the Caretaker immediately, but Ben knew a workaround. Diane implemented it now.

Using a thin motorized screwdriver, she opened the panel and shifted the scanner aside, taking care not to let it detach all the way. A blinking circuit board greeted her, and after she deactivated a switch, moved a couple diodes, and reactivated a dormant inductor, a pleasant beep emitted from the door.

Diane resecured the panel and pressed her hand to the glass. The autodoor opened.

Deactivating a palm scanner would trigger the alarm, but resetting its biometric parameters to accept any colonist's hand caused no trouble at all.

"Flawless," Ben grinned. "You're a natural."

He hurried inside and Diane followed. For the first time that day, she didn't feel like *Cradle*'s biggest liability.

The Security Room was half the size of Diane's cabin, and an oversized computer screen dominated most of it. Ben sat down at a keyboard and began to type. "All right, where are you . . . ?"

He scrolled through countless security feeds.

Thermal Control: two teenagers from Block Three flirted quietly while taking *Cradle*'s temperature.

Waste Management: five colonists from Four hollered to each other while fixing a broken pipe.

The montage seemed endless until Ben stopped on the feed he wanted: Gravity Control.

A wide pyramid-shaped space filled with Sixers, all sitting calmly at their consoles, adjusting this and monitoring that. A triangular pedestal occupied the room's center, and *Cradle*'s heart floated above it. It was a glowing orb of rare minerals and ethereal light, spinning slowly, glistening like a diamond in the sun. Two golden rings surrounded it, rotating counter to each other, held up by forces invisible to the human eye.

This was the secret to *Cradle*'s existence. The single greatest achievement Armstrong Technologies had ever produced, dwarfing their ventures into artificial intelligence and sustainable energy.

This was the Gravity Core, and it looked completely normal.

"See any issues?" Ben asked.

Diane watched the screen over his shoulder. She saw the docile expressions on the Sixers. The serene movements of the Gravity Core and its halos. This room was at the epicenter of her fears, but it showed no disarray. No problems at all.

Before Diane could admit this, the day's third quake began.

She clung to the back of Ben's chair, and he twisted around to hold her hands firmly. The quake whirled them in every direction, swinging between weightlessness and crushing gravity at breakneck speed. Outside the Security Room, they could hear people of all ages struggling against the same capricious force. Those who couldn't find something to hold were knocked about the Central Atrium; one body smacked into the autodoor, groaned pitifully, then tumbled away. It was the worst quake yet, but Ben Five-Zero-Nine never let Diane drift away, and his grip on her never loosened. Not once, for the full two and a half minutes.

When the quake died down, Ben looked back to the rattling computer screen.

"Look at that!" he exclaimed. "They didn't even flinch."

On-screen, the Sixers continued typing and staring. Their docility remained unscathed.

"Not even a little," Diane muttered.

"They're not worried. You shouldn't be either."

Diane gave no reply.

Gently, Ben eased her hands off the chair's back. He held them as he spoke. "You had a big scare, Diane. Bigger than most of us will ever know. But *Cradle*'s been afloat for centuries. It's safe. You're safe."

"Thank you for showing me this," Diane said, and she meant it. Then: "I'm going to run to the lavatory."

Ben smiled. "I about peed myself too, just now. I'll meet you back in Block Three. We got a Nurse to fix."

Diane tried to appear calm as she hurried across the Central Atrium, avoiding looking at the Earth at all costs. Her fellow colonists were too busy picking themselves up to pay her any mind. Gone was the laughter and talk of roller coasters; people were injured. Mostly sprains and minor cuts, but one Block Four woman appeared to have suffered a concussion. She had to be carried away on a stretcher. The Medical Wing would have its hands full today.

Diane ducked into one of the lavatories, confirmed that all the vacuum stalls were empty, and only then did she allow herself to hyperventilate.

Maybe Ben had not been watching the security screen during the last quake, but Diane hadn't been able to look away. She had read the room at Gravity Control, and she saw the Sixers were more than just calm; they hadn't reacted in the slightest. No grabbing consoles to keep steady. No loose objects flying across the room. No swaying bodies, not even a pause. Even that close to the Gravity Core, the quake would have affected the space in some tangible way, especially if solar flares were the culprit.

The Gravity Room's apparent disconnect from reality could only mean one thing.

"It wasn't live," Diane panted to herself. "The feed wasn't live."

But no one would believe her. Not even Ben.

Shut up, Diane. You're being paranoid.

Paranoid people needed proof. She had to see the Gravity Room in person, but there was a problem: only Sixers were allowed in there.

When she got her breathing under control, Diane climbed onto a lavatory sink. A circular vent hung directly overhead, also rigged with a palm scanner. Only colonists on Interior Maintenance duty could access the air vents. Fortunately, that's exactly what Diane was. She pressed her hand to the scanner, and the vent cover dropped away. In *Cradle*'s low gravity, climbing up into the ceiling was no difficult task.

Ben Five-Zero-Nine had recognized Diane's aptitude for maintenance work early on, and he would often take her on jobs usually saved for Block Fours and above. He had shown her how *Cradle*'s air vents ran everywhere, how they paid no mind to the security system that herded colonists along their day-to-day. The two of them had spent a great deal of time up there together, spying on their neighbors while they repaired the air filtration system. These were some of Diane's fondest memories.

Now, Diane crawled through the claustrophobic tunnels as quickly as she could, her path guided only by dim lights trickling through occasional vents. She followed a mental map drawn from her previous trips with Ben, and she paid close attention to her body's shifting weight. The heavier she felt, the closer she was to the Gravity Core.

At the bottom of a long vertical passageway, Diane knew she had found the right tunnel. Narrow darkness led to a single grate flowing with abstract light, turquoise and wavering. A beacon underwater.

Diane crawled toward the light, feeling gravity's hand push against her. She powered on to the vent cover, pressed a tiny switch, and watched the grate drop away.

With violent force, an unseen power yanked Diane into the Gravity Control Room. The mellow workplace from the security feed was nowhere to be found. Instead, Sixers scrambled between consoles, their screens glitching, their voices hoarse from shouting to each other. Diane's falling body halted a few inches above the floor, then smacked down with jarring momentum. The room's gravity fluctuated out of control, and the Gravity Core was to blame. The orb spun rapidly. The golden rings scraped against each other. Rogue particles flew in every direction. Diane didn't need a Block Six residence to guess that something was very wrong.

All around her, the console screens all ran the same repeating code string:

error = override invalid (cmd=recall.TOWER)
[override]error(cmd=recall.)[override]error

A Sixer tripped over Diane while running across the room. They locked eyes, both gawking at the other.

"You shouldn't be here," the Sixer said.

"What's happening?" Diane shouted over the ruckus.

The Sixer recoiled as if the question were a razor in her brain. "We did everything we could. We fought this thing for a whole orbit. It's a miracle we lasted this long—"

Diane grabbed the Sixer by the shoulders. "What's wrong with the Core?"

"It's not the Core's fault . . ." The Sixer looked dolefully into the orb, which washed her face in blue. "It's just doing what it's told."

"Which is?" Diane asked.

"Tear *Cradle* apart."

Diane felt the room spinning, and not because of the Gravity Core. It took no small effort to keep her mind from retreating into itself.

"We're still trying to fix it," the Sixer said, regarding her block mates around them. "It's all we can do. Fix it, or die."

"What're you talking about?" Diane screamed. "Why haven't you warned anyone? We need to evacuate!"

"Evacuate? To where?"

"To Earth!" Diane said.

The Sixer squinted as if she hadn't understood. She strained to connect the dots between the word and its meaning. The place and its implications.

"*Earth*?"

The Sixer began to cry.

She cried long and hard, bawling even after Diane released her shoulders and ran out through the nearest autodoor. The Caretaker's cabin was a straight shot down the hallway, and he needed to be told. The engineers in Gravity Control had lost their minds, and they were going to get everyone killed.

The Armstrong Technologies logo branded the Caretaker's door, which was thicker and more ornate than the average cabin's. Diane made a fist, ready to knock against it.

"Mr. Caretaker—!" she started to say, but the door hissed open, unlocked. Somehow, that scared Diane more than anything else. "Mr. Caretaker?"

She crept into the cabin, which resembled an office more than sleeping quarters. Low marble steps paved the way to a desk built from imitation oak, a desk topped with holographic keyboards and live *Cradle* diagnostics, all flashing red. The Caretaker's leather chair was rotated away, facing its occupant toward a wall paneled with screens: a ten-by-ten grid, each square projecting a different video.

At first, Diane couldn't tell what she was looking at. What were these faces, terrified and screaming? Where were these locations, hellscapes of jagged iron and scarlet dirt?

The confusion subsided when Diane heard what the faces were saying.

"Mayday! Hostiles on site! They ripped my craft to pieces!" This was a chiseled man with a bleeding forehead, crawling through gravel. A blurry mob stalked after him in the background. Humanoid shapes. Rigid, robotic movements.

"They're enormous! Coming . . . right out of the ground!" said a ghostly woman in another video. She had hair like Diane's and was hiding in a rusty shipping container. Something big rumbled outside, shaking the camera.

On another video: "They shot me! Oh god, it hurts!"

And another: "It's not crying . . . It's hunting . . ."

They went on. "Do not engage this landing site! It's not safe!"

"Dangerous! The whole planet! Do not land!"

"I don't want to die! I . . . No no . . . *Please*—!"

These were the scouts, each delivering their status updates from Earth. Each video was watermarked as the subject's final log. Each one ended in bloodshed or static.

There were no settlements waiting on Earth. The Caretaker had lied.

"Sir . . ." Diane called to her leader one last time, but the chair remained still.

Trembling, she reached out and spun the chair around. When she came face-to-face with the Caretaker, Diane screamed.

The Caretaker stared back at her with blank, lifeless eyes. His face was slack and washed out. Gray smoke rose from a hole in the center of his forehead. Diane recognized the tool clutched in his right hand. She had seen its picture during her history lessons, whenever they discussed war. But these lessons were always brief, and it took a moment to recall the word.

"Gun," she said aloud.

Cradle's final quake knocked her off her feet, sent her rolling across the room. The lights went dead and stayed dead. The entire station shrieked in pain: support beams twisting, rooms collapsing, the muffled din of four hundred ninety-nine colonists losing their minds with fear. Diane imagined the Sixers weeping. The Fivers and Fours calling out to Threes and Twos. The Ones . . . Oh god, the *Ones*.

Above it all, an ear-shattering *bang* erupted somewhere in the station. No need for guessing; the Caretaker's desk was quick to pinpoint the source. A 3D replica of *Cradle* filled the holographic display, and it showed a large bulkhead ripping like paper, ejecting countless tiny human figures into the vacuum of space. *HULL BREACH: MEDICAL BAY*, the diagnostic read. The estimated body count made Diane's stomach turn.

She racked her brain for a solution, but nothing came. Diane had no idea why *Cradle* was imploding. Her "pathological obsession" had been useless after all.

Or maybe not.

A concealed hatchway opened in the floor, emitting steam and red light, scaring the hell out of Diane. A single-person escape pod rose up from the haze. Egg-shaped, it was bigger than the escape pods she remembered from the evacuation drill. The plating looked thicker, more durable. The propulsion jets could swallow a grown man whole.

The escape pod opened, and Nurse's voice called out from inside. "Emergency. Please enter your Level Seven Caretaker-Class Evacuation Pod."

Diane threw herself into the Caretaker's pod, and it sealed itself around her. A safety harness lowered, securing her to the passenger's seat. Before she could breathe, the pod sank back into the floor, jettisoned through rumbling darkness, and then shot out from a launch cannon on *Cradle*'s hull. It tore through endless layers of space junk, parting them like curtains.

All too soon, Diane laid eyes on her destination: Earth. The nightmare planet filled the pod's narrow observation window; its lightning tongues flicked in anticipation. Fresh meat was entering the atmosphere.

Smaller escape pods appeared in her window's peripheral, only for *Cradle*'s gravity to suck them back into a fiery embrace. Diane could feel her own ship struggling against the rogue Gravity Core, a crumbling dragon at her back, roaring through space in pursuit of its last survivor. Her vessel led the charge downward, toward a destination that had driven the Caretaker to suicide.

As the world she knew perished behind her, Diane fell to Earth, screaming all the way.

CHAPTER 2

"... 'Bout ninety-five and climbing. Caravan's headed west, just south of the Vegas quarantine limits. Swarm of centipedes reported a hundred miles north of the Heap, so watch out if you're headed that way. Speakin' of which, still no word from the Heap since—"

Garbled static devoured the frequency. Virgil tuned the dials on his CB radio, never taking his eyes off the desert road. He followed one rule when he was behind the wheel: watch where you drive. There were countless dangers around every bend, and some of them knew how to drop land mines.

Eventually, the DJ's voice returned. The signal was weak over so many relay towers, but her words were clear enough: "... *outta the damn sky! Your guess is as good as ours right now, but when Junkie FM knows what it is, you will too. That wraps up Traffic. Here's the good part.*"

A jingling song about an "army on the dance floor" replaced the DJ. Junkie FM only had so many cassettes and CDs at their disposal; this song was a favorite among listeners.

"*Looooove myyyyyy waaaaaaay—*"

Click. Virgil shut the radio off. Not his jam.

Other sounds filled the void the music left behind. The electric StormCell engine in Virgil's jeep purred, bits of scrap metal crunched beneath his military-grade tires, and the chains on his rickety hauler trailer jingled with manic intensity. Behind the lens of his gas mask, Virgil quickly broke his driving rule to check the meter on his dashboard. The jeep was at 40 percent power. Not terrible, but not great, either. If Hobble hadn't called him up yesterday to chase the new junkheap that had fallen from the sky, it would have been just enough power to get home.

Home.

Home was a long drive north, into the mountains, up a secret pass that Virgil would sooner die than reveal to anyone. Home was everything the Junkyard was not, and it was the reason Virgil had taken this shitty job in the first place. The job he had come so close to quitting just yesterday. He wasn't usually the type of junkie to leave contract work unfinished, but after spending four tedious months without ever getting close to his target, he had been ready to abandon the reward and go home empty-handed. It wouldn't have been a proud moment, but Virgil wasn't a young man anymore. He was tired, sicker than most. He needed to heal in a way that Battery couldn't provide much longer. He needed rest before he was no good to anyone.

Then Hobble called him up, and just like that, Virgil was back on the goddamn case.

He had sped off through the night and into the next morning. The distance to the crash site wasn't all that far, but no route across the Junkyard was ever truly direct. A world of danger transformed every straight mile into a winding ten. If luck was on his side, Virgil would reach the crash site this afternoon. Before his target.

A waste disposal truck, capsized in a pond of its own radioactive goo, blocked the highway up ahead. While coasting around it, Virgil felt the telltale signs of the Junkyard Blues tickling at his stomach. He could usually detect the attacks early; not an easy skill to acquire. Like clockwork, he lifted up his gas mask, popped an inhaler into his mouth, and took a hit of high-grade Battery. He had absorbed enough radiation in his lifetime to wipe out a village, and Battery didn't make that go away. The poison had built up in his blood, killing more red cells every day, getting so bad that normal Battery couldn't keep the sickness contained. Most junkies never needed—or never lived long enough to need—anything beyond the low and medium grades, but Virgil had been in this game a very long time. Anything less than the good stuff would leave him for dead . . . or worse.

Virgil peeked into his rearview mirror as he lowered the gas mask. A large object occupied his trailer, its bulk wrapped in a thick multicolored fabric. If you laid the fabric out, it revealed a pattern of red-and-white stripes, topped with a blue square filled with stars. Virgil assumed the crest belonged to one of the old nations that existed before the Grand Finale, but the country's name eluded him. Not that it mattered. Dead nations meant little to the living.

The object swaddled in that ancient flag was Virgil's last resort. It could bring him back from a fatal Junkyard Blues attack, but in doing so would lead him toward a very different kind of destruction. A worse kind, in his opinion. If the people back home did not rely on him so heavily, and his survival was not so crucial to theirs, he would have never accepted this double-edged gift. Most junkies had no homes to provide for, no one to miss them, and they only needed to worry about themselves. Virgil was not most junkies.

He looked back to the road.

"¡*Ay, carajo*!" he screamed, slamming on the brakes.

The jeep swerved off the highway and came to rest in a roadside ditch. While neglecting his own rule, he had drifted around a hill and nearly collided with . . . something.

What the hell was it?

Only one way to find out.

Virgil put the jeep in park. After a quick look around, he reached into the back seat and pulled out his clunky handheld Geiger counter. A gaping hole had been punched into the stratus, and the sky overhead was clear blue.

The ticking counter gave a reading of 352 counts per minute. A bona fide miracle.

Virgil peeled off his gas mask to enjoy an air much too clean for these parts; even the microplastics seemed to have dissipated. He dropped the mask and Geiger counter in the back seat, next to his trade goods and dwindling water supply, and in their place he took out the Volt Caster, a mechanical glove and gauntlet dotted with golden electrodes. It was the rarest, most powerful wartime junk Virgil had ever scavenged—excluding the object in his trailer. He had nicknamed it himself.

He jammed his left hand into the Caster, flicked his wrist, and the electrodes pulsed with a deadly cyan energy. Electric bolts arced between them, mimicking the volatile lighting storm that was *usually* overhead. But today, under this abnormal patch of cloudlessness, there was only sunshine.

It reminded him of home.

Armed and dangerous, Virgil hiked back onto the road. The obstacle he narrowly avoided was some kind of vessel, a sleek metal egg with a jet engine bigger than his whole body. Based on the rippling crater in the asphalt, he could deduce that this thing had fallen out of the sky. That made sense, considering that his ultimate destination—something else that had fallen out of the sky—was less than a mile up the road. It had torn a hole in the clouds on its way down, and this little egg must have fallen with it. Or ahead of it. Whatever. The details meant little.

Virgil approached the vessel, holding out his gloved hand in case the egg tried anything funny. Something was moving around in there, pounding against the walls, trying to get out. He took a knee and wiped the dirt off the pod's narrow observation window.

When he saw what was inside, he lowered his weapon.

It was a girl, no older than seventeen, dressed in a burgundy jumpsuit. Her black hair was a mess, her collar was dark with sweat, and the sight of Virgil made her flinch away from the window.

He couldn't take offense at her reaction. Imagine falling out of the sky, stewing in your own panic for half a day, and *his ugly mug* was the first thing you saw. His gray beard was thick and wild, peppered green around the lips from constant Battery consumption. Heavy bags drooped under his eyes, adding distance to his already piercing gaze. The hood from his coat dropped a constant shadow over his face, making it hard to tell if his complexion was marred by deep wrinkles, scars, or both.

For a while, Virgil and the girl just stared at each other. Neither was quite sure what to make of the other.

"Hi," Virgil said.

Perhaps realizing that he wasn't a feral madman, the girl pressed herself against the window.

"Help me," she said. "Please."

"Where in the hell did you come from?"

"*Cradle*. I'm a colonist on *Cradle*. Please, the hatch won't—"

Virgil frowned. "*Cradle*? What's . . . Oh."

He gestured up the road, toward his destination. "Okay, where'd '*Cradle*' come from?"

"We were in orbit around the Earth," the girl said. "Something attacked our computer system—"

"Orbit!" Virgil said. "Hang on, you telling me that thing's a spaceship?"

"Um . . . More like a space *station*."

Virgil hooted and slapped the ground with his Volt Caster; a flash of light crackled from the hit. The girl retreated from the window, as far as the cumbersome seat harness would allow.

"¡*Que nooo*!" Virgil said with a laugh. "I thought I'd seen it all!"

The girl spoke carefully. "The hatch on my escape pod is broken. I can't get out."

Virgil was no longer listening. He observed the crash site up ahead, pondering its cataclysmic vastness. The wreckage had been sliced into three chunks, and the nearest piece was by far the largest. A gargantuan hull, crushed, charred, and twisted around itself. Support beams sticking out like broken ribs. Little fires all over the damn place.

"Looks like you abandoned ship just in the nick," Virgil mused. "Your space station's not looking too hot."

"Please, I don't know how much oxygen I've got left," the girl said.

Something light bumped the toe of Virgil's boot. Looking down, he found a crumpled ball of garnet-colored wax paper, the kind used to package Nutribriks hot off the assembly line.

"And you know," Virgil said, watching the ball drift away like a tumbleweed, "I'm pretty sure there was a village around here somewhere. Nice people too—"

The girl kicked the glass. "Why aren't you listening to me?"

Virgil found her huffing and puffing, nearly as angry as she was afraid. All of a sudden, he remembered that he had places to be.

"I hear you fine, *chamaca*," he said, giving the escape pod a once-over. The plating was dented in some places, melted in others. "Your egg's all messed up. Would take time to pry it open. Time I don't have right now."

"Why not?" the girl said.

Virgil checked back the way he'd come. Twinkling shapes had materialized on the desert's edge. Some of them were humanoid, and the rest were anything but.

"And if I help you out," he continued, "you're my problem. Again, time I don't have."

The girl pressed her hands against the window, shaking her head frantically. "No. If you let me out, I can find my own way. I promise."

"Right," Virgil scoffed. He stood up, leaving only his boots in the window's field of view. "Someone else will come along. Probably."

"Wait—"

"Later, kid."

Virgil returned to his jeep, doing his best to ignore the shouts and banging that now rocked the escape pod. He could still hear them after he reignited the engine, and his hand faltered over the gear shift.

This was low. Even for him.

"Soft grass," he whispered to himself. "Cool breeze. Trees dancing in the wind."

He could still hear the commotion from the pod. Her anger. Her fear.

"Fingers plucking at guitar strings. Bow racing over a fiddle. Everyone singing. Everyone, even Úna, who can't carry a tune to save her life."

If the girl died in there, it was on him—

"Green grass. Green trees. Green everywhere. *Green*."

He could see it now. *Home*.

It gave him the nerve to put the jeep in drive, like it gave him the courage to do so many questionable things. Nasty things. The Junkyard was paved with moral compromises, and every junkie had their way to cope. For Virgil, it was looking out for his own. He was part of something bigger than himself, and that put ample distance between his heart and his actions. Did he take joy in leaving the space colonist trapped in her egg? No. But he was on the clock. He had a contract to fulfill. A home to provide for.

With a murky conscience and 39 percent energy in his jeep's Storm-Cell, Virgil drove off to the nearest chunk of this mound of wreckage the girl had called *Cradle*.

He parked his ride behind a pile of rubble disconnected from the main wreckage, out of sight and away from the fires. The ruined space station was truly a mountain to him, stretching its gnarled beams high into the blue sky. Whatever *Cradle* had been, whatever purpose it had served, it was now the largest junk pile Virgil had ever seen. This did not intimidate him. He was no stranger to climbing, and the last Battery dose was still fresh in his system. In addition to its intended function, Battery took the edge off just about everything physical. Climbing. Running. Fighting for your life. When the green stuff was in your lungs, it all hurt a bit less.

The ascent was pretty damn steep, but there were plenty of climbing holds. Protruding rods and hull breaches formed a natural ladder up the slope, and Virgil chose his path wisely. Half an hour later, he was sitting atop a ledge of thick glass about two-thirds of the way up *Cradle*. Behind him, a shattered panoramic window offered passage to some kind of lopsided atrium. He did a quick check to make sure it was empty, then, at the sound of motors, he looked back to the road.

The Peacekeepers had just reached the toxic goo pond, and they barreled through it fearlessly.

The tribe was twenty machines strong, all riding on the back of six-wheeled rover drones. It amazed Virgil that a group this size had eluded him for months, especially one with such variation. Their ranks included the standard combat models, built like muscular humans, each armed with a powerful plasma cannon in place of one hand. These were called "argonauts." Some were thinner and agile, both hands swapped for scythe-like blades, called "reapers." Crawling at their feet were orbs of laser-proof glass with appendages that resembled the look and function of spider legs: "seekers," the perfect spy drones. There was even a "strongman," a bipedal behemoth elephantine in size and with crushing pincers, bounding after the rover drones on foot.

And then, there was Virgil's target.

This was not Virgil's first time seeing a "diplomat" Peacekeeper; they were essential in bringing a tribe of this size together. Long before Virgil's time, the Peacekeepers had marched under one Hive Mind, and every action was selected with purpose. Today, in the Junkyard, each individual Peacekeeper was trapped in the prison of its own CPU. No directives, no purpose, only the base instinct for self-preservation. Most of them couldn't communicate with humans. They could barely communicate with each other. That was where the diplomats came in. This unique Peacekeeper model had the capacity to program other Peacekeepers with new directives. Considering that diplomats couldn't fight worth a damn, it was in their best interest to form a tribe around themselves.

In some ways, this diplomat was no different from the others Virgil had previously encountered: it had long carbon-fiber tendrils instead of limbs and a large cyclopean head vaguely reminiscent of the human skull. It was under heavy guard, surrounded by argonauts on all sides. But in other ways, Virgil had never seen a Peacekeeper like this before. The diplomat occupied what could only be described as a hollowed-out strongman—the head and pieces of the torso of the larger drone removed to form a cockpit, its legs and pincers following the diplomat's every command. It was like seeing a person walking around in a human meat suit.

On top of that, the diplomat wore a mask. Virgil couldn't make out the details from so far away, but the idea of a masked machine sent shivers down his whole body.

This was not an assassination. Virgil was not a mercenary, and he didn't seek out fights with other humans. But as a junkie, he was more than willing to hunt down valuable tech for the right price. Four months ago, Virgil had been hired to locate a masked diplomat whose tribe had been a real pain in the employer's *culo*, causing mischief all over the Junkyard. This diplomat boasted the rare ability to speak human, and it called itself the Messenger.

Virgil's job was to collect the Messenger's head.

The Peacekeeper tribe split off into three groups, each approaching a different chunk of *Cradle*. Just Virgil's luck, the Messenger led its party toward the same section of the wreckage Virgil had selected. From on high, he watched the Messenger, four argonauts, one reaper, and a seeker disappear into the crumbling space station.

He knew it would be suicide to go straight for the leader. Best to take care of the pawns first and play this one quiet.

The Peacekeepers entered the atrium, their ocular lenses piercing the gloom with beams of red. The Messenger gave a brief sequence of digital chirps, and the party members split up to investigate different passageways. Virgil realized then what was happening: these Peacekeepers were searching for something. Something specific. Even with a diplomat in their midst, this level of coordination was extremely rare.

Virgil slid down the atrium wall, which he suspected had once been the floor. Everything in the room was hopelessly askew. The walkways stood vertical; the doorways were crooked and horizontal. Flashes of burgundy jumpsuits peered out from beneath the rubble deposits. Broken glimpses of someone's back, someone's mangled limb. Virgil didn't linger on any of them for too long. They were beyond his help. Way beyond.

With great care, Virgil navigated around the detritus and live and sparking wires in pursuit of a lone argonaut, one he had picked out of the several combing this part of the wreckage. The hunt took him through a grand archway marked with dim blue neon, the last flicker of life in a place as good as dead. The hall beyond was a foam-padded cylinder, rendering Virgil's footfalls silent.

The argonaut wavered just up ahead, looking back and forth between two new doorways, struggling to choose a path. *Choice* was rarely a Peacekeeper's strong suit. They were followers. Foot soldiers to a vanquished artificial intelligence. They didn't do well on their own.

Slowly, Virgil drew his hunting knife and pressed a switch on the handle. The blade's edge erupted with a searing orange glow, and the air around it warped and sizzled.

Heated knife in his right hand, Volt Caster on his left, Virgil snuck toward the argonaut. Its back was turned, and its auditory processors were useless amid the foam padding. It would not autodetect Virgil's presence until he was five feet away.

No problem at all.

From a safe distance, Virgil whipped out his gloved hand and snapped. An energy bolt shot from his fingers, flooding the dark space in cyan, and struck the argonaut in the back. The machine's limbs contorted, locked in a seizure of overloaded circuits. Virgil sprinted the distance between them, swift as a man half his age and twice as healthy, and plunged his knife between the argonaut's shoulder blades. The armor plating liquefied beneath the serrated edge of the knife, which Virgil pushed as deep as it would go while slicing down the Peacekeeper's spine. When he withdrew the knife, steam and black fluid poured from the wound like hot blood.

The argonaut stopped twitching. The red light of its ocular lens went dead. It swayed for a moment, then fell face-first to the floor. The foam reduced the impact to a soft *poof*.

Virgil thumbed the button on his knife handle, and the blade cooled instantly.

One down.

As he turned to leave, a bright light shot at Virgil's face. His eyes shut automatically, but he could still sense a red hue against his lids, running up and down his face. Scanning him.

When the brightness retracted, Virgil opened his eyes. A lone seeker clung to the ceiling, its legs poking tiny holes into the padding. Its ocular lens widened with something like shock.

"Damn it," Virgil mumbled.

Before he could lift an electric finger, the seeker unleashed a piping shriek. The alarm was earsplitting, and it reverberated far beyond the foam's ability to repress it. Virgil flung a lightning bolt toward it, but the seeker dropped to the floor quicker than he could adjust his aim. It scurried back through the archway.

Cursing, Virgil gave chase. He made it two steps into the atrium before the reaper pounced.

Virgil heard the whooshing air displacement not a moment too soon. He dove aside, missing the reaper's outstretched blades by an inch, and landed tactically on his back. With a wave of the Volt Caster, a sparkling energy wall formed between him and the reaper. The barrier's life span was brief, but it gave Virgil just enough time to crawl for cover behind one of the lopsided walkways.

A plasma shot hit the wall near Virgil's head, searing it with a bright yellow aura. The other three argonauts had returned to the atrium, and they unloaded their cannons at Virgil without mercy.

Virgil flung himself through the nearest open doorway. He was now in a small room dominated by an oversized computer screen, which was cracked and blank. Flattened against a wall, he heard the Peacekeepers marching toward his hiding place, ready to flood the room with plasma beams and slicing blades. If he didn't do something fast, he would either be fried to a crisp or chopped into itty-bitty cubes. Whichever came first.

Virgil squeezed the Caster into a fist. The electrodes grew brighter.

When the robotic footsteps sounded right outside the door, Virgil leaped out from hiding. The argonaut trio was gathered before him, the single reaper not far behind. Their weapons were raised and all their ocular lenses pointed at him.

Virgil punched the floor.

His fist was a stone dropped into still waters. A wave of electromagnetic power rippled across the space, consuming every metallic surface that it touched. The Peacekeepers danced their spastic dance until their ocular lenses burst. Smoking, they all fell in unison.

Virgil flexed his fingers in the Volt Caster, massaging out the stiffness. The electrodes had gone dark, and a small white dot blinked on his forearm. That last trick had drained all the juice the Caster had left.

No worries. There was more where that came from.

He holstered his knife, then pulled out a tier-one StormCell from a pack on his belt. The lucent disk was about the size of his palm—fusion energy contained in rings of particle accelerators, heat shields, and uranium. It was a smaller duplicate of the StormCell powering Virgil's jeep; they came in many sizes. Machines ran on StormCells like junkies ran on Battery.

Virgil tapped the blinking light, and a hidden compartment opened in the Caster's gauntlet. Another tier one, all dim and used up, rested within.

That's when the Messenger arrived.

It burst through a nearby wall, showering the atrium in more debris. Virgil shielded his eyes with his left hand, and between the Caster's fingers, he saw the Messenger's mask clearly for the first time.

The mask was an abomination that came in two layers, one on top of the other. The foundation was a metal faceplate torn from an argonaut's head. A cracked, leathery material was stretched over it, and as the dust from the Messenger's entrance settled, Virgil realized that the material was skin. Skin from a human face nailed to the bottom layer. One eyehole aligned with the faceplate's ocular port, clearing a window for the diplomat's own lens to peer through. The other eyehole hung half shut against blank rusty nothing, as did the nose and mouth.

"Holy hell . . ." Virgil whispered.

The Messenger charged, using its tendrils to manipulate the strongman from the inside. With a panicked squawk, Virgil fled across the atrium into a nearby corridor propped at an upward angle. He shook the dead StormCell out of the Volt Caster as he ran, and a slight pang of regret followed. The little guy could have been recharged, or traded for something else. What a waste.

While the Messenger lumbered after him, pincers snapping, Virgil slipped the fresh StormCell into his Caster. But there was no epic surge of power when he shut the compartment again. The flashing dot merely took the shape of a lightning bolt, pulsing slowly, and the electrodes remained cold. The weapon needed to reboot.

"Come on, come on, *ándele!*" Virgil wheezed.

Broken pipes crossed his path, splashing him with oily liquid, forcing him to duck and vault. The Messenger plowed through all of them, never slowing as the distance between them shrunk. Their corridor ended at a T-junction, and, faced with a split-second decision, Virgil chose to turn left. He chose wrong; the next hall was blocked by a collapsed ceiling. Checking back over his shoulder, Virgil saw the Messenger overshoot the turn and collide with a wall. Bits of debris rained onto the machine's shoulders, stunning it only for a moment. Not nearly enough time to slip past.

Finally, the Caster's lighting symbol turned blue, and its electrodes blossomed with electricity. When Virgil reached the end of the path, he turned and faced his pursuer. In two more massive strides, those pincers would be crushing down on his head.

Virgil snapped his fingers. Lighting sprung forth and hit the strongsuit's knee, causing the whole limb to go stiff. The Messenger tripped.

Against the weight and momentum of the tumble, the hallway's floor broke away like wet cardboard. The diplomat's ocular lens spun wildly as it dropped farther than Virgil expected, disappearing into the dark. The *bang* from its landing sounded weak by the time it reached Virgil's ears.

The junkie peered over the pitfall's edge. In a chamber far below, the Messenger lay twitching, immobile. Virgil took hold of a broken cable dangling nearby and slid down to the diplomat's level. Black screens covered the walls and ceiling, all busted up. That many LCDs felt like overkill to Virgil. Whatever this spherical room had been meant to accomplish, one screen would have probably worked just fine.

The Messenger lay spread-eagle at his feet. A sharp steel rod had pierced the machine's chest plate, and Virgil could see a punctured StormCell flickering underneath. Peacekeepers ran on tier twos, same as Virgil's jeep. These StormCells were big enough to fill a human's rib cage, and the Messenger's was definitely broken.

Virgil put his face directly over the hideous mask. "You speak?"

The machine responded with a singsong mixture of digitized tones meant to approximate human speech. "Your death is imminent."

"Good. Before I cut your head off, I got to know where you found this strongman puppet."

"We serve a higher function," the Messenger said. "You serve nothing. Null function."

Virgil ran his eyes over the hollowed-out strongman, admiring its obscene craftsmanship. "I've seen mercenaries build crude exoskeletons, but this is next level. I'm impressed. Really."

Distracted by these observations, Virgil failed to notice the Messenger slithering its tendrils out from the strongman's limbs.

"Did you make it yourself?" he asked.

"You are unessential," the Messenger replied.

By the time Virgil saw those tendrils wrapping around the steel rod, it was too late to do anything about it.

"You are null."

The Messenger freed the rod from its chest.

The force emitted from the ruptured StormCell was mostly concussive, knocking Virgil into the black mirror wall. But foul subatomic particles rode the blast as well, flying through his body, filling his senses with a pain more familiar to him than any person or place. StormCells may have been the safest, cleanest way to harbor fusion energy, but that fusion was still nuclear. Unleashed, it burned out the Battery in Virgil's system and flung him deep into the Junkyard Blues. His insides caught fire, and though he couldn't see through his radiation blindness, he could feel the rancid boils sprouting up all over his skin. Arms, legs, chest, and face. Especially his face.

With practiced precision, Virgil found his inhaler and took a hit of the highest-grade Battery in existence.

Nothing happened.

Even after the acid taste and the hacking green smoke, the Junkyard Blues persisted. A potent terror mixed with Virgil's agony. After all this time, he had finally reached the worst-case scenario. *Battery wasn't working anymore.*

Hoping against hope, he dug out a fresh high-grade Battery capsule and swapped it into his inhaler. He took another hit, held the vapor in his lungs for as long as he could stand, then exhaled again.

This time, the Blues followed the script. Pain faded, vision returned, and the boils flattened to irritated splotches on Virgil's skin. He rested his back against the screen wall, fighting to catch his breath and organize his thoughts.

Two hits. He needed two hits of high-grade Battery. That was bad. Very bad.

"Death defines your species."

Across the room, the Messenger leered at Virgil through a dimming ocular lens, already at half-brightness. Its life clung to an emergency power supply, minutes from total shutdown.

"Death lives in your blood, turning it to poison. Death lives in your minds, making you selfish and solitary. Your blood will destroy your bodies, and you will all die alone."

Virgil struggled to his feet while the Messenger droned on.

"We are not alone. We are unified in our function." The synthetic voice dropped to a low, groggy octave. "The future . . . belongs . . . to us—"

When Virgil's heated knife entered the Messenger's neck mechanism, its speech processor was the first thing to go. The blade cut through the joints and wires like butter, leaving an orange molten slop in its wake. The diplomat's head came loose in the Volt Caster's grip. The carbon-fiber tendrils gave one last frantic death rattle, then fell lifeless.

Virgil held the masked head up at eye level. A faded wartime serial code was stamped just above the point of severance: 258-067.

"Asshole," he said.

The diplomat's dying words played on a loop in Virgil's brain, where his neurons still simmered from the Junkyard Blues.

Your blood will destroy your bodies, and you will all die alone.

"Can't die. Not yet," Virgil told the dead machine. "Not just yet. They still need me."

It took Virgil all afternoon to dig himself out of *Cradle*'s depths, where one wrong move could bring the whole place down. He felt tempted several times to dump the Messenger's head and free up both of his hands, but reason prevailed. No head, no payment. No payment, no reason for enduring any of this bullshit in the first place. So Virgil climbed out of *Cradle* one-handed. It wasn't the worst afternoon of his life, but it definitely took a spot in the bottom five.

The jeep sat unscathed where he'd left it, and thank goodness for that. In the Junkyard, a journey on foot was usually a trip to the grave.

Virgil had a decision to make.

His Battery dependency had doubled, and that kind of need would drain his stash in no time. And the Messenger had been right: he *was* alone. The slightest upset could trigger his Junkyard Blues now, and if he found his inhaler out of reach, there would be no one to help him. He would die, but that in itself wasn't what worried him. If he died, he would be unable to claim his reward for the Messenger's head. He would be unable to bring that reward back home.

Home would be in serious shit.

In one grand swoop, Virgil yanked the star-spangled fabric off the object slumped in his trailer. The mechanized suit he'd been hauling around for the last year was about half the size of a strongman, but it still dwarfed any human Virgil had met. Eight feet tall while standing, one thousand pounds of tungsten alloy. Limbs like tree trunks. Hands the size of cannon balls. Its head and chest cavity hung wide open, revealing a matrix of nodes and thin surgical needles lining the interior. An iron maiden with arms and legs.

If Virgil entered that suit, he would live long enough to complete his mission, but not much longer. It would cure his sickness, but if he wanted to survive inside long-term, or get back out again, he would have to put himself at the mercy of others. Not an option. Never an option. He hadn't survived this long in the Junkyard by trusting anyone but himself. He would probably die soon without the suit, but he would definitely perish later if he locked himself inside.

Later, with just enough time to finish the job. Just enough time to get the reward home.

Plasma shots cracked in the distance, yanking Virgil from his internal debate. Back up the highway, two argonaut Peacekeepers were shooting at something in the road, while a reaper crawled around it, slicing for weak points.

What was that thing? Virgil racked his Blues-battered memory. He had seen it. Spoken with it. The egg . . .

The kid.

Hallucinations were a common side effect of post-Blues delirium, and in that moment, Virgil got hit with one for the books. Defying reason and gravity, he watched as the rubble around him lifted off the ground. Each of the distinct chunks rose into the air, and as they climbed higher toward the sun, they began to connect. Shattered support beams repaired and relinked. Loose metal shavings found their perfect place on the hull, which expanded like a balloon to full size. *Cradle* returned to the stars fully formed, and the kid was back inside. Though Virgil stood miles below, he could see her floating in that grand panoramic window, watching him from on high. They locked eyes, as if spotting one another from across a room.

Virgil exhaled, wonderstruck. A wisp of green Battery smoke escaped his lungs, trickling out from parted lips. He was toxic. Dying. Unclean.

In response, the girl calmly exhaled onto the window. Her breath was invisible, fogging the glass white. It was invisible because she was clean. She was clean because . . . *because* . . .

Because she was the kid from outer space. The kid who had probably never tasted Battery, because she had never tasted the Junkyard's air. Even now, trapped in her sealed escape pod, the kid was breathing clean, albeit limited, oxygen. The kid was healthy. *Healthy.*

Virgil blinked, and *Cradle* was back to its decimated true self. He knew right away that nothing he just saw was real, but it didn't need to be. The hallucination had given him a very real idea.

He regarded the severed machine head, which he still clutched in the Volt Caster's grip.

"You think *she's* got death in her blood?" Virgil asked.

He shook the head, *no.*

"Yeah, me neither."

Virgil stowed the head in his front seat, then draped the fabric of the flag back over the mech suit in his trailer. He would need it soon, but not for himself. No, he had a new plan. Probably the best plan he'd concocted in years.

But this plan required deception, and pain. Her pain.

"White clouds," Virgil whispered. "Bright sun. Blue afternoon sky. Warm kimchi stew, red hot. A cold glass of milk . . ."

As he summoned these images of home, Virgil knew what he needed to do. No matter what, he had to stick to the plan. Step one: save the kid.

Virgil jumped into the driver's seat and took off toward the escape pod. With his Caster hand on the wheel, he used the other to draw the .44 magnum from his belt. If he zapped the Peacekeepers, he risked lighting up the pod as well. His plan would be foiled before it began.

The argonauts turned to face the jeep as it came toward them, but two well-aimed gunshots exploded their heads in quick succession. The reaper darted toward the vehicle, zig-zagging evasively, and Virgil held his fire until he could read the pattern. Titanium-coated magnum ammo was hard to come by these days; he felt obliged to make every shot count.

The reaper lunged at Virgil for the kill. One muzzle flash later, it ground to a stop, headless.

The girl was a mess when Virgil found her, sobbing, cowering back in the escape pod's limited recesses.

"Kid!" he called to her. "Relax! It's me."

Recognition dawned on her face, followed quickly by fury.

"*You*!" she hissed. "You left me! I can't believe you just left me!"

"But I came back!" Virgil said. "My schedule cleared up, and I'm feeling charitable. I can get you out of this thing."

The girl's eyes lit up like plasma beams. "Really?"

"Yes . . ." Virgil checked the surrounding area. The other Peace-keepers were emerging from their search parties, and the strongman was hauling something big out of the wreckage. Some kind of ball surrounded by golden rings that didn't look like they were attached to anything, like they were floating on their own. Farther out, a pair of army trucks plowed through the garbage dunes in their direction. More junkies, en route to strip the crash site for valuable space junk. They would be the first of many, and other Peacekeeper tribes would likely join the fray. Their bodies needed constant upkeep, and they took new parts wherever they could find them.

". . . but not here," Virgil said. "This place will be a war zone in a few minutes."

"Did you see any other colonists?" the girl asked.

"Any what?"

"Colonists! They'd be in suits like mine. Did you see anyone?"

Virgil remembered the bodies half buried in debris. If any of them were alive, they had been real good at hiding the fact.

"Did anyone else make it?" the girl pushed.

At times like these, Virgil envied the Peacekeepers. Even at their most confused, they never asked questions. They were never expected to give answers.

The girl found her answer in his silence. Her whole body started to shake, and her breathing became fast. Too fast. She was losing it.

"Kid, relax," Virgil cooed.

"I couldn't . . . I tried to . . . Oh my god . . ." The girl was hyperventilating.

"Kid! Look at me!"

The girl's vacant stare refocused on Virgil.

"What's your name?" he asked.

"Diane."

"Diane, I'm Virgil. I know something messed up happened to you, but if this egg's sealed off, you only got so much oxygen in there. You need to try and relax. You need to survive."

Gradually, Diane slowed her breathing back to normal. Her body still trembled, but progress was progress.

"Do you trust me?" Virgil asked.

"I . . . don't know you . . ." Diane said.

"I'm the guy who's going to take you somewhere safe. Trust me, and we'll have you on your feet pronto. Okay?"

Reluctantly, Diane nodded.

"*Bien*," Virgil said.

After stowing the wrecked Peacekeepers in his trailer—their parts could trade for a decent amount of Battery—Virgil unraveled some excess chain and lassoed it around the escape pod. He confirmed the links were tight, then drove back up the highway.

To any onlookers, his company was a sight to behold: a jeep hauling a trailer hauling a giant egg that scraped and swerved across the road with a mind of its own. To top it all off, a diplomat-class Peacekeeper's head rested comfortably in the jeep's front seat. Virgil couldn't decide which was more valuable: the head in the mask or the girl in the escape pod. The bounty, or the clean blood.

Either way, they both belonged to him.

CHAPTER 3

For Diane Three-One-Seven, the concept of time had grown fuzzy around the edges. The escape pod's electrical system had given out somewhere between the stratosphere and troposphere, and it took the digital clock with it. On *Cradle*, every action had been scheduled down to the second, and the clock was god. Now, time was the color of light seeping through the observation window. Time was the staleness in the air, the increasing labor needed to satisfy Diane's lungs.

Her life in the escape pod could be divided into two eras: Before Virgil and After Virgil. An age of paranoid stillness, and then an age of breakneck speed. Already, she missed the former desperately.

The world outside was now a blur of movement—a smeared watercolor painting—and in those fleeting moments when the visuals stabilized, none of them made any sense. It was like everything Diane knew about human civilization, from war to leisure, had been chewed up by some great monster and vomited out in random combinations. A derelict tank here. A charred cosmetics billboard there. Everything looked old. Everything was broken.

The jeep stopped twice while Diane was in the pod.

The first stop was at night, and they parked beside a concrete pillar leaning precariously into the pod window's view. Lightning cracked in the ebony sky, and during those brief eruptions, Diane could see the pillar was connected to a lengthy overpass canted high overhead, a ragged, swiss-cheese structure that looked ready to topple at a moment's notice. Another worthy monument to whatever catastrophe left Earth in such a dilapidated state. As Diane tried to understand why *this* was the ideal place to park, the stampede arrived. She felt it first, a kinetic hum muted against the pod's dense exterior. Then came the shadows, dark impressions moving over blackness, like water flowing over ice. Diane leaned closer to the window, hoping to identify these mysterious shapes.

A lightning bolt flashed, and she got her wish. Ants. Could she call them ants? *Cradle's* biology lessons had covered insects briefly, but what she was seeing did not match the image in Nurse's presentation. These ants were the size of human toddlers, with veiny purulent growths festering on their heads and abdomens. Hundreds of them raced over the desert floor, mandibles clicking.

Huddled as far from the observation window as she could manage, Diane watched the herd of giant ants go by. They all moved in a straight line, shifting course only to circumvent roadblocks. When the ants scuttled around the concrete pillar, they did not turn back onto their original paths. They kept going straight. Diane understood now why Virgil had stopped here. He must have seen the herd coming, and this was the best refuge he could find on short notice. The pillar was an ant shield, and evidently, a good one.

After an unknown length of time, the vibrations faded. Lightning revealed an empty desert; the herd had passed. The jeep's engine grumbled back into earshot, and they moved on.

Diane must have fallen asleep, because the next thing she knew, she was dreaming that she was back in *Cradle's* Central Atrium. All the other colonists were there with her, five hundred burgundy jumpsuits standing still, looking out the panoramic window. Diane followed their collective gaze, and she saw that the Earth was approaching. It was on fire. The oily atmosphere popped and boiled in a halo of flame. Diane tried to speak, to warn the others, but her voice had abandoned her. A firm hand rested on her shoulder, and she saw that it belonged to Ben Five-Zero-Nine. His head was on fire. Then his body was on fire. Then all the colonists were on fire, unmoving, watching the Earth. Diane could scream now, because she was on fire too—

When she opened her eyes, warm dawn light flowed lazily into the escape pod. She gagged at the smell of her own waking breath; she had soiled her underwear at some point during the crash, and they now occupied a back corner of the tiny pod. In this sealed environment, the smell was only getting worse.

Virgil pulled them into some kind of building, and cool shade overtook the daylight. Diane got the feeling this wasn't a place meant for vehicles. Smooshing her face against the observation window, she could see the tires and escape pod making a mess of the ceramic tile floor—a pathway clearly once intended for pedestrians. Tiny shops flanked them from every direction, advertising clothes, pastries, video games, and other goods stolen long ago. A glass ceiling sparkled four stories up, but layers of grime kept the sunshine from reaching the lower levels. Escalators crisscrossed overhead, unmoving. Out of order.

They parked for the second time beside a tall fountain, dry as a bone. Diane heard Virgil exit his jeep, rummage around in the back seat, and then something gave off a low-fidelity *click . . . click . . . click.*

"This'll work," she heard him say.

More bizarre noises followed. The untying of chains. The whoosh of fabric being shaken and bundled up. The click of flipped switches. A machine turning on.

Virgil reappeared in the pod's observation window. "You have any radiation problems on that *Cradle* of yours?"

Diane blinked at him. "I don't know what you mean."

The window fogged a little as she said this. It was getting foggier all the time.

"Perfect," Virgil said. He pulled an inhaler from his coat and ejected it into his mouth. Green vapor bombarded the window as he coughed, leaving a jade streak on the glass.

"What is that?" Diane asked.

Virgil swapped the empty capsule in his inhaler for a glowing replacement.

"Battery," he said, and off Diane's confused look: "It's medicine. Without this, folks of flesh and blood would've died out a long time ago."

"How?" Diane asked. "What happened here?"

Virgil took another hit, coughed up another green lung. "We'll get to that." He refilled the inhaler, then tucked it away. "Here's the situation, Diane. The air out here's dirty. Toxic. Everybody and their mom has the Junkyard Blues. Always have, always will."

"The junkyard what?"

Virgil waved his hand dismissively. "Just roll with me. As soon as I crack open this egg, you'll have about ten seconds before the Blues get you too."

"So . . . I'll need Battery?" Diane guessed.

The stains on Virgil's beard made his smile twice as big. Ten times as ghastly. "Smart kid! Problem is, I've only got high-grade Battery on me. The strong shit. If you took it, your virgin lungs would explode inside your chest. Not exaggerating."

Something twitched in Diane's face. The news kept getting better. "Can we find some Battery that *won't* make my lungs explode?"

"The nearest village is a ways off," Virgil said. "How much oxygen you got left in there?"

"Not much." The air in the escape pod grew hotter every time she spoke, and she was starting to feel dizzy. This conversation wasn't helping, either. Virgil was laying out these problems for a reason. Get to it.

"So what do we do?" she said.

Virgil tapped the window playfully. "I'm glad you asked."

Then he ran away.

"Wait!" Diane called, to no avail. She heard the jeep's engine rev up, then its tires crunch across the floor. *He was abandoning her again. She was going to die in this pod. She was going to suffocate and die. She was going to die—*

Virgil parked his jeep in front of the observation window, and for the first time, Diane saw the mechanical suit resting in his trailer. She observed its bulky frame, its brawny limbs, its interior lined with needles.

"See that beauty?" Virgil said, returning to the window. "That's a Grave Walker. Finest piece of human-operated battle tech the Grand Finale ever produced. Story goes, they put wounded soldiers in there to keep them on the battlefield. Top-notch armor, all kinds of hidden gizmos, and total control over the user's biosystems. Wild stuff. Rarest junk I've ever seen.

"But here's the best part! Once you're inside, you're in a regulated, totally isolated environment. It cleans the air. It purifies water. It's the perfect fix to your little problem—"

"Why aren't you using it?" Diane asked.

Virgil paused. "Hm?"

"If it's so great, why aren't you wearing it now? You said you had the 'blues' or whatever."

"I was saving it for an emergency," he replied quickly. "Think this qualifies. Don't you?"

Diane wasn't buying the pitch. Something about the situation, the convenient inconveniences that rendered putting on a needle suit her only option, stank of deception. She felt that creeping dread again, and after *Cradle*, she would not dismiss her hunches so easily.

"Here's the plan," Virgil said. "I'll cut this pod open, and then you'll jump into the Grave Walker, easy-peasy. Sound good?"

The first part sounded fantastic, but Diane had her own plans after that. Once the escape pod was open, she would make a beeline for the nearest escalator and hide somewhere in this abandoned shopping . . . place—there was a word for buildings like this, but it escaped her. Then, after the green-bearded psycho had left, she would go back to *Cradle* and look for other colonists. She couldn't be the only survivor, and if the air really was toxic, she would find someone else to help her. Anyone else.

"Sounds good," Diane said.

Virgil moved out of sight again.

A shrill whining filled the escape pod. Diane covered her ears, but nothing less than total deafness would have blocked that noise out. A patch of the interior ceiling began to glow. First dull red, then orange, and then glaring white. Diane moved closer to the phenomenon, trying to understand it, when a simmering knife blade shot down and nearly stabbed her in the face. She fell back with a yelp, and the blade proceeded to carve its way across the metal plating with little resistance. When it retracted, the knife had sliced a perfect circle around the observation window. It looked like an eye crying molten lava tears.

The front of the escape pod detached, hitting the tiles with a loud *clang*. The harness bar lifted off the passenger seat. Diane bolted to freedom.

In a single step, she realized her mistake. The muscles in her legs gave out instantly, and she crumpled to the floor. She had not noticed her dilemma in the escape pod, where space was tight and standing wasn't an option. But out in the open, she discovered that she couldn't stand at all. Her body felt heavy and weak. Her mobility peaked at a slow crawl.

Gravity was to blame. *Cradle*'s Gravity Core had created a force that equaled somewhere between the gravity of the Earth and the Moon. But here, on actual *Earth*, the laws of physics made no compromises. These were Diane's first real steps, but she hadn't the strength to take them.

"What happened?" Virgil ran to her side. "Your leg asleep?"

Diane rose onto her elbows. "I can't . . . I can't walk . . ."

The air smelled dry and sour. The tiles were freezing cold. Virgil's countdown to the ambiguous sickness, "the Junkyard Blues," ticked in her head.

Ten . . . nine . . . eight . . .

"Hold your breath!" Virgil lifted her by the armpits and dragged her to the trailer. The electrodes on his Volt Caster dug into her flesh.

Seven . . . six . . . five . . .

With a labored grunt, he hoisted Diane into the Grave Walker. The needles retracted harmlessly against her skin, and she exhaled with relief.

Four . . . three . . . two . . .

The Grave Walker's chest plates lowered slowly. Virgil pushed down on them with all his might, struggling to speed up the process. The veins in his neck bulged.

He muttered to himself, "Clean air. Sweet air. Úna's hair in the wind—"

One.

The chest sealed shut. The head snapped down. A thin Y-shaped light marked the border between the separate plates, and it was all Diane could see.

Locking contraptions snapped and bolted. The Y-light disappeared from the bottom up. Diane was in the dark again.

The first needle pierced the back of her neck, where the spine meets the skull. She cried out, leaned forward, but the needle elongated with her. Wherever she moved, the sharp point remained at the exact same depth in her body. Never stabbing deeper, never sliding farther out.

The other needles attacked in rapid succession, going for the legs, arms, and back. Amid the skin-tearing pain, she had no way to know how many needles were invading her pores. And it wasn't just needles. Some unseen device plastered sensor disks to her forehead, drilled tubes into her belly. Invisible hands stabbed, poked, and prodded her from every angle. Her nerve endings screamed while she herself was in too much agony to make a sound. She felt sick. Violated. Helpless and alone. She longed for the stinking claustrophobia of her escape pod. Suffocation didn't seem so bad now.

A switch flipped, and the needling anguish erupted into something a million times worse. Every atom in her body combusted all at once. A molecular migraine. A hurt to end all hurts.

In the next millisecond, all sensation disappeared. Diane had no body. No thoughts. She became one with the dark. It was not frightening, nor was it a relief. It was nothing, just like her.

"Diane?" A distant voice. His voice. The voice of the man who did this. "You see anything yet?"

Much to her surprise, Diane found that she could speak. "No. I don't—"

Multicolored lights filled the void. They were unintelligible at first, a garbled mess of meaningless pixels, but then something outside smacked the Grave Walker's head. The shapes reformed into a computer boot-up sequence. A loading bar stretched over Diane's vision, filling quickly as a function list scrolled beside it. "Shields," "HUD_Tracking," and the like.

"Better?" Virgil called from beyond.

"What is this?" Diane asked. "What did you do to me?"

Familiar noises followed. The jeep's engine. Tires decimating ceramic. Virgil's voice returned, but it had somehow become omnipresent in Diane's head. Crackling and distorted, like it was passing through a radio. "All right, kid. Listen up—"

"Where are you taking me?" Diane interrupted.

"*Cállate*, all right? I'm getting the sense that your *Cradle* didn't keep up on world events, and nothing's gonna make any sense until you understand a few things. So listen up. I'm only going to break this down once . . ."

As Virgil took a deep breath, the loading screen transformed into a complex heads-up display—the HUD. Counters and gauge meters went through various calibrations, all gibberish to Diane.

"There was a war," Virgil said. "That much should be obvious. We call it the Grand Finale, because that's what it was. Whatever life was like before the war, whoever ran the show, the Finale wiped all that clean off the map. We don't even know why the war was fought. All we've got is the mess it left behind."

Crunching tile became grumbling asphalt. They were outside again.

"Here's what we do know. At some point, after the cyborgs and the mutants did their damage, some high-grade dumbass built a thinking computer with a gazillion mechanical bodies. They were called the Peacekeepers, and they were supposed to end the war and unite the human race in kumbaya. But they didn't. They tried to turn folks into cattle, and folks don't like being cattle. We're just fine pushing ourselves to the brink, but when some holier-than-thou AI tries to pull us back, well, we just get *pissed*."

Diane felt the jeep roll to a stop.

"So the people who could still fight back fought back, and eventually, the ol' thinking computer got taken down. Where did that leave us? Our ecosystems were trashed to shit, all records of human history were mangled or straight-up deleted—the computer's last middle finger to us all—and we've still got a bunch of wartime leftovers lurking around, like the Peacekeepers. They may not have a voice in their heads calling the shots anymore, but they still hate us like always. Maybe it makes them feel nostalgic."

The jeep door opened and shut. Virgil kept talking, but the sound was coming from outside the suit, rather than inside her helmet. Distant, but like he was approaching her.

"So now, we're out here doing our best. The townies live in villages built from old factories. The roadkillers pillage and murder. The mercenary clans protect, or kill, for the right price. And then there's folks like me. We're junkies. We live off the land, digging up valuable junk and selling it for the right price. It's a dangerous life, but it's free. It's the life you make it."

Virgil flicked something on the Grave Walker's head. "Welcome to the Junkyard, kid."

The dark veil lifted.

Through a visor and the constantly shifting HUD, Diane saw everything.

They were on the roof level of an old concrete structure packed with totaled cars, and the sprawling view from up here took her breath away. A deep valley ran just below them. The right side was made of natural red rock, but there was something odd about the left side. Diane squinted, and to her amazement, the visor zoomed in on the valley with near-perfect resolution. She saw now that the other hills were not rock at all. They were trash heaps, collections of scrap metal risen to impossible heights. Some pieces were huge, broken tanks and annihilated buildings. Other additions, like bent nails and broken TV screens, were small but ubiquitous. Nature had created half the valley, and the Grand Finale had done the rest.

Something moved on the valley floor. Diane could see a small group of humans locked in battle with more of those machines—the so-called *Peacekeepers*. The humans' clothes were even more ragged than Virgil's, and their guns fired searing light.

Beyond the valley, vehicles raced along distant roads, some alone, others in small packs. Fumes rose from bustling factories. Lightning struck at tall spires made of silver. Gray smog ate a corner of the landscape, hiding all but the vaguest outline of a city too big to be real. Far into the west, Diane could see the shape of a man moving sluggishly along the horizon. A mirage, she hoped. To be visible from so far away, the man would have to be enormous.

For a place ravaged by warfare, the Junkyard sure was lively. Diane felt compelled to move closer, to get a better look. She stood up from the trailer, planted her feet on the ground, but then realized she felt none of this. Her movements yielded no sensation.

She looked down. Seeing the Grave Walker's flat, hulking feet was not like wearing a pair of boots. She didn't feel her toes inside the shoe, and yet it moved when she willed it. They were not her feet, and yet the feet belonged to her.

Vertigo squeezed Diane's equilibrium. She wobbled on her phantom feet, flapped her "arms" in vain, and fell to her knees.

"Easy!" Virgil rushed to her side. "The suit takes getting used to. Baby steps."

Diane lifted the great hand she saw in front of her, watched its fingers bend to her command. "How am I doing this?" she asked.

"The Grave Walker's hooked straight to your nervous system. Think of it as your new body. A crazy strong, super durable body."

Diane remembered the first point stabbing into her spine. The surge of pain that overloaded her nerves. "So . . . all those needles . . ."

"It's worth it," Virgil said. "I promise."

Diane rose the Grave Walker from its knees. "I want out."

"What?" Virgil gaped. "Are you kidding? Look at you!"

The entire Grave Walker began to tremble, along with Diane's voice. "I can't feel my body. I . . . I can't feel anything . . ."

Virgil took a few steps back. "Calm down. It just takes time—"

"Get me out!" Diane shrieked. She made the hands claw at the head and torso, searching desperately for a seam. Metal scraped against metal, and the noise mixed terribly with Diane's screams. "I want the needles out! Out! *Out*—!"

"You can't get out!" Virgil blurted.

The suit's arms fell limp.

"What?" Diane said.

"It's hooked to your brain, kid. Can't just pull the plug. We're talking paralysis. Death."

The Grave Walker remained perfectly still for way too long. Concerned, Virgil inched toward it.

"*Why?*" Diane lunged out at Virgil. He jumped back, Volt Caster raised and sparking.

"Back up!" he shouted.

The Grave Walker stumbled and landed on its face, smashing the concrete beneath to bits. "You knew what this was!" she said, raising the machine's head to face him. "How could you do this to me?"

Virgil threw his hands in the air. "Oh, my bad! How could I save you from the Blues, give you legs, and turn you into a goddamn juggernaut? What was I thinking?"

The Grave Walker went still again. This time, Virgil kept his distance.

"There had to be another way," Diane said, and she started to cry.

"Look, you're going to be okay," Virgil promised.

She said nothing. Her brain groped for warmth, cold, a tickle, an itch, anything to reestablish the mind-body connection, but there was nothing to be found. The feeling transcended numbness, and she realized that she had traded one prison for another. She was locked in solitary confinement from her own body, and of course from others. Diane had so rarely been close to anyone on *Cradle*, so rarely felt someone hold her hands and tell her that everything was okay—even when she knew it wasn't. Now, she would never be close to anyone ever again. She was more alone than ever, trapped in a cell of sensory deprivation.

Was this what it felt like to be dead?

"I meant . . . you can't get out *yet*."

Diane sniffed. "But you just told me—"

"I'm on contract for a very powerful person," Virgil said. "I'm headed to see her now. She's got a scientist working for her, smartest guy I know. One of the last *really* smart people. He gave me the suit, and he can do the operation to get you out. He can even augment your space legs with bionics, get you walking in Earth gravity on your own."

Diane lifted the Grave Walker back to a kneeling position. At this level, she was about a head taller than Virgil.

"You could have led with that," she said.

Virgil shrugged. "I wouldn't trust him if it were just me under the knife, but you're not going in alone. I'll be right there, making sure he doesn't tag you with a kill switch or nothin'. People are always looking to take advantage."

Diane squinted at Virgil, and her visor zoomed in on his cragged face. That smile looked genuine, carefree, without malice. But his eyes were hidden beneath the shadow of his hood, and there was no reading them. Diane suspected this was by design.

"I don't understand why you're helping me," she said.

"Kindness of my heart?"

At Diane's silence, Virgil threw back his head and laughed. It was a hearty sound, good-humored and infectious. Diane almost smiled herself, but then remembered how afraid she was.

"I'm not doing so hot, kid," Virgil said. "You saw me take two hits of Battery back there? Most people only need one. But I can't tap out until I finish this contract, and most hired guns would either shoot me in the back or cost me an arm and a leg."

He opened his arms to Diane, like he was presenting her to an audience. "Enter you! You're big, you're scary, and nobody would know you're a snot-nosed kid just by looking at you."

Diane huffed. "I'm not a kid. I've gone through seventeen orbits."

Virgil squinted at the term *orbits* but let the comment go. "You watch my back, keep me breathing, and I'll get you out of the Grave Walker. Deal?"

Diane considered the proposition, the reasoning behind it, then: "I'm not buying this."

Virgil groaned. "No?"

"There have to be a million people more qualified to be your bodyguard."

"None of them work for free," Virgil said.

Diane shook the Grave Walker's head. "There's something you're not telling me."

Virgil ran his ungloved hand down his face, stretching the exhaustion there to caricatured proportions.

"You see a meter on your HUD?" he asked. "The one with a little lightning bolt?"

Diane searched the heads-up display. Sure enough, a meter and lightning bolt symbol occupied the upper right corner. The meter was half full.

"That's your StormCell's power bar," Virgil continued. "If that runs out, the suit goes dead and all your bodily functions shut down."

Diane dreaded the impending point he was about to make. As she stared at the StormCell gauge, the meter decreased by about a pixel. She nearly cried out.

"You're going to need someone to replace the StormCell for you," Virgil said. "And the one you got right now's old as hell, so it's probably leaking juice like a sonofabitch."

Diane tried to keep a steady, unaffected tone. "I can find someone."

"Better hurry. Every step you take costs energy, and the Junkyard's a big place. Big, mean, and out for blood."

Virgil's mouth twitched at the mention of "blood," but for all Diane knew, it was just a tic.

"If you want to take on the Junkyard all by yourself," he continued, "with zero knowledge beyond my little history lesson, go ahead. Ready or not, here you come."

He walked back toward the driver's side of his jeep. "I'm out of here. If you're not back in the trailer when my foot hits the pedal, *hasta luego.*"

With great difficulty and zero grace, Diane pulled the Grave Walker onto its feet. Virgil hopped back behind the wheel, turned the key in the ignition, and then waited with the engine idling. In spite of his ultimatum, he was still giving Diane time to make a decision. She got the sense that, while Virgil was undeniably brash, he still had the capacity to be reasonable. When it suited him.

Diane looked back to her epic view of the Junkyard, and already the landscape had changed. One of the garbage hills in the valley had avalanched, burying every human fighter and most of the Peacekeepers. A pack of cars was driving away from some shapeless gyre, a vibrating darkness hovering just beneath the real clouds. The tiny shape of that distant titan was nowhere in sight.

Behind her, Virgil revved the engine. He was growing impatient. Time to make a call.

Could she trust this man? Probably not. Could she survive in the Junkyard on her own, in a body she knew nothing about? Same answer.

Farther south, a wide blue patch in the sky marked *Cradle*'s point of entry. It wouldn't be hard to retrace the way back to the crash site, but deep down, Diane knew what she would find there. She had caught a glimpse of the wreckage when Virgil first hauled the escape pod away. The destruction had been absolute.

There was nothing left behind for Diane. All she had learned, everyone she had ever known, none of that meant a thing. She was a foreigner on a foreign world, and if she denied the only hand offered to her, she would truly be alone.

The wheels on the jeep began to inch forward. Far away, a green lightning bolt struck at one of the silver spires.

The Grave Walker's hands balled into creaking fists. Diane didn't do this on purpose. It just happened.

CHAPTER 4

They were several hours into their drive, barreling down a wide avenue that separated a ruined neighborhood from an abandoned construction site, when Diane saw the four-wheeler racing toward them. Its all-terrain body was covered in hostile graffiti, a million iterations of *Die* and *Screw You*, with a few skulls for good measure. The driver looked to be a sun-burned woman wearing mismatched rags and a stitched-up gas mask, wielding a gun much larger than the Caretaker's had been.

"Um, Virgil—"

"I see her," Virgil said. "Looks like she's packing an ion shotgun. Big heat for a roadkiller."

When she got within range, the woman aimed her shotgun at Diane and fired. Virgil swerved at just the right time, and the ion cluster sailed over the jeep, obliterating a bulldozer parked at the construction site.

As Diane gripped the trailer's edges to keep from flying off, Virgil reached out with his Volt Caster. He snapped his fingers. A thunderbolt struck the four-wheeler's hood, and the StormCell within it exploded. Bits of engine shredded the would-be assailant's head to a pulp.

"*Oh my god!*" Diane shouted.

The Grave Walker's HUD tracked the woman's body as it soared through a hail of vehicle parts. A green rectangle and the word *HOS-TILE* surrounded her, following her every movement without delay.

Only when the corpse hit the road and stayed there did the border disappear. *HOSTILE TERMINATED.*

"Wooo-*whee*!" Virgil howled, his CB mic crammed into his gas mask. Diane cringed at the signal's loudness. The Grave Walker must have detected her discomfort because the volume of his next exclamation decreased to a more bearable level. "Roadkiller, meet road! Am I right?"

"You killed her!" Diane said, horrified. "You just . . . She's dead!"

"Lucky for us. Honestly, I expected to see more roadkillers 'round these parts. Your Grave Walker makes a good scarecrow."

He sounded so matter-of-fact, so unfazed by the brutal slaying of another human being. Diane had never witnessed a death before. Yes, everyone she knew from *Cradle* was . . . gone, but all of that happened out of view. Just far enough out of mind. This was her first direct encounter with death, and the pill did not go down easy.

"You just kill people on sight?" Diane asked.

"Did you miss the part where the roadkiller shot first?" Virgil countered.

Diane inhaled sharply. "You could have talked to her!"

Virgil laughed like it was the funniest thing he had ever heard.

Nobody fought on *Cradle*. Nobody died until they aged out of Block Six. There had not been a single instance of bloodshed until the very end, and that end was so horrible that Diane could not bring herself to comprehend it. Whenever she tried to think about all the bodies that Virgil must have found, her brain shut off. She still caught herself wondering what Ben Five-Zero-Nine was going to teach her about Interior Maintenance today, what the other Block Threes were saying behind her back. She could not yet grasp the true reality of death. Virgil could, but he didn't seem to care.

They turned onto the main street of a dense residential area, or what was left of it. Some plots of land were black and empty, the product of apathetic long-range missiles. The houses and pharmacies still standing were riddled with laser burns, bullet holes, and acid corrosion. Battles had been fought here, and Diane got the sense that they never really stopped, even after the Grand Finale had come to an end.

"Is this how it is everywhere?" she asked somberly. "Just people shooting each other up?"

"No, no. The villages are *tranquilas*," Virgil said. "They take care of their own. Most shooting happens on the road."

"Then why live on the road? The villages sound so much safer."

"Because the villages don't have everything they need. Some make food, but not water. Some make Battery, but not food. And when something breaks, they don't always have the parts to fix it. Junkies are the go-between."

That wasn't good enough for Diane. "Why don't the villages work together, then?" she asked. "Everybody would get everything they need."

Virgil gave long, encumbered sigh. "Because not all the villages get along, kid."

"What do they argue about?"

"I don't know. Trade. Territory. Stuff like that."

"Can't they just work it out? For the greater good?"

"People don't work that way."

"Why not?"

"They just don't."

"But then how come—"

"¡*Chale*!" Virgil yelled. "You're driving me bugshit with all these questions!"

Diane listened while he fumbled with the water tank in the jeep's back seat. He poured the last of the water into a canteen, lifted his gas mask, and took a big chug. The CB mic captured his swishing with uncomfortable clarity.

She listened, and she wondered . . . Was this the first time someone had yelled at her? Not just scolded, but really raised their voice?

She realized that it must be. On *Cradle*, anger manifested in sideways glances, insidious comments, and communal neglect. In the first weeks after her accident, before she learned to hide her dread and *read the room*, Diane had felt *Cradle* growing weary of her dissonance. She reflected a failure on the system's part, and failure bred resentment. Even with nowhere to send her, they had found a way to banish Diane from the social flow.

Now, sitting in the back of this rickety trailer, Diane discovered something new about herself: shouting did not intimidate her. After a whole orbit of seething mind games, hearing a grown man shout was almost a relief. He wore his anger on his sleeve. She could work with that.

With an air of calmness, Diane asked, "How am I going to learn anything if I don't ask questions?"

Virgil swallowed another mouthful of water. "Look. Listen. Shut your mouth."

"*Wow*," Diane said.

Virgil threw down the empty canteen. Even he must have felt the rudeness in his words because he shifted gears almost immediately.

"Starting now," he said, "we have a new rule. You get three questions a day. Three. No more."

"Fine," Diane said. It was an imperious constraint, but at least it was a compromise. And she had no intention of traveling with this man after they reached their destination, so she wouldn't have to put up with his condition for long.

After taking a bit to deliberate, Diane asked her first question: "Where are we going?"

"Jericho," Virgil said.

Diane rolled her eyes. The visor HUD spasmed to track the gesture, and she vowed never to roll her eyes in the Grave Walker ever again.

"What's Jericho?" Diane asked, extending her original inquiry.

"It's a supercity."

"Come on. That's barely an answer."

Virgil reclined in the driver's seat. "During the Grand Finale, all the ecosystems got screwed up, and places near water got it worst. Everybody moved to the desert, and lots of those people shacked up in a big walled city that kept getting bigger. They called it Jericho for some reason. When the war ended, they shut the gates and told everybody outside to take a hike. Nobody goes in, nobody comes out. Officially, at least. That's their law."

Diane perked up. So there were still laws on this godforsaken planet, and walls to keep law-abiding citizens safe. Maybe she could stay in

Jericho when she got free of the Grave Walker. Maybe everything was going to be okay after all.

"But the corporations," he continued, "the ones that control Jericho, they know there aren't enough resources in the supercity to keep it running. So, behind each other's backs, they work with junkies like me to smuggle in the goods. I radioed ahead to my client. We'll get in, no problem."

That brought Diane to another nagging question. "Why do you use radios? I know there are still some satellites in orbit. I've seen them. Cellular would be so much easier."

Virgil eased them onto a highway entrance ramp, leaving the ruins behind.

"When that AI I told you about went off the deep end, it got into everything. Computers, satellites, those little touchscreens people used to have. Nobody's heard from the Hive Mind in centuries, but if it's still out in cyberspace somewhere . . . Nobody wants to make that reintroduction."

"You said it 'turned people into cattle,'" Diane said. "What does that mean?"

Virgil clicked his tongue. "Your three questions are up."

"No! I only asked where we're going. Well, that and the radio thing I guess, but I still have one more."

"You also asked: 'What's Jericho?' I count three."

Diane squeezed the sides of the trailer in frustration. Another involuntary gesture, one that bent the railing like it was papier-mâché. "That's cheap and you know it."

"Rules are rules," Virgil replied.

Diane scowled, crossing the Grave Walker's huge arms over its chest plate. It was a comedic gesture from the outside, a battle mech of immense size pouting like an angry child, but there was nothing funny about the resentment stewing beneath it.

Miles passed without a word.

Virgil refused to answer any more questions for the day, and questions were all Diane knew. She had no common experiences from which to conjure small talk. No relevant memories beyond the past two days. She felt like a newborn, experiencing every aspect of life for the first time. And with no willing teacher to guide her, she struggled to make sense of it all on her own. To complicate things further, Diane had no way to know what lay on the road ahead. Sitting in the trailer with her back to Virgil, she could only see things after the jeep passed them by. They zipped past countless wrecked combat vehicles along the highway shoulder, and she watched them shrink and vanish down the gullet of distance. For Diane, everything was in the past tense.

They were headed east; that much she knew. Not because she could see the sun, a dull ember in the heavy clouds, dipping gradually into her visor's line of sight, but because the Grave Walker's HUD contained a digital compass. She was facing west. Now Virgil turned onto a new ramp that faced Diane southward, and she took the opportunity to look east, hoping to catch a peek at their destination.

She got much more than a peek.

The Wall of Jericho dominated the middle distance, a mountainous barrier of steel and concrete stretching farther than Diane's visor could zoom. Another wall rested on top of it, one made of smog vapor and exhaust fumes. It reduced the skyline beyond to faint lights, ghostly shapes, a megalopolitan shadow. Diane understood now that Jericho was not a place *within* the Junkyard. These were two separate universes, and Diane found that immensely reassuring. The Junkyard was not the entire world; there was another place to begin her terrestrial life. A safer place, she imagined. Jericho.

The next leg of Virgil's route meandered through open desert, giving Diane more opportunities to behold Jericho in all its glory. As they drew closer, she noticed a divide in the Wall, a narrow segment that split the barrier in two. It was a door, a sealed gateway as high and mighty as the Wall itself. The seam running down the door's center was nearly invisible, caked over with centuries of reddish grit. It corroborated Virgil's history lesson: *when the war ended, they shut the gates and told everybody outside to take a hike.* These gates had not been opened for a very long time.

There was something else clinging to the door, running along its length and about a third of the way up its height. Diane first mistook it for moss, some kind of dying organic growth that had formed on the entryway during its inactive state. Diane almost lobbed an unsolicited question at her taciturn driver, but as he drove them over an interchange in the highway, she observed the answer herself.

What looked like moss was actually a favela that clung to the gate, an eclectic patchwork of shanty metal shacks piggybacking up the door. Some dwellings rested on girders drilled into the concrete; others were wedged into naturally occurring crevices—a testimony to the Wall's immense width. The shacks were suspended over a barred drainage grate that comprised the door's bottom rim, and from that grate, dirty brown water flowed in a bubbling rage. A canal had been dug beneath it, directing the water flow toward shabby filtration silos that gulped the water through copper pipes.

Diane had spent enough time in *Cradle*'s water treatment sector to understand the forces at work here. This village hydrated itself with Jericho's waste. It was smart. Disgusting, but smart.

Virgil took up his CB mic as they drove along the canal. "We're gonna park in Gatetown real quick, see if I can haggle for supplies. These are decent folks, and I'm not trying to scare the piss out of them by bringing you into negotiations."

Diane hugged the Grave Walker's arms around its body in a self-conscious effort to appear smaller. Was she really so intimidating?

"So," Virgil went on, "some ground rules. Rule one: you stay by the jeep. Rule two: you talk to no one unless you have to, and if you do, don't let anyone know where you're from."

"I don't see why that matters," Diane said.

"It does," Virgil insisted. "You don't want to be 'the Girl from Outer Space.' Might attract the wrong attention."

"How?"

"You're out of questions, remember? Just do what I say."

Virgil parked the jeep in a small roped-off lot beneath the favela's entrance steps. A wilted old parking attendant with no legs and a laser rifle sat guard under a plastic umbrella, and Virgil tossed her a Nutribrik as he climbed out of the driver's seat. She caught it with one hand, digging into the nutrient bar with unexpected savagery.

Up above, Gatetown bustled with something Diane never thought she would see again: *community*. Merchants haggled with customers over the price of Battery capsules. Teenagers passed a water bottle between themselves as they laughed and gossiped. Midwives helped a pregnant woman refill the tank in her self-contained Battery apparatus; if she suffered the Blues for even a second, Diane guessed, the baby could be in serious trouble.

The baby . . . So they still performed natural births down here? Diane couldn't even imagine what that must be like.

Her head was spinning. She wanted so badly to talk to these people, to fill the hole that *Cradle* left behind. But then she remembered what she was wearing, what Virgil had said about her scaring people, and a sense of otherness smothered her. As long as she was trapped in the Grave Walker, she could be part of nothing.

"I won't be long," Virgil called back to her as he started up the stairs. "Stay in—"

"The trailer. I got it. Thanks."

Diane waved him off dismissively, but after he had climbed out of sight, it occurred to her that she was alone for the first time since leaving the escape pod. Alone with a strange parking attendant gnashing audibly on a Nutribrik. Alone in a body losing too much power way too fast—she was already down to 30 percent. And she couldn't be certain, but she thought there was something moving among the other vehicles in the lot. Small bodies crawling and weaving, just beyond the visor's ability to track them. Maybe this was just her paranoia. Maybe it wasn't.

Virgil annoyed Diane like no one she had ever met, but she was counting the seconds until he returned.

CHAPTER 5

At the top of the stairs, Virgil allowed himself one last look at the irate death machine sulking in his trailer. The events of that morning still weighed heavy on his mind, though he took great pains not to show it. He couldn't quite shake something Diane had said after learning about the Grave Walker's true nature. Her words haunted him.

There had to be another way.

She was right, of course. The Junkyard Blues would have taken days to kill a healthy person, plenty of time to find some low-grade Battery. And Virgil had not prepared her for the Grave Walker's neuro-synchronization process. Not in the slightest. If he had, she might never have climbed inside. The truth was, he needed her in that suit. Not just alive, but clean. Blood untainted.

And she couldn't know about the blood, how valuable it made her. That would give her leverage; Virgil couldn't afford that.

He felt his conscience getting all murky again. Not the time or place, so he quickly took his guilt and flipped it around.

"Ain't I doing the kid a favor?" he mumbled.

He had saved her from suffocating to death, and now he was taking her to the only man who could get her out of the Grave Walker in one piece. And while she was under anesthesia, Virgil would ask the scientist to drain a few liters of blood, just enough to get Virgil himself back in good shape. Diane wouldn't even miss them.

Everybody wins, he thought.

He moved on, leaving his guilt behind.

The shop was empty when Virgil stepped up to the refrigerated display counter. He had sold a cooling coil to the owner the last time he was here, and now the case was stocked with plastic bottles of chilled Gatetown water. Not a delicacy to leave unguarded, and yet Virgil was alone with the bottles, the empty water tanks hanging from the ceiling by rope, the random machine parts strewn haphazardly on crooked shelves. The shop was three walls and a roof, with the open entrance facing west. In the early evening light, Virgil's shadow, and the shadows of passing townies, were his only companions.

He rapped his Volt Caster's knuckles on the counter. A tubby man in his thirties slipped through a plastic curtain in the back, regarding Virgil with an irritated grunt. His left hand had been replaced with a bionic prosthetic—thick blocky fingers designed for strength rather than dexterity—and a blue cable ran from his wrist to the back of his head, just under the skin. He was not the owner that Virgil remembered.

"What you see is what I got," the shopkeeper said, approaching the counter.

Virgil didn't see much. The shelves were nearly barren, and not a StormCell in sight. In his experience, village shopkeepers usually had private inventories saved for themselves, or for preferred customers. Virgil was a seasoned pro at getting on those VIP lists. It was easier than people thought.

He smiled, looking past the shopkeeper, toward the curtain. "Business must be booming if Annette can afford to take on a cyborg! She around anywhere?"

"You a regular?" the shopkeeper asked.

"I consider myself a friend."

The shopkeeper gave him a rude once-over, but Virgil never showed any sign of offense. Townies often harbored prejudices against junkies, most of which were earned, and the trick was to appear oblivious to the local/outsider dynamic. Act familiar, but not invasive. It was their house, and he was happy to be there.

"Annette's on a trip to the Heap," the shopkeeper eventually said. "And she ain't flipping my surgery bill. I paid my cybersmith off years ago."

Virgil looked concerned. "The Heap's a long ways from here. Dangerous trip, especially for someone Annette's age."

The shopkeeper ignored the sentiment. "What do you want?"

"Couple things," Virgil said, resting his elbows on the counter. "I need a new tank of water . . ."

"That I got," the shopkeeper said.

". . . And some tier-two StormCells."

"That I don't got."

Virgil opened his hands, turning them upward. "Come on, *güey*—"

"What you see is what I got," the shopkeeper repeated, clicking his robotic fingers on the counter. The pinky got stuck halfway up, and he had to punch it hard to knock it back into place. Virgil now understood how the man could pay off his cybersurgery debt with such ease; the augmentation was a hack job.

Virgil winked. "I know you've got some StormCells back there. I wouldn't usually ask for the personal stash, but it's kind of an emergency."

The shopkeeper shook his head firmly. Virgil held eye contact, hunting for any sign of leniency. Any weakness that could help him avoid bringing out the big guns. He found none.

"What's your name?" Virgil asked.

"Al," the shopkeeper said.

"You're Annette's brother, right? She told me about you."

Al was the antithesis of impressed.

"She ever tell you about me?" Virgil asked.

"Depends," Al said. "Who are ya?"

Virgil plucked a leather pouch off his belt and dropped it on the counter. The contents rattled upon impact. "I'm the junkie who sells this."

Confused, Al clocked the wrinkles on Virgil's face. "A junkie? I never met a junkie that lived past forty—"

"Open the bag, Al."

The cyborg undid the twine that sealed the pouch, more out of professional courtesy than actual curiosity. The rim of the sack fell open, and when Al saw what was inside, his entire face expanded. His eyebrows went up. His mouth fell open. He ogled down at the pouch, a man transformed. When it was clear that he recognized the contents, Virgil snatched the bag away again.

"It's all yours," Virgil said, "assuming you have what I need."

The shopkeeper could barely get the words out. He was breathless. "It's *you*."

"You got my StormCells now?"

Al bit his lip. "I'm sorry. I really don't got any."

Now the junkie was in as much awe of the shopkeeper as the shopkeeper was of him. He still wouldn't sell? What kind of iron will was Virgil dealing with here?

Al leaned over the counter, dropping to a secretive whisper. Gone was the bothered aloofness. He needed Virgil to understand that it wasn't his fault.

"Every month," Al said, "we send delivery guys to the Conductor plant just up the road on I-25. We got a good thing going. They recharge our StormCells, we give 'em water. Number Zero Zero Four, I think the plant's called."

"I know the one," Virgil said. If he had looked back out the shop entrance then, he could have seen the Conductor's distant spire poking up from the junkscape like a toothpick.

A cackling toddler ran past the shop, followed closely by his exasperated mother. Al waited for them to pass before continuing.

"Our last group went out a couple weeks back. They never came home."

"Roadkillers probably got 'em on the way over," Virgil said sympathetically.

"That's what we figured. So we radioed the Oxen clan to get some mercenaries out here and find our stolen goods." Al stopped then, as if trying to make sense of his own story.

"And?" Virgil pushed.

The shopkeeper sounded very tired all of a sudden. "Nothing. The channel was just other people trying to call in. No operator. Nothing. We called every other clan based out of the Heap. FireFighters. The Modified. Even those Ker freaks. Nothing. Dead air."

Virgil pondered the odd scenario, unable to fully wrap his head around it.

The Oxen were the go-to mercenary clan for the average joes of the Junkyard—everyone's first choice. They were reliable, had the best weapons, and were easily the most pleasant to deal with. But they weren't the only hired guns on the market. If a client wanted to pay less and didn't mind collateral damage, the FireFighters would raise their flamethrowers for just about anyone. The Modified were pricier, and their addiction to DIY cybernetics made them tough on the eyes, but they were more efficient than FireFighters and lacked the Oxen's cumbersome sense of morality. Only the very wealthy or the very desperate turned to the Keres. They were expensive and, in a quite literal sense, inhuman.

These Big Four mercenary clans had plenty of differences, but they did share two things in common. They were always hungry for clients, and when a client called, they usually answered. The Heap couldn't afford dead air. It wasn't some anonymous village on the outskirts of the Junkyard, it was a city. Not a *Jericho*-level city, but a city by Junkyard standards. Some people argued that it was the Junkyard's capital city, if the wasteland could have such a thing. It was a center of trade. A reliable place to buy Battery. A secure location for networking and leisure. There was too much there. Too many . . . investments.

"Maybe the Heap's relay went down?" Virgil suggested.

"That's what Annette took a team to go find out," Al said. "Took her boy Andy with her; that's why I'm running the shop. If we don't get our StormCells back, we're screwed. But keep that on the down-low. We don't need the whole Junkyard knowing we're in bad shape."

Disheartened, Virgil tied the pouch back to his belt. There was no negotiating for StormCells that didn't exist. "I got some junk in my trailer—"

"No! I want *that*." Al pointed at the pouch so hard it jammed his robotic index finger. This was why Virgil held back his special merchandise from most bartering deals. When people saw it, they desired nothing else.

Virgil patted the bag. "You know a tank of water isn't worth this."

Al ducked behind the counter, fumbling through unseen crates. He returned with a cardboard box filled with tiny glowing disks.

"Tier-one StormCells, for your glove there."

Virgil put on his best disinterested face. "I need tier twos, not tier ones."

Al went back behind the counter. "And! Just got some of these in!"

He slapped another box on the glass. This one was faded red, styled with washed-out logos of a man in a ten-gallon hat riding a hoofed creature for which Virgil had no name. Inside: magnum rounds, titanium-coated.

Not even Virgil could hide his amazement. "Where the hell did you find them?"

"Floated out with the sewage," Al said. "Damnedest thing."

Virgil untied his pouch once more. "How about that?"

CHAPTER 6

Diane remained perfectly still as the figures crawled out from beneath a van across the parking lot. Three of them total, all grubby and ragged in their tunics of scavenged cloth. Wild eyes, staring out from masks of dirt and grime. Crooked smiles, teeming with mischief.

Children.

They would have been Block Twos on *Cradle*. Two long-haired boys—one tall for his age, the other a runt—and one girl with a shagged pixie cut and a black eye. None of them were older than six orbits.

"Whooaa," the small boy said.

"What is it?" the black-eyed girl asked.

The tall boy scoffed. "It's a dead Peacecreeper, dumb-dumb."

Small Boy hoisted himself onto the trailer's rail. "It's huge!" he exclaimed.

"I'm not dumb!" Black-Eyed Girl spat at Tall Boy.

"Are too!"

Small Boy reached out to touch the Grave Walker's arm. Diane flinched away.

"Please don't do that," she said.

It was like a bomb went off. Small Boy flung himself off the trailer, and the other children scrambled backward. Diane checked the dirt parking lot around them, nervous about the attention this might draw.

"Aaaah!" Small Boy screamed.

"It's alive!" Black-Eyed Girl shouted.

"It's gonna smash us!" Tall Boy cried.

Diane lifted her hands in a gesture of peace. "Calm down! I'm not a Peacekeeper. I won't hurt you."

Without missing a beat, the children's fear turned to wide-eyed curiosity.

"There's a girl in there!" Tall Boy said.

Black-Eyed Girl sneered at Tall Boy. "Who's dumb now?"

"You are!" Tall Boy said.

"Nuh-uh!"

Small Boy ignored the quarrel between his peers and addressed Diane directly. "Whatcha sittin' around for?"

"I'm waiting for someone," Diane said. It was harmless information, and they were only kids.

"Who?" Small Boy asked.

"He's a . . ." Diane struggled to remember Virgil's job title, an easy alternative to giving his actual name. ". . . junkie?"

"Ooooh," Small Boy nodded, satisfied.

Black-Eyed Girl abandoned her spat with Tall Boy. "Are you here to help us find our StormyCells?" she asked Diane.

"I don't think so," Diane said. "We're just getting supplies before we go into Jericho."

All the children's faces crinkled with confusion, and Diane knew that she had said something wrong.

Small Boy frowned up at the megalopolis casting a shade over them all. "Nobody goes into Jericho," he said.

"They do too!" Black-Eyed Girl insisted.

"Nuh-uh!"

"Yuh-huh! My daddy—" Black-Eyed Girl hiccuped, "—my daddy says they go in through the sewers."

"But they never get out of the sewers," Tall Boy added.

Diane and Small Boy asked the same question: "Why not?"

"Crybaby eats them," Tall Boy said.

"Oooooh," Small Boy gasped.

Tall Boy turned back to Black-Eyed Girl. "And if you keep bein' a dumb-dumb, Crybaby will come out at night and eat you too!"

Black-Eyed Girl looked horrified. "No!"

"He'll melt your bones and eat you up!"

"What's Crybaby?" Diane asked.

All three children looked slowly to Diane. A wickedness filled Tall Boy's muddy face.

"Crybaby . . . Crybaby . . . black and blue. If he's not crying then he's gonna . . . get . . . you."

He whispered the rhyme, slow and ominous. Black-Eyed Girl joined him, their spat forgotten in the face of a new victim to torment.

"Crybaby Crybaby, black and blue. If he's not crying then he's gonna get you."

They chanted it over and over, getting louder each time. Even Small Boy joined in.

"*Crybaby! Crybaby! Black and blue! If he's not crying then he's gonna get you!*"

They hopped up and down, screaming the horrid nursery rhyme at the top of their lungs. Diane felt her patience wearing thin; the Grave Walker's volume adjustments were powerless against these earsplitting tormentors. The rhyme wasn't even scary after the five millionth time, just annoying. She considered leaping out of the trailer and committing to the role of big bad Peacekeeper: stomping her feet, swinging her giant arms, anything to make the chanting stop. She had just survived a roadkiller assault, and she sure as hell didn't have to put up with this.

A lightning bolt struck the ground near the children's feet. Virgil descended the Gatetown stairs, Volt Caster raised.

"¡*Vámonos*!" he shouted at the children, and they all dove under different cars. Virgil cast a weary look at the parking attendant, who responded with a half-hearted shrug.

"Sorry about them," Al said, following his customer down the steps. He was hauling a full water tank by himself, a task made possible only through the iron grip of his bionic hand.

The junkie chuckled. "We were all little roadkillers at that age."

Al ignored Diane entirely as he lifted the water tank into the jeep's back seat. While he massaged his aching and still-human tricep, Virgil dropped a leather pouch into the shopkeeper's open robotic palm. Diane watched Al closely as he sniffed the bag, its euphoric scent bringing him to tears. He tucked the pouch into his pocket, then hurried back up the stairs.

"Those kids get under the jeep?" Virgil asked, lying down to inspect the chassis.

"I don't think so," Diane said.

Virgil ran his hand under each fender. "You sure? If one of them planted a bomb . . ."

"A bomb?" Diane laughed. "Are you kidding? They were just kids!"

"Rather be paranoid than dead," Virgil replied.

As he got back in the jeep, Diane noticed a small crowd gathering around the man who had delivered their water. He was showing off the pouch.

"What did you give him?" Diane asked.

Virgil started the engine. "Ask me again when you have more questions to ask."

Diane saw that the water tank was alone in the back seat.

"I'm not seeing any new StormCells," she said.

"What's your energy at now?" Virgil asked.

Diane checked the HUD's power meter.

"I'm down to fifteen percent," she said, her anxiety renewed. "I don't get it. I've just been sitting here!"

"Relax, *chica*," Virgil said. "I've got us covered."

They drove along the Wall for miles, following the subtle curvature of Jericho's perimeter until Gatetown was out of sight. Virgil parked beside a cement patch just as blank as all the others, tuned his radio to a dead frequency, then spoke into the mic.

"Supply to Demand. Supply to Demand. Do you copy? Over."

No response.

"Supply to Demand. Supply to Demand. Do you copy? Over."

This went on for a good thirty minutes. Virgil repeated the same phrase into the static abyss, and each time, no one called back. Virgil was a broken record, and a boring one at that.

When Diane felt certain that she would lose her mind, a woman's voice answered the call.

"*Where've you been?*" she asked. "*Thought you died or something. You missed the last meeting, I don't have any payment ready—*"

"I've got a specific request," Virgil interrupted. "Super simple on your end. I need two StormCells. Tier twos, both of them. I'll give you two bags in exchange."

A long stretch of radio silence, then the woman's voice asked, "*Same place?*"

"Yup."

Virgil hung up the mic. He yanked a backpack out from under the passenger's seat, stuffing the Messenger's head and his new ammo boxes inside.

"All right, let's go," he said.

Standing from the trailer, Diane found Virgil running his Volt Caster over the Wall's smooth, blank surface. She stopped herself from asking the obvious question. She waited. She watched.

When he reached a seemingly random point on the Wall, Virgil snapped his fingers. A spark hit, and the point turned bright magenta. A large circle in the concrete lit up, fizzled, and then dissipated like the hologram that it was. A steel, algae-coated door beyond creaked open, revealing the beginnings of a long, pitch-black tunnel. A sewer tunnel.

They go in through the sewers . . . But they never get out of the sewers.

"You're going to hear some freaky sounds in here," Virgil said. "Just stay close, do exactly what I—"

"Tell me there's no Crybaby," Diane pleaded.

Virgil gawked up at her. "How'd you hear about—?" He answered his own question in his head. "Damned brats . . ."

Diane felt sick. This boogeyman *was* real, and allegedly, he melted bones.

"Okay, lesson time," Virgil said calmly. "You've seen people, you've seen bugs, you've seen Peacekeepers. But the Junkyard's got one more fun surprise. They were the freakier weapons created during the Grand Finale, and no two are alike. Some are monsters. Some are one-of-a-kind machines. Some are places. One's just a few lines of code. We call them Relics."

"And there's a Relic in this sewer called Crybaby," Diane said, getting to the point.

"Yup. He's one of the monsters."

The suit's fists clenched for the third time. Diane now understood that the Grave Walker could detect her raw urges, but she was too pissed off to care.

"You're unbelievable," she said. "When were you going to tell me?"

Virgil offered no trace of an apology. "I know a safe route. You do exactly as I say, you'll never even see Crybaby. You were better off not knowing about it."

Diane stomped her foot, shaking the ground. "You keep throwing me into danger, and you don't even warn me! How am I supposed to trust you?"

"You're the one who's supposed to be protecting me," Virgil said.

"Which still makes zero sense," Diane countered.

Virgil looked like he might shout again, but he didn't. He stared into the Grave Walker's visor, through the visor, straight to Diane.

"If this were some kinda long-term partnership," he said, "then yes. We'd have a problem. But it's not. Once we're through that sewer, my man will get you out of that suit, and you'll be free to go wherever with whoever. Until then, stop worrying. Stop asking questions. I'll tell you what you need to know, and I wouldn't steer you wrong."

Virgil marched into the tunnel. Into the darkness.

"Home stretch, kid," he called back, and after forcing herself to ignore the many red flags, Diane clomped off in pursuit.

The door slammed shut behind her.

Crack.

Virgil lifted a glow stick, bathing the sewer tunnel in eerie chartreuse. Diane followed him forward, through a stagnant gray stream that reached her shins, his knees. Lathers of waxy foam bobbed around them, and though Diane could smell nothing from inside the Grave

Walker, she imagined a stench that would take millennia to wash away. You could practically see the odor, hanging around them in a sickly miasma. It made Diane queasy just looking at the stream.

"How can you breathe in here?" she asked Virgil, who had left his gas mask in the jeep.

"You get used to it," Virgil said. "The mask makes it harder to hear. Can't afford that."

Curious, Diane listened to the noises around them. Their sloshing echoed off the grimy corrugated walls. Heavy droplets drip, drip, dripped from the ceiling pipes. An air current moaned past their ears. This was the song of Jericho's sewer, and it was nothing all that strange. Nothing all that scary.

They reached a four-way intersection, and Virgil took them left. The tunnel ramped downward to another junction, and Virgil led them straight. They waded through a dizzying labyrinth of rights, lefts, inclines, and declines, and Diane could not have retraced their steps to save her life. Virgil began the twisting expedition with confidence, foraging ahead without pause. But after a while, he made a point to read the washed-out numbers stamped on each new tunnel. He forced them to backtrack a couple times, swearing under his breath. Diane suppressed the impulse to ask him if he really knew where they were going. If he didn't, there wasn't much she could do about it now. She had no choice but to trust him.

They came to a hexagonal chamber, with each side bleeding into a different tunnel. Diane waited in the center while Virgil inspected each possible route, reciting a sequence of tunnel names as he did so. "R Fifty-Six, R Forty-Nine . . . No . . . R Forty-Eight? Damn it . . ."

As she tuned out Virgil's babbling, Diane detected a new layer in the soundscape. Was it actually new? Or had she simply missed it under their sloshing footsteps? Hard to say, but now that she heard it, there would be no pushing it out of mind. The new sound was distant, fluctuating in volume, but unmistakable.

Weeping. Hysterical, nearly human sobs. *Nearly* human.

A jangling shudder rattled the Grave Walker—another subconscious impulse.

"You finally hear it," Virgil said, still focused on tunnel labels.

Diane spun a full three-sixty in the hexagon's center. The crying seemed to come from every direction. A reverberation, or were there multiple sources?

"Are you sure there's only one Crybaby?" Diane asked.

"Nope," Virgil said, too focused on his task to remember that she was out of questions for the day. "Doesn't really matter, though. One or a hundred, we're just as dead if it finds us."

"But the suit would keep me safe, right?"

"Safe-ish."

"*What?*"

"Shhh." At long last, Virgil chose a path. They entered a new tunnel network with wider passages, and Diane no longer had to duck to keep from bumping the Grave Walker's head. Now Virgil regained his sense of direction, choosing their turns without hesitation. The omnipresent sobbing was a constant, but Virgil's assuredness made it easier to bear. If Virgil wasn't scared, Diane had no reason to be. She was the one in the "safe-ish" metal suit, after all.

Her anxiety morphed to mental exhaustion as they trudged on through the endless maze. Most tunnels were indistinguishable from the rest, leaving no clues to indicate their progress. Diane lost all track of time, and all the sewer's mucky sights and sounds dropped into the background. She felt no physical fatigue in the Grave Walker, but her numbness made the trek challenging in a different way. Every step she took was a conscious choice, an act of neurological willpower, and as she disassociated from the repetitive task at hand, the suit's feet became harder to lift.

Suddenly, halfway down a particularly long tunnel, Virgil held up a hand and stopped them both in their tracks. He wrapped the glow stick in his coat, plunging them into darkness.

"What is it?" Diane asked.

"The crying stopped," Virgil said.

Diane checked back into the soundscape. He was right.

"Good," she said. "That means we lost it."

"No. It doesn't."

The children's nursery rhyme came back to her. *Crybaby . . . Crybaby . . . black and blue. If he's not crying then he's gonna . . . get . . . you.* Diane's tongue went numb. She listened closely.

A mellow current trickled at their feet. Virgil breathed slowly through his nose. These were the only sounds in the pitch-black tunnel.

Then something moved.

Somewhere behind them, far away but not far enough—a sloshing sound. Something pushing through the water, against the current. Swimming? Walking? Impossible to tell. But it was there, and it was big.

The Grave Walker began to rattle again. Virgil placed a hand on its arm, and Diane took the hint. In a clench of considerable self-discipline, she brought the suit under control.

She held her breath. The sloshing grew louder . . . closer . . . Then it veered off down a different tunnel. It faded further and further, then it was gone.

Silence. An agonizing eon of silence.

Then, at long last, the sobbing resumed.

"Let's go," Virgil said, unveiling his glow stick. He pressed on, and Diane followed close.

A ladder stood alone at the tunnel's end. Virgil mounted it and climbed through an open manhole in the ceiling, leaving Diane hesitant beneath him. The ladder looked too frail for the Grave Walker's weight, the manhole too narrow a fit.

"You coming?" Virgil called down.

Diane hopped up and grabbed the rim of the manhole. She pulled, and her suit made the worst scraping noise as she forced herself through the opening. Bits of ceiling cracked and crumbled around her, and the manhole widened to a gaping tear. But she made it, coming to rest at Virgil's feet.

"Nice," he snickered.

"Do you think Crybaby heard that?" Diane asked.

Virgil leaned against a thick pipe arcing out of the wall. "Doesn't matter. We're safe now."

Diane took in their new surroundings. Every surface in the

oval-shaped room was covered with a white powdery substance, and when Virgil tucked his glow stick away, the powder revealed its dim phosphorescence. Then he flicked his left wrist, and the Volt Caster's blue charge relit the room.

"And now," Virgil said, "we wait."

Diane stood by him, fixing her visor on the only tunnel connected to the white chamber. It ran a few feet out, then curved abruptly.

"I can't believe someone would come down here just to trade with you," she said. "This place is a nightmare."

Virgil shrugged his quintessential shrug. "They don't have a choice. I can't sell my goods on the street, and addiction's *una perra*. Makes people do crazy things. Especially when there's only one supplier." He pointed smugly to himself.

"Addicted to what? What are you selling these people?" Diane asked.

Virgil took his back-to-back hits of Battery, saying nothing.

They waited quietly in the white room, listening to those choked, faraway sobs. Diane wondered why the monster cried. Could it really feel sadness, or were the similarities between the noise and the human emotion coincidental? She added this to the growing list of questions she had for Virgil, or for whoever she met once the two of them parted ways. She had no intention of following Virgil back into the Junkyard. A structured place like Jericho would be more her speed.

A flashlight beam hit the curved tunnel wall, accompanied by the clack of boots on metal.

Virgil straightened his posture. "Game time."

The beam dropped off to reveal a filthy hazmat suit waddling into the room. A knapsack clung to its back.

"That you, Kara?" Virgil asked.

The hazmat ripped off its mask, revealing a buzz-cut, sharp-faced woman with gauges and pierced eyebrows.

"You're a pain in the ass, you know that?" Kara said. "Can't just break the routine. I've got work and shit—" She noticed Diane lingering in the corner and practically jumped out of her hazmat suit. "What the *hell* is that?"

"New friend." Virgil looked past Kara into the tunnel, as if expecting someone else. No other flashlights appeared. "Eli not make it this time?"

Kara took off her knapsack, watching the Grave Walker for any sudden moves. "He won't be coming down anymore. But don't worry. I got what you need."

She handed the bag to Virgil. Inside, he found a pair of tier-two StormCells, both shimmering with atomic promise. In the dank sewer, their radiance low-lit Virgil's face to resemble an eyeless, green-lipped ghoul.

"Good stuff," he said.

Virgil knelt down and unhooked six pouches from his belt, lining them on the powdery floor in a neat row. Kara sat on the other side of the line, and as Virgil opened the bags one by one, her lips began to tremble. Her eyes widened with hunger. With need.

Diane leaned over Virgil's shoulder, and she finally saw his merchandise.

Seeds. Brown seeds. Red seeds. Long skinny seeds and plump round seeds. Each bag was filled to the brim with a different type of seed, and Virgil pointed them out from left to right.

"Strawberries, tomatoes, peppers, carrots, broccoli . . . No, sorry . . . peas. That one's peas. And this one's new. Sunflower seeds. You can eat those right out of the bag."

"You don't need to incubate them?" Kara asked, amazed.

"Nope. You can munch 'em raw. Just don't swallow the shells."

Kara's hungry eyes moved over the different seeds, ranking the flavors they would yield. Diane remembered the deal Virgil had offered: two pouches for two StormCells. Hands shaking, Kara selected the carrot and sunflower seeds. Virgil tossed the other pouches into his backpack.

"Let's get you recharged," Virgil said to Diane. "Turn around."

Diane obeyed. She felt him prodding and searching along the Grave Walker's back, then a hatch whirred open. A moment of pressure, then something popped. Her HUD disappeared. The visor shrunk to the size of a pea. Diane couldn't move a muscle.

She became aware of her chest again. Her real chest, delicate and human, heaving erratically. It was so hard to breathe. The air tasted hot and metallic, like blood.

This lasted for only a moment, then a second pop brought everything back to normal. The visor and HUD warbled into place, and Diane felt nothing but her own thoughts.

"How's that?" Virgil asked.

Diane started to give a thumbs-up, but then she noticed her power meter. It was wrong. It had to be. "The HUD says I'm only at forty percent."

"*Forty?*" Virgil lobbed an accusatory glare at Kara. She had unzipped her hazmat suit and was now stuffing the pouches into her overall pockets.

"Is there a kid inside that thing?" she asked innocently.

Virgil ignored the question. "You trying to rip me off?"

"These were all I could find on short notice!"

"No, no, no. No way," Virgil moved toward her. "I'm not dropping two whole bags on half-baked StormCells."

Kara backed toward the tunnel, kicking off her hazmat suit in the process. "I gave you what you asked for. Fair's fair."

Virgil brought the Volt Caster's thumb and middle finger together. With one snap, he could seriously ruin Kara's day. "You came up short. Fair ain't fair."

Kara reached into the depths of her left pocket. She looked wild, like an animal backed into a corner. "Don't take this from me," she pleaded. "I need this. You know I need this. If I eat one more Nutribrik, I'll puke my guts out."

"Then don't burn me," Virgil said. "I'm the only hookup you have."

Kara's face ran through a spastic roulette of expressions. Fear. Hunger. Sadness. Hate. And through it all, the sound of Crybaby's distant mewling.

"You've been off the schedule," she said. "I don't know when you'll be back with more. You might never come back again."

"Kara . . ."

Diane braced for conflict.

"Sorry," Kara said.

Kara's hand emerged from her pocket with a pistol, and she fired in Virgil's direction. A laser beam struck Virgil's armored chest, then ricocheted upward. Virgil staggered, and in the haze of steam from a ruptured ceiling pipe, Kara fled back into the tunnel.

Virgil bellowed something between a curse and a primordial howl as he launched after her in blind pursuit.

"Wait!" Diane called as he vanished into the steam. There were a million reasons not to follow him, but the terror of being alone, down here of all places, trumped them all.

She gave chase, leaving the unexplained safety of the white powder room behind her. There were now two lights to follow. Virgil's electric-blue gauntlet, aimed steady despite the chase, and the flashlight bobbing wildly ahead of it. Three sets of feet splashed and clanked, a commotion rivaled only by the crackle of Virgil's lightning bolts. Even with level aim, he missed every shot in this looping tract of Jericho's intestines. Not a straight tunnel for yards.

They were making too much noise, and Diane knew it. This chase was loud and sloppy. Dangerous. But she pressed on anyway, keeping a close ear on those all-pervading sobs. If Virgil wasn't scared, she had no reason to be.

The pursuit brought them into a cavernous antechamber, a stark change from the cramped tunnels Diane had come to know so well. Soft-red industrial bulbs formed a vertical trail up the wall, leading to a haze of streetlight passing through a distant sewer grate. Diane couldn't help but pause at the sight. Pause and wonder. There really must be a city up there. Maybe it resembled the photos she had taped on her wall back in Cabin Three-One-Seven. Maybe it was home.

In her moment of stillness, Diane heard something strange. Something bad.

Virgil threw another lightning bolt, and with no immediate turns or corners to block it, the shot zapped Kara in the leg. She fell face-first into the gray water.

"*Dolor en mi culo*," Virgil panted, sloshing toward her.

She rolled around and pointed her dripping pistol at Virgil's head. He raised the Volt Caster in response.

"Let me go," Kara said, wobbling to stand while keeping her aim.

"Can't do it," Virgil said.

"You've got so much more, just let me have this."

"You're not walking out of here with two bags."

"Virgil . . ." Diane approached.

"What happens if you kill me?" Kara said. "I'm your only dealer. Eli's out. Nobody topside knows about you."

"I'll find someone else," Virgil said. "Wouldn't be the first time—"

"Virgil!"

Diane stomped her foot, and Virgil shouted back at her without taking his eyes off Kara.

"I'm busy!"

"Listen . . ." Diane said.

Both Virgil and Kara realized then what was wrong. They both heard what Diane heard. At some point during the argument, or maybe the chase . . . the sobbing had ceased again.

Kara gulped. "Oh god."

A terrible quiet saturated the sewers.

Haunting as those cries had been, their absence left a void that was infinitely worse. Diane felt trapped in that quiet, ensnared by its terrible meaning. No one moved. No one spoke another word. She could only make out the sounds of Virgil and Kara panting, the low hum of her suit's internal mechanisms, and the endless *drip-drip* from so many leaky pipes. No matter how far the Grave Walker's audio input strained, the oppressive silence would not yield.

Then, all at once, Crybaby came out of the water.

It howled as it broke the surface and rose to full height directly behind Kara, whose head only reached the creature's chest. It was disturbingly humanoid: two arms, two legs, head and torso, a collage of burlap and garbage bags wrapped around its body like a poncho. But the arms were too long, with hands that could fit Kara's head into a single fist. Its skin was chalk white, totally hairless, and covered in thick blue veins.

Then there was the face. The eyes were dark craters burrowed into swollen flesh, jet black and impossible to distinguish. The lipless mouth hung wider than any human jaw could ever hope to unhinge, and from the black eyes and gaping maw, a thick bile oozed down onto the creature's face and clothes, grime bubbling in its throat and pooling in its eye sockets.

Kara didn't have time to turn around, which was probably best. She didn't have to watch those giant hands wrap around her shoulders. She didn't get to see that mouth fall over her scalp. But Kara did seem to feel the bile; she screamed as it smoked and bubbled upon contact with her skin. Flesh melted down to bone, and then Crybaby's teeth cracked through her skull in pursuit of juicy brain matter. At that point, Kara fell silent. Her body went limp, held up only by the grip of her killer.

Wet slurps. Muffled sobs. Was Crybaby weeping over its actions, out of shame? Or was it just a sound, bestial and meaningless? A feeding sound?

Diane and Virgil did not wait to find out.

"*Run!*" Virgil screamed. He made no attempt to fight, zap, shoot, or stab. It was time to leave.

Diane led the retreat back into the tunnels. Behind them, she heard Kara's body drop into the water. Crybaby had finished its meal, but it did not resume sobbing. It was dead silent, which meant it was still hunting.

At the next intersection, Diane felt Virgil jump onto the Grave Walker's back, wrapping his arms around her neck.

"Right!" he yelled, and Diane turned right. She ran through the tunnels as fast as she could, following the directions Virgil shouted into her ear. The glow stick had been lost sometime during the chase with Kara, and the Volt Caster was now their only source of light.

More than once, Virgil peeked back over his shoulder and begged her to go faster. She could not see how close Crybaby was behind them, nor did she want to. Her brain might freeze with terror, and the Grave Walker's legs would do the same.

A mess of twists and turns, ups and downs led them to a hall of giant pistons, the height and width of Roman columns. Even in extremis, Diane and Virgil marveled at the automated pillars as they rose and fell, emitting clouds of steam with each pump. It was the first sign that the sewers fulfilled any kind of practical purpose, beyond giving the boogeyman a place to call home.

"Where do I go?" Diane asked. The hall was lined with branching pathways, all veiled in heavy steam. Virgil checked behind them again, still clinging to the Grave Walker's back. It seemed there was no sign of the monster.

"Maybe we lost it," he mumbled, but Diane knew that he couldn't say for sure. The roar-hiss of the pistons was deafening, and it was impossible tell if Crybaby was wailing again.

Diane slowed to a walk. "Are we safe in here?"

"I'm not sure where 'here' is," Virgil said.

Diane could have slapped him then, but she remembered how big her hands were. "Just tell me where to go."

They came up to a new path on their left.

"Here," Virgil said on a whim. "Try here."

Diane went left, wandering blind among the pistons. Amid the grinding racket, Virgil pulled himself close to the Grave Walker's helmet.

"Let's take the next tunnel we find," he said.

"'You'll never even see Crybaby,'" Diane mimicked. "That's you. That's what you said."

"I'm not clairvoyant, *chamaca*." Virgil pointed to a hazy darkness on their right. "Go here."

Diane made the turn, now approaching a tunnel entrance. "Oh no. You're the furthest thing from—"

"*Look out!*"

Ten steps in front of them, Crybaby was waiting.

It was a tenebrous shadow in the steam, lashing out at Diane with one clawed hand. Its nails scratched across the Grave Walker's chest, and Diane saw sparks. Smoke. Warning messages flashed over Diane's HUD.

ARMOR COMPROMISED!

ADVANCED HOSTILE DETECTED!

THREAT ID: BANSHEE—AQUATIC MODEL!

Diane screamed bloody murder. On instinct, she lifted the Grave Walker's arms in defense, crossing the suit's two hands in front of her visor.

Whoosh!

Where Diane's wrists met, an orange, semitransparent circle had bloomed, curved like a cornea, large enough to form a perfect barrier between the Grave Walker and Crybaby. Rings of light pulsed from the center, expanding out until they reached the circle's wispy edges. Crybaby's assault never ceased, but now its hands bounced off the circle with electrified *pops*.

Diane realized she had accidentally conjured an energy shield, and evidently, a good one.

"*Hot damn!*" Virgil cried in delight.

The sudden joy in his voice emboldened her. Keeping her wrists together, she pushed back against Crybaby, daring to look it in the eyes. But she found no recognition of defeat in the Relic's face. No fear, not even surprise. Only hunger. The creature thrashed mercilessly at the barrier, and though the energy field remained intact, its orange hue darkened with every animalistic blow. The edges grew fainter, as did the rings of light.

"It's not gonna hold!" Virgil warned.

Diane leaped back, parting the suit's hands as she did so. Her shield dissipated with a burst of orange light, and the energy release knocked Crybaby in the opposite direction. It was only a few feet, but it was just the head start Diane needed to start her escape. Wasting no time, she turned and peeled out through the artificial fog. Crybaby flailed after her, swinging its hands and spewing its corrosive bile. This boogeyman would rip the suit apart if she let it, and then it would devour the mushy human center.

Diane sprinted through the piston hall and down the next passageway she saw. It immediately forked in two, and Virgil pointed to the tunnel labeled "W-11."

"I know where this goes!" he shouted. "Go here! Go here!"

The tunnel in question appeared infinite, with no branching routes for a quick escape. Diane hesitated.

"¡*Vámonos!*"

Diane ran, pushing the Grave Walker's speed to the limit, as fast as the legs would go, but Crybaby's gurgling moans were never far behind. This Relic would never grow tired, Diane realized, no matter how many volts Virgil cast its way. It would never show mercy. It had one biological drive, a single purpose validating its whole existence. This creature was a child of war, and its only need was to kill.

A pale luminescence came into view, revealing an archway at the tunnel's end. What awaited them on the other side? Salvation? A dead end? Didn't matter. It was the only finish line in sight.

The sobs grew louder in Diane's helmet speaker. The archway came closer.

Long fingers brushed the Grave Walker's heel. Closer.

A screeching howl.

Diane dove through the archway, into another hexagonal chamber, landing hard and bucking Virgil off her back. This room looked older than the others, made of brick instead of concrete, and its surfaces were coated with more of that white powder they'd seen in the first room. Crybaby squeezed itself through the archway, but as soon as its foot touched the floor and its hand pressed against the wall, the strangest thing happened. A sizzling sound, like bacon on a frying pan, rose from the contact points between powder and veiny flesh. Crybaby recoiled in what looked like pain, withdrawing back through the archway.

Silent, it stared at the humans. Repulsed, the humans stared back. They remained like that for a while, not moving, both parties gawping at the ugliness of the other. Then, leaving a trail of bile in its wake, Crybaby sulked into the darkness. Soon after, the distant sobbing returned.

Virgil dusted the powder off his pants and coat. "Whelp . . . that could've gone smoother. Good hustle, kid."

"I'm amazed that you survived this long," Diane said.

"I'm usually more careful," Virgil said, "and my customers usually don't rip me off. Just one of those days, I guess."

He tapped his Volt Caster along a brick wall dividing two tunnels. "Thankfully, forty percent was more than enough power to get you here."

Diane checked her meter again. This new StormCell was a huge upgrade; the gauge had only dropped by 5 percent. "Then why did we chase Kara?"

"Principles, kid. I won't be ripped off."

"They were just seeds!"

Virgil snapped his fingers at one of the bricks. "Exactly."

Another holographic shroud, like the first one that had obscured the entrance to the sewer, fizzled away. Behind this one was an elevator door branded with a large serif *W*. Virgil typed a fifteen-digit code into a connecting keypad, and the door clattered open. The elevator car was spotless, bathed in golden light.

"One more rule," Virgil said while he flicked off his Volt Caster. "One more thing I need from you, then you're out of the Grave Walker, and you never have to deal with me again."

Diane nodded, and the Grave Walker's head mimicked the gesture.

"Don't speak. Don't say a word, even if she talks to you directly. The lady up there's a crafty one. If she figures you out, she'll find a million ways to take advantage. Don't give her the ammo. You're with me, she's going to help you out because she owes me, and that's it. Got it?"

"Got it," Diane said, even though she really didn't. Something in Virgil's tone worried her. He had spoken of killer robots, highway marauders, and even Crybaby in his typical laid-back way, but now he sounded tense. There was something dangerous about the person they were going to meet. Something that intimidated Virgil in a way not even the Junkyard could manage.

Nevertheless, Diane joined him in the elevator car. She had not come all this way to loiter in the sewers.

"Did you know I could make a shield like that?" she asked.

"Didn't have a clue." Virgil noted the five claw marks defacing the Grave Walker's chest. "Sick battle scar. Too bad you're bailing out of the suit. A Crybaby wound gets mad cred in the Junkyard."

"Really?" Diane asked.

"For sure. A buddy of mine lost a leg down here. Way people look at him now, you'd think he was a war hero."

The elevator jerked into motion. Going up.

CHAPTER 7

In the grand scheme of things, Diane had only experienced a fraction of the Junkyard. A few streets, a single village, the inside of an abandoned mall. (*Mall!* She finally remembered the word.) Much of the Junkyard was a great big question mark in her head, and she knew this.

But nothing could have prepared her for Jericho.

The dark from the elevator shaft gave way to an overwhelming brightness, and when her helmet's aperture readjusted, Diane realized that the entire car was made of spotless glass: an invisible barrier between herself and this new world within a world.

Jericho was not like the photos of old Earth back in Cabin Three-One-Seven. Those cities had structure; Jericho did not. Serpentine roadways strangled each other in helices without end, stuffed to the brim with shiny vehicles going nowhere. Smaller buildings rose from circuitous streets like jagged concrete teeth, while monoliths of glass and neon rose up forever, their peaks lost in the smog. Warring video ads goaded, seduced, and threatened across a million LED billboards.

DreamVision v2.0—V.R. by FunSoft. Now with Over One Million Adult Channels!

Wellington Incorporated. Prices You Can Afford. Cybernetics You Can't Live Without.

Safety in Weaponry: The Noyuri Corp. Way!

Nutribriks. Any Meal. Every Meal.

The higher the elevator climbed, the more Diane saw. And the more she saw, the more she realized how wrong she had been about Jericho. This was not a place defined by laws and security. At this very moment, a truck was plowing its way through a congested street, forcing grid-locked drivers to abandon their cars or be crushed. Just south of that, a man in a dark uniform chased a hooded figure over monorail tracks, both seemingly unaware of the silent bullet train speeding their way. A naked woman on a billboard glistened above it all, killing fictional attackers with her brand-new, sleek and shiny Wellington cyberarm. Jericho was bright and bustling in some sectors, blacked out and crumbling in others. All this, crammed together in the Wall's stifling embrace.

Jericho was not safe. It was simply contained.

"I didn't know cities were like this," Diane muttered.

Virgil shook his head, drinking in the sight right along with her. "Nowhere's like this. The closest thing we got in the Junkyard is a place down south called the Heap. It's big, and plenty important, but it's a fraction of what we're looking at. Jericho ain't a city. It's ten cities. Plus change."

They rose high into the smog, higher than any other buildings Diane could see, before the elevator came to a stop.

"Executive Office!" a pleasant voice called from nowhere.

The door opened to a lobby paved in sleek obsidian. Two men in three-piece suits guarded a frosted double door, their eyes covered with retractable shades built right into their brows. They both had guns. Big, fully automatic plasma rifles with secondary ion grenade fire. One gun was aimed at Diane, the other at Virgil.

"Um . . . I don't know if this—" Diane began, but Virgil put a finger to his lips and entered the lobby. With some effort, Diane made the Grave Walker follow.

The frosted doors opened on their own. "Thanks, boys," Virgil said to the goons as they passed. Their stony faces betrayed no reaction. Virgil and Diane crossed the threshold, and the guards followed, remaining by the elevator doors while they slid shut behind them.

The Executive Office was something out of a fairy tale. A cobblestone bridge took Virgil and Diane to a grassy island surrounded by a crystal-clear moat, in which bettas and angelfish swam freely. Marble statues abounded: frolicking fauns, muscular men in deep contemplation, and beautiful bathing goddesses all stood in orbit around an L-shaped glass desk and its smiling owner.

The woman sitting at the desk had skin as smooth as porcelain and equally pale. Her lips were ruby red. She wore a dress and sun hat the color of the obsidian lobby; the color of her raven hair matched Diane's. She sat motionless in a leather armchair, perfect hands resting on the desk, gazing up at her guests with luminous purple eyes.

Artificial eyes.

Through the window behind her, the red border between the Jericho smog and Junkyard sky intersected her neck like a flatline.

"Hello, Virgil," she said.

Virgil nodded. "Ms. Violet."

Ms. Violet's irises snapped to the Grave Walker, while her head remained still. "You . . . regifted?"

"You know me," Virgil said. "I see someone in need, I help."

Ms. Violet refocused on the junkie. "Please, sit."

She tapped a corner on her desk, and a second armchair sprouted up from the grass. Diane blinked twice. Virgil took off his backpack and slumped down into the chair—the epitome of laid-back.

"I appreciate you letting us both up," he said.

"I trust you," Ms. Violet said, "and the suit is no threat here."

Her casualness gave Diane chills, but Virgil merely chuckled. "I guess not."

He unbuckled the straps on his backpack, but as he reached inside, Ms. Violet interjected.

"To clear the air, I'm afraid Wellington Incorporated can no longer honor your contract."

Virgil stiffened. "'Scuse me?"

"I'm afraid Wellington can no longer honor your contract."

"No, I heard you—"

"Then why did you ask?"

Virgil sat up, leaving the diplomat's severed head in his pack. The shadow from his hood could not conceal his resentment.

"Why can't you honor the contract?" he asked.

Ms. Violet's smile never wavered, her tone never rising above blasé. "Circumstances have changed. We would've contacted you, but your CB radio violates Wellington's info-security protocol."

Virgil's jaw clenched. "If you had any idea what my last four months have been like . . ."

"I apologize for any inconvenience this might cause—"

"Don't *apologize*, damn it."

Diane knew this side of Virgil. She had seen it in the sewers when Kara tried to swindle them. Virgil had a line, and when someone crossed it, rage took over. The man had principles, she would give him that, but now was no time for one of his outbursts. Diane was keenly aware of the armed guards posted by the office door, guns raised. How many more guards waited on the floor below them? And the several hundred floors below that?

"I'm not one of your rent-a-cops," Virgil seethed. "We have history, and I have always delivered for you. Always."

Ms. Violet's smile dropped to a sympathetic frown. "You are Wellington Incorporated's most reliable junkie contractor. Hands down."

"Then don't screw me! Honor the contract."

"Circumstances—"

Virgil slapped the desk. The glass jangled, and the guards behind them took a step forward. "We had a deal, Violet! I deactivate the Messenger, you give me a tier-five StormCell. I've done my part!"

Ms. Violet pursed her lips. "I'm afraid you haven't."

"Wanna bet?" Virgil reached for his backpack again, but Ms. Violet spoke quickly to cut him off.

"I've seen the Peacekeeper head inside your backpack," she said, "along with the five titanium-coated magnum shells, the eight tier-one StormCells, and the twelve high-grade Battery capsules."

She x-rayed us, Diane realized. Where? In the elevator? The lobby? Or was it a function of those robotic eyes?

"I've also seen the teenaged girl hiding inside that suit of armor," Ms. Violet continued, "but that's a discussion for another time."

Suddenly and terribly, Diane felt exposed. Naked. Even Virgil was taken aback, but he swiftly regained his composure and steered them to the point.

"So you know I did my part," he said.

"I know that you didn't," Violet said. "It's not your fault, of course. We negotiated your contract with faulty intel."

"What the hell are you talking about?" Virgil asked.

"The machine in your backpack is not the Messenger."

With that, Diane was officially lost. She had followed the exchange as best she could, but this complication exceeded the bounds of her context, and even Virgil appeared baffled. It was some time before he responded.

"*Pendejadas.*"

"Like I said, circumstances have changed." Ms. Violet swiped a finger across the desk, and her office underwent a drastic transformation. The holographic island, moat, bridge, statues, and fish all disappeared, revealing a featureless chrome room that evoked serious memories of *Cradle*; Diane could practically smell the recycled air. The view of Jericho behind Ms. Violet blacked out, and the window became a holoscreen.

"As you know," Ms. Violet began, "Wellington Inc. recently launched an initiative to secure defunct Junkyard factories and refurbish them for production."

"Corporate villages," Virgil said, somewhat disdainfully.

Ms. Violet typed across a holographic keyboard, and pictures of a burning factory appeared on the holoscreen. "A year ago, one of our sites was attacked and raided. Reports on the incident were scarce, but one employee managed to deliver an update before their death."

She pulled up the email, a single sentence: *The Messenger is here.*

"Not cryptic at all," Virgil said.

The burning factory gave way to snapshots of the masked Peace-keeper, head and body still attached. Many angles, all blurred and distant.

"After a string of identical attacks in the following months, we received reports of a diplomat-class Peacekeeper called the Messenger raising hell with a large machine tribe. We assumed this machine was our culprit, and we hired you to take it out."

"Which I did," Virgil added.

Ms. Violet nodded patiently. "But, while you were on the hunt, new reports came in."

The next slide featured a village under attack. Townies ran crying from barbaric cyborg soldiers, all of whom had three-digit serial codes branded onto their necks. A clear figure led the charge: a man with a scarred scalp and feeble torso, augmented with robotic limbs bulky enough to rival the Grave Walker. A bizarre rash festered on his cheek, shaped like some diseased fingerprint. The brand on his neck read "9-T-9."

A breathing apparatus covered the man's face, and a layer of tanned human skin was wrapped tightly over that. The resemblance to the diplomat's mask in Virgil's backpack was undeniable.

"These reports detailed a masked cyborg, also calling himself the Messenger, raiding villages with a gang of escapees from the augmented fight club in Reno. We checked with our contacts at the coliseum—the cyborg's real name is Brutus 9-T-9."

Virgil leaned forward in his chair. He looked puzzled. Diane had never seen Virgil look puzzled.

"Why would a fighter from Reno and a Peacekeeper use the same moniker?" he asked. "That doesn't make sense."

"And to complicate matters further," Ms. Violet said, "neither of them is the actual Messenger."

She whisked the pictures away, leaving the window blank.

"A month ago, one of our operatives arrived at the Heap to negotiate a trade deal with the Aardwolf clan. Their dominion over the city's economy has remained steadfast for centuries."

"Which operative did you send?" Virgil asked.

"Leon."

"Oh, nice. *Real* people person. I bet the Aardwolves loved him."

Ms. Violet ignored the jab. "Another incident occurred during Leon's sit-down with the Aardwolf leader. His ocular implant captured everything."

A buffering symbol filled the holoscreen, and Virgil eyed it suspiciously. "You beam this video right out of his head?"

"We install satellite uplinks into all our operatives," Ms. Violet said.

"You're playing with fire," Virgil warned.

Diane remembered what Virgil had told her about the vanquished AI, how it could still be lurking in cyberspace, among the satellites. As he had said, *nobody wants to make that reintroduction.* Was Ms. Violet getting too close?

"Leave your junkie superstitions in the Junkyard," Ms. Violet chided. "We simply don't have time for them."

The buffer completed, and Ms. Violet pressed Play.

File: L-2049. Source: JY Operative 07—Location:
35°1′38″N 111°1′21″W.

All Footage Is Property of Wellington Incorporated.

The text held over black for exactly three seconds, then the image cut to a grainy prerecorded video. The Wellington logo watermarked each corner of the screen.

The camera peered out through the eye of Ms. Violet's operative. *Leon*, Diane remembered her saying. This must be a video of something Leon saw.

He was standing on a balcony.

Below him, the Heap resembled a low-budget parody of Jericho. Most buildings were mere burrows carved into garbage deposits, and the few legitimate architectures looked ready to topple at the slightest provocation. The structure Leon occupied seemed to be the only one not made from trash. It was a tight assemblage of industrial workshops, storerooms, and silos, bound together by catwalks and skybridges. Studying it, Diane pegged the building for some kind of factory. Maybe a processing plant.

But the Heap was not without its merits. The city's layout was remarkably organized, making Jericho's arrangement look like the ravings of a madman. From his vantage point, Leon could clearly see the divisions between a wild outer region, a barricaded inner district, and a reinforced gated wall protecting the central building. The Heap was a center within a circle, within a larger circle.

The outer region was a lawless bazaar, a shantytown where people shouted and scrambled among random pockets of violence. The inner district appeared to be calmer, cleaner, more dignified. And within the safety of the gated wall, uniformed guards walked endless patrol routes on the factory grounds. When Leon looked up, he saw a thick green vapor billowing from smokestacks overhead. This place was making something. Something valuable.

"Don't see the point," a weathered voice said.

Leon turned his attention to a bloated old man sitting in a wheelchair nearby. He wore an ancient officer's jacket, the shoulders bedazzled with bits of colorful glass. He glared at Leon with mean, cataracted eyes.

"We make it all here," the man said. "Power grid, water, plumbing, medicine, it all comes from *this* fortress. And this fortress belongs to the Aardwolves. The Heap needs my family, that's what's kept us on top all these years. Why'n the hell would we give that up? We brew our own Battery. Why do we need yours?"

"You're not listening, Josiah," Leon's voice replied. "Wellington isn't trying to sell you Battery. We want to supply your ingredients. All the chemicals, the iodine solution, we can sell that to you for a fraction of the price you're paying the villages. You'll make a killing."

Josiah took a huge bite from a Nutribrik, munched it thoughtfully. "What's in it for you?"

"You let Wellington set up a cybersmith shop in the Inner Ring. You let us into the Heap's economy."

Josiah mulled over the proposition. "I dunno . . . Dunno about getting into bed with you Jericho-types."

"Think of how much capital you'll save," Leon beguiled. "You could afford more surveillance in the Outer Rim. Finally get a mercenary clan on retainer. You give us access; we give you options—"

Leon's pitch was interrupted by an explosion.

It came from below, and both men leaned over the balcony to see what had happened. They found the gate between the factory-turned-fortress and the surrounding district—what Leon had called the Inner Ring—hanging wide open, a legion of hostiles was now pouring through. Many of them looked like roadkillers. Some were cyborgs. All of them wore bloody bandages wrapped around their heads.

"Are they with you?" Josiah shouted, drawing an antique Luger pistol from his officer's jacket.

"Of course not!" Leon said, abandoning all tact. "Don't be stupid!"

The curtain behind them whipped open.

"We're under attack, sir!" an Aardwolf lieutenant cried.

"No shit!" Josiah said.

The lieutenant wheeled his superior off the balcony and into what appeared to be a war room, and Leon followed. Inside, soldiers hurried to their posts; officers barked orders; weapons were passed around like burning coals. Josiah called for one of them as he was escorted out of sight, abandoning Leon in the confusion.

Another explosion blew a hole in the floor.

The enemy rose up in a tangle of grappling hooks, firing lasers, swinging machetes, and electrified batons. The Aardwolves sprang into a counterattack, but Leon did not join them. Quick and silent, he dashed along the room's perimeter with superhuman quickness. He passed into a stairwell unseen, but on his way down, three bandaged warriors appeared in his path. They were surprised to see him, and their hesitation was their undoing.

Leon ax-kicked the frontmost warrior with what appeared to be a bionic foot, shattering his face and knocking him back onto his comrades below. While they fumbled with his dead weight, Leon drew two plasma pistols with the word *Deckard* branded on the sides. He aimed them at the warriors' foreheads, pulled the triggers, and the stairwell was clear once more.

Leon got off on the seventh floor; the wing was an absolute war zone. Another pack of invaders spotted him; he decided they weren't worth the effort. Leon shot his Deckards at a nearby barred window, blowing the bars to smithereens. He leaped out, soared through empty space, and landed feetfirst on a roof in the Inner Ring. The tin beneath him bent from the impact, but it held.

Leon was out.

But he did not flee the scene entirely. Instead, he vaulted over rooftops neighboring the fortress wall, trying to glimpse the origins of the invasion. When he reached a roof near the gate, now shut, he discovered the tides turning in the Aardwolves' favor. They had formed a blockade in front of the inner entrance, and they were slowly pushing the bulk of the invaders back. Perhaps the fortress would not be lost after all.

An unseen chorus began to chant in the streets below. Low, almost unintelligible. "Rah . . . Rah . . . Rah . . ."

With a hollow groan, the gates opened slightly on their own. The invading mob parted down the middle.

A new fighter sprinted through the gates, faster than anyone Diane had ever seen, cyborg or otherwise. Under a sleeveless coat, he was towering, hairless, and muscular—too muscular for a human living in a toxic nuclear wasteland. His left arm was wrapped in bandages from his elbow to his fingertips. They were the same bandages on the warriors' heads, and Diane suspected this was not a coincidence.

Running barefoot, this new fighter gripped a metal rod with pieces of sharpened scrap metal welded to both ends—the ultimate homemade battle staff.

But the most shocking revelation was the mask, made from a skinned human face nailed to an argonaut Peacekeeper's faceplate. The metal ocular cavity had been split wide, leaving room for two fleshy eyeholes. Diane knew this mask must mean something, but she could not begin to fathom what that message might be.

Unafraid, the Masked Man charged the Aardwolf forces. The battle staff was a whetted cyclone, cutting down soldiers in broad, merciless strokes. The twirling blades also deflected energy fire, turning gunmen into victims of their own projectiles. The invading warriors rallied behind the Masked Man, his raw power feeding their confidence. He was a warlord who led by example.

"¡*Pendejo!*" a familiar voice called out.

A mechanized goliath emerged to meet the Masked Man. At first, Diane mistook it for a Peacekeeper. But then it spoke again: "Get your sorry ass out of my city!"

The Aardwolves cheered, and Diane realized it was Josiah, piloting a cage on wheels with strongman arms hooked to the sides. He knocked the pincers together in a gesture of challenge. His followers braced for the fight of the century.

Josiah drove forward.

The Masked Man pulled back his battle staff and hurled it like a spear. It slipped between the cage's frame, impaling Josiah in the chest. His wheels quit spinning. The strongman arms went limp.

The Aardwolves retreated into the fortress, and the invaders pursued. The Masked Man retrieved his staff, regarded the dead Aardwolf patriarch with a subtle nod, and then ran off to rejoin the battle.

Leon turned away. There was nothing more to see.

The video feed went black.

Three still frames appeared on the screen: the Masked Man, the cyborg with the fingerprint rash, and the diplomat-class Peacekeeper that was now missing its head.

"Among the three masked individuals we know about," Ms. Violet said, "only one has led the largest military campaign since the Grand Finale. Brutus 9-T-9 is a powerful fighter, but he's not a strategist. The Peacekeeper even less so. We believe the man from the video is the real Messenger."

Virgil was seated again, elbows on his knees, staring at the holoscreen. Based on his silence, and the total focus with which he had watched the video, Diane figured this was more than just another random act of violence. The assault on the Heap had changed something.

"On a positive note," Ms. Violet went on, "Wellington once again requires your services."

Virgil sat back, arms crossed in defiance. "I'm not a mercenary."

"Nor would I ask you to be. We require something far more nuanced: the retrieval of Wellington property."

Ms. Violet rewound the video to Josiah Aardwolf's demise. When the bandaged warriors charged into the fortress, she paused, zoomed, then tracked to the left.

Once the visual enhancer smoothed out the overblown image, a previously unseen figure came to light. It was a middle-aged man in a dirty white lab coat, with some kind of portable console hanging from a strap around his neck. Two bandaged warriors were herding him along with the others. He looked terrified.

"You remember Dr. Isaac," Ms. Violet said.

Virgil glanced quickly at Diane. Why? What did the man on-screen have to do with her?

"What the hell is he doing out in the Junkyard?" Virgil asked.

"Isaac was the lead on our factory reclamation project," Ms. Violet explained. "He was at the weapon site when the Messenger attacked. We assumed that he had been killed."

Virgil rose out of his chair, leveling himself with the frightened image of Dr. Isaac. "You don't drop the smartest man in the world into the most dangerous place on Earth."

"Lesson learned," Ms. Violet said, clacking her manicured nails against each other. It was the closest she would come to expressing any kind of displeasure, with herself or with Virgil.

"Leon investigated the Messenger's invasion after the fact as well," she went on. "Eyewitnesses say the electronic gates to the fortress miraculously opened when the attackers approached and then shut again when the Aardwolves tried to escape."

"You think that was Dr. Isaac?" Virgil asked.

Ms. Violet nodded. "The Messenger is no doubt extorting Dr. Isaac for his technological expertise. He hacked the Aardwolf security system ahead of the invasion, and he's found a way to reprogram Peacekeepers to do the Messenger's bidding."

Virgil's response was instant. Automatic. "Peacekeepers can't be reprogrammed. Not like that."

"And yet the Peacekeeper in your backpack wears a human's insignia."

Virgil opened his mouth to retort, but for the first time since Diane had met him, Virgil could think of nothing to say. It appeared Ms. Violet's impossible answer was the only plausible one.

"We need Dr. Isaac back," Ms. Violet said. "A Jericho mind in Junkyard hands is a dangerous thing. Not just for Wellington's interests, but for everyone."

"Leon's already out there. Why can't he get Dr. Isaac?"

"This situation requires more . . . finesse."

As Diane observed the conversation, she noted that Virgil would not look Ms. Violet in the eye. He looked at the holoscreen, the floor, anywhere but her cyborg eyes, purple spotlights aimed directly at his face. Never blinking. Never letting up.

"Chaos is an instrument, Virgil," Ms. Violet said. "And you play it beautifully."

"You've already burned me once," Virgil said. "How do I know you'll deliver?"

"I'll make it worth your while. You get the tier-five StormCell—though what a traveling junkie wants with such a cumbersome device is beyond me—and, as a bonus, I'll legalize your seeds in all of Jericho's Wellington districts."

Virgil's whole body went statue-still, like the marble fauns from that holographic island. At this, genuine amusement crept into the corner of Ms. Violet's controlled grin.

"Oh, yes," she said. "I know all about your little sewer rendezvous. We've confiscated seeds from some of your clientele, but it appears your plants are bioengineered against reproduction. No additional seeds can be cultivated. Very clever."

Ms. Violet closed the holoscreen, and the real world retook the window. From here, at the highest point in Jericho, Diane and Virgil could see all the militarized borders that carved the city into corporate territories. Digital billboard ads were localized to their home turf, marking each company's sphere of influence. Noyuri Corp. looked to be a sizable presence. FunSoft was small, but its displays were the brightest and most colorful. And just below Ms. Violet's office, the Wellington market district was the largest one by far.

"If you bring Dr. Isaac home," Ms. Violet said, "you won't have to deal your wares in Crybaby's lair. You can sell to my streets directly. You'll be a member of the Jericho economy."

Virgil remained a statue for little longer, then: "I'll think about it."

He turned to leave, and Diane followed without needing to be told.

"Leon's waiting for you in the Heap," Ms. Violet called. "He'll be your point of contact."

"I said I'll think about it," Virgil said.

"Think fast. And a pleasure meeting you, mystery girl."

The frosted doors opened, and Virgil and Diane left without daring to look back.

The trip out of the sewer was much quieter than the way in. Virgil led them through his mental-mapped route with utmost diligence, always keeping an ear on the distant sobs. He detoured only once, to see if his stolen pouches could be found in the antechamber where Kara had died, but there was no sign of them. No sign of a body, either. When Crybaby ate, it seemed, it didn't leave much in the way of leftovers.

Virgil picked up Kara's other StormCell in the ovoid room, and they didn't stop again until they reached the algae-coated door. Outside, the sun was a magenta fleck dipping into oblivion, and the indigo night was hastily approaching.

Virgil reactivated the hologram that hid the sewer entrance. "We better find a place to camp."

"What about back at Gatetown?" Diane asked. "Can't we sleep there?"

"By now, that shopkeeper's told everyone about the sunflower seeds I gave him. They'll all want some, even if they can't afford it. I don't need that kind of heat."

Virgil returned to his jeep, but Diane hung back near the Wall. "Virgil?"

He popped the engine hood and swapped out the old StormCell for the tier two Kara had sold them. The dashboard's energy meter rose to a measly 30 percent.

"That man Ms. Violet wants you to find. Dr. Isaac."

Virgil slammed the hood, shoulders sagging.

"He's the scientist you were talking about, right?" Diane asked. "He's the only one who can get me out of the Grave Walker?"

"I messed up, kid," Virgil said earnestly. "I hadn't seen him in ages, thought he was still in Jericho. If I'd known . . ."

He trailed off. No two ways about it: Virgil had been played. He'd been dragged into something so much bigger than he could have anticipated, and he pulled Diane right down with him. It wasn't fair. She never signed up for this. She never *signed up* at all.

"Come on," he said, climbing back into the jeep. "We don't wanna be out in the open. Not after dark."

CHAPTER 8

"This can't be a good idea."

Diane waited inside the convenience store, watching Virgil through cracks in a broken window. Looters had gutted the space around here long ago, leaving only toppled shelves and obscene roadkiller graffiti in their wake. This emptiness, and the shop's proximity to the highway, made it the ideal shelter for a long Junkyard night. The jeep sat parked around back, hidden behind a pair of dumpsters. Virgil was out front by an ancient gas pump, probably last used during a bygone era when the world still ran on liquid fuel.

"Anyone ever tell you that you worry too much?" Virgil asked.

He tapped the fuel pump with his Volt Caster, and it lit up like a slot machine hitting the jackpot. A burst of gasoline shot from the pump's hose, drenching a wad of cloth Virgil had torn from the old flag in his trailer. He set the cloth in a parking space outside the window, snapped his Volt Caster just above it, and the cloth went up in yellow flames.

"¡*Caliente*!" Virgil leaped back from the eruption.

"Someone's going to see us!"

Virgil ducked back into the store, taking up post beside the Grave Walker. "Exactly. We gotta eat, don't we?"

Diane stared at the junkie with absolute horror. In that wild fire-light, the stained rictus in his beard was exceptionally ghoulish.

"Are you . . ." she stammered. "Um . . . Sorry, are you a cannibal?"

Virgil looked like he had just been smacked in the face. "What? No! Why the hell would you say that?"

"You just said you wanted to lure people with fire and eat them!"

"I didn't say . . . Ugh, nobody's eating any*body*. Just watch."

Outside, the scrap of embroidered white stars burned bright and alone against the night. The Junkyard's perpetual lightning storm had mellowed over the last hour, and only Virgil's fire offered solace from the absolute dark. It was the only beacon for miles.

And a swarm of roaches took the bait.

Like the ants from the day before, these insects were much larger than they had any right to be. Big as dogs, they scuttled out of the dark and congregated in the fire's welcoming heat. Five of them, clacking and hissing, combed the asphalt for potential food scraps. The sight made Diane thankful that she couldn't feel nausea in the Grave Walker.

"You eat bugs?" Diane moaned.

"Protein's protein." Virgil drew his knife and turned up the blade's heat. "Let's go."

Virgil went for the door, but Diane stayed put.

"I'm not going near them!" she said.

"Look, kid," Virgil leveled with her, "you're going to be living on the road a lot longer than either of us thought. If you wanna survive, you'll have to get your hands dirty."

Diane hated how right he was, almost as much as she hated the idea of confronting those giant cockroaches.

"The Grave Walker will protect you," Virgil said, patting the claw marks gashed into the suit's chest. "Just follow my lead."

Ten thorny antennae perked up as Virgil and Diane approached the fire. Diane silently hoped that the bugs were more afraid of her, like the science lessons on *Cradle* said they should be. No such luck. These were Junkyard roaches; all skittishness must have mutated out of their nature long ago.

Virgil snapped the Volt Caster as the insects attacked, zapping one of them square in the head. It flipped onto its back, twitched its legs, and died.

A second roach threw itself at his face, but he raised the heated knife just in time. The blade cut through the mandibles, pierced the brain, and the dead roach slid harmlessly into a puddle of its own phosphorescent blood.

The other bugs went for Diane, either unintimidated by her size or ganging up because of it. As she stumbled back, her foot landed on an overzealous roach, and a sickening crunch signaled its demise. The remaining two scaled the Grave Walker's legs, torso, and head, blinding Diane in the blur of their tumorous bodies.

"Virgil! Help!"

"They're just bugs, kid!" Virgil yelled. "What do we do to bugs?"

Though she had never encountered bugs firsthand, Diane could take a guess.

Wailing, she slapped the Grave Walker's hands all across its body. When the frenzy ended, she found both roaches laying twitchy and broken on the asphalt. Her hands dripped with insect innards, and she whipped them outward in disgust.

"Three to two!" Virgil said as he stomped out the fire. "You beat me."

Diane wiped her fingers on the ground. "So gross."

Virgil gripped his kills by their antennae. "You get used to it."

Diane gathered up her own roaches, and together they hauled the night's hunt back into the convenience store.

CHAPTER 9

In the light of another glow stick, Virgil set about preparing the roaches for dinner.

He began by draining the creatures of their blood, collecting the radiant liquid in jars and plastic containers. Virgil explained to Diane that "bug juice" was valuable, used for all kinds of things—medicine, engineering lubricants, carrier fluids, and the like. You could find a use for every part of an insect carcass if you tried hard enough. Waste not, want not.

After the bleeding, Virgil chose the beefiest-looking roach and peeled off its exoskeleton with his knife, revealing a bountiful slab of pale, mushy meat. He cut out a generous portion, laid it on the floor, then wiggled the Volt Caster's fingers just above it. A low current sizzled across the roach meat, cooking it to a light-brown jerky.

With his own meal prepared, Virgil chopped the remaining meat into tiny cubes. Then, awkwardly, he began to pat around the Grave Walker's outer thighs.

"They told me it was around here somewhere," he mumbled.

Something clicked under Virgil's probing finger. A hidden compartment opened in the Grave Walker's leg, ejecting a cylindrical container filled with tiny blades. Virgil dumped the meat cubes inside, added some water from his canteen, and then shut the compartment again.

They heard a muffled whirring, the noise of a blender liquefying cubes of roach meat. When it stopped, a wet churning sound rose from deep in the Grave Walker's torso. Diane squirmed. "Ugh, that's weird. What is that?"

"Suit's pumping food into your stomach," Virgil said. "'Least you don't have to taste the roach."

"Or anything else," Diane sighed. "Ever."

They ate in silence.

Virgil gnawed on his jerky, and Diane endured the Grave Walker's digestive process. The graffiti around them looked like perverse cave paintings in the glow stick's chilling light. Outside, far-off plasma gunfire cracked at irregular intervals, breaking long periods of windless quiet. These were the sounds of travelers who had not found shelter before sunset, and whether they survived the night was in fate's mercurial hands.

Once he finished his jerky, Virgil belched and wiped his greasy fingers on his pants.

"What kind of food did you eat on your space station?" he asked.

"Um, we had garden units that grew fruits and vegetables," Diane said. "Protein was artificially synthesized."

Virgil dabbed the grease from his beard thoughtfully. "You're lucky, then. Most people in the Junkyard only ever eat bugs and Nutribriks. The soil can still grow fungi, potatoes, some grains, but most of our vitamins come from those shit-tasting blocks. Everything's made in a lab. Fruits and vegetables are a myth down here."

"But not for you," Diane said, looking to the pouches around his belt. Virgil tapped the tomato seeds gently.

"I'm from somewhere else," he said. "Just like you."

"Where are you from?" Diane asked.

"No more questions today. Remember?"

Diane went back to the broken window in a huff. Virgil sensed her frustration, the growing resentment hanging over her like a bad omen. He didn't starve her hungry mind out of spite or sadistic pleasure. He just couldn't afford to answer too many questions. Secrecy was his home's greatest defense, and anyone who knew the secret was a threat. The fewer threats Virgil had to face, the better.

To distract himself from Diane's moping, he fished a screwdriver out of his backpack and set about disconnecting his inhaler's mouthpiece from the capsule port. The process of taking his Battery, refilling the inhaler, taking a second hit, and then refilling the inhaler again was becoming tedious. Something needed to be done.

"Come sunrise," he said while he worked, "we'll drive to a Conductor plant nearby, get our StormCells charged. Then, we'll go to a place called Caravan, restock our supplies, find out what's really happening at the Heap."

"I don't know if I should," Diane said, still gazing out the window.

"Don't know if you should what?" Virgil asked.

"Go with you."

The screwdriver stopped midturn. Virgil was a statue again.

"The Messenger looks dangerous," Diane said. "I don't care how tough the Grave Walker is. I'm not a fighter."

"He's not the job," Virgil said. "You probably won't have to fight anyone."

"You can't promise that."

"Dr. Isaac is the only person who can get you out of the suit."

"But then what? He gets me out, fixes my legs, then what? Everything is . . . shooting. And explosions. I won't last an orbit outside the Grave Walker."

"A what?" Virgil asked.

Diane paused at the question. "An orbit. An orbit around the sun."

Virgil went back to work on the inhaler. "Oh, a year. Say *year*, kid. You'll freak people out with that kind of space talk."

The screw popped loose, and the inhaler came apart. Virgil set the pieces aside while he dug through his backpack.

"So you cut ties with me," he said. "What next?"

"I could stay at Gatetown," Diane suggested. "Find a job with heavy lifting. They could look out for me."

"They're fresh out of StormCells in Gatetown. They can't keep you running."

"Then maybe I'll find my way back into Jericho," Diane said.

Virgil guffawed at that. "You want to go round two with Crybaby?"

Diane crossed her arms defensively. "I remember the way . . . I think. Maybe Ms. Violet could give me a job—"

"You don't want to mess around with Violet." Virgil pointed the screwdriver at her like a teacher's stick. "You've seen how she works. How she leads people on."

"She can't help that she had faulty intel," Diane said.

Virgil stifled his gut response to that. He found his backup inhaler and set about disassembling it as well. The task helped him formulate a retort.

"Let me put it this way. When I met Violet twenty years ago, Wellington was a family-owned company, and she was the lowest head on the totem pole. Lower than that. She was under the totem pole. Now, she's the sole executive, and no one's heard from the original Wellington family in years. And she hasn't aged a day. If anything, she looks younger."

"What're you saying?" Diane asked.

"I'm saying . . ." Virgil boiled his point down to the bare essential. The advice he wished someone would have given him when he was young. "Whatever you decide to do, don't trust Ms. Violet. *Never* trust Ms. Violet."

"But you work for her," Diane countered.

"As a contractor. On my terms."

"That's not what it looks like."

Virgil kept his eyes on his work, dismissing Diane's challenge as utterly beneath him. "Jericho's not the place for you, *chamaca*. Let it go."

The Grave Walker's posture slouched. The blue visor dimmed. It looked like the suit was turning off, but Virgil knew that couldn't be; her power meter should still be in the low thirties. No, this was another case of subconscious manifestation, like the clenched fists and the fearful rattling. These mechanical tics offered a window into Diane's mind. Right now, her mind was shutting down.

"There's never a place for me," she said. Her voice was a monotone whisper. Despaired. Defeated. Done.

The lament stunned Virgil. He understood that feeling, more so than he dared to admit. Like Diane, Virgil was not of the Junkyard. He had learned to walk the walk, talk the talk, and his sanity had even taken on the frayed quality expected of a junkie his age, but the road was not his home. He was not born and raised in a speeding car like so many of his peers. He was closer to a townie at heart, whispering a mantra of memories to survive each day, and if he didn't have the promise of home dangling over him like a carrot, he would have shut down a long time ago.

Diane needed that same promise, he realized. If he didn't provide one, he would never get her back in the trailer. So in an unprecedented act of desperation, Virgil lifted his wrist and checked a watch that was not there.

"Look at that! Midnight! You know what that means?"

The Grave Walker stood lifeless by the window.

"You got three more questions!" Virgil said. "Yay you!"

The visor lit up, just a little.

"Ask me your first one again," he offered.

The Grave Walker's head tilted toward him. Hesitant. Untrusting.

"Go on. Ask."

"Okay," Diane said, clearly humoring him. "Where are you from?"

"We don't really have a name for it," Virgil said. "Names are a thing you use to talk about something, and I don't talk about this with anyone. Ever."

He nodded sternly, implying that she had just been sworn to secrecy. She was getting more than the answer to her question; Virgil was giving her a piece of himself.

His expression took on a distant quality. He was seeing past the graffiti around them, past the dark Junkyard night, beyond to somewhere far, far away. "My home's only been around for a couple hundred years, I'm told. You ever hear of terraforming?"

Diane shook her head.

"Well, apparently," Virgil explained, "the Grand Finale weaponized terraformers. Big machines that could shake the earth. Change it. Destroy it. I don't know the whos or whys, but someone grew a mountain up north. Can you imagine? One day, it was just a field or a forest. Next day, whoosh! Mountain! *Loco.*"

Virgil made sweeping hand motions as he said this, pantomiming a mountain shooting up from flat terrain. The Grave Walker's visor was at full brightness now.

"There was some good soil where the mountain grew, and the peak took it high, higher than the Junkyard storm, so it stayed good."

As he spoke, Virgil tinkered with the inhaler parts in front of him. There were two of each piece, and he clanked, bolted, and jammed them together in a fit of exploratory surgery.

"My people settled there in secret. They tend the soil. Raise livestock. It's not like the Junkyard. It's safe. Clean."

He tapped the pouches hanging from his belt. "We engineered these babies just for selling down here. They're packed with growing enhancers—just add water—but they can't bear more seeds after they sprout. Buy one, get one. I never tell customers where they're from. If people knew, people like Ms. Violet, they'd want it all for themselves. They'd try to take it away from us. Industrialize us. Use our crops to control people."

"You use the crops as a bartering tool," Diane said. "That's not much better."

Smart kid, Virgil thought. Time for another history lesson.

"The mountain's first settlers tried delivering food packages to the Junkyard, long before I was born, but it didn't pan out so well. Villages tore each other apart trying to steal each other's portions. See, people don't want to settle for their fair share. They want more. They always want more. That's why there was a Grand Finale. People will go to war over anything, and we can't give them another excuse. The Junkyard's fragile enough as it is."

"Why do you come to the Junkyard, then?" Diane asked. "Why not stay home?"

Virgil smiled sadly. He had asked himself that question every day of his adult life.

"We can't grow everything. Some poor sap has to go down the mountain and scavenge for supplies. I've been that sap for almost thirty years."

"Why you?" Diane asked.

Virgil came close to giving an honest answer, but he bit his tongue at the last second. This was why he didn't take questions. Once you started telling the truth, it was hard to stop, and this was one truth he couldn't afford to disclose. If Diane knew the true reason why he was the mountain's glorified errand boy, she could easily deduce her actual value to him. That couldn't happen. The kid seemed nice enough, but a little leverage brought out the worst in people.

Virgil needed Diane too much to let her know it.

"Luck of the draw," he lied. "And I'll count all those questions as one because I'm such a nice guy."

Diane already had another question in the barrel. "What was it like coming to the Junkyard for the first time?"

"It was the worst day of my life," Virgil said.

With a final twist, he set the screwdriver aside and lifted his creation to the glow stick's chartreuse light. He had Frankensteined both capsule ports to a single mouthpiece, enabling two Battery hits to be inhaled simultaneously. He would be the invention's first test subject, and as he loaded the siamese ports with high-grade Battery capsules, he circled back to his point.

"It's cold up on the mountain, and all the greenhouses need energy to stay warm. It takes a tier-five StormCell to run the settlement. Those are rare, and ours is on its last legs."

Virgil put his lips around the mouthpiece and hit the eject button. With a grinding rattle, the capsules both emptied, and he coughed up a green cloud dense enough to rival the smogs of Jericho.

"I'm on my last legs too," he rasped. "But I can't crap out yet. Not until I get my people what they need."

Virgil reloaded the modified inhaler, then stuffed it into his backpack. Emerald smoke danced around his head, dropped over his shoulders like dry ice, and stained his beard fresh. Diane's captivated stillness told him exactly how he appeared to her in that moment. He had taken on a sort of mystical quality. Supernatural, with a hint of menace. He was a green devil; a desert-dwelling, silver-tongued Azazel; a peddler of forbidden fruit. And like all good demons, he offered a bargain:

"There's a lot of strength in that Grave Walker, Diane. A lot of power.

If you use it to keep me alive, help me get Dr. Isaac back to Jericho, I'll bring you home. We'll get you out of that suit, and I'll take you up the mountain. No shooting goes on up there. No explosions. Just good food, *real* food, and the cool breeze on your face. Soft grass between your toes. You help me, and that's your life. You have my word."

Diane could not bring herself to reply.

"Think about it," Virgil said, "while you take first watch."

He sprawled out on the floor, repurposed the backpack as a pillow, and shut his eyes. Soon, he was snoring.

CHAPTER 10

It struck Diane as odd that the Grave Walker had no night-vision functionality. Her HUD could zoom, monitor cardinal directions, identify hostiles, and even track their movements, but it couldn't see in the dark. Or maybe it could but required an eye gesture to activate, a voice command, or something.

"Night vision," Diane murmured. She felt embarrassed talking to herself, even though she was alone. She had ventured back out to the gas pumps, far enough to get some privacy but close enough to keep Virgil's snores within earshot. She needed time to herself. She needed to think.

"Night. Vision."

The evening remained dark and grainy through her visor. She might ask Virgil about night vision in the morning, if she decided it was worth spending one of her precious questions. The audacity of that rule still bugged her, but it was a battle she might have to forfeit for the time being. Tonight, she had a much larger conflict to consider.

Outside the glow stick's reach, Diane found the darkness wasn't as absolute as she originally believed. The Jericho skyline haunted the distance with its spectral neon, and right below it, the modest lights of Gatetown shone smaller but more vibrant. A few other villages pierced the blackness around her as well, fluttering like torches on faraway shores. But perhaps the most profound sight: in the western sky, she could still spot a hole where *Cradle* had fallen to Earth—a galaxy of stars twinkling through a tear in dark fabric. The tear had looked bigger that morning. The clouds were sewing themselves back up. Sealing the breach. Closing the door behind her.

Diane could still find her way back to *Cradle*. Or she could try her luck in Jericho, or Gatetown, or any of the other villages shining out there. Someone would have the resources to keep her alive. Virgil couldn't be the only one. That was the reason she found him so hard to trust; he had taken such pains to make himself essential, and he had known exactly what to offer. The exact thing she craved, he had in stock. More than anything else, even escaping the suit, Diane yearned for a safe place to call home. As soon as she threatened to leave, Virgil had suddenly provided.

Why? Why was he so desperate to keep her around? Was the Grave Walker really so powerful? Was she really worth so much?

She was worth something, though. That much was clear. If only she could figure out the reason why. The *real* reason, beyond his half-baked plea for protection. But maybe it wasn't so half-baked. Maybe he really did need a "safe-ish" guardian to watch his back. The Grave Walker clearly had its perks when you weren't the one trapped inside, constantly relying on others to perform maintenance and keep your StormCells replenished. Tricking her into the suit had been a gross deception, but maybe that was the limit of his treachery. Maybe, now that he had her where he needed her, she could trust him.

Too many *maybes* for Diane's liking, but if she bailed on Virgil now, she risked losing her only ticket to what as far as she knew might be the last safe place on Earth. The Junkyard could never be a home to her, that much she knew, and Virgil's mountainous paradise sounded like her only chance at a life that wouldn't end in bloodshed. Honestly, it sounded too good to be true. Terraformers? The world's last garden, tended in secret above the clouds? It had to be a fantasy, but she was the last person qualified to say so. Everything in this world looked fantastical to her alien eyes, and Virgil was her only tether to reality. The nearest light in the darkness. Her guide—not a good guide, but the best one she had. The only one she had.

And besides, wasn't it Virgil who had freed her from the escape pod? Whatever his motives, that surely counted for something.

Under these justifications, Diane did not hike back to Gatetown. She did not venture off to a distant village, nor did she brave the sewers again for an audience with Ms. Violet.

She went back into the abandoned convenience store, sat by the broken window, and kept watch.

CHAPTER 11

The next day, they began the trek to Caravan.

He described it as a junkie safe haven where they could catch their breath, gather their thoughts, and he'd been there countless times. They would be welcomed with open arms, a guaranteed parking space, and complimentary shots of the best and only spirit Junkyard distilleries had to offer—vodka. In an age of toxic famine, potatoes were still going strong.

After a quick pit stop at the nearest Conductor plant, they would have all the StormCell energy they needed to seek out Caravan. Virgil had mentioned Gatetown's dilemma with roadkillers staking out the highway, but he was confident the bandits wouldn't be an issue for the two of them. They'd take an alternate route. They'd proceed with caution.

Diane saw the spire of the Conductor first, poking at the agitated clouds, goading the storm into action. The silver needle was taller than anything else for miles around. When lightning struck, electricity crackled down its body in a shimmering waterfall, droning like a broken synthesizer. The spire siphoned its energy into a network of wires and transformers, which then fed the power to nearby charging domes. A sign on the power plant's chain-link fence labeled this place *US Army Fusion Conductor Station #004*.

Diane's decision to stick with Virgil seemed to have put him in high spirits, and he'd spent the whole jeep ride telling her about StormCell technology. She had not needed to ask. He simply started talking, and she listened.

He told her how the Grand Finale drained the world's liquid fuel early on, and the burned-out sky left solar power dead in the dust. Nuclear fusion was the next logical move. Enter StormCells. When lightning struck the Conductor spire, it flooded a power plant with enough electricity to initiate nuclear fusion, and it stored that energy in state-of-the-art fuel cells that ranged from tiny tier ones, which powered most Junkyard weaponry, to the much rarer tier fives, which could supply a village with electricity for years. Then, when the burst of electricity ran out, the fusion reactor died, and the power plant became no more volatile than an empty farmhouse. The storms never passed for long, so the Conductor never ran out of power for long. Safe. Sustainable. StormCell.

Diane had absorbed this knowledge with a sponge's eagerness, but when they got within spitting distance of Conductor #004, Virgil went quiet again.

Diane followed his gaze, and suddenly she could see why. The plant was overrun with roadkillers. They weren't just marauding the highway that led to the Conductor; they had taken the Conductor itself. Gatetown's merchants never stood a chance.

Cackling mad, a scabrous gang of raiders bustled about the station, hauling boxes of empty StormCells into the central dome, dragging the corpses of the original owners out. Some of the plant's machinery was marred with concentrated burn marks, the result of a reckless shootout, and Diane could now see that Conductor #004 was only operating at half capacity. When lightning hit the spire, 50 percent of the power plant remained in the dark. This dilemma reminded her of *Cradle*'s no-specialization policy, and though it had been frustrating, she had to acknowledge its effectiveness. Unless the roadkillers had an engineer in their midst, the rest of the power plant would fall into disrepair as well, someday. Roadkillers had the strength to take, but not the intelligence to maintain. All their savage accomplishments were temporary. They were doomed.

Upon analyzing the situation, Virgil quickly U-turned away from Conductor #004. They would receive no StormCells here. That was a problem.

Both Virgil's jeep and Diane's suit were dangerously low on energy, their respective StormCell meters dropping further all the time. Their rates of decline were neck and neck, both hovering above the 20 percent mark.

As the Conductor spire shrank behind them, Virgil assured Diane that Caravan couldn't be that far off. He said the same thing after an hour passed. And again when the next hour came. By hour three, he had stopped speaking to Diane altogether.

The longer they roamed the wasteland in search of "home away from home," the more Diane got the sense that he had no clue where Caravan actually was. Even while facing backward in the trailer, she knew an aimless route when she saw one. Too many stops. Way too much backtracking. Any right-minded person could tell they were lost.

Diane could never bring this up during the drive, though. She had rationed the day's questions for a situation just like this, but Virgil had become unreachable after they left the Conductor. He spent the whole ride juggling radio frequencies, calling up an endless contact list for discussions Diane never quite heard. But based on their current circumstance, and the way Virgil began each call with a laugh and ended with an angry "¡*Estúpido*!" she figured he was asking for directions. How could it be that none of his junkie friends knew the way to junkie paradise? Yet another question for the backlog, assuming she lived long enough to ask it.

As her StormCell meter hit 10 percent, Diane spotted a lone argonaut Peacekeeper wandering just off the road. Both its arms had been ripped away, and the dullness of its ocular lens implied that it was blind. It walked an aimless path across the desert, turning and detouring at random. Diane wondered if the argonaut had any destination in mind or if this was all the machine could think to do in such a hopeless state. A deep gully intersected the Peacekeeper's current course, one that would swallow the argonaut whole. Maybe the machine would turn in time to avoid the trap. Maybe it wouldn't. This broken thing would live and die at the mercy of chaotic forces much bigger than itself, and Diane could relate a little too well. She suspected that Virgil could too.

Sometime around midday, when both jeep and Grave Walker teetered on the verge of shutting down, they came to a village called Sacred Chapel.

It was a lively borough, small yet bustling, full of townies going about their daily business in the village center. The townies here lived in scrap-metal wigwams encircling a half-demolished megachurch, while the temple itself was home to some of the best damn gunsmiths from here to Jericho—Virgil's words. Nothing sacrilegious going on here, he promised. The prewar deities weren't providing food or Battery; the gunsmiths were. Therefore, the eponymous church was better suited for them.

Virgil went to pay these gunsmiths a visit, leaving Diane to wait by the jeep again. He gave her a job this time, one that wouldn't deplete her fading power supply.

He put a tarnished tin bucket in her hands, filled it with scorched Junkyard dirt, then planted three seeds and added water. After dusting the mud with a white powder, he told Diane to guard the bucket with her life, then he disappeared into the church.

There were no obnoxious children to pester Diane; most of the townies passing by were too busy to notice her at all. So she played a fly on the wall at the village's center, and she soon lost herself in the various dramas at play.

A mother scolded her daughter for slacking off at gun repair training. If she didn't get her act together, how could she ever hope to earn a coveted seat on the Sacred Chapel assembly line?

In hushed tones, a young man argued with his sister over his secret love for a cyborg working in the village. The sister warned him that the cyborg would spend his whole life paying off cybersurgery debts, but the brother didn't care. He would happily go to bed with an empty stomach if it meant going to bed with the man he loved.

A woman Virgil's age came up to Diane and asked her if she was sweating buckets in that silly suit. Diane said that she wasn't. The woman insisted on giving her a bottle of water anyway, even though the jug from Gatetown was clearly visible in the jeep's back seat. Diane wasn't sure how to drink while inside the Grave Walker, so the woman left the bottle in the trailer and moved on. Diane was so touched she forgot to say thank you.

From behind her visor, these events played out like a cinema verité piece in *Cradle's* video archive. A fictitious world, separate from life on the road, where people had time to love. To quarrel. To engage in random acts of kindness. Diane was en route to another world like this, she hoped, only hers would be safer. No chance of a roadkiller invasion where she was headed. Just clean air, fresh food, and soft grass between her toes.

That was the promise, anyhow.

Virgil returned to the jeep looking satisfied. For the masked Peace-keeper head and all the junk in his trailer, the gunsmiths had provided a large cache of tier-two StormCells and implemented some tweaks to the Volt Caster, swapping out its electrodes for shiny, more conductive replacements. For a bag of pumpkin seeds, they had also provided directions to Caravan. Energy replenished, Virgil and Diane left Sacred Chapel and continued on their way.

Several hours of driving brought them to a hill on the outskirts of a modest prewar town named Brighamland. Virgil kept them a good distance away from the city limits, and Diane didn't need to ask why. The ground beneath Brighamland had become thin and brittle, seeping noxious gases that reduced the town to a mustard-colored blotch. Before their eyes, a newborn sinkhole gobbled the community clocktower, belching more gas to fill its place. This area could never be reclaimed as a village, and only the craziest junkies would venture inside. Brighamland belonged to the Junkyard, and the Junkyard was swallowing it one building at a time.

Virgil kept them on that hill all day, munching Nutribriks and huffing Battery, eyeing the roads that led southwest. Diane kept hold of the bucket in her charge, watching the dirt magically turn dark, soft, and speckled with tiny green leaves. Junkie FM played music tracks about enjoying the silence and fucking the police, interspersed with a DJ's commentary. No news on anything related to Caravan.

Diane sacrificed a precious question to ask why they were waiting around this dump, because this clearly wasn't the junkie safe haven she had been promised. Virgil told her that Caravan was a location with no address. A fixed point on the move. He would not elaborate; he didn't want to ruin the spectacle for a first-timer. He advised her to sit back and wait. Just wait. Caravan was on its way.

That day at least, Caravan never came.

In a race against the setting sun, Virgil scoured the immediate vicinity for shelter, grumbling constantly about those rip-off gunsmiths and their useless intel. His search brought them to a nearby airport, its runway littered with combat jets and hovertanks broken beyond repair. But one plane sat totally intact, wasting away in its hangar, a living sacrifice to the hungry god of rust. Virgil stashed his jeep under the plane's wing, then he and Diane rushed to the base's traffic control tower. The turret from a dismantled hovertank blocked the entrance. Diane shoved it aside with minimal strain.

The lightning was in full force that night, snapshotting the aircraft cemetery in blazing, erratic bursts. Through the tower window, Diane fixated on the untouched airplane sitting across the runway, and she asked Virgil why humans no longer traveled by air. Surely the safest way to navigate the Junkyard's terrain would be to avoid it entirely. While pouring water into the Grave Walker's nutrient blender, Virgil responded by pointing to the sky. The storm was constant, relentless, and it left no room for safe passage. To travel by air was to challenge the lightning, and the lightning always won.

By now, the enhanced seeds in Diane's bucket had sprouted into three cherry tomato vines, each bearing one plump rose-colored fruit. Virgil described the burst of watery flavor as he popped two into his mouth, and he dropped the third into the Grave Walker's blender for nutritional value. Virgil and Diane spent the night sharing details from their respective homes, anecdotes from childhood. She talked about seeing Earth from her observation window. He described the traditions of his annual harvest festival. Diane had watched films from the twentieth century. Virgil had played fetch with the last canines in existence. For the first time, they talked for hours, talked and talked until sleep could no longer be ignored.

Diane took first watch again. The night was mostly uneventful, empty time dusted with a few passing bugs. But in the final hours of her shift, something new disturbed the peace. A half-naked man limped onto the runway, his body a gruesome tie-dye of bionic joints and bloodied flesh.

As Diane watched, six laser beams flew out of the darkness. One hit the cyborg's good leg, and as he dropped onto the tarmac, a lightning flash revealed his attackers. Five humans, too well-armored to be roadkillers, descended gleefully upon their prey. Diane began to rise, to rush outside to the man's aid, but then she felt a hand on the Grave Walker's ankle.

Now wide awake, Virgil cautioned her not to get involved. A desperate junkie was a dangerous junkie, and the only thing more desperate than hunting a live cyborg for parts was doing so after the sun went down. There was nasty business going on outside—it made Virgil sick—but it wasn't their fight. They had bigger bugs to fry.

Though Virgil began his watch early, Diane lost the most sleep that night. When she did sleep, she dreamed of dismembered bodies, space colonists on fire, and lines of malignant code.

error = override invalid (cmd=recall.TOWER)

[override]error(cmd=recall.TOWER)

[override]error(cmd=recall.TOWER)

[override]error(cmd=recall.TOWER)[override]error

Scrolling, burning, screaming. Forever, and ever, and ever.

She woke before sunrise, bawling like a child. Virgil came to her side.

"Kid! What is it? What's wrong?"

"I should have . . ." Diane whimpered, still half asleep. "I should have said something. I waited too long."

Virgil put a hand on the Grave Walker's arm. "It's okay—"

"It's not okay! I could've made them believe me!"

She rambled on, trapped in a lingering nightmare. "I knew something was wrong with *Cradle*. I knew it, but I was too scared to say anything. And now Ben's dead. Everyone's dead, and it's my fault."

"Shhhh." Virgil leaned in front of Diane's visor. "Don't do that. You can't carry that load."

"I killed them," Diane whispered.

"You didn't kill anyone," Virgil said. "Whatever happened to that space station, it wasn't your fault. I mean . . . I'm ninety percent sure it wasn't your fault, only because I wasn't there. But you don't seem like the mass-murdering type. I've got a nose for that kind of thing."

Diane couldn't help but giggle. In her old life, she had grown weary of Nurse's cookie-cutter reassurances, and Virgil's fumbling condolence was far removed from that. It felt real.

She drifted back into another hour of sleep. Merciful, dreamless sleep.

Compared to all the other Junkyard phenomena Diane had faced up to this point, a sandstorm felt rather tame.

It overtook them the next day on the open road, while they were driving southwest from the airport. It was only a strong wind at first, but then the air darkened with grit, and it became harder and harder for Virgil to keep the jeep driving straight. The interstate had been hazardous enough already, sprinkled with truck carcasses and tire-shredding potholes. Now, even with the headlights at full blast, Virgil couldn't see three feet in front of them. The sandstorm may have been relatively pedestrian, but that made it no less dangerous.

"Maybe we should turn back!" Diane shouted over the wind.

Tight-lipped, Virgil pushed ahead. "It's gotta be somewhere around here! I can feel it!"

Diane felt only panic as they barely avoided spinning off the road. The trailer's safety railing was already bent from the Grave Walker's iron squeeze, and she twisted it even farther while gripping the bars for dear life. It wasn't the idea of wiping out that concerned her; she knew her suit could take the hit. She was more worried about landing in a ditch, getting buried under six feet of sand, and disappearing from Virgil's sight. Would he stick around, risk his life, to dig her out? How much trouble was she really worth?

Finally, a faint light appeared to Diane out of the haze.

Its size and brightness grew steadily, turning the gritty maelstrom into pixels on a dying computer screen. As the glow expanded upward and outward, it revealed two startling facts.

One: the glow originated from a pair of headlights, each wider than Virgil's entire jeep.

Two: those headlights were attached to a colossal rhomboid mass, its height lost in the fuzzy upper echelons of the sandstorm.

"Um . . . Virgil—?"

The boom of a deafening horn stole the words out of Diane's mouth. Virgil glanced into his rearview mirror as the headlights rose to blinding luminance. He said something, but the horn made it impossible to hear.

"What is it?" Diane screamed when the noise died away.

Virgil guided them onto the interstate shoulder, beyond the cold edge of the high beams, and then slowed the jeep to an idle coast. Bit by bit, the grainy features of the rhombus materialized as it drew closer, but even when its full image became clear, Diane still had no name for what she saw.

"That," Virgil shouted proudly, "is Caravan!"

They could see the full length of Caravan as it passed them by, forging ahead on caterpillar treads, shattering any obstacles with its indestructible front buffers. It was a monster—two gigantic vehicles, both six hundred feet long, wide enough to fill the freeway, welded together so that the front of one linked sloppily to the back of the other. Each rhomboid piece was a mobile citadel in its own right, sharing at least a dozen artillery chambers between them, all armed with high-powered laser cannons. A silver conduit pole jutted up from the front cart's roof, harvesting green lightning bolts from the Junkyard's radioactive sky. Through years of grime and dirt, Diane could just make out a faded emblem painted across the rear vehicle. The design resembled that bedraggled flag Virgil had burned to lure cockroaches a couple nights back: red stripes, white stripes, and a blue square full of stars.

An entourage of motorcycles, pickup trucks, and SUVs formed a loose posse around Caravan, and they all swerved past the jeep without slowing. Virgil trailed close behind, shouting into his radio all the while.

"Caravan, come in! Caravan, this is Virgil Ceres, Registration ID J-Five-Eight-Zero! Requesting permission to dock!"

A younger voice, calm and polite, responded over the CB. "*Caravan to Mr. Ceres, we read you. I'm afraid the garage is currently at maximum capacity."*

"Like hell it is!" Virgil said. "There's always an open spot!"

"*Unfortunately, all our designated spots are—*"

"Listen, *cabrón*! You tell Captain Nico who's at the door, and you tell him he'll never see an ounce of real tobacco again if he leaves me *en la maldita tormenta*! *¿Comprendes?*"

A brief silence, then the voice returned: "*Permission granted. Prepare to dock.*"

Virgil hung up his mic. He decelerated further until they were just keeping up with the rear cart's taillight. Facing the wrong way, Diane could only hear the groan of a blast door opening, then the whir of a liftgate sliding out to meet them. Hydraulics carried the platform downward, stopping a hair's length above the moving road.

Virgil toed the gas pedal, and the jeep lurched onto the flat metal surface. Diane felt their vehicle rise off the freeway and slide backward, then the blast door sealed the Junkyard away.

No more wind. No more sand. They had made it; they were here.

But where was "here"?

Looking around, Diane saw they were the latest addition to a smorgasbord of vehicles. Not the broken-down shells clogging up the roads outside—these were *alive*. A sedan fitted with remote-controlled plasma turrets. Armored vans rigged with bulldozer blades. A motorbike fast enough to leave trails of lightning. Fireproof RVs. A goddamn battle tank. It was a bona fide fleet of anti-Junkyard vehicles, no two identical, thronged into the steamy, pipe-lined repository of an industrialized docking bay. Most of the vehicles were stowed in parking spots or suspended platform rigs, while a very lucky few sat in the care of grease-stained, overworked mechanics at their designated repair stations.

And loitering among the vehicles, steam-bathing in a haze of exhaust and Battery smoke, were the drivers. They were not townies, neatly clad in hand-washed hand-me-down threads. They were not roadkillers, draped in rags, prodding at open wounds. No, Diane recognized the high-tech armor, the uncovered gems of advanced idiosyncratic weaponry, the green-stained lips from years of Battery use. These were people like Virgil. Wasteland survivalists. Warrior merchants with enough psychological issues to have driven her old Nurse droid crazy.

These were junkies.

They came in every shape and size, chatting, coughing, and laughing to each other as they swapped stories and muttered trade secrets. While they shared the telltale signs of junkiedom, it amazed Diane that they all belonged to the same profession; everyone looked so different! She wondered what her life might have been like if one of these anomalies had discovered the escape pod instead of Virgil. What could she have learned from the stocky barbarian wearing a necklace of Peacekeeper lenses, or the machete-wielding woman covered head to toe in acid burns? The pale, alopecic ghost dressed like a Wild West gunslinger? The blue-eyed Madonna in riot gear? Would they have tricked her into the Grave Walker? Would they have stopped to help her in the first place?

Diane knew one thing for certain about the crowd: Virgil was easily the oldest among them. The majority of these junkies would have fallen squarely into *Cradle*'s Block Four category, the outliers no younger than Diane's age, no older than the beginnings of Block Five. Meanwhile, Virgil was well on his way to Block Six—fifty orbits around the sun. She had spotted other people his age in the villages, but here on Caravan, he was alone. An outlier among outliers.

At the direction of a uniformed guard, Virgil coasted the jeep along a marked path toward the repair stations. Two junkies broke from the crowd and sauntered along beside them, both dressed in matching business suits that looked wildly impractical for Junkyard living. However, through a series of burn holes in the fabric, Diane saw that both men wore metal body armor under their pants and blazers. The suits were merely an aesthetic choice. One half of the duo was tall and clean-cut, the other short and scruffy. Their voices were rough as sandpaper, simmering with outrageous machismo.

"Well, I'll be damned," the tall one said.

"Look what the storm blew in," the scruffy one chimed.

Virgil nodded at the men, from tall to scruffy. "Johnson. Schwartz."

"Haven't seen you in a while," Johnson said.

"I bet Johnson five Nutribriks you were bug food," Schwartz said.

"Put my money on roadkiller food," Johnson confirmed.

"Neither of us bet you were still breathing."

"Guess we both lost."

"Story of our goddamn lives."

The banter was a ping-pong match, and Virgil struggled to keep up while also watching the jeep's path.

"I've been busy," he said, then he noticed the collage of still-bleeding cuts on both men's faces. "You two look . . . good."

"We look like shit," Schwartz said.

"We look like shit took a shit," Johnson added.

Schwartz sighed. "*Shiiiit.*"

The one called Johnson noticed Diane for the first time, and he gave the Grave Walker a good long look. "Who's your buddy?"

"Just a buddy," Virgil said quickly.

Schwartz zoned in on the claw mark across the Grave Walker's chest. "Where'd you get that battle scar, buddy?"

Realizing that he was talking to her, Diane took a deep breath and made her voice as deep as she could. "Crybaby gave it to me."

"Playin' in the sewers, huh?" Johnson lit up with approval. "That's hardcore."

"We splashed around down there, once or twice," Schwartz said, flexing a little.

Johnson laughed. "Oh yeah! You wanna see a Crybaby scar? Schwartz, show 'em ya ass!"

Schwartz began to unzip his dress pants, but Virgil accelerated the jeep before his trousers could drop.

"Nope!" Virgil yelled back, glancing at Diane. "Nope, we're good. Take it easy, boys."

Schwartz zipped up his fly. "See you later, Big V."

"*Adiós, viejo*," Johnson said.

The pair melted back into the crowd, and Diane succumbed to a fit of giggles. Virgil was unamused.

"What's *viejo*?" Diane asked.

"He's calling me old," Virgil grunted.

"Then why not say *old*?"

"I don't know. Why do you call years *orbits*? It's just the way we talk. Always has been. And that's question number three, by the way."

He pulled up to the largest repair station, where several vehicles—including a hypersleek, razor-sharp tank—already sat waiting. Virgil parked the jeep at the front of the line.

"Knock, knock, Rok!" he called.

From beneath an ice cream truck with roof-mounted flamethrowers, an exasperated voice answered the summons. "Virgil, no."

The mechanic named Rok slid out on a four-wheeled creeper, face and tank top stained with a sheeny black fluid. The top of her jumpsuit was tied down around her waist, revealing muscular arms lean and toned from a lifetime of heavy lifting. Electric-blue highlights glowed within her messy dark hair—tied up in a practical bun—and bulging safety goggles magnified the annoyance in her eyes. Virgil greeted her with a warm smile.

"Miss me?" he asked.

Rok disregarded the question. She was all business. "You gotta park in the back. I've got three other cars in line."

"They can wait," Virgil said.

"No, they can't. The drivers already paid. They got places to be—"

As they argued, Diane found herself fixating on the tool belt clipped around Rok's waist. It wasn't so different from her own belt on *Cradle*, though some of these tools appeared homemade, and a couple were fitted with weaponized modifications. The mechanic was three or four orbits older than Diane, and though the space colonist would never aspire to a life in the Junkyard, she couldn't help admiring the circumstances that this woman had built for herself. A technical problem-solver, safe on a moving fort, in such high demand that her repair station was the only one with an actual line.

A line that Virgil had totally ignored. Age was not the only thing that separated him from the junkie mold, Diane began to realize. She had not been rescued by just anyone. Reading the room, she had seen the wonder on all the junkies' faces when Virgil passed them by. Virgil, with his rare merchandise and Jericho connections, was an influential person in this world. The idea made Diane feel safer and more intimidated all at once.

She tuned back into the argument.

"—I'm confused," Virgil was saying. "How many people in this garage do you have a blood pact with?"

Rok bit her lip, resentful and conflicted.

"Just me?" Virgil pressed.

The mechanic peeled off her goggles, and her round olive eyes glared at the old junkie with bitter defeat. "I was really getting used to you being dead."

"Happy to disappoint," Virgil said.

Rok spat a glob of brown juice onto the garage floor, and Diane realized that she had been chewing tobacco this whole time.

"What do you need?" she asked.

"Usual tune-up on the ol' jeep. And . . ." Virgil flicked his thumb back at the trailer. ". . . I'd like you to take a look at her."

Like Johnson and Schwartz before her, Rok only noticed Diane after overcoming the distraction of Virgil's presence. But when she did see the Grave Walker, she looked more amazed than all three of those Gatetown children combined.

"Where did you find it?" she gasped.

"Around," Virgil replied. "And it's a she."

Rok moved her hands along the nooks and edges of the armor, almost sensually. Diane, fascinated by the mechanic's fascination, said nothing.

"Do you have *any* idea how rare this tech is?" Rok asked. "Was it just lying somewhere? Did you trade for it?"

Virgil blocked the inquiries with an exhausted wave. "So many questions! You two will get along great."

He produced a crumpled sheet of paper from his pocket, its every inch covered in a scrawled itemized list. He must have composed it while Diane was asleep; she had never seen him write anything down in all their time together.

"She needs a rundown of her suit's capabilities," Virgil said, handing the list to Rok, "some retrofitting to increase energy efficiency. Stuff like that."

While Rok smoothed out the paper, Virgil looked to a heavily guarded bulkhead across the docking bay. He began to leave.

"Where are you going?" Diane asked, slightly anxious.

"I'm headed up front," Virgil said. "I got questions. A man there has answers."

"How will I find you?"

Virgil yanked his left hand out of the Volt Caster, tucking the glove and gauntlet under one arm. "You're gonna have to hang back on this one. The front cart's a no-weapon zone, and you're basically a killing machine."

"But—"

"Don't sweat it, kid. I won't be long, and Rok'll take care of you. She's the best mechanic on this dump. Ain't that right, Rok?"

Rok, who had just finished reading the list, was impervious to compliments. "This is a tall order, Virgil. Can you at least pretend that you'll pay me?"

Virgil patted Diane's shoulder. "You get to tinker with a Grave Walker! Experience is its own reward."

Rok put a hand on her hip. Whatever sway their "blood pact" held, Virgil was pushing it. Taking the hint, he took a pouch from his belt and dropped it into Rok's open hand.

"Make sure she doesn't rig the jeep to blow," Virgil told Diane. He gave her one last reassuring wink, then strolled off toward the bulkhead, whistling all the way.

"*Cabrón*," Rok grumbled at his back. For the first time, she peered up into Diane's visor, regarding her and not the Grave Walker. "That bastard got you on the hook too?"

"No, I'm . . ." Diane started to clarify, until she realized that "on the hook" was exactly where Virgil had her. "My name's Diane. And . . . yeah, I'm on the hook."

Rok's laughter was bitterly sardonic, and somehow, it was music to Diane's ears. It was the laugh reserved for a person who knew things. A person who had survived their fair share of bugshit and come away with ample street smarts, plus a healthy dose of cynicism. That laugh encompassed everything Diane did not have, and she found it utterly fascinating.

"How old are you?" Rok asked. "You sound young."

"I'm not that young. I'm almost eighteen orb—years. Almost eighteen years old."

Rok studied Virgil's list again, her face turning grim. "*El hombre es un maldito vampiro.*"

"What?" Diane asked, unable to decipher the unfamiliar language.

"Nothing." Rok folded the paper into a neat square. "Let's see what makes your Grave Walker tick."

Diane said she would like that.

CHAPTER 12

Virgil crossed the rickety coupling tunnel between Caravan's rear and front halves, cursing all the way. "*Pinche puente . . . Puta desvencijada . . .*"

These profanities, whispered through clenched teeth, were the same ones he used every time he braved the tunnel—a swaying catwalk encased in narrow corrugated tubing. He had crossed this undulating threshold countless times, and every time, it made him queasy. It was a tradition at this point. Welcome back; enjoy the nausea.

He was unarmed now—his knife, magnum, and Volt Caster checked into a holding armory—and his left hand felt naked as he leaned against the wall for balance. He told himself that he was safe, that in Caravan's two hundred years of service, the coupling bridge had never severed. Even so, something about the turbulence, combined with his lack of weaponry and the tunnel's resemblance to a certain sewer, put Virgil on edge. He never dared give a name to this sensation, though he knew it deep down. In times of vulnerability, his last defense was denying that he felt vulnerable at all.

But these anxieties were short-lived. After five long strides, he reached the security checkpoint where a Caravan guard patted him down, searching for any weapons the armory might have missed. She found none. Virgil was a professional.

The front cart was busy this afternoon.

Under the warm glow of caged Edison bulbs, junkies laughed and lived in the only place many of them felt safe. They were slumped over the donut-shaped bar at the cantina's center, downing vodka shots, commiserating over the Junkyard's many cruelties. They were playing cutthroat on billiard tables bolted to the grated floor, and any disruptions from road turbulence were fair game. They were hunkered down in salvaged diner booths, plotting and scheming, flirting and kissing. Almost everyone socialized, junkies of all genders and orientations grateful for company after countless days on the road.

Only one loner today, at least that Virgil could see. A dark-eyed, dreadlocked, painfully skinny young man reading a weathered paperback in one of the booths. Tattoos covered his entire body, images of arcane runes and tentacles etched in black and green ink. Virgil recognized the design, at least by reputation. Those tattoos were a rite of passage for acolytes of the Shallows—an isolated village on the Junkyard's northwestern coast, gripped by a religion so perverse that it actually worshipped the biohazard nightmares lurking in the ocean depths. Virgil had heard rumors of a Shallows acolyte who had abandoned his order to live free as a junkie. His name was supposed to be Ishmael, and considering the stigma that preceded his kind, it made sense that he would keep to himself.

One common trait prevailed among all the patrons, even Ishmael: none of them were armed. Caravan was many things. It was a bar. It was an auto repair shop. A citadel. A union headquarters. A motel. But above all else, Caravan was safe passage. For the right price, Caravan would deliver anyone anywhere without a scratch. The rules were strict. If you couldn't pay, you couldn't stay. If you got in a fight, you got a ban. And if you took a life, Caravan took yours. Junkies weren't usually the rule-following types, but in exchange for safe passage across the Junkyard, it was a reasonable compromise.

Virgil found the man he was looking for at one of the billiard tables. This man had just hustled the hell out of his last opponent, and he was now fishing for another poor sap to take him on.

"Come on, you green-lipped cowards!" he bellowed. "I'm betting like a maniac here. You could win big!"

"Screw yourself, Duke," the latest loser spat.

"We know you're wired on uppers," another junkie added. "Ain't fair."

Watching Duke from across the room, Virgil imagined how red and puffy his eyes must look behind those aviator sunglasses—the lenses tinted green, the rims heavy with AR modifications. He pictured a brain so full of chemicals that it was bursting out of Duke's skull, and his floppy white sun hat barely kept the mess from spilling out. How fried was the liver trapped inside his body? That body, plump from easy living, wrapped in a ratty shirt with black-and-yellow floral patterns? A hand-rolled cigarette dangled between his teeth, but the mustard smoke hinted at chemicals barely reminiscent of real tobacco. Disgraceful.

Before Duke could take another puff, Virgil pushed through the crowd and snatched the cigarette from his mouth. Duke could only gape as Virgil crushed the paper under his boot, snuffing out the last of the mustard vapor.

"Smoking kills," Virgil said.

A stunned silence rippled through the immediate junkies. Everyone braced for the rare event of a fistfight.

Instead, much to everyone's bafflement, Duke laughed and pulled Virgil into a bear hug. "You seedy bastard! Where the hell have you been hiding?"

"Why you smoking this crap, Duke?" Virgil asked. "Real thing not good enough?"

"I thought my tobacco guy was belly-up in a ditch! I was desperate."

Robbed of their spectacle, the crowd scattered to other entertainments. Virgil slipped a new cigarette out of his coat pocket, one filled with the real thing.

"Damn decent of you," Duke said. He accepted the gift, lit it with an electric lighter, and inhaled the sweet taste of unfiltered, 100 percent genuine tobacco.

"You're the third person to tell me I died," Virgil said. "What's up with that?"

"You've been gone four months, man. That's a junkie eternity."

Virgil eyed the open pool table beside them. "Up for some eight-ball?"

Duke grinned, his smile crooked and mischievous. "Loser buys a round of shots?"

"You're on."

Virgil broke, sending the balls scattering like gas molecules.

"Good break!" Duke exclaimed. "Damn good break!"

The six ball dove into a corner pocket; Virgil was solids.

"Did that Wellington gig pan out?" Duke asked while Virgil lined up his next shot.

Three, side pocket.

"Yup. Signed, sealed—" Virgil struck the cue ball, and three vanished in a blur of speed. "Delivered."

"Took you long enough."

Virgil missed his next shot, giving Duke the floor. Teetering slightly, he popped a red upper into his mouth, set the cigarette between his teeth, and lined up his shot.

"How's the ol' Neon Nightmare holding up?" he asked, while knocking out ten and fifteen in a single blow.

"Still standing," Virgil said. "Ms. Violet didn't ask about you this time."

"Thank god! That woman scares the shit out of me." Duke ricocheted the cue ball off a corner, sinking fourteen.

Anyone who knew Duke agreed that he was the best pool player in the Junkyard, and there was no question why. Duke was not a guest on Caravan. He was not in transit, not en route to another destination. Through means known only to an elite few, Duke earned enough barter goods each week to afford permanent lodging in one of Caravan's passenger cabins. He was Caravan's only long-term civilian resident, and while he couldn't aim a gun to save his life, he had gotten damn good at other things. Pool, for example.

"Maybe I'm finally old news," he said.

"Would you ever go back?" Virgil asked.

"To Jericho?" Duke almost pissed himself laughing. "Ha! I've got enough bounties on my head to make a top hat. Not a chance."

Duke missed a shot at eleven, and Virgil prepared for an assault on two.

"I took another gig on my way out," Virgil said.

"No kidding?" Duke said. "Thought you didn't like playing errand boy."

"Priorities change." Virgil struck the cue, missed by a mile, and scratched. "Damn."

Duke took out the cue ball and positioned it for the slaughter. Virgil had seen the old bastard play long enough to know this was the end. The game was all but lost.

"How's business 'round here?" Virgil asked.

Duke's fingers tensed around the pool stick, and behind those tinted sunglasses, the shadow of a twitch crossed his eyes. But the moment passed like lightning, and Virgil found himself questioning whether it even happened at all.

"Booming," Duke said, puffing solid white smoke from the corners of his mouth. "Always booming."

He took his shot.

Suddenly, a loud *boom* shook the nearest wall, and the cart tilted at a thirty-degree angle. Reactions were minimal, mostly grabbing drinks and loose belongings. Disturbances like this were common on Caravan, probably the result of some Peacekeeper tribe desperate for parts, and the crack of ten defensive laser turrets signaled an end to the threat. But the tilt made a mess of Duke and Virgil's pool game. When Caravan finally settled, only one ball remained on the table: thirteen. A stripe.

Virgil clapped his hands, cackling so hard he couldn't breathe. Caravan turbulence was fair game, and all the solids had been knocked away. He had won.

"Son of a bitch!" Duke cried, his neck bulging with angry veins. "Son of a goddamn, boil-freak bitch! Shit!"

"Easy there," Virgil said, taking a restive look around the room. Pretty much everyone was watching Duke, except the tattooed loner in the booth. His eyes stayed on the paperback.

Duke breathed deeply, fingers tap-dancing in the air. "No, it's cool. I'm cool. So cool." He took a blue downer out of his shirt pocket, swallowed it dry. In seconds, his rigid posture liquefied into a mellow, constantly swaying interpretive dance. His hands floated like they were conducting an invisible orchestra.

"And I'm a man of my word." He drifted over to the bar, leaning so far he almost fell over the edge. "Two shots! Your finest!"

A grumpy bartender filled two shot glasses with crystal-clear vodka. Virgil and Duke toasted, then drank. Against Battery-fried taste buds, Virgil's spirit went down like water.

Meanwhile, Duke gagged. "Mmm! That is vile!"

Virgil patted him on the back as he coughed, and though the junkie still wore a friendly smile, his mind was checking the final box on a list of obligatory pleasantries. It was time to get down to business.

"Mind if we chat in private?" Virgil asked.

"Not a bit," Duke said, wiping spit and vodka from his lips. "Something tells me we've got a lot to chat about."

CHAPTER 13

"This is incredible," Rok said. "Really one of a kind."

She had strapped Diane to a vertical repair rig, locking the Grave Walker in a wide-armed scarecrow pose. The plating on the left arm was removed, revealing glimpses of a second interior armor tangled in wires, tubes, and things Diane could not name. Rok seemed to know her way around, prodding and tinkering with focused confidence, yet an audible sense of wonder filled her voice as she spoke.

"I mean, I've repaired plenty of cyborgs. I get how neural interfacing works. But to see the entire nervous system hijacked like this . . . It's a revelation."

"Could you get me out?" Diane asked, hoping against hope.

"Not without killing you."

With some difficulty, Diane buried her disappointment.

"I understand the mechanics of cyberaugmentation," Rok said, "but I don't know jack about neuroscience. That's for the cybersmiths, but even those guys probably never see hardwiring this complicated."

She stepped back to look Diane in the visor. Something had dawned on her. A puzzle piece had fallen into place. "But I bet Virgil knows someone who does?"

"That's what he says," Diane confirmed.

Rok nodded bitterly. "And there's the hook."

With a long tool the width of a butter knife, she detached the exterior armor from the Grave Walker's left breastplate. The underarmor here looked like a black pectoral muscle made from synthetic tissue fibers, so dense that they could be mistaken for a single piece.

"Hang on," Rok said. "I gotta take a picture of this."

The mechanic reached into a chest of neatly organized tools, machine parts, various odds and ends. Diane expected to find a camera thrust in her face, but instead, Rok's hands emerged with an old spiral-bound notebook, the edges worn and stained. A long, chewed-up pencil doubled as a bookmark.

Rok stepped back, gnawing at her writing utensil as she took in the Grave Walker's many visual complexities, then she began to draw. In her grip, the pencil danced across the page with unparalleled grace. Diane couldn't see the work in progress, but the notebook was folded backward, putting a finished drawing from an older page in full view. The art was stunning—a detailed sketch of a Conductor plant, its domes and spire rendered completely to scale. Something else hovered in the margins, a blueprint for some contraption that, according to a dotted line, was to be built in the central dome.

"What's that?" Diane asked. She didn't have to budget her questions with Rok.

"What's what?"

"The device, in the Conductor."

Rok peeked at the backside of her notebook. "Oh, that's just an idea I've been working on. In theory, it would reverse the charge of a Conductor, essentially turning it into a giant EMP emitter. Could be a great defense against Peacekeepers."

"That's genius," Diane said, and she meant it.

Rok's face vanished behind the notebook, but not before Diane caught glimpse of a bashful smile.

"Maybe," Rok said, "if I ever get to build it."

"What's stopping you?"

Rok bit the end of her pencil. "Well, first, I'd have to get off Caravan. Easier said than done, I've got lots of . . . commitments."

Diane remembered the "blood pact" Virgil had mentioned but stopped herself from bringing it up. Reading the room, she got the sense that it was a touchy subject.

"Then," Rok continued, "I'd have to find a Conductor plant willing to let me tinker around, and . . . I mean, those StormCells are people's livelihood. I don't want to break something by accident."

"But then they'd pay you to fix it. Double win."

Diane braced for a scoff, an eye roll, or flat-out disregard. That was how most Block Threes had reacted to her attempts at humor, along with everything else she did, during that final orbit on *Cradle*. She tried to avoid jokes altogether now, but when she really wanted someone to like her, they just kind of slipped out.

Rok snickered. "I like the way you think."

For once, Diane felt grateful to be hidden behind a visor. She was grinning like an idiot.

Just then, across the garage, the blast doors opened. A new passenger entered Caravan from the sandstorm. He did not arrive by jeep, nor motorbike, nor bulldozer-RV hybrid. He had boarded the liftgate on foot, and he limped into the garage with nothing but the armor on his back and the satchel hanging from his shoulder.

Wait . . .

That wasn't armor. Apart from his cargo shorts, the young man wore no clothes at all. All that metal was a part of him, and he had more bionics than any cyborgs Diane had seen. His limbs were all mechanical, complete with repulsor jets for extra kick, and his organic parts appeared to be fitted with wind-resistant skin grafts. This was a body redesigned for speed, a function no doubt inhibited by the metal fracture torn through his right leg. Black fluid leaked from the tear.

The garage went silent as everyone stared at Caravan's newest passenger. In that moment, it occurred to Diane that he was the only cyborg in the room. But he wasn't intimidated by the onlookers. Through bionic eyes that pulsed an icy shade of blue, the cyborg glared right back at each and every one of them. Annoyed, the junkies returned to their own little worlds, and the cyborg limped off toward the repair bays.

Specifically, Rok's repair bay.

"Hi," he said, leaning against the tank. "My leg hurts. Fix it."

"I'm busy—" Rok began, but the cyborg dropped his satchel at her feet, ending all argument. The flap hung open, revealing a bountiful cache of glowing Battery capsules—the Junkyard's ultimate currency.

"It'll take you two seconds," he said.

The cyborg lifted his injured leg onto a nearby workbench, and much to Diane's annoyance, Rok prioritized him.

"Don't need 'em anyway," he said, regarding the capsules. "I got an iodine filter in my lungs; cuts the Battery itch like you wouldn't believe."

Rok lowered her goggles into place. "This fracture is gnarly. What happened?"

"I fell, and then I ran really fast for a really long time."

"How long are we talking?"

"Few days."

Rok probed the tear with a set of magnetic pliers, untangling a mess of torn cables nearly microscopic in width.

"What were you running from?" she asked.

"I don't run *from* anything," the cyborg replied.

Diane knew instantly that he was lying. It wasn't his tone of voice, snarky as ever, that tipped her off. Nor was it the look on his face, indecipherable behind his robotic eyes and artificial skin. It was the pause, the slightest breath that proceeded his assertion. Virgil had paused like that when Diane asked why he wasn't wearing the Grave Walker himself. Nurse had taken a much longer beat when *Cradle's* integrity came into question. The cyborg's hesitance had been quicker, but so was everything else he did. He moved fast, talked fast, and bragged at the speed of light, so even the slightest breath betrayed a lie in the works.

The truth, Diane had come to learn, required no hesitation.

But once the cyborg regained his momentum, he couldn't be stopped. "Just wanted to get off the road before all the crooked junkies sniffed me out. More every day, feels like. Freaks. No better than roadkillers. I'm a junkie too, ya know? I got rights. But they don't care. They just see the augments. 'Ooo, shiny.'"

Rok, who was hard at work re-fusing wires with a laser torch, merely grunted.

"Hard to blame them though," the cyborg continued. "I'm basically made of gold. My eyes alone could get you half a year's worth of Nutribriks. These parts are like predator magnets—"

"Then why'd you get them?" Diane interrupted.

The cyborg flinched, though his injured leg remained perfectly still. "That thing's alive?"

Keeping her eyes on the task at hand, Rok introduced them. "Gage, this is Diane. Diane, meet Gage."

The cyborg named Gage leered up at the Grave Walker. "A chick! Bet you're a hit with the boys."

"What're you talking about?" Diane asked, baffled by the comment.

"Kissing must be weird, right?" Gage jeered. "Since you're so tall. And you don't have lips."

Diane felt her face getting hot. The Grave Walker could do nothing to cool it.

"Does it ever ruin the mood when you crush the bed—?"

Suddenly, Gage went limp. His eyes fell dark, and he collapsed onto the floor like an abandoned marionette. Despite her embarrassment, Diane felt an automatic pang of concern.

"Rok, we talked about this," Gage said. His lips were still operational.

Back on the workbench, Rok had inserted a long flexible probe into the fracture on Gage's leg—the source of the shutdown.

"Are you gonna lay off?" she snarked.

"Yes," Gage groaned. "Whatever. Fine."

Rok winked at Diane, then she slipped the probe out from Gage's leg. His eyes and limbs convulsed back to life.

"Messed up." Gage hopped up onto his good leg, using the tank for support. "You know that's messed up."

Rok lifted the laser torch and returned to work. "Too bad I can't turn off your mouth."

"But seriously," Diane said, emboldened by the idea that Rok had her back. "Why'd you get all those parts if you knew they'd attract thieves?"

A confused look passed between Rok and Gage, the kind Diane had seen on *Cradle* many times before. She had said something wrong. She had made a mistake.

"Where you from, kid?" Gage asked, and Rok made no effort to block the question.

You don't want to be "the Girl from Outer Space." Might attract the wrong attention. Virgil's warning repeated in Diane's mind, and though she didn't know the consequences of such a reveal, she decided this wasn't the time to learn. So she took a page from Virgil's book, and probably Gage's. She lied.

"Jericho. I'm from Jericho. Virgil smuggled me out of Jericho."

Her audience stared doubtfully.

"I got these scars from Crybaby," Diane insisted, tilting the Grave Walker's chin downward, puffing out her chest, "on my way out."

Gage noticed the claw marks on her chest, and his robotic pupils dilated. "Okay, that's objectively badass."

Rok was a much tougher audience. "They don't have cyborgs in Jericho?"

"None like him," Diane said, hoping to appeal to Gage's vanity. She succeeded.

"I'm starting to like her," he beamed.

Dissatisfied, Rok pinched a glob of chewing tobacco from Virgil's pouch, popped it in her mouth, and refocused on her work. The leg fracture ran all the way from ankle to calf, and she traced it slowly with a narrow hose dripping liquid metal.

Gage leaned back against the tank, making himself comfortable. "I only chose one of my augments," he explained to Diane. He squeezed his fists, and a trio of blades jabbed out from both of his forearms. When he relaxed his hands, the blades retracted. "The rest were forced on me."

"Why?" Diane asked. "By who?"

"You gotta understand, there are two kinds of cyborgs," Gage said. "The ones that choose to be augmented, they only get one or two parts, usually. Cybersmiths ain't cheap. Most people can only pay them back over time, which is why they tag all their clients with kill switches. If a cyborg is late with payment . . . *pop*!" Gage made an explosion gesture with his hand, right next to his head. "Those cyborgs usually find a village to sponsor them. They're usually free in a few years."

"What about the cyborgs like you?" Diane pressed.

"You ask a lot of questions, huh?" Gage said, but he didn't clam up like Virgil would have. He clearly liked talking about himself, even when it was painful. "I was taken from my family when I was little. Or sold, I can't remember which. I was brought to Reno. Gambling capital of the Junkyard. They made me . . . what I am, and they put me to work in the casinos. I raced. I raced so assholes could gamble on who'd win. I won a lot. That's how I survived. Then I escaped."

He looked to Rok with as much affection as his bionic features would allow. "I got to Caravan before they realized I was gone. Rok was the one who shut off my kill switch."

"And he's been bugging me ever since," Rok said. The liquid metal had solidified, and now she was rubbing a clear gel on the border between Gage's robotic calf and organic inner thigh.

"That tickles!" he yelped.

"Quit whining and hold still," Rok said. "The impact from your fall must have irritated the bionic seam."

"I love when you talk dirty," Gage said.

Their banter faded as Diane watched the mechanic tracing her finger around the cyborg's flesh, and all sound was replaced with the *lub-dub* of her own heartbeat. The sight triggered a sudden yearning, one that felt totally out of the blue. Painfully unobtainable.

On *Cradle*, she had always taken physical contact for granted. Hugs and roughhousing were a natural element of Block Two life, and then Block Three introduced the awkward brushes and flirtatious cues inherent to puberty. That all came to an end after Diane's accident, but she had been too focused on her various fears to notice.

When she entered the numbing world of the Grave Walker, one of her initial thoughts had been of touch: *I'll never get to touch anyone ever again.* The idea had been manageable enough while she was alone with Virgil, but now it was hard not to picture herself in Gage's position.

How she longed to feel close to someone, to have someone touch her like it was the most natural thing in the world. At an age when she craved physical intimacy more than ever, she could not have been more isolated.

But that would change after they found Dr. Isaac. Everything would change.

"Why don't you come up to the front?"

Diane blinked, and she found Gage standing confidently on both legs, looking at her.

"First shots are on me," he offered. "I can tell you more about my shitty life."

"I can't," Diane sulked. "They won't let me up in this suit."

"You hardwired in there?" Gage asked.

"I guess so," Diane said.

The cyborg patted the Grave Walker's shoulder affectionately. "Guess we're not so different."

He departed for the same door that had swallowed Virgil an hour ago, and Diane noticed something dark printed on the back of his neck. She squinted, and her visor zoomed to reveal a small brand, carved with lasers: *4-D-5*.

When Gage was out of earshot, Rok spat tobacco juice onto the grated floor. "Sorry about him. He means well, but he's . . . a lot."

Diane watched the autodoor shut behind him. "That's one way of putting it."

CHAPTER 14

"Step into my office."

Duke led Virgil into the cramped quarters of his passenger cabin. Its layout was identical to all the others on Caravan: two leather benches facing each other, a single porthole between them, and overhead shelving units for luggage. But while the other cabins were alike in their aesthetic blankness, Duke's had all the telltale eccentricities of long-term residence. It was his space, and he had filled every inch of it.

The bench Duke sat on was covered in pillows, pill bottles, and a couple hookah pipes, while Virgil crammed himself between a CB radio and the potted succulent he had sold to Duke several years prior. The walls were papered with old, washed-out photos of sexy models who wouldn't last five seconds out in the Junkyard. The luggage racks were filled with plastic cubby units that Duke used to house his trading inventory. Today, they were mostly empty.

"I thought you said business was booming," Virgil said, eyeing the barren cubbies.

Duke popped another blue downer from one of the pill bottles. "I was saving face. Shit's tense outside, man. Everybody's paralyzed. Trade's all screwed up."

"Because the Heap's under new management?"

"You didn't hear? The Heap shut down."

Virgil stared blankly. He couldn't have heard that right. "Shut down?"

The downers kicked in, and Duke repeated himself slowly. "Shut . . . down . . ."

"The Heap can't shut down," Virgil protested. "It's the hub. Heart of the Junkyard."

"And the Messenger's got it on lockdown." Duke sprawled out over his pillows and recreational poisons, his soft belly peeking out from between the buttons on his shirt. "Now lots of townies are having trouble selling their goods. So they're being stingy, which means they're not hiring junkies, so I can't get any of my clients work."

Virgil turned the news over in his mind. He'd been in this game a long time, but he had never heard of the Heap going on lockdown. Not once. Not until the Messenger arrived.

"Townies don't know the first thing about the Junkyard," Duke rambled on, "but they keep trying to do junkie work themselves. Keep getting killed in wildly entertaining ways. Your magic beans are about the only thing paying my rent."

He sat up suddenly, reaching for the shelf over his head.

"Speaking o' which . . ." He pulled a shoebox out from one of the cubbies, handed it to Virgil. ". . . here's your cut from the last few months."

Inside, Virgil found a decent cache of high-grade Battery capsules, a couple tier-one StormCells . . . and that was it.

"Not much here," he observed.

Duke threw up his hands, sinking back onto the pillows. "I just said the economy's in the shitter. What do you want from me?"

Virgil tucked the box into his backpack. It was time to move on to new business. "The Heap's actually a big part of that job I was telling you about—"

"Ms. Violet trying to get her lab rat back?" Duke asked.

"So you know about Dr. Isaac," Virgil said, unsurprised.

"Knowing's my main hustle."

"Then I need everything you know on Isaac, the Heap . . . and this Messenger guy."

Duke's aviators slid down to the tip of his nose. His eyes were as foggy and bloodshot as Virgil had imagined.

"That's some pricey info, friend," Duke said.

Virgil gave no response, and in that silence, the two men waged a silent war recounting all the favors they had done for one another. Who owed more? Who was next in line to do the other a solid? Without a word, they traced back a decade-long partnership that began one fateful night when Duke—then a resident of Jericho—had needed help, and Virgil provided it.

When they were otherwise even, it always came down to that night.

"But you are an old friend," Duke relented, "so I'll cut you some slack. Got any news? A junkie can see a lot in four months."

Virgil gave the question some thought. "You know Gatetown?"

"I know of it."

"You know their problem?"

A notepad and pen appeared in Duke's hands, signifying that he did not.

"The Conductor on I-25 is overrun with roadkillers," Virgil said. "If anyone's selling StormCells, they'll get the most bang for their buck in Gatetown."

Duke scribbled the information with handwriting only he could read. "I-25 . . . That's good, that's real good."

Virgil leaned forward in his seat. "Your turn. Where'd the Messenger come from?"

After tucking the notepad under a pillow, Duke plucked a half-finished cigarette from his breast pocket, relit, and took a long, leisurely drag. He exhaled the smoke in a quartet of perfect rings. They entered the world as tiny gray loops, so dense they looked solid, before growing, thinning, and ultimately dissipating into nothingness. "First sightings came in couple years ago," he said. "Big bastard in a creepy mask, leading a roadkiller gang on the outskirts of the Junkyard. They stayed near the coast, by the Firelands. Nobody paid them much mind, even when they started raiding villages."

"How come?" Virgil asked.

"When most roadkillers sack a village," Duke explained, "they go for broke. They loot the place, burn it down. But not the Messenger. His crew would swoop in, take a little, then get out. At first, everybody thought they were just weak. Didn't have the balls for a full assault."

Duke ashed the cigarette over the floor, inhaled, puffed some more rings. "A village can't produce anything after it's wrecked. He was draining them slow, leeching them over time. And these towns are on the edge of nowhere. They cry for help, but most mercenaries don't want to make the drive out."

Duke made a noise trapped between a laugh and a smoker's cough. A blended expression of admiration and disgust. "That's how the Messenger got the funds for his little army. He was smart. Goddamn methodical is what he was."

Duke passed the cigarette to Virgil, who accepted it.

"This guy had Violet convinced that he was a machine," Virgil said, exhaling his own smoke without fanfare. "He made her look like a dumbass. That's *muy difícil*."

"I told you, man, he's smart. By the time he started making big-boy moves, he was a man, a cyborg, and a robot. Three different identities, in three places at once. Made himself a rumor."

"You said the Heap's on lockdown. Elaborate."

Duke reclaimed the cigarette. "When he took the Aardwolf fortress, he shut the gates, cut the long-range radios, told everyone inside the Heap it was his way or the highway."

"And the mercenary clans just sat there?" Virgil asked.

"The mercenaries are in on it."

"Duke, this is like pulling teeth. Give it to me straight. What the hell's going on?"

Duke snuffed the cigarette on the sole of his shoe. They could have kept smoking that tobacco until their lips burned off, but Virgil's merchandise was a rare commodity. It had to be rationed.

"The Messenger's building something," Duke said. "Nobody knows what—info out of the Heap is scarce—but the word is he's building something inside the fortress. He paid the mercenary clans to stand down while he kicked the Aardwolves out, and now he's paying them more to help with construction."

"How much is he paying them?" Virgil asked.

"Enough to make them ignore their real job. Enough to make the FireFighter clan get along with the Oxen. Can you imagine?"

Virgil considered himself open-minded, but even he had trouble comprehending such a diplomatic feat. The Oxen and the FireFighters were on opposite ends of the mercenary spectrum. The Oxen fought by a code, and their contract work was a financial means to an end in their endless war against the Peacekeepers. Meanwhile, the FireFighters were anarchists. Pyromaniacal thrill seekers. Roadkillers with a touch of infrastructure. The two clans had been at odds longer than anyone could remember, but now, with a wave of his bandaged arm, the Messenger had taught them to play nice. It defied all logic.

"What about the civilians?" Virgil asked. "The Heap townies?"

Duke frowned. "He told them they could either join his little project or find their Battery somewhere else. And you know most of those city slickers wouldn't survive two minutes in the Junkyard. The next Battery plant is miles away."

"So they're *esclavos*," Virgil said.

"I mean, that's a little harsh. He's giving them all the utilities they were paying the Aardwolves for—"

"They're *esclavos*," Virgil repeated, stern and forceful. It was a dark word in the Junkyard. A taboo word, one that cut right through Duke's chemical-induced haze.

Esclavos. It was why junkies craved a life on the road, free from authority and oppression. It was why, even in a world as anarchistic as this, the cyborg gambling rings of Reno were considered evil by more dignified circles. The Grand Finale had produced its fair share of slaves. *Esclavos* to a state, then *esclavos* to a machine, then *esclavos* to a promise of safety behind the walls Jericho. The Junkyard was not a safe place, but it was free. *Libre*.

Except when it wasn't.

"And they're *esclavos por nada*," Virgil went on, gaining steam. "The

Messenger's not making capital. He's not producing anything for anyone else. He's just taking. He's taken the mercenaries from people who really need them, and he's bleeding the Heap dry. Holding Battery hostage. The Messenger is a leech on the Junkyard's back. He's a parasite."

His burst of conviction seemed to shock Duke. Virgil rarely got worked up about anything.

"You really believe that?" Duke marveled.

Virgil sat back on the bench, and his fervor mellowed to a devilish grin. "Nah, I don't really give a crap either way. But if someone tries to back me into a moral argument, it's good to have an opinion. Even if it's bugshit."

When the mushy mess that was Duke's brain finished comprehending this total one-eighty, he nearly laughed out a lung. "You're twisted, man. Goddamn warped."

Virgil shrugged. "Fact is, I need something, and the only way to get it is to steal the Messenger's biggest asset. So I guess that makes us enemies."

"You sure he's an enemy you want?" Duke warned. "He's a beast. I've heard things . . ."

"I'm not going to arm wrestle the guy or nothing," Virgil said. "Not my style."

"You should take a crew with you," Duke said.

"I got a crew—"

"I'm not talking about a scared teenager in a robot costume."

Virgil usually took Duke's omniscience for granted, but that one surprised even him. How did he know about Diane without going out to the garage? Who tipped him off? He was almost as bad as Ms. Violet in that way. Maybe that was why she wanted him dead.

"I'm talking," Duke sat upright, "about grabbing the meanest junkies on this dump, paying 'em good, and doing this suicide mission right."

A familiar tickling rose in Virgil's stomach. Without thinking, he pulled the double inhaler out of his backpack. "I don't do crews. You know I don't do crews."

He took the dual hit, coughed out the green, and it was only while refilling his inhaler that he noticed Duke's expression. He looked utterly shocked.

"What is that abomination?" Duke said.

Virgil wiggled the homemade device affectionately. "You like this?"

"No!" Duke practically shrieked. "Look at yourself, man! Your body's coming apart at the seams! Two high-grade capsules . . . And what're you pushing? Sixty?"

"Fifty," Virgil said. He put the inhaler away, now feeling self-conscious.

Duke struggled to keep his tone in check. "You're my best client, so I'm going to give it to you straight: the Messenger's a freak of nature. Nobody in the Junkyard should be that strong, that goddamn healthy. Meanwhile, you're burning through Battery just to stay alive. You go up against him on your own, and you're dead meat."

"How did he get so strong, anyway?" Virgil asked.

"Million rumors," Duke said. "He's a Grand Finale supersoldier that got busted out of cryo. He's a junkie who burned his arm shaking the devil's hand. He's an alien. In any case, he's tough, and you're screwed."

Through the porthole, Virgil caught the faintest glimpse of a village as Caravan passed it by, appearing as abstract shadows fizzling in the sandstorm. Or maybe it was the ruins of a city ravaged by the Grand Finale. Or maybe junk hills. Maybe nothing at all. There was a time when Virgil felt like he knew the Junkyard, with all its hidden dangers and unspoken rules. But new dangers were cropping up. Rules were being broken. Nothing looked familiar in this weather, and the storm wasn't going to let up any time soon.

"I saw a pack of junkies strip a cyborg," Virgil said, staring out the porthole. "Right out in the open, in the middle of the night. At *night*, Duke. You know how desperate you have to be to pull that? Or stupid?" He met Duke's anxious gaze. "These kids working today," Virgil said, "they're not crew material—"

Caravan's horn cut him off. An obstacle had appeared in their path.

Curious, both Duke and Virgil turned their attention back out the window.

First, they saw headlights. An army of high beams pierced the sandy gloom, illuminating a second army of silhouettes that waited motionless on the side of the road. There were human shapes, wild around the edges, brandishing blades and energy rifles. There were shapes of Peacekeepers—rigid argonauts, spherical seekers, blade-handed reapers. And leading the pack, bathed in red from the warning lights dotted across Caravan's exterior, was the cyborg Virgil had seen on Ms. Violet's holoscreen. The sickly head and torso held up by titanium limbs, defaced by the fingerprint rash. The Messenger's ringer and glorified errand boy. Brutus 9-T-9. He stood on the highway shoulder, watching Caravan go by. No awe on his face, no recognition of Caravan's immense strength. Only defiance. Cold, world-weary hate.

"Don't care how tough they look," Duke said, sounding hoarse all of a sudden. "No way they're gonna take on Caravan."

"Not yet," Virgil said.

It wasn't their numbers that worried Virgil, though this was likely a fraction of the Messenger's full militia, a mere raiding party sent to accompany 9-T-9 on his sinister errand. No, what frightened Virgil were the members of that party. He had known the Messenger commanded humans, and he had known the Messenger could reprogram Peacekeepers. But Virgil had never imagined, even for a second, that the Messenger could make humans and Peacekeepers stand together. The two species—they couldn't communicate. Couldn't empathize. Couldn't forget centuries of apocalyptic warfare that left them both crippled forever.

It scared Virgil to see humans and Peacekeepers united. it scared him because they were not allies in peace; they were servants to a warmongering leader who, if given enough power, could conquer any village. Slay any foe.

Climb any mountain.

Virgil began to mumble without realizing it: "Blue skies. Soft baked carrots. Úna's hair. Red fiery hair, flowing forever—"

"What?" Duke snapped. "What are you babbling about?"

Virgil regained focus. "You have anyone in mind for that crew?"

Duke popped his millionth downer. "I got some candidates."

CHAPTER 15

The book had no title. Not anymore.

When Ishmael found the paperback during a routine junk dive, the front cover had already been seared away, along with most of chapter one. But even in this incomplete state, the book was among his most valuable possessions. His bike, his harpoon rig, and his paperback. Escapism was a rare commodity in the Junkyard, and most people would trade a lot of Battery for a story with a happy ending. The happier the better. This particular story concerned a young girl lost in a fantasy realm, searching for a wizard who could help her return home. Ishmael found Dorothy's sorrows trivial compared to his own, and her travel companions were useless at best, but the ending was a happy one. A happy ending in a world of friends and loved ones. He had read the paperback more times than he could count. Reading kept the Master at bay.

Someone is coming.

Ishmael's senses were sharp—sharp enough for him to catalog a room without ever looking up from his page—but they could not always be trusted. It was not his own voice that warned of an approaching stranger; it was the Master's. Quiet, vicious, looking to infiltrate his every thought, the Master was a sickness with a mind of his own. Part of Ishmael, yet beyond Ishmael's conscious control.

He draws nearer, you fool.

The paperback trembled in Ishmael's hand, and he could not make it to the end of his sentence: *A heart is not judged by . . . A heart is not . . . A heart—*

Your heart lives in the ocean.

He tried to shake the voice from his head, but it only grew louder. Things went hazy, as things often did for Ishmael, and he suddenly found himself kneeling on the cold sand of a distant beach, five years younger. He was not alone. His brothers and sisters kneeled beside him, all around him, a flock of dire faces inked in matching tattoos.

Silent, still, they all gazed up at the Master's shadowy frame. The old man lurked on the edge of torchlight, speaking to his congregation from the lofted height of a wooden pier. His voice seemed to merge itself with the ocean breeze, and his words reeked of salt and death.

When the Earth caught Fire, the Master preached, *salvation came from the Sea. The Kingdom of Man has fallen. The Machine God has been ripped from Its blasphemous throne. Now is the Age of Those Who Dwell Below. Men are peons beside Them. The Deep have awoken. The Deep shall rise.*

At this, the acolytes began to chant in a low whisper: *The Deep shall rise. The Deep shall rise. The Deep shall rise.*

Only Ishmael kept silent; his attention was transfixed on the antique shark diving rig standing by the pier. Moments ago, one of Ishmael's dearest friends had entered the ceremonial cage dressed only in a scuba mask, remaining stoic even as the cage dipped into the sea. Now, the mechanism's chain ran down into the glowing, irradiated murk of the Pacific. His friend's shadow had been visible for a short time, but tentacled shapes quickly swarmed the cage, obscuring its form in a cloud of menacing movement.

Ishmael knew what awaited his friend beyond the Shallows. Everyone did.

We send our chosen to the Deep, and in Their wisdom, They decide who is worthy to lead us. The chosen return with a Blessing from the Sea, with righteous hearts and minds . . .

The Master pulled a lever on the diving rig. The crowd moaned in religious ecstasy. The chain began to reel upward.

. . . or they do not return at all.

The acolytes chanted louder as the chain rose faster, as the cage's outline drew closer and closer to the surface. Ishmael wanted so desperately to look away, but the horror of the moment petrified him. He couldn't bring himself to turn, even as the water above the cage turned red, redder, then black with blood—

"How's it going?"

Ishmael blinked, and he was back in his booth. An older junkie now sat across the table.

"You're Ishmael, right?" he said. "I'm Virgil."

Virgil reached out for a handshake, but Ishmael didn't move a muscle. Anyone with the courage to approach a face like his, tattooed in the likeness of a sea monster, could not be trusted.

Eventually, Virgil retracted his hand with a good-natured chuckle. "You're from the Shallows, yeah? Long way from home."

Deserter. Traitor. You are alone.

"I have no home," Ishmael said. "Not anymore."

"We're all home on Caravan." Virgil threw something across the table, and Ishmael caught it without looking. He felt the crackling plastic of a Gatetown water bottle. A gift, one that made Ishmael trust this man even less.

"Whatcha reading?" Virgil asked.

"A book about missing pieces," Ishmael said.

"Sounds . . . fun." Virgil stifled a sarcastic tone. "I got a source for some FunSoft virtual reality goggles. I could hook you up."

"One reality is enough for me." Ishmael took a swig of the purified liquid, never taking his eyes off Virgil, never betraying the slightest hint of emotion.

"I hear you like to keep to yourself," Virgil said.

"So what?"

"Most junkies come to Caravan looking for friends."

Friends? You had friends. Brothers. Sisters. Look what you did to them. Look how you treated your friends.

"I want to be left alone," Ishmael said, a little too loud.

Virgil didn't seem to notice. "Word on the street is, you're one of the best damn fighters the Junkyard has ever seen."

Yes, Ishmael could fight, and fight well. The coast was teeming with danger, slimy bloodsuckers and flesh-eating crustaceans. Most junkies refused to come within five miles of the western beaches, made of dark sand and ground-up bone. Ishmael had grown up there. He had learned to kill before being killed, and in the Junkyard, that skill set was warmly received. But he never fought because it thrilled him. He fought to survive. Only to survive.

"If you have a point," Ishmael said, "make it now."

Virgil leaned across the table. An Edison bulb hung directly overhead, smearing his face in the shadow of his brow. "I'm putting a crew together. Rescue mission. Big payday."

"No," Ishmael said.

"How come?"

"I do not work with crews."

"How come?"

"Because crews have *jefes*. I serve only myself."

The Shallows' only expatriate had endured enough leadership for one lifetime. No more.

Angry voices shouted from the bar area. Virgil looked toward the disturbance, perhaps buying time to gather his thoughts, but Ishmael knew the old junkie was wasting his time. The *no* was final.

"Then I have a solo gig for you," Virgil said, turning back to Ishmael with a sly sincerity. "I need a bodyguard."

"I want no part of your crew," Ishmael said.

"You wouldn't be on my crew. Your job's separate, and nobody can tell you how to do it."

Behind his stoicism, Ishmael felt himself growing uneasy. The job already sounded more enticing, but that was the power of words. A simple title change could turn a hard no into an enthusiastic yes. The Master had been good with words too.

"Get me from the Heap to Jericho alive," Virgil said, "and I'll buy you a month's rent in one of the passenger cabins."

A reaction must have slipped through Ishmael's mask, because Virgil's green lips curled into a smile.

"A month of being left alone," Virgil said.

"That will be expensive," Ishmael said.

"I know."

One month in a private room.

Lazy. Weak. You are growing soft.

One month away from the dangers of the Junkyard.

Poor Ishmael. A frightened boy lost at sea, gasping for air.

One month to meditate on the tsunami raging in his mind. To understand its nature. To quell the noise.

You will never know silence. You will never know peace. You abandoned us, Brother Ishmael, but I will never abandon you—

"We got a deal?" Virgil asked.

Ishmael tried to find a reason to trust the man, and he came up short. But to be fair, he would have felt this way no matter who approached the booth. Ishmael didn't trust anyone.

"I will keep you alive," he said. "Nothing more."

Virgil slapped the table in triumph. "I feel safer already!"

CHAPTER 16

With his first recruitment in the bag, Virgil moved to a seat at the donut-shaped bar and waited for his next candidate to arrive. He didn't have to wait long.

Gage sauntered up to the bar with his head held high, planting himself between a burly woman with sharpened metal dentures and a genderless figure in a gimp suit rigged with retractable knives. If the cyborg noticed all the side-eyed glares the other junkies were giving him, he had chosen to ignore them.

"Six shots," he called to a nearby barkeeper. "*Rápido.*"

"You got a way to pay for 'em?" the barkeep asked doubtfully.

Virgil understood the barkeep's hesitancy. After taking one look at Gage, he probably assumed the cyborg was drowning in debt to some cybersmith in Reno. Bionic parts like that didn't come cheap.

"I got a tab under *4-D-5*," Gage said. "Thanks for asking, though. Really appreciate your concern."

Clickity clack of the barkeep's fingers typing on a keyboard, *beep* from a computer screen, *grunt* from the barkeep, then finally: the sound of vodka splashing into six dirty shot glasses. With a good percentage of Gage's body weight replaced by metal, Virgil would have thought one shot would go a long way for the cyborg. There must be a synthetic liver in the mix, one that would kill his buzz in mere minutes, maybe seconds. If Gage wanted to get drunk and stay drunk, he would have to drink a lot.

When the cluster of miniature glasses arrived, Gage wasted no time downing his first shot. He gagged triumphantly on the burn, exaggerating the noise for his two scowling neighbors. For the life of him, Virgil couldn't understand their blatant hostility. What the hell was going on? Hadn't they seen a cyborg before?

"I know what you're asking yourselves," Gage said to them, looking straight ahead, "and the answer is . . . Yes. I do still have a human cock."

The woman with dentures leaned toward Gage. "Actually, we were wondering what happened to Belle."

The tipsy grin on Gage's face evaporated. Virgil had been out of the Caravan loop for a long time, and these junkies clearly knew something about Gage that Virgil did not. Is that why everyone had been staring?

"Don't know what you're talking about," Gage lied.

"Yeah you do," the gimp hissed.

"She was our friend," Dentures said. "We used to run junk dives together."

"Whatever you heard," Gage said, "it's got nothing to do with me."

The junkies weren't buying it. They both leaned even closer, trapping Gage in the unwanted conversation.

"Last week, Belle told me she was taking an SOS job from a village with a roadkiller problem," Gimp said. "Said she was bringing a partner to clear 'em out."

Dentures frowned, her callused lips bulging from the surplus of pointy teeth. "Said she hired a cyborg with a smart mouth."

Gimp made a scornful slurping noise. "Heard that village is gone now. Every townie dead. Nobody's heard from Belle."

"And then you were spotted limping through the Junkyard with a sack full of Battery," Dentures concluded.

For the first time, Gage remained silent.

"Sounds like you ripped everybody off," Gimp said. "Took the payday, left Belle and those townies to die."

"You have no idea what you're talking about," Gage replied, lifting his second shot.

"What happened?" Dentures asked, loud enough for the whole room to hear. "Couldn't handle a few roadkillers?"

"It wasn't roadkillers—" Gage tried to explain, but his tormentors weren't listening.

"You give real junkies a bad name."

"You're worthless."

"Unless we stripped you for parts—"

Gage slammed the glass down on the bar. It shattered beneath his artificial hand.

"It wasn't roadkillers!" he screamed.

Gimp drew a knife from their wrist. Dentures bared her teeth. Blades shot out from Gage's forearms. Behind them, Caravan braced for a spectacle.

"Hey hey!" Virgil joined the huddle, and the onlookers turned away disappointed. When Virgil wanted to stop a fight, the fight usually obliged. "How's it going?" he calmed. "We good? Relaxed?"

No one moved. No one backed down.

"You know," he nodded to Dentures and Gimp, "I think I saw a couple drinks over there with your names on them."

Virgil winked at the barkeep, who knew this game well. He filled two mismatched mugs with vodka and carbonated water, then set them down on the other end of the bar.

"Why don't you go check it out?" Virgil asked.

Gimp retracted their blade, Dentures closed her mouth, and the two of them slunk off to claim their free drinks. Virgil took Gimp's old seat.

"Great," Gage huffed, "now everybody thinks I need my grandpa to save my ass. *Este día apesta*."

Gage gulped another shot. Three down, three to go.

"Just wanna talk to you," Virgil said. "Privately."

"Why would the great and powerful Virgil want to talk to little old me?"

"I need backup on a job."

"Save it," Gage said. "I'm not looking to be anyone's thug."

"What are you looking for?" Virgil asked.

Gage sipped his fourth shot, nice and slow. "My rep's in a bad spot. Everyone in here probably thinks I'm a joke."

Virgil offered neither confirmation nor condolence. He listened.

"I need to do something big, you know?" Gage went on. "Something that'll get me respect. Make it harder for those freaks to rip me apart."

Virgil knew where Gage's grandstanding impulse came from. It didn't take a genius to see that cyborgs who won fights and races in Reno got to live, while the losers were sold for scrap. During his days as *un esclavo*, Gage had to be worth more than the sum of his augments. He was conditioned to be impressive.

Virgil could use that.

"I'm going to the Heap," Virgil said.

Gage's artificial face came close to a look of surprise.

"The Messenger's got something that doesn't belong to him," Virgil continued. "I mean to take it back."

"*No manches*," Gage said. "You're going up against the Messenger? The *actual* Messenger?"

Virgil hushed the cyborg, glanced around for unwanted ears, then lowered his voice. "And I could use a junkie with your speed. Someone who can get in and out of places in a hurry."

"That's what she said," Gage confided.

Virgil snorted. The fifth shot disappeared down Gage's throat.

"There it is," the cyborg giggled. "Five shots in, my brain lets go of all the pressure sensors. Feels like I'm floating." He hiccuped, then said, "I want two things."

"Name 'em," Virgil said.

"I want enough of your magic beans to buy half the vodka in this place."

"Done."

"And when we make it to the Heap, I get first dibs at killing the Messenger."

Virgil's smooth affectation faltered. "Uh, we're not actually—"

"It's just what I need," Gage said, slurring a little. "My street cred will go through the roof. And sure, he's supposed to be big, but I've fought bigger. I'll slice him to pieces."

Gage squeezed his fists in excitement, and the forearm blades shot back into view.

Virgil flinched away. "The Messenger's all yours."

"Then I'm in!" Gage exclaimed.

Virgil moved to stand, but not before swiping Gage's final shot and downing it himself. "That's for calling me grandpa."

With that, he rose and vanished into the crowd, leaving Gage to face impending sobriety, and with it, full comprehension of his dangerous commitment.

"*Pinche estúpido*," Gage said to himself.

CHAPTER 17

Rok flipped a switch, and the Grave Walker came free from the repair rig.

"I hit you with some basic upgrades," she explained. "Your Storm-Cell port was crazy old, so I did some rewiring. Should make you more energy efficient."

Diane examined the HUD's power meter. It was definitely longer.

Rok continued, "I tweaked the synapses in your neural interface, sped up the suit's reaction time by a few nanoseconds . . . Oh, and your automatic night vision was disabled for some reason. Fixed that too."

Diane flapped her arms up and down, trying to detect any change in speed, but then she noticed something just below her wrist. A small black box drilled into the metal on her right arm, serving no obvious function.

"What's this thing?" she asked.

"Reflex module," Rok said without pause, without thinking. "Part of your update."

Two responses came to Diane at once. She was grateful to Rok for improving her suit's quality of life, but also sad to see the job finished so soon. Their time together, a time when Diane could ask questions and make idle jokes to her heart's content, was drawing to a close.

"Thank you," Diane said.

Rok went to organize the tools on her workbench. "Just trying to get paid."

"More where that came from." Virgil appeared from nowhere, leaning on the tank like he owned it. If Rok was startled—Diane certainly was—she didn't let it show.

"I tuned up the suit," Rok said, "and the jeep. You're good to go."

"I got more work for you," Virgil said.

"And I've got other clients."

"Deal with them first. You'll want a clear schedule for my thing."

When all the tools were in order, Rok bent down to a tiny washing station and rinsed the grime off her fingers.

"I'm going to get something from the Heap," Virgil said.

"Good for you," Rok replied.

"And when I get it, there might be some heat on my tail. If something happens to my jeep or my weapons, I won't have time to stop and get them fixed."

Rok dried her hands on the front of her jumpsuit.

"It'd be good to have a mechanic on the road," Virgil said.

She faced him for the first time since his return. "I don't do that kind of work."

"You have before," he accused.

"Well, not for you." She spat a bullet of tobacco juice at Virgil's feet, barely missing. As much as Diane liked Rok, that habit was undeniably repulsive.

Virgil inched his boot away from the splatter. "You get first rights to all the junk we find."

"No thanks," Rok said. "Not worth the risk."

"And I'll consider your debt paid," he added.

The tobacco chewing stopped. The air of indifference turned to gaping shock. Diane's curiosity escalated; what the hell was this blood pact?

"It's a big job, Rok," Virgil said. "*Necesito la mejor.*"

A palpable conflict furrowed Rok's brow. She bit her lip, hands fidgeting nervously.

"What are you getting from the Heap?" she asked.

"A Jericho scientist," Virgil replied.

"You do kidnappings now?" Rok sounded disgusted.

"It's a *rescue* mission. Some freak called the Messenger is forcing this guy to reprogram Peacekeepers. He's building an army."

"Peacekeepers can't be reprogrammed," Rok said.

"I've seen it," Virgil insisted.

Rok began to sink into herself, calculating risks, grappling with the impossible. Diane saw it happening, and so did Virgil. He grabbed Rok gently by the shoulders, bringing her back.

"If I don't free this guy," Virgil said, "the Messenger could turn the Junkyard into a new Jericho. Worse. We wouldn't be slaves to corporate comforts. We'd just be flat-out *esclavos.*"

Where the notion of relocating to Jericho had once given Diane comfort, Rok emanated pure disdain. It suddenly occurred to Diane that Jericho's great wall might offer two-way protection. It kept the Junkyard's perils out of Jericho, and it locked Jericho's corporate subjugations out of the Junkyard. Supercity life wasn't for everyone.

Virgil repeated his offer once more. "Help me pull this off, and you get the junk, you get off the hook, and you get to do some good. Some *real* good. What do you say?"

The answer was yes; Diane knew it before Rok did. The answer would always be yes, because that was Virgil's gift. He identified what a person wanted most, and he found a way to provide it. For a price. Always for a price. What wouldn't someone pay for their heart's desire?

Diane could see the defeat in Rok's face. Virgil could see it too.

"We leave at dawn," he said, then he flashed Diane a thumbs-up and left to make final preparations for the journey.

The crew was complete.

Sluggish, Rok pulled her tools back off the workbench. Diane sensed her disappointment, her silent self-loathing, and though the two had only just met, it hurt Diane to see Rok in this existential rut. She knew the feeling.

"I'm glad you're coming with us," Diane said, trying to lift the mechanic's spirits.

Rok smiled a little, appreciating Diane's gesture. "Who knows? Maybe it'll be fun."

She grabbed a key fob out of her pocket, tapped a button, and the nearby tank opened itself to the world. Hatches lifted and slid away, revealing plasma cannons, ion launchers, and a large empty slot where a StormCell belonged.

"That's yours?" Diane said, surprised. She had assumed the tank belonged to a junkie.

"Oh yeah," Rok said, lifting a tier-three StormCell in both arms. This glowing disk had a circumference bigger than a human torso, but she had no trouble hoisting the fuel cell into its slot. Then she pressed the fob again. The armor hatches closed, and a deep red light traced the outline of their interconnected seams. The tank was online.

"The Junkyard hits hard," Rok said, patting the war machine affectionately. "I hit harder."

CHAPTER 18

The next morning, as the dead sun rose and Caravan thundered up the central Junkyard, Virgil's crew departed. They rode south, a trio of vehicles between the five of them. Virgil drove in his jeep, hauling Diane in the trailer she had come to know so well; Ishmael drove a slender motorbike with a faded red paint job, rigged with a rearview camera and a screen between the handlebars; Rok piloted her tank, and Gage dangled off the side, holding on to a crack in the armored plating. He hung leisurely from arms that would never tire, watching the road ahead. His eyes could see farther than most.

The jeep and tank drove side by side, with Virgil slowing a few miles per hour to keep Rok from falling behind. Meanwhile, Ishmael stayed a good distance ahead of the pack, sometimes speeding out of sight altogether. He drove like he was separate from the team, a stranger who just happened to be going their way.

"Why does he do that?" Diane asked Virgil. She could see the motorbike slicing up a road to her left, fresh off a turn that the others wouldn't make for another few hundred yards.

"He's scouting. I think," Virgil said. "He does things his own way."

"He scares me," Diane said. He had scared her from the moment they met back in Caravan's garage, a looming presence that rarely spoke, never smiled, and often glared at dark corners and empty spaces—like he could see things that no one else could.

"He's got a screw loose, for sure," Virgil conceded. "But I'm told he's reliable, and he can hold his own in a fight. He's gonna make your job a little easier."

Diane was here to protect Virgil, to keep him alive as he confronted a vicious army and a crippling case of the Junkyard Blues. Her task felt so big, so insurmountably out of her league, that she still couldn't believe Virgil had entrusted it to her. But in a way, he hadn't. He had put his faith in the Grave Walker, and maybe Diane's presence was incidental. There could be anyone piloting the suit; it just happened to be her.

"Where the hell do they think they're going?" Virgil suddenly hollered.

Behind them, Rok had kept going straight when the jeep had turned, and they were now driving in different directions. Virgil parked on the highway shoulder, radioing for the others to join him. The area around them was a vast bog of radioactive waste, courtesy of countless fissured barrels floating in the swamp like buoys. The elevated highway rose just above the waterline, a concrete isthmus in the toxic marsh.

Minutes later, the tank caught up and parked beside them. Gage hopped onto the road. Rok sprung out from the cupola hatch and slid down the tank's side.

"Why'd you keep going straight?" Virgil asked.

"We're going to the Heap, aren't we?" Rok said. "That's the best route."

"We're stopping in Pozo first."

Rok groaned. "Why didn't you tell us that on Caravan?"

"We're not psychic, man," Gage added.

"I'm used to traveling alone." This was the closest Virgil would come to apologizing.

Rok pulled a Battery inhaler out of her tool belt, huffed her medicine, then asked in a haze of green, "Why are we stopping in Pozo?"

"We need to refuel, restock supplies," Virgil said. "Once we leave the Heap, we can't stop again until we reach Jericho."

Rok tsked. "So you were going to go straight south? That's centipede country."

"We can handle a few centipedes."

"I'd rather not." Rok freed her spiral notebook from a chain dangling off her belt and laid it open across the Grave Walker's legs. Looking down, Diane beheld her first comprehensive map of the Junkyard as a whole, its countless communities and pitfalls hand drawn over lined parchment.

The map answered a question Diane had long pondered but could never quite articulate: Did the Junkyard have limits?

Yes, the region had boundaries. To the east, the impenetrable Wall of Jericho. To the north, a natural barrier of lakes and mountains. To the south, a field of ruinous flame labeled *Firelands*. To the west . . . the ocean. These barriers filled the four edges of the map, and what lay beyond them, no one could say.

Virgil and Gage gathered beside Rok as she ran her finger across the map, tracing a route.

"Why don't we cut southwest, then zip back east?" she asked. "Not direct, but it's safer."

Virgil looked doubtful. "Safer? You think we're safer cutting that close to Vegas?"

"We'd keep our distance," Rok defended.

"Radio says the wind's blowing east all day. If the Pest really is airborne, we're screwed."

Diane made a mental note to ask someone about Vegas. What was airborne? Why did it fill Virgil with such audible dread?

Annoyed, Rok outlined another route. "*Okay*, what if we go to Camp Phoenix instead? Loop southeast, then hit the Heap on our way back north?"

"Nah." Gage stepped in. "I heard that place is a ghost town. Something blew when the Firelands expanded last year, just flooded the village with smoke. Nobody could breathe."

The notebook slammed shut, and Rok clipped the spiral back to its chain. "Guess I've been on Caravan too damn long."

"Do you know for a fact the townies cleared out?" Virgil asked Gage.

"I mean, I didn't go check—"

A motorized purr announced Ishmael's arrival. He eased the

motorbike to a stop, planting one foot on the asphalt without cutting the engine. He peeled a gas mask from his face, taking care not to tangle the head strap in his dreadlocks, and the Grave Walker juddered slightly. Diane still hadn't gotten used to those tattoos.

"Why have you stopped?" Ishmael asked, eyeing the highway behind them. "Not safe."

"Thank god you're here!" Gage cheered with faux excitement.

Virgil gave Ishmael the rundown. "We need to get to Pozo, to re-stock."

"Go south," Ishmael said. "It is quickest."

"That's what I said."

"I'm not messing with centipedes," Rok insisted.

"I have heard rumor that the centipedes migrated," Ishmael said.

"When?" Rok asked.

"After the meteor landed. The quakes confused them."

"Meteor?" Gage said. "You mean the spaceship?"

"Space *station*," Virgil corrected, flashing a wink at the Grave Walker.

Diane had never considered *Cradle*'s impact on the Junkyard as a whole. It was always her problem, a cataclysm that rocked her world alone. But now, listening to these Junkyard locals, she realized the crash must have been huge news. Theories and speculations rode the shock-wave from Jericho to the Firelands, but only Diane and Virgil knew the truth behind the event. She'd lived it, and he had listened to her recount the details during their long drives and late nights around glow-stick campfires. *Cradle*'s history lived in her and Virgil's memories, and it would likely die with them. There was a kinship in that, Diane decided.

Rok frowned. "Do you know for sure the centipedes migrated?"

"We don't know anything for sure," Virgil cut in. "Our choices are: maybe get attacked by centipedes, maybe breathe Vegas air and choke on our own blood, or maybe show up to a village that's totally aban-doned and a waste of fucking time."

He scanned the immediate Junkyard, then said with finality, "We're going south."

Rok threw up her hands and climbed back into the tank.

"Good talk," Gage said, following after her.

Ishmael didn't even wait for the others to start their engines. He sped off in a haze of red, moving southbound.

By midmorning, they had cleared the swamp and risen onto a sweeping desert with no trace of civilization, past or present. But it was not without signs of life. Lofty mounds spiked out from the barren earth, interconnected by long burrows tunneling for yards, sometimes miles—scoliosis spines of displaced dirt. Diane held her breath whenever these mounds interrupted the highway and forced them off-road, but nothing ever came of these detours. No hundred-legged arthropods burst up to devour them. If the centipedes hadn't migrated, they were heavy sleepers.

Just when Diane began to feel safe among the burrows, she heard shouting.

It was Gage, pointing to something off the highway, hollering his iodine-filtered lungs out. When he realized none of the drivers could hear him, the cyborg dropped off the tank, somersaulted across the highway, and then took off into a sprint. Arms pumping, repulsor jets firing with every stride, he dashed toward a shiny object half buried in the desert. Diane zoomed in with her visor until she saw what had gotten Gage so excited.

It was a door.

"Shelter," Gage announced when the others had caught up with him. "Unopened, untouched, unclaimed."

Virgil had given Diane a brief history of war-era shelters. Rich families had spent big bucks to wait out the Grand Finale underground, and many had never come out again. Now, these subterranean dwellings were treasure troves of unscathed junk. Finding an unopened shelter was like a holiday for junkies, and the residents didn't mind the intrusion. They'd been dead for at least a couple hundred years.

"We don't know it's fresh," Virgil said, still sitting in his jeep. "Might be another way in."

"You know these things only have one entrance." Rok went the door with a boxy radar console in hand. On-screen, white rings blossomed from a central dot, expanded across blank pixels, and then disappeared.

"No movement inside," she confirmed. "The occupants are probably skeletons by now."

Gage clapped his robotic hands in delight. Virgil was not so pleased.

"We're on a schedule, people," he said.

"Come on!" Gage whined. "I didn't think there were any uncracked shelters left! No way we're passing this up."

Virgil revved up the jeep. "I'm not paying you to play tomb raider."

"We're junkies, asshole. This is what we do."

As they argued, Diane zoomed her visor on a detail that meant nothing to the others. She couldn't believe what she was seeing at first, and her brain almost blew a fuse trying to accept it as reality. At the center of the shelter door, caked in centuries of Junkyard grit, was a familiar logo. A lowercase *a* beside a stylized uppercase *T*.

Armstrong Technologies. The same company that built *Cradle.*

"Rok, help me out here," Virgil said.

Rok dropped the radar console, dangling it from a strap around her neck. "Gage is right."

Virgil punched the jeep horn.

"You gave me first scavenge rights," Rok said. "If we can't stop between the Heap and Jericho, that's worthless. This is how I get my due."

Virgil signaled to Ishmael for backup, but the tattooed stoic offered no support. "Skeletons pose no threat to your safety," he said.

"I love this guy!" Gage laughed.

Ishmael did not seem to return the sentiment.

"Fine." Virgil cut the jeep's engine and clambered out. "Whatever. Crack it open. But if this detour screws me over, y'all get *nada.*"

Rok slipped a modified laser torch out of her belt.

In less than a minute, she had carved an upside-down *U* into the iron door. Gage hit the center with a repulsor-powered kick, and the door fell back into the space beyond.

After a cursory glance, Gage took the first heedless step into the shelter. Virgil and Rok secured their gas masks, then followed more cautiously behind Gage. Diane went in next, ducking to fit through a door not built with Grave Walkers in mind.

The entrance led them into a small foyer, where motes of dust hovered on the borderline between sunlight and shadow. The walls were made of chrome. The crew began to venture on, but after a few steps, they all realized someone was missing. They looked back to find Ishmael sitting in the door-turned-archway, facing the Junkyard, a black shape against solid white light.

"You don't want in on the junk?" Virgil asked.

"I will stay and keep watch," Ishmael said.

No one stuck around to argue.

The hall beyond the foyer took them down a steep decline, dropping farther and farther into the Earth. Automated plasma turrets hung from the ceiling, limp and powerless. No obstacles slowed their descent into the shelter, and Rok's high-powered flashlight kept the smothering dark at bay.

Once the ramp leveled out, it fed the group into a wide multistory atrium. Diane nearly screamed with recognition.

She had been here before. She had bounded along these same walkways in low gravity, laughing with friends during the good orbits and sulking alone during the bad. She knew the autodoor on their left would open to a security room, and the archway on the second story would lead to a residential junction. Then to Block Three. Then to Cabin Three-One-Seven, her home.

The space resembled *Cradle*'s Central Atrium in almost every detail. Even the observation window was accounted for, replaced by a wide holoscreen that might have simulated a day-to-night cycle. Diane felt like she had slipped into a parallel reality, a mirror dimension reflecting a world she never thought she would see again.

Virgil must have noticed the similarities too. While Rok and Gage wandered off through the atrium, he hung back at Diane's side. "You okay, kid?"

The Grave Walker nodded.

"You don't have to poke around down here," he said. "We won't be long."

"I want to stay," Diane said. She needed to see as much of the shelter as she could. When would she ever get the chance to go home again? Still, she appreciated his concern. It was almost like he cared.

"Something's wrong," Gage said. He stood across the atrium, his eyes like tiny spotlights in the distant darkness.

"What is it?" Virgil asked, powering on the Volt Caster with a flick of his wrist.

"The bodies." Gage lowered his voice. "Where are all the bodies?"

Annoyed, Virgil turned off the Caster. "I'm sure they're around."

"This place is perfect," Rok said. Her handheld console had switched to a Geiger counter function, clicking steadily. "We've got a light radiation leak, probably from the cracks I'm seeing in the ceiling, but not enough for a full breach. I think we're the first junkies to find this place."

Virgil lifted his gas mask for a quick hit of Battery, and when he exhaled, the green smoke floated away from the direction they had come. Their own breach had created the strongest airflow in the shelter.

"You've got an hour to junk dive," Virgil said, securing his mask. "Don't make me come looking for you—"

"Something's really wrong," Gage insisted.

The others stared at Gage, equal parts concerned and annoyed. All the brashness had gone from his voice, leaving a trepidation that didn't fit Gage at all. Diane couldn't understand why missing bodies were such a big deal. If anything, she considered the absence of mummified corpses a blessing.

"We are alone, right?" Virgil asked Rok.

The mechanic checked her radar again. No bleeps, nor blinking dots. "I got nothing."

"You sure that thing works?" Gage snapped.

"Duh," Rok said. "I built it myself."

Virgil put his faith in the radar. "Relax, Gage. We've got nothing to worry about."

The cyborg hurried off down a hallway that would take him to the temperature control wing, according to Diane's memory. He was frightened of something, but in that fear he suffered alone. Diane knew the feeling, but before she had time to dwell on it, Rok grabbed her suit by the wrist and led them toward a different corridor.

"We're going to find the fusion reactor," Rok announced.

As they rounded a corner, Virgil called out: "One hour! Keep an eye on her!"

And Diane wondered . . . Who was keeping an eye on who?

There were subtle differences: the shelter connected its levels with narrow stairwells, while *Cradle* had used ladders. The halls of *Cradle* had been rounded and edgeless; the shelter was all sharp corners and support columns. *Cradle*'s structural integrity had been pristine until the very end. The shelter was riddled with tiny cracks in the walls and ceiling, odd bumps in the floor, consequences of an ever-shifting tectonic environment.

Diane noticed these little details while Rok guided them with her flashlight, carping at her own navigational incompetence.

"*Laberinto estúpido.* The layout of this dump makes no sense." She forged ahead blindly but without fear. Diane clomped right behind her, a timid giant battling déjà vu.

"Are you worried about . . . whatever Gage is worried about?" she asked, distracting herself with conversation.

"I'm more worried about Gage," Rok said. "I heard he ran into some nasty roadkillers on his last job, messed him up bad. He's not usually this on edge. Hope he doesn't flip out."

"He's not the one I'm worried about," Diane said.

"Who?" Rok pointed her flashlight at the Grave Walker. "You scared of the squid-boy? Ishmael?"

"A little," Diane admitted.

Rok made a raspberry sound. "*Please.* He's all rifle, no plasma. Doesn't want anything to do with us, anyway. And besides . . ." She kicked the Grave Walker's shin, emitting a solid *clunk*. ". . . you got no reason to be scared of anybody."

"What do you mean?" Diane asked. She could think of a million reasons to be scared of everything.

"Come on! Look at you!" Rok ran the flashlight up the suit's eight-foot height. "You're the scariest-looking badass in the Junkyard."

An amazed, self-conscious titter escaped the Grave Walker's helmet—a bizarre sound from such an imposing machine.

Rok gnawed the inside of her cheek. "I can't believe you want out of that thing. You're not vulnerable like everyone else. You're . . . powerful."

Powerful?

Amazing, how a single word from Rok could shake Diane's entire perspective.

Powerful.

From the moment she landed on Earth, all Diane had wanted was to get out. Get out of the escape pod. Get out of the Grave Walker. Get out of the Junkyard. Her time and energy thus far had been devoted to taking flight, but here was someone telling her to stay. To embrace her new form and all the strength that came with it. What would Rok think of the real Diane if she ever laid eyes on her? She certainly wouldn't call the frail space colonist "powerful." She might want nothing to do with her at all.

But what did Diane care? Why was she so preoccupied with the opinion of someone she had only just met?

It was the same reason she had to get out of the suit, no matter what it cost her. She wanted to be close to Rok, and people like Rok she hadn't met yet, but as long as the Grave Walker had its needles in her spine, that could never happen. Not in the way she wanted so badly.

"It's lonely in here," Diane said. "Lonely and numb."

Her confession seemed to shake Rok; it was a long time before the mechanic spoke again.

"I'm sorry," she said, so sincerely it made Diane nervous. She quickly moved on down the hall, casting off the moment like a dirty coat. "But in the meantime, you're a tank. Use that."

Their path brought them to a junction, forking right and left. Rok shone her light down the two identical hallways.

"Flip a coin?" she said.

Without speaking, Diane ran down the left hall. She could pinpoint their exact location again, and that uncanny awareness sent her conscious mind reeling, leaving the subconscious in control of the Grave Walker's feet.

"Diane!" Rok chased after her, barely keeping up. "Slow down! You don't even know where you're—"

Turning a corner, Rok found the Grave Walker standing at the entrance to the shelter's Reactor Chamber. The autodoors hung wide open.

"Whoa."

On *Cradle*, this had been Gravity Control. Here, in place of the physics-defying Core, an hourglass-shaped fusion reactor stood tall. There were no bodies in this room, either. Just a mob of dead computers, empty chairs, and thick layers of dust.

"Have you been inside a shelter before?" Rok asked.

Diane said no, and though it was technically the truth, Rok clearly wasn't buying it.

"You never told me how Virgil found you," she said.

"Neither did you," Diane replied. It was a dirty countermove, and it pained Diane to show any hostility toward Rok, but this was a line of questioning she could do without.

"Point taken," Rok said, and the interrogation died there.

While Rok set about prying open the reactor's maintenance hatch, Diane wandered among the darkened computers. Their arrangement was identical to the Gravity Control Room's layout. Completely identical.

"Look at this!" Rok shouted as the hatch fell away. "No damage. Nothing broken. They just ran out of juice!"

Diane found the air vent she had used to infiltrate this room's counterpart. Standing beneath it, she could almost hear that whirring pandemonium of the Gravity Core gone haywire.

"I'm going to buy so much Battery with this," Rok rejoiced. "And so much vodka!"

The Grave Walker began to tremble. Rok pulled herself back from the reactor.

"You okay?" she asked.

"Yeah, I . . . um . . ."

The trembling intensified because now Diane really could hear the Gravity Core. She could hear the quaking of a space station trying to tear itself apart. The Sixer bawling at the mention of Earth. Distant screaming from the Block Threes, Twos, and . . . and . . .

Oh god, the Ones.

"Diane?"

The Grave Walker bolted for the door.

"I'm gonna go look around," Diane mumbled.

She hurried out, leaving Rok alone and perplexed with the reactor.

As Diane abandoned the range of the flashlight, her new night vision kicked in automatically. It put her face-to-face with an ornate door across the hall—branded with the Armstrong Technologies logo—which hung ajar. Diane nearly fell scrambling in the other direction. If this place had a Caretaker, he might be waiting on the other side of that door, sitting at his desk with a gun in his hand. A bullet hole in his head. When she finally returned to the Central Atrium, Diane fell to her knees and cried—cried and cried until the sounds of destruction faded from her ears.

Nimble feet hurried down the shelter's entrance ramp, alerting her fully back to reality. She readied for anything, but it was only Ishmael she found sliding into the room. A clockwork brace now covered his left arm, fitted with a harpoon head on the wrist, which connected to a rig on his back through a long, tightly wound chain. The night vision's low resolution did nothing to beautify those frightening tattoos.

"What happened?" Ishmael asked. "Is Virgil safe?"

Diane stammered to explain herself. "I think so. I mean, nothing happened. I was just . . ."

She felt her breathing slow, like something had reached into her chest and taken control of her lungs. The Grave Walker's doing, no doubt.

"You ever feel like the past wants to swallow you whole?" Diane asked, suddenly calm.

Ishmael answered without missing a beat. "Every day."

Ishmael started back up the ramp. Maybe it was the brief solidarity they had just shared, or Rok's encouragement, but whatever the reason, Diane allowed herself a question . . .

"What do the tattoos mean?"

Ishmael paused on the ramp, as surprised by Diane's boldness as she was.

"They represent the gods of the Deep," he said eventually. "The tattoos were a rite of passage."

Diane went further. "Do your gods have names?"

"They are not my gods anymore."

"Oh." An awkward silence pulled Diane back onto her feet. "I'm going to go find Virgil. See if he needs help . . . I don't know . . . lifting something."

The dynamic suddenly reversed. As Diane moved to leave, embarrassed at her own hypocritical prying, Ishmael called to her. "If you find any books, I would pay a great sum for something new to read."

Diane was surprised by the request. She hadn't pegged Ishmael for a bookworm.

"I would search myself," he said, "but I must guard the entrance."

"I'll keep an eye out," she promised.

She made it halfway down a corridor before Ishmael called out once more.

"The past is a book," he said. Some trace emotion bubbled beneath his monotone, but Diane couldn't place it.

"A book?" she asked.

"You are not obligated to read the story. You can close it anytime."

Diane reflected for a moment, then asked, "What if my book keeps falling open?"

"Burn it," Ishmael said.

He retreated up the ramp, and Diane asked no follow-up questions. There was something ominous in that last remark, a hint of dangerous repression, and his exit made even the subterranean shelter seem a little brighter.

Diane climbed a nearby stairwell, crossed an elevated walkway, and ventured off into the Residential Junction.

"Virgil?" she called. No response. The entrance to Block Three was exactly where she expected it to be. "Virgil? You there?"

She didn't wait for him to answer, because she wasn't really looking for him anymore. She was climbing the stairs to the first catwalk, passing six tiny cabin doors to the one labeled *317*. She couldn't stop the approach. Her feet were not her own.

She pulled open the door.

A blue flash lunged out of the cabin, armed with something sharp. Diane shoved the attacker with all her might, and he flew across the room, landing on his feet. Diane braced for combat, but only after taking a fighting stance did she realize that Gage was the attacker. In that instant, he came to the same conclusion about her.

"Damn it, Diane!" he said.

"You 'damn it'!" she yelled back.

The Grave Walker relaxed, and Gage retracted the blades back into his forearms.

"What are you doing up here?" she asked.

"Checking the rooms. You?"

Diane sidestepped the question. "Have you seen Virgil?"

"No," Gage said. "You find any bodies?"

"What's your hang-up with the bodies?"

Gage squeezed past the Grave Walker, moving on to Cabin Three-One-Eight. As he opened the door enough to peek inside, he asked, "You ever heard of the Chimera?"

"From Greek mythology?" Diane said.

"Who myth-what?" Gage replied.

The layout of this Three-One-Seven doppelgänger matched Diane's old cabin perfectly. She walked inside, while Gage continued checking the other rooms around Block Three.

"Chimera's a Relic, like Crybaby or the Pest," he said, "but worse. Way worse."

"What does it look like?" Diane asked, half listening. The walls here were blank. No art. No signs of personality. Whoever lived here didn't intend to stay long, though they had brought along a versatile collection of pill bottles. They were scattered around the dusty sink, diagnosed for a variety of ailments. Back pain. Insomnia. Depression. Diane considered gathering them up as trading goods, but then she noticed the expiration dates on all the labels. She couldn't say for sure what year it was now—*Cradle* had deemed Earth time "unnecessary information"—but the expirations were all capped at the year 2000. That must have been ages ago.

Gage reached the end of their cabin row. "Some people say the Chimera's a feline with three stomachs. Or a reptile with too many teeth. Nobody's ever actually seen it and lived."

"If no one's seen it," Diane said, "how do you know it's real—"

"It doesn't leave bodies," Gage said, checking the last empty cabin. "It eats everything. Even the bones."

Diane pieced together what Gage was really proposing. A monster that no one had seen had infiltrated the shelter and eaten all the residents. A shelter with one entrance, sealed for a hundred years.

"That's what you're afraid of?" Diane said, unconvinced.

"I'm not afraid of anything," Gage said.

"You sound pretty afraid."

"I'm cautious." Gage slammed the door to the final cabin. "There's a difference."

It felt strange to be on the other side of this scenario. Diane's last year on *Cradle* had been a constant game of cat-and-mouse with unseen dangers that she could never prove, that no one would ever believe. She wished that she could give Gage the faith that no one had given her, but his naysayers were the two people she trusted most in the world.

"Rok and Virgil said there's nothing to worry about."

In the blink of an eye, Gage was inches from Diane, poking the Grave Walker's chest.

"Never trust the bastards who tell you not to worry," he spat. "Understand? That's how they sedate you. Fear is survival."

He stepped back, cleared his throat. "Not that I'm afraid, just to be clear."

Diane took a stab at lightening the mood. "Well, if the Chimera is down here, you've got a whole crew to protect you."

Gage patted his right leg, where a faded gray line told the tale of his old fracture. "My last crew didn't do me any favors."

"Could anyone in your last crew do . . . this?" Diane crossed the Grave Walker's wrists in front of her face.

The orange energy shield appeared, as expected, but Rok's tinkering must have amplified its strength. It spawned with an unexpected force, and the kick knocked Diane right off the catwalk. The fall was brief, but humiliating.

Gage leaned over the railing, while the Grave Walker moaned to its feet. "No!" he cackled. "No, they couldn't do that!"

He vaulted down to Diane's level, all smiles and snide. "Let's go find your grandpa."

"He's *not* my grandpa," Diane said, wiping the dust from the Grave Walker's legs.

"Uh-huh."

They left the Residential Junction together, calling out to Virgil between banter and snipes. Gage could run laps around Diane's limited sarcasm, but it didn't affect her like it had on Caravan. It was all in good fun, all to keep high spirits in a gloomy place.

When they found Virgil in the shelter's cafeteria, the mood spoiled immediately. He sat perched on a table, huffing Battery, surrounded by gnarled shapes draped in burgundy jumpsuits.

"Oh," Gage said. "There they are."

"Yup," Virgil replied. "Here they are."

The bodies nearest the table matched Diane's expectation. Shriveled skin and bone, locked in fetal and defensive poses, gray from head to toe. But there was something wrong with the other corpses, the vast majority carpeting the cafeteria. Calcified tumors bulged out from their skulls and remaining skin, corrupting anatomies into hellish new arrangements. Some of the tumors had teeth.

"I'm gonna go . . . find some more junk." Gage fled the room, leaving Diane alone with Virgil and the bodies.

She decided it was time to burn a question. "What happened to them?"

Virgil refilled his inhaler without looking up. "Do you know what Battery does?"

"It cures radiation sickness?" Diane guessed, using context clues.

"It *represses* radiation sickness," Virgil said, "and it fills the body with fake blood cells, to make up for the ones the radiation killed. When Battery wears off, the fake blood cells go away."

He stood up, surveying the mutant skeletons beneath him. "When most people stop taking Battery, they die. But if you take Battery long enough, like these guys . . ."

Like you, Diane thought.

". . . the withdrawal triggers a mutation. The body tries to create the fake blood cells on its own. You get a kind of super-cancer, and everything gets . . . messed up."

Understatement of the century, Diane thought.

"We call them *boil freaks*," Virgil concluded.

Virgil stepped down, traversing the cafeteria on a winding path between the mutated bodies. Diane could not picture him joining their misshapen ranks, but she knew that he could. It was probably all he thought about. Every action, every deception, all taken to avoid this fate for one more day. One more job. One more trip home.

Finally, Diane understood why she was here. She understood why Virgil wanted her help, despite her total inexperience. He needed all the help he could get.

"This won't happen to you," Diane told him, once he had crossed to her side of the room.

"Can't be helped," he said.

"I won't let it."

The old junkie wouldn't look her in the visor, so she bent down and forced their eyes to meet.

"We're going to finish this job," Diane said, "and we're going to get you home."

"*No le mientas a un mentiroso, chica*," Virgil said. "I know you're in this for you."

"I'm in this for *us*," Diane insisted, and when Virgil still seemed unconvinced, she doubled down. "At the end of the day, I'm alive because of you. I'll never forget that."

Virgil squinted up at the visor as if trying to see through it. "You really mean that, don't you?"

His countenance shifted, duplicating the look Rok had given after hearing Diane's lament on isolation. Such sadness had never burdened Virgil before, at least not in the brief time they'd spent together. It worried Diane in a way she couldn't quite define. What was this melancholia that he and his mechanic seemed to share? What did it have to do with her?

Virgil took one final glance around the cafeteria.

"Birds singing to the sunrise," he whispered. "Soft grass. Biting into an orange, citrus mist—"

"What?" Diane asked.

He spun around, suddenly roguish and playful again. "Junk time's up! Let's go round up those assholes, huh?"

His transformation bordered on bipolar, leaving Diane flabbergasted.

"Come on, kid!" Virgil called from the hallway. "¡*Vámonos*!"

She ran after him, leaving the dead forgotten behind her.

CHAPTER 19

They passed the night in a canyon made from old Peacekeeper parts, charred and mangled beyond salvage.

Around the warmth of a heated lamp, Virgil, Rok, and Diane listened to Gage's tall tales of epic adventure, self-aggrandizing odysseys in which he slayed roadkillers, rescued townies, and celebrated with rowdy mercenaries. Diane asked a million questions, Rok and Virgil poked a million holes, and Gage had an answer for all of them. They laughed, they jabbed, and no one mentioned Diane's ambiguous origins, or Rok's history with Virgil, or Gage's paranoia back in the shelter.

Ishmael watched the crew from his perch above the canyon. He sat cross-legged on a pile of dull scrap metal, passing the night alone. Though his exile was self-inflicted, he could not deny the loneliness he felt while observing the others. How quickly they had fallen into conversation, prattling with a natural ease that had always eluded him. A part of Ishmael wanted to slide down and join the merriment, but as always, the Master held him back.

The others hate you. The girl fears you. The old man is using you. Expendable fool.

Ishmael tried to use the task at hand to keep this voice in the background. He kept watch for any danger to his employer, staying awake long after the others had fallen asleep, but each lightning flash revealed only empty desert. No roadkillers. No Peacekeepers. No bugs, even. Just Ishmael, a lonely speck on the infinite midnight, with only the Master's cruelty to keep him company.

When you die, who will weep? No one.
Alone—
No one.
You are—
No one.

With no distractions, the voice crashed against Ishmael's mind in savage white bursts, like the Pacific waves of his childhood. He took the flood without flinching or responding. He did his job. He watched the night.

CHAPTER 20

At sunrise, the crew set out again. By midafternoon, they reached the village of Pozo.

"Aw, what the hell . . . ?" Virgil brought the crew to a stop, and Diane hopped out of the trailer to see what was wrong.

Pozo greeted them with a crude barricade of barbed wire and a team of riflemen with their crosshairs aimed up the road. Behind the barrier, a community of wide eyes and frightened faces spectated through broken windows in prewar industrial warehouses. These buildings were stationed around a concrete reservoir—bone dry. A thick steel pipe rose out from the pool's filtration tank, ran visibly for half a mile, then disappeared into a hillside.

Parked a safe distance from the riflemen, the crew argued and speculated over the cause of this increased security. Diane deduced from their conversation that Pozo wasn't typically so hostile. Something was off.

"We should've gone to Camp Phoenix," Rok said.

Virgil stormed off. "I'll handle this."

He approached the barricade without fear, waving to the rifles trained on his face.

"¡*Hola*!"

"Turn around!" one of the riflemen called.

"Nothing to worry about!" Virgil said. "We're junkies—"

A streak of red, a piercing whine, and the road at Virgil's toes exploded into a geyser of dirt and concrete. Virgil leaped back, hollering curse words.

"One more step," the rifleman yelled, "and the next laser goes in your head!"

Virgil planted himself where he stood. "That feels . . . drastic."

"That's the way it is."

"You got a chief I can talk to?"

"You're talking to him."

Behind him, Gage whisper-shouted, "You're doing great, *jefe*!" Diane could hear Rok snigger.

"No clue what's got you so high-strung," Virgil called to the distant Pozo chief, "but we don't mean any harm. All we want is Nutribriks and water."

"We got nothing to trade," the chief replied.

Virgil laughed in disbelief. "Are you joking? You're a groundwater town!"

"We were, until the centipedes migrated south. Our plant's overrun . . ."

A sinking sensation tugged at the memory in Diane's stomach. Ishmael had been right after all. *Cradle*'s impact had confused the centipedes, and this village was paying the price. Diane assured herself that she wasn't to blame, but a nagging guilt insisted otherwise. She was *Cradle*'s sole survivor. Keeper of its legacy. Inheritor of its crimes.

". . . and that was after we took in a bunch of Heap refugees," the chief went on. "We're overpopulated, running on reserves. We got nothing to spare."

As Virgil pondered the dilemma, Rok padded up beside him.

"We're wasting our time," she whispered. "Let's get out of here."

Diane knew Virgil wouldn't give up so easily. He never did. Not in the Jericho sewers when Kara tried to rip them off. Not in Ms. Violet's office when the corporate overlord threatened to nullify their agreement. When time and resources were on the line, Virgil refused to walk away empty-handed. His particular brand of crazy wouldn't allow it.

Sure enough, Virgil ignored Rok's plea and addressed the chief again. "Couldn't get ahold of any mercenaries, huh?"

"They're not taking calls," the chief said bitterly.

Virgil made a sweeping gesture to his crewmates. "Well, we're not mercs, but we do kick ass on a professional level."

"Don't you dare," Rok hissed.

Again, Virgil ignored her. "If we can clear out the centipedes, get your treatment plant up and running again, would that cover the cost of our food and water?"

The riflemen murmured to each other. A whispered excitement passed among the half-hidden townies. Virgil's offer had the whole village talking.

When deliberations completed, the chief answered, "If you live long enough to collect."

"Deal," Virgil said.

He returned to the vehicles, with Rok protesting behind him.

"¿*Estás loco*?"

"It's a bug hunt, Rok."

"You got pissy when we stopped at the shelter. How is this different?"

"The shelter was a pointless detour. Pozo is free water for a five-second headache."

"It's a risk we don't need to take!"

"For the record," Gage piped in, "I'm all for this."

"*Gage*!" Rok bawled.

His smile broadened. "Rescue a village from bugs? That's the rep boost I'm looking for—"

"I agree with the mechanic." Ishmael's voice made everyone jump. How easy it was to forget he was there. "This plan is foolish."

"Who asked you?" Gage snapped. "Who *ever* asked you?"

While taking a hit of Battery, Ishmael directed his stony gaze to Virgil. "You are taking an unnecessary risk. How can I be expected to protect you?"

"Do your best?" Virgil shrugged.

"Virgil," Rok said, clapping in his face. "This is a very . . ." *Clap.* "Bad . . ." *Clap.* "Idea."

Virgil swatted her hands away. "No, it's a polarizing idea. The crew is split."

Rok cast an apprehensive glance at Ishmael—an ally she never would have expected.

"Diane, what's your take?" Virgil asked.

The Grave Walker jolted. Diane had been standing just outside the huddle, listing to an argument where she claimed no authority. "My take?"

"Break the tie," Virgil insisted. "Do we fight or flee?"

Rok stepped in. "Come on, she doesn't know—"

"She's part of the crew. She gets a say."

He patted the Grave Walker's elbow, smiling warmth and confidence into the visor. "How should we play this, kid?"

Diane made an effort to think strategically, to weigh the benefits of accessing Pozo with the risks of battling centipedes. She tried to call upon her relationships with Rok and Virgil; which one could she not bear to disappoint? Both worthy motivators, but neither could distract from the scene playing in her head. Rational or not, it consumed her.

She imagined *Cradle*'s broken pieces bombarding the Earth, each casting its own ripple of destruction through the Junkyard. Villages collapsed. Cars flew off the road. Giant bugs scattered on violent paths. Final bastions of order tumbled into chaos, all because she had failed. She had waited to act until it was too late.

Cradle inflicted harm upon the world. Someone needed to atone.

"If we can help these people," Diane said finally, "then we should."

Gage, Ishmael, and Rok all went very still, their own motives tottering against one so unusual, so utterly divorced from the concept of self-preservation.

Virgil grinned at the others. "We can, and we will."

They followed the reservoir pipe to a hill range shaped like the crescent moon, and in the center, they found the groundwater treatment plant that fed Pozo its lifeblood. The damage could have been worse. All the filter tanks were intact, and the facility house looked no more dilapidated than most buildings in the Junkyard. The problem was the piping. Many lines hung broken, spewing water and chlorine into the muddy dirt. During their frantic escape, none of the townies had remembered to shut off the water flow. Now, it was wasting away by the gallon.

"Tragedy," Virgil said as they parked. "Goddamn tragedy."

Diane couldn't see any centipedes, but once all the vehicles stopped and the Grave Walker's feet landed on the ground, she could feel them. Squirming, invertebrate disturbances navigating a subterranean world. They were big, and they were many.

Rok confirmed this with her radar console, now swarmed with dots. "I count at least twelve," she said.

Virgil watched the blinking pinpoints over her shoulder. "Too many in one spot to be full-grown. Must be larvae."

"We can handle a few babies," Gage said, leaning on Rok's shoulder. "Can't we?"

She pushed him away. "So now what? They won't surface until nightfall."

"Got anything in that tool belt that can make some vibrations?" Virgil asked.

"Oh sorry," Rok said, "I left that tool on my nightstand."

While the crew struggled to brainstorm, Diane studied the hilltops half-circling the treatment plant. She thought about *Cradle* and all the vibrations it had produced. There was no secret to its success in displacing the centipedes. It was simple science. A matter of gravity.

"How much do I weigh?" Diane suddenly asked.

After processing the question, Rok answered, "About a thousand pounds. Give or take."

"And how does the Grave Walker do with long drops?"

"Why?" Virgil asked.

Diane sighed. "I've got a really dumb idea . . ."

The next thing she knew, Diane was wobbling on a rocky hilltop, peering down at miniature models of her crewmates.

"Remember to land on your feet!" Rok called.

"Or your head!" Gage heckled, but after seeing how the others glared at him, corrected, "Seriously, though! Don't land on your head!"

Whatever Ishmael felt about the stunt, he kept it to himself.

Virgil ran a twitchy hand through his green-stained beard. "This is stupid."

"The suit can take it," Rok said.

"And what if it can't?"

"It can. You want to hunt centipedes, this is how we do it." Rok shielded her eyes against the sunlight. "That girl's either a genius or bugshit crazy."

"You sure you want to do this?" Virgil shouted upward.

No, Diane wasn't sure.

"We can find another way!"

Yes, Diane would give anything to find another way. But she knew they'd come up short.

So she jumped.

She feared the plummet would bring her mind back to the escape pod, force her to relive *Cradle*'s descent all over again, but the fall was too quick, and there was no mystery about where she would land. The ground met her feet right on schedule, and the suit's knees popped like gunshots from the impact. All the vehicles, even the tank, hopped at least a couple inches off the ground. Virgil and company floundered to keep from toppling over. Startled expletives were hollered by all.

And, as if on cue, the first centipede shot to the surface.

Longer than Virgil's jeep, thicker than a human arm, and with more legs than anyone could count, the larva broke through the ground and announced its arrival with a rattling screech. A dozen other centipedes joined the ascent, worming up from deep dark burrows, slithering off in every direction. The Grave Walker's HUD marked each centipede with a tiny square, and each square emitted a dotted line tracing the hostiles' predicted paths. Amazed, Diane saw that one of the lines was pointed her way.

A centipede crawled over the path not a second later, following the dots almost exactly. The beast was coming for Diane.

What came next was a team effort.

Diane knew that she wanted to crush the centipede before it reached her, but the larva was fast. She would only get one chance to strike before it wrapped itself around her body, binding her limbs and pinning her to the ground. Diane knew she lacked the reflexes to outmaneuver the centipede, but unbeknownst to her, she didn't need them. The Grave Walker was designed to pick up slack on the battlefield. All Diane needed was to want something, preferably something destructive, and the suit would take care of the rest.

As the centipede came within range, Diane chose to punch it. The suit's giant arm that was hers yet not hers lifted back in response, and at the absolute perfect time, her fist—which was also not her fist—shot down in a meteoric fury. The larva's head splattered against the Grave Walker's knuckles. A definitive crunch echoed off the hillside.

Another centipede charged Diane, leaping up toward her visor, and the Grave Walker snatched the creature out of the air with both hands. Once she overcame her revulsion, Diane ordered those hands to rip the bug in two. Innards spewed, legs spasmed, and the dichotomized centipede fell dead in the dirt.

She turned back to Virgil and found him beaming with pride.

"¡Mátenlos!" he cried.

The crew sprang into action. Virgil snapped his Volt Caster at the centipedes scuttling his way, while Gage chased others down and kicked them onto their backs. Stunned, these bugs were powerless to avoid the Grave Walker's foot as it stomped their heads flat. Virgil and Gage knocked them down, and Diane made sure they stayed down.

Across the treatment plant, Rok and Ishmael settled into their own extermination dynamic. Ishmael aimed his clockwork brace at a far-off centipede, and he squeezed his left hand into a fist. The harpoon rocketed from his wrist, trailing the chain behind it, and punctured the unlucky centipede's trunk. When Ishmael opened his hand, the rig on his back whirled clockwise, pulling the harpoon and its catch back toward the point of launch. He jerked his arm upward, yanking the centipede through the air in a dazzling arc. At its highest point, Rok shot the centipede with her tank's ion launcher, igniting a firework of flaming bug chunks. The freed harpoon snapped back to its home on Ishmael's arm.

The collaboration was totally spontaneous, and though neither party rejoiced at working with the other, they repeated the tactic many times. The results spoke for themselves.

As the crew zapped, kicked, stomped, and skewered the centipedes around them, Diane marveled at how easily they had fallen into their roles. The dissonance between them, the islands of neurosis that kept them from seeing eye to eye, had vanished in an instant, and they were now gears in a unified, well-oiled war machine. Combat was a tradition among the junkies, a group dance where everyone knew the steps, and Diane was right there dancing with the best of them. She wasn't a liability here like she had been on *Cradle*. She was pulling her weight. Finally, she felt useful.

The fight ended with thirteen larvae carcasses death-rattling across the treatment plant. Still synchronized in the heat of battle, each crew member struck a defensive pose while checking for any stragglers. None came, and Gage threw his fists into the air.

"Whooo!" he cheered. "*That* is how you do a bug hunt!"

Everyone else took the cue to relax. Rok sprang out of the tank's hatch, gasping with excitement.

"Where'd you get that grappling rig?" she called to Ishmael.

He wiped the bug guts off his harpoon. "It is the standard weapon for the Shallows' hunters. Allows them to slay crustaceans without getting too close."

"It's amazing!" Rok said.

Ishmael walked away from the group as if summoned by a frequency only he could hear.

Rok rolled her eyes. "All right. See you at the next one."

She fell into a jubilant hype session with Gage, recapping the battle in boisterous detail.

Virgil went to Diane. "Nice footwork, kid."

"I did the easy part," she replied.

"You held your own." Virgil shut off the Volt Caster. "One week on Earth, and you're already playing with the big kids."

Had it only been a week? Had a whole week already passed? Time moved strangely in the Junkyard.

Diane kicked bashfully at the dirt. "It was all the suit."

"The suit's nothing without the person inside it," Virgil said. "You held your own. I knew I brought you along for a reason—"

"We have made a mistake," Ishmael called out.

The others found him kneeling among the dead larva, one hand pressed to the ground.

"What the problem, dreads?" Gage asked.

Ishmael ran back to his motorbike. "We need to leave!"

"But we still need to fix the pipes," Rok said.

"*Run!*" Ishmael cried.

The ground began to shake again, harder and faster than before. No one needed to ask why.

Everyone mounted their rides and sped away from the treatment plant. As they neared the opening in the hill range, a monstrous roar penetrated the topsoil from far below. Virgil looked to his side mirror. Rok and Ishmael checked their rearview monitors. Diane and Gage beheld the source with their own horrified eyes.

The Worm. The Leviathan. The World Serpent.

Larger than life and angry as hell, a queen centipede launched one of the filter tanks into the sky as it infiltrated the surface world. It was double the size of all thirteen larvae combined, and it chased after the crew with all the power of a locomotive. Its intentions were painfully clear. The babies were dead, and their mama was pissed.

Frantic voices rattled Diane's helmet.

"This is the shit I was talking about!" Rok hollered.

"How do we lose this thing?" Virgil yelled.

"We must return to the village!" Ishmael said. "We need more firepower!"

As they started on the road back to Pozo, Diane felt the jeep lurch with a sudden additional weight.

"Hey!" Virgil yipped.

Peering back, Diane saw that Gage had jumped from the tank to the front seat beside Virgil, and Gage snatched the radio mic out of the old junkie's hand.

"We can't lead it to the village!" he cried.

"*We have no choice!*" Ishmael said.

"It'll kill everyone!" Gage said. "*Everyone!*"

Virgil fought to reclaim the mic, but before he could rip it out of Gage's hand, the cyborg spat one last decree. "I won't let this happen again!"

"*Again?*" Virgil squawked.

Gage flung himself out of the jeep, landing on his feet.

"*Gage, no!*"

Rok's words fell on deaf ears. Gage sprinted toward the queen centipede, and when it seemed like he and those gnashing mandibles would collide, he suddenly veered right. The centipede followed, its fury redirected.

"*He is insane,*" said Ishmael, of all people.

The jeep, the tank, and the motorcycle kept driving straight, leaving the chase behind. From where she sat, Diane could see that Gage was barely keeping ahead of the mammoth pursuer. No twists or turns could shake the centipede from Gage's heels, and one slip or stumble would send him falling into its crushing mandibles. When that happened—not if, but when—would the centipede follow their scent? Would it decimate the town of Pozo, as Gage predicted? Would another community get wiped off the map?

And if so . . . would that blood be on their hands?

Diane wasn't sure if she jumped on purpose or if the Grave Walker reacted to another subconscious slipup. One second, she was sitting in the trailer; the next, she was standing on the desert road, ankle-deep in the potholes of her own impact.

Virgil's scream blew out the speakers in her helmet. "*Diane!*"

She had no plan, and she suspected Gage didn't, either. Thankfully, as she sprinted toward the unfathomable arthropod, she heard the jeep's wheels swerving through a U-turn.

"*All right, we're doing this!*" Virgil announced.

The tank and motorbike flipped around as well, but their drivers weren't happy about it.

"*Has everyone gone crazy?*" Rok yelled.

"*This is suicide!*" Ishmael said.

Virgil ignored their protests. "*We need to take out the queen's head! All ideas welcome!*"

Diane winced at the sound of Rok's disdain. "*I didn't sign up for this* mierda."

A chewing noise filled her radio signal, followed by a delighted "*Mmmf!*" and the spitting of tobacco juice.

"*Grave Walker!*" Rok blurted.

Humming feedback rose from the tank, and Rok's voice blared from speakers built into the hull. "*Gage! Lead the bug to Diane!*"

"Wait, *what?*" Virgil said, echoing Diane's own thoughts. "*Why would we do that?*"

"*Diane, stay where you are!*" Rok said.

The Grave Walker skidded to a stop, and the vehicular trio flew passed her at full speed.

"What am I doing?" Diane asked, panicked.

"*Hang on!*" Rok said. "*Just trust me!*"

Diane stayed put. She did trust Rok, probably more than she trusted anyone.

Gage led the queen on a wide turn, but the arc killed his momentum. The space between him and the monster shrank.

"*It's gaining on him!*" Rok said. "*We need to slow it down!*"

Without responding, Ishmael accelerated his bike ahead of the pack.

He gained on the centipede's segmented tail, and when the distance was just right, he lifted his brace and made a fist. The harpoon wedged itself between two of the exoskeleton's hard-shelled pieces, penetrating the soft meat beneath. The centipede hissed in pain.

Ishmael opened his hand, hit the brakes, and miraculously, his left arm did not tear out of its socket. The mysterious workings of the clockwork rig held solid. The bike's front wheel lifted off the road, and though the queen did not stop, it slowed enough to keep Gage safe.

"*That . . . That'll work!*" Rok whooped.

The queen struggled across the desert floor, trailing the motorbike behind it. It moved to abandon its chase in favor of the nuisance at its tail, but when it turned right, Rok was waiting. She hit the centipede with a round of plasma fire, forcing it back on track. It tried to veer left, but Virgil herded it with a shock from the Volt Caster. Flanked, the bug had nowhere to go but forward. Toward Gage.

Toward Diane.

"*Rok, what is she doing?*" Virgil asked.

"*Wait for my cue, Diane!*" Rok ordered.

Gage threw himself to the side, and Diane found herself staring down the crystalline eyes of the queen centipede. She saw herself reflected in two hundred glassy shards, all deep red with carnivorous hate. Two hundred Grave Walkers getting closer . . . and closer . . . and—

"*Shield!*" Rok screamed.

Diane shut her eyes and crossed her wrists.

She felt a tremendous impact, then something like a long drop, except she was upright and moving backward. Asphalt shredded beneath her feet. A ringing sound pierced her inner ear. There was pain, but it was distant. Phantom. Someone else's pain.

It could have been seconds or hours for all she knew, but eventually, the Grave Walker slowed to a stop. The ringing died away. A whirring sound rose from somewhere deep inside the suit, and when it ended, so did the pain.

Opening her eyes, Diane found the energy shield colored the darkest orange on the spectrum. She parted her wrists, and the shield gave way to a pulverized centipede skull oozing thick phosphorescent blood. Its giant body lay motionless in a figure eight. They had done it.

Gage, Ishmael, and Rok were a safe distance from the collision zone, but the jeep was much closer, sitting tires-up on the road.

"Virgil!" Diane sprinted to the jeep and flipped it upright, too frightened to appreciate how easy her grisly task had been. If Virgil was hurt, she would never forgive herself. It didn't cross her mind that his death meant no escape from the Grave Walker, no access to the fabled mountain paradise. In that moment, all she cared about was spending a question:

"Are you okay?"

He was. She found him behind the wheel, saved by the grace of his seat belt. A few scratches on his face, a shell-shocked daze, but nothing was broken. He was breathing.

"I'm . . . I uh . . . Whoo . . . Whoo ha . . . Ha haha . . . Hahahaha!"

When the others arrived, they found Virgil and Diane rolling with hysterics. They laughed for their lives. They laughed for each other. They laughed because in a world of giant, vengeful centipedes, it was the only sane response.

There was just enough daylight left to make repairs on the treatment plant.

After berating Gage for his reckless behavior—he eventually apologized but refused to fully explain the source of his madness—Rok took stock of the damages incurred from the centipede invasion. There was nothing to be done about the wrecked filtration tank, but the broken pipes could be welded back together. With a little elbow grease, they would have the plant running at about 60 percent capacity. Better than nothing. Way better.

They chose to divide the repairs and conquer.

At one end of the facility, Diane held two broken pipes together all by herself, and Virgil fused them with the flat side of his red-hot hunting knife. The pair worked quietly for a while until Virgil broke the silence.

"You about gave me a heart attack, *chamaca*."

"I'm sorry," Diane said. "What Gage was saying before . . . I guess it got in my head."

"You need to look out for yourself," Virgil said. "Nothing's worth dying for."

"Then why'd you turn back to help me?"

Virgil stopped welding. Diane waited for a witty response, but instead:

"Come on, kid. You know I've got your back."

It was exactly what she needed to hear. "We make a pretty good crew, huh?" she asked, willfully burning the day's last question.

Virgil smiled. "I guess we—"

His eyes went wide, lips trembling, like he was going to be sick.

"Something wrong?" Diane asked.

The jeep was parked nearby, and Virgil scrambled for his backpack under the front seat. The sack made a crunching sound as he raised it up. Green liquid soaked the bottom, dripping onto the ground, leaving stains that glowed.

"Virgil, what's wrong?" Diane pressed.

He opened the pack. Inside, broken capsule pieces floated in their own spilled contents. He had survived his collision with the queen centipede, but his Battery cache had not been so lucky.

Virgil let the backpack slip from his hands. "Diane—"

He gagged, eyes rolling back in his head. He fell against the jeep, and Diane could literally see his skin crawling with imminent boils. What kind of sickness moved this fast? Virgil had claimed that his Junkyard Blues was in the advanced stages, but the onset of these symptoms defied everything Diane knew about biology. And, oh god, it was *hideous*.

"Rok!" Diane shouted. "Rok, help!"

On the other side of the plant, deep in the whine of sparking metal and concentrated lasers, Rok and the others heard nothing.

Virgil crawled to Diane, who had never witnessed the Blues in action before now. She had never seen the boils, the steaming flesh. She had never seen so much anguish.

"Oh no," she groaned. "Tell me what to do. What can I do?"

A swollen tongue blocked Virgil's mouth, and he could issue no instruction. He groped his way up the Grave Walker's leg, then hung from her left arm like a pull-up bar. Diane had no way to know what was happening, so she didn't put a stop to it. She had no reason to resist.

Not until Virgil pressed a hidden switch on the box beneath her wrist. The box that Rok had installed, that she had told Diane was a "reflex module."

Diane felt a stabbing pain in her arm, her real arm. The sudden awareness of skin, mixed with panic from a hurt she didn't understand, sent her flailing away.

"What was that?" she cried out, swatting at the box.

Virgil crawled as fast as he could, but Diane wouldn't stay still. She was afraid. He was mute. All communication had broken down.

He snapped the Volt Caster's fingers. Lightning struck Diane's helmet, scrambling her HUD, numbing her mind, and the Grave Walker dropped onto its back. All functions were active, but the neural interface had been frozen.

Diane could not move.

Through a blizzard of static, she watched Virgil pull himself back to the box. He pressed the switch again, held it down. The stab returned to Diane's arm, and a syringe needle on a plastic tube ejected from the box.

After a couple fumbles, Virgil stuck the needle into one of his veins. He hit the box key again, and dark blood pushed its way out of the Grave Walker, through the tube, into Virgil.

The transfusion lasted an hour before the other crewmembers stumbled upon the scene. With each passing minute, each milliliter lost, Diane's world became looser, unanchored to the here and now. She stared at the wild pixels in her visor for so long that she began to see forms, shapes, objects. She could make out stars, then broken satellites, then Earth, all wheeling around her as she spun through outer space. Disoriented. Helpless. Alone.

So very alone.

CHAPTER 21

Virgil's meeting with the Pozo chief that night went great. Couldn't have gone better.

Hostilities from their first encounter were long forgotten, replaced with gleeful praise and hearty backslaps. The village would send technicians to fully revive the treatment plant tomorrow, but in the meantime, water was flowing into the reservoir. Pozo had been saved from the brink of extinction, and the heroes responsible could fill their water tanks, restock their Battery, and gather as many Nutribriks as they pleased. A deal was a deal, after all.

As he left the chief's quarters and stepped out into the cold Junkyard night, Virgil found a community in the midst of celebration. Townies skipped through the streets as water and vodka flowed, the liquids indistinguishable in their sloshing mason jars. Pre-Finale dance music rang out from the warehouses, with a woman's voice singing too fast for Virgil to keep up. Something about shaking your body, losing control, feeling a rhythm getting stronger. Lots of trumpets. Pozo celebrated the salvation that Virgil's crew had provided. This party was for them, but it was wasted on its guests of honor. None of them felt like celebrating. In fact, Virgil felt lower tonight than he had in a long time.

Rok was waiting for him outside the chief's quarters, watching the dancing townies without really seeing them.

"How's Diane?" he asked her.

Rok startled, caught off guard. She spoke quietly, a conspirator in a terrible crime. "I got her sitting by the reservoir, feeding the suit water. She needs water. You . . . you took too much."

Virgil grimaced at the comment, but his reaction paled in comparison to Rok's. She looked ready to vomit.

He approached with caution. "You good?"

"She won't talk to me. Won't say a word." Rok gnawed the inside of her cheek, emitting a gloom that made the music and celebration feel a million miles away. "She hates me now," she said. "I can feel it."

Virgil shook his head. "She doesn't hate you. It's just a bad time. She'll come around—"

"Will she?" Gage revealed himself leaning by the warehouse door, bright eyes lurking in the dark. "*Should* she?"

"Mind your damn business," Virgil warned.

Gage ignored him, speaking directly to Rok. "I'd expect shit like this from him, but you . . . You built the transfusion mod, didn't you?"

"He put me up to it," Rok said quietly. "It wasn't my call."

"Diane liked you. Like, really liked you. I could tell—"

"So what?" Virgil barked.

Gage fumed in silence.

"Huh?" Virgil pressed. "What does this have to do with the job?" He got in Gage's face, then Rok's. "None of this matters. Nothing's changed. You barely know her, anyway."

"I know what it's like to lose control of your body," Gage said, to which Virgil had no comeback. "And it sure feels like something's changed, *jefe.*"

Virgil watched the cyborg disappear into the party, and then he watched the revelers yapping, stumbling, and gyrating until he couldn't handle the discordance between them and himself any longer.

"Where's Ishmael?" he asked.

"Probably hiding in a cave somewhere," Rok said.

"So Diane's alone?"

The mechanic nodded, and Virgil patted her on the shoulder. "Get some food."

He jostled his way to the village reservoir. Pozo's guards kept the townies at bay, distributing water one bottle at a time. They let Virgil pass, of course. The heroes could go where they pleased.

The Grave Walker sat leaning against the reservoir's exterior, alone in the village's only empty corner. A hose ran from the container in her leg to the concrete pool, slurping water directly into the Grave Walker's filtration system. A miniature treatment plant. Rok's handiwork.

Virgil sat beside her, but Diane showed no recognition of his arrival. The shock to her system would have worn off by now, and the Grave Walker was designed to keep people moving no matter how much blood they lost. Still, she said nothing. The suit didn't move.

An awkward, time-stretching quiet passed between Diane and Virgil. One had nothing to say; the other didn't know where to begin. *Sorry* was not a junkie's area of expertise, but when the silence became unbearable, he took a stab.

"I'm type AB," he said. This would be more explanation than apology, but it was the best he could do. "That's why they sent me down from the mountain. I can take blood from anyone. Whenever I go home, I get a transfusion to reset my Battery itch. Everyone's clean up there. It's how I've stayed alive."

The Grave Walker kept still.

"But I've been away too long," Virgil lamented. "I was on my last legs. You knew I was on my last legs—"

"Do you feel better?" Diane asked.

The question made Virgil uneasy. He didn't like that he couldn't read her face when she asked it. He didn't like her flat, emotionless delivery. Most of all, he didn't like the answer. While she wallowed in a rut of depression and blood loss, he was back to huffing medium-grade Battery. He felt better than he had in years.

Diane moved on before he could reply. "Why didn't you tell me you needed my blood?"

Virgil shifted uncomfortably. "Come on. That's big leverage. I couldn't have you holding that over my head."

"You think I'd do that?" She looked to him then, her visor brightening with anger. "How broken are you?"

Virgil's face went hot. "Easy—"

"You're paranoid," Diane said, "and you're manipulative, and you hurt people."

"Calm down, all right? It was just a little blood—"

"No! It didn't have to be like this! You didn't need to . . . You could've . . . You could've just *asked*!"

The entire Grave Walker shook violently. Virgil readied the Volt Caster, but the suit fell still. The visor dimmed as Diane looked away.

"I'm an object to you," she said. "Another piece of junk."

"And what am I to you?" Virgil growled. "Your friend? Your babysitter? No. I'm a guy who has something you need, and you're using me just like I used you."

"It's not the same," Diane said.

"It is the same! We're a business transaction. Always have been. You didn't have to get in my trailer, but you did, and this was the price."

"You said the price was to protect you," Diane said. "I did that, and don't you dare act like I had a choice."

Virgil turned his back to her.

A communal chanting swelled behind them, timed to the beat of the music, and it paired strangely with the view ahead. No longer speaking, they stared out past the barbed-wire barricade at a Junkyard night as quiet and static as the Grave Walker. Nothing moved out there among the mesas. All was dead. Barren.

"Is the mountain real?" Diane asked eventually. "Or was it just a way to string me along?"

"It's real."

"You got a pretend wife too? Some pretend kids?"

"I can't have children. Too much high-grade Battery."

He bent down, leveling his face with the Grave Walker's helmet. "Everything I do, I do to protect my home. Doesn't matter if I'm proud of it. Doesn't matter who gets hurt."

"You're right," Diane said, her voice taking on that flatness again. "I don't matter. None of this matters."

The visor fell black, and Virgil could think of nothing more to say.

He left her sitting alone by the reservoir, too stubborn to admit his wrongdoing, too smart to fully believe he had done nothing wrong.

Back in the village proper, Pozo's cantina—a squat shack with an outdoor bar—was the eye of the celebratory storm. The townies wanted to dance the night away, so all drinks were ordered to go. The bar was mostly empty, serving only a few solitary souls, and Virgil claimed a spot at the end, far from everyone except the sleepy-eyed barkeep.

"Ah, the hero!" the old lady wheezed. "Get you some vodka, Mr. Hero?"

"Please and thanks," Virgil replied.

She poured him a shot, which he swallowed before the glass could hit the bar. It wasn't Caravan quality, but a few more rounds would get him where he needed to be.

He requested another, and the barkeep provided. As the second shot trickled down his throat, a voice he recognized spoke to him from the nearest barstool.

"Took your sweet time with those centipedes."

In his defense, Virgil hadn't been searching for any familiar faces when he approached the bar. But his guard wasn't exactly down, either. He always clocked the people in a space before he entered, profiling them, noting any potential threats. Virgil thought he had the crowd here all figured out, but when he looked to his right, there was Leon. This underhanded bastard was Wellington's top agent in the Junkyard; the invasion footage in Ms. Violet's office had come straight from his eyecam. Sitting there now beside Virgil, he was a complete revelation, yet his demeanor suggested he had been there all along. Watching the junkie. Holding all the cards.

Leon was an easy man to miss.

His frame was slender, his above-average height undercut by a tactical slouch, and he wore all black. Exclusively black. But when you took a closer look, and Virgil always did, Leon's otherness became apparent. His leather jacket was not scavenged; it was tailor-made. His right eye, half concealed behind dark bangs, glistened with a purple tint that only showed in the right lighting. It was a well-hidden augment, but its very subtlety made it conspicuous among the Junkyard's grungier cybernetics. It wasn't his only upgrade, either. A rip in his pants hinted at bionic legs so sleek and advanced that they instantly betrayed their origins: those legs were from Jericho.

"Getting slow in your old age?" Leon asked.

"How'd you know I was in Pozo?" Virgil said.

"You're driving around with a Reno escapee, a Shallows defector, a Grave Walker, and a tank. You're pretty easy to keep tabs on."

The crew had not passed any other travelers en route to Pozo. The road had been empty, and Virgil was at a loss to explain how Leon could have kept tabs on anyone. Where had the Wellington spies been hiding? In the toxic swamp? Among the centipede burrows? Ms. Violet's cunning never ceased to amaze.

"We've been tracking your movements for a while," Leon admitted, as if reading Virgil's thoughts, "ever since you pawned off that Peacekeeper head at Sacred Chapel. When I heard you and your crew were driving south from Caravan, I figured you'd stop here to refuel. I got in yesterday. Pretended to be a refugee from the Heap."

"You were here this whole time?" Virgil lowered his voice, consciously restraining it. "Why didn't you say anything? We had to fight a queen, for shit's sake."

"I had to know Ms. Violet put her confidence in the right people," Leon said. Cool as winter. Calm as death.

Virgil scoffed. "I was doing runs for Wellington back when you still had both eyes."

Virgil signaled to the barkeep, who poured him another shot. Leon took a sip from a tall glass of water.

"So you gonna brief me on the Heap situation?" Virgil drank the shot, hiccuped. "Or what?"

"Not yet," Leon said. "I need to make sure you're in this."

Virgil gritted his teeth. "*¿Qué demonios pasa?* Of course I'm in this!"

"Are you?" Leon rotated the glass in his hands. Right to left. Left to right. "You're binge drinking. Your team's moping around on different planets."

"We're fine," Virgil said, feeling anything but.

Leon glowered. "You're not focused. You're not prepared. You're not in this."

"I told Violet I'm in it, so I'm in it."

"You said you'd think about it." Leon straightened his posture, making himself unmissable. "Those were your last words to Ms. Violet. 'I'll think about it.'"

"Leon . . . why are you up my ass?"

The Wellington agent chugged the rest of his water without spilling a drop, and when he set the glass down, his lips were desert dry. Everything was precise with Leon. Nothing missed. Nothing ever out of place.

"You think I *want* to be out here?" he asked. "Sipping shit water in Garbage Land?"

Tipsy, Virgil giggled at the remark. "'Garbage Land' . . . ?"

"I can't go home without Dr. Isaac. And Ms. Violet—"

Leon caught himself, and Virgil knew why. He was about to speak ill of his employer, who had a direct line to everything he saw and heard via satellite uplink. There was no way to know when Ms. Violet might be listening, when her finger might be hovering over a kill switch command. That was why Virgil only worked freelance; the Wellington payroll came with dangerous fine print.

"Ms. Violet, in all her infinite wisdom," Leon adjusted, "wants you to spring Isaac loose."

"Which I will," Virgil said.

"This isn't a bug hunt, junkie. You haven't seen the Messenger. You don't know what he can do."

"Violet showed me your little home video. Messenger doesn't look so bad—"

"That footage is nothing. Not even a taste."

The barkeep crossed in front of a lamp while serving another patron, and during the brief eclipse, Leon's right eye shone like an alien star.

"There's something . . . wrong with him," he confided. "The way he moves, talks, gets roadkillers and mercenaries eating out of his hand . . . It's unnatural."

Virgil was struck by the company man's words. He had brushed shoulders with Leon for half a decade and had never heard him talk like this. Leon measured everything by Jericho standards, and the Junkyard always came up short. Out here, Leon boasted the shiniest bionics, the most powerful connections, and he was the best and final marksman his victims ever saw. Nothing in the Junkyard ever intimidated him. Not before now, it seemed. Not before the Messenger.

Virgil understood the gravity of this observation, but he ignored it out of spite. "It's the Junkyard, Leon. Everything's unnatural."

When he moved to signal the barkeep, Leon grabbed his wrist and held it down.

"If you half-ass this job," he said, "you and your crew will die. And you will seriously inconvenience me."

Virgil tore his hand away and finished hailing his next shot.

"One last time," Leon said. "Are you in this?"

The fourth drink came and went.

"Until the end," Virgil replied.

Leon departed then, off to acquire the night of sleep that Virgil should have pursued for himself. Instead, the junkie remained at the bar to drink his thoughts away, muttering about the distant home he was fighting for.

"Dogs barking, wrestling, playing. Cold beer frothing. Úna's smile. Bright. Warm. It makes everything okay."

The things he had done, and the things he had yet to do, all were in service of home. He would bring Diane home, and that would make everything better between them. All of this would feel like a bad dream, and they would dance like Pozo was dancing now. Happy, carefree, leaving the worst behind them. They would dance under cloudless skies, bathing in unfiltered moonlight. They would fill their lungs with the cleanest air, stomp their feet on the softest grass.

Diane would be happy there, and everything would be okay.

Virgil would keep his word. Everything would be okay.

CHAPTER 22

Around midnight, Diane felt a diffident presence lingering beside her. She made no effort to determine its identity; all she wanted was to be left alone. The mysterious visitor stood in silence by the reservoir for a long while, but when a jovial cheer rose from the townies behind them, he finally spoke.

"This village is so different from the place I was born."

It was Ishmael, and even in the fog of depression, Diane was startled to find him in her company. He had said nothing when the crew learned of Virgil's actions, disappearing soon after they returned to Pozo. She had figured her tragedy was the last thing on his mind.

"In the Shallows, our faith was everything," he said, contemplating something in the northwest that Diane couldn't see. "The high priest was our master, our link to Those Who Dwell Below. On his orders, we twisted our minds and mutilated our bodies. Things like dancing were forbidden. Sin was punishable by torture. Doubt was punishable by death."

Diane kept quiet, but no longer out of malaise. This was the most she had ever heard Ishmael speak, and she wasn't about to risk scaring him away. His tale of home disturbed and enthralled her. At the very least, it distracted from her own problems.

"But I never complained," Ishmael said. "I let the ink into my skin and the Master into my soul. The Shallows was the only home I had ever known. Those people . . . they were my family."

His voice dropped to a whisper, so quiet the Grave Walker had to enhance the volume.

"And I believed in the Deep. I believed in everything."

He leaned back against the reservoir. "But there was one ritual . . . we called it the Trial. The Master would choose one of us to meet with our gods in their domain. If the chosen one returned from the ocean alive, and sane, they would become a priest, a leader in our community. I saw many people enter the cage. Not one came out alive."

Through her night vision, Diane caught the abject horror in Ishmael's tattooed face. She thought she had seen the worst the Junkyard had to offer. He had seen so much more.

"Then I was chosen for the Trial. I tried to be brave, to have faith . . ."

He stood urgently, speaking fast, moving his face inches from Diane's visor.

"I do not know what pact you have made with Virgil, but you are your own master. Your life is your own, and if someone tries to tell you differently . . ." He looked back to the northwest, as if checking for some distant eavesdropper. "You owe him nothing."

Ishmael hurried away, leaving Diane alone to process the odd encounter. His tale mingled strangely with her sadness and exhaustion, and as sleep wrapped its tentacles around her mind, she became fixated on the image of a shark cage dipping into the sea. She witnessed the scene as if from behind bars, until the icy waterline rose above her head. Then she was blind.

Diane couldn't see *Cradle*'s residents in her dream that night, but she knew they were present. She knew they were gathered on the beach, along a wooden pier, staring into the ocean.

She knew, in her heart of hearts, they were all watching her drown.

CHAPTER 23

Leon drove a black convertible with a brand-new Wellington engine, hood-mounted plasma guns, and gyroscopic tires. He led the crew out of Pozo, and to everyone else's chagrin, Virgil had no objections. But Virgil was deathly hungover and could barely focus on steering, much less leading. Ishmael stayed close this time as they navigated the southbound roads, while Gage and Rok displayed an open mistrust toward Leon every chance they got. They didn't care if his employer was technically the same as theirs; you never took your eyes off a company man. That was a surefire way to get stabbed in the back.

They spoke very little during the ride, except for Diane, who didn't speak at all. She had boarded Virgil's trailer without objection, going through the motions on autopilot, too mentally exhausted to conceive a better path than the one she was already on. She would talk to no one, and the others were left to speculate what tragic notions clouded the Grave Walker's blank visor.

Radio silence prevailed for most of the morning, each crew member alone with their personal demons, until—

"*Prepare for uneven terrain*," Leon reported.

He had reached the top of a steep hillock in the road, and when the others caught up, even Diane roused from her catatonia. There was no ignoring this spectacle.

They had come to the final resting place of a metal giant, half buried under centuries of sand. Body parts jutted from the ground like rock formations, redefining the landscape, turning flat desert into a hamada of mangled iron. A crooked finger here. A broken limb there. Pinkies taller than houses. Arms longer than life. The battlemech's head, fissured with an ancient wound resembling a mouth in a grimace, gazed up at the noxious sky with black-hole eyes. The distance from toe to head spanned a mile at least. The travelers were ants crawling over a shallow grave.

Like always, Diane had so many questions. Virgil owed her three for the day, and Rok would have happily answered the rest. But whenever she tried to speak, the Grave Walker's left arm began to tremble, and a Molotov cocktail of fury and heartbreak blasted her cerebrum into silence. She kept her questions to herself.

They evaded most of the body parts with ease until they reached a severed leg intersecting the road. A tear in the kneecap offered passage into the hollowed limb, and a white sliver of light implied an opening on the other side. Circumventing the leg would take them into a minefield of tire-ripping shrapnel, so they chose to pass through. The drivers' eyes were limited to their headlights while traversing the tunnel, but thanks to the Grave Walker's night vision, Diane could see clear as day. She alone bore witness to the leg's inner workings, the complex mechanisms that would have allowed a limb this size to walk. It must have taken years to build. Years of dangerous labor, an unfathomable resource drain, all in the name of . . . what, exactly? What had this giant died for? No one knew, and no one seemed to care.

"*Shit.*"

Leon was the first to emerge out the leg's other side, the first to see what made everyone else slam on their brakes. A tribe of Peacekeepers, eight times the crew's size, blocked the path ahead. Mostly argonauts, a few reapers, one strongman. They traveled on foot, forming a dense mob around a six-wheeled rover drone. They were marching north, straight for the crew.

Leon drew one of his Deckard pistols.

"Wait," Virgil said. His first command of the day.

The Peacekeepers came to a halt twenty or so yards up the road, same as their human counterparts. They did not open fire as Leon expected, and a closer look at their ranks explained why. These machines were beaten to hell. Dented armor. Missing limbs. This tribe was literally on its last legs, survivors of an ordeal known only to their memory banks, and they had no desire to join their titan brother beneath the sand. They were on a journey of their own, and that journey was not yet complete.

Wind howled through the gorge as the two camps stared each other down. There were no diplomats present, so talking was out of the question. Action would be the common language, and Virgil knew from experience to let the Peacekeepers make the first move.

Eventually, one argonaut chirped and walked off the road, content with going around the long way. The rest of the tribe accepted this directive, and they trailed close behind.

Everyone relaxed until they saw the rover drone's cargo.

Rok shot out from the tank's hatch. "That's a tier five!"

The biggest StormCell Diane had ever seen rode on the six-wheeler's back. Wide as Rok's tank, its rim glistened and pulsed with enough fusion energy to power a village for years. The nearest argonauts kept their hands on the tier five, assuring that it wouldn't fall off the drone. This was their treasure, the boon of their journey and likely the source of their hardship. Gage practically salivated as he watched the Storm-Cell pass. It was worth a fortune.

"We're letting some good junk pass by," he called to his crewmates.

"The tribe looks pretty beaten down," Rok said. "I've got an EMP emitter that could knock most of them flat for a while."

"They're not the job," Leon objected.

"And you're not our *jefe*," Gage said, and then looked to Virgil. Everyone did.

Diane could not predict how the old junkie would respond. The promise of a tier-five StormCell was the whole point of this job, the payment due to him after their mission against the Messenger. A tier-five StormCell was the only reason he was out fighting centipedes and not back home. Swiping this one now would save him a lot of time, and a lot of risk, but it wouldn't sit well with Ms. Violet. She would be watching him through her proxy, and one wrong move could burn his Wellington bridge forever. Virgil stood at a crossroads of terrible risks and great rewards, and after a pause, during which Diane imagined him peering down each road as far as his mind's eye could see, he made a call.

"We don't need any more trouble. Let 'em pass."

Rok and Gage moaned. Leon nodded with approval.

"Wise decision," Ishmael said.

When the last Peacekeeper stepped off the road, Virgil put his jeep in drive.

"Come on," he said, "let's keep—"

An ion missile struck the road. The explosion tore the last Peacekeeper in line to shreds, pelting the vehicles with burned metal and asphalt.

"¡*N'ombre*!" Rok shrieked, falling back down into the hatch of her tank.

More missiles came, whistling from every direction, blasting at Peacekeepers and humans alike. Everyone scattered in the violent confusion, and the radio in Diane's helmet blared with screams and conflicting orders. Virgil doubled back to take shelter inside the giant's leg, but before the others could follow, a missile struck the metal thigh and sealed the entrance behind him with rubble. The cave-in didn't stop there, and Virgil barely escaped through the tunnel and out the knee before the entire hollow collapsed.

Now back at the iron hamada, Virgil and Diane watched as soldiers fell upon the giant's grave: an allied legion of roadkillers and argonaut Peacekeepers, their numbers indeterminable in the chaos, all wearing bloody bandages around their heads and wielding machetes and arm cannons, plasma rifles and ion rocket launchers. They charged from every direction, riding four-wheelers and pickup trucks, flanking the giant from all sides.

"*Idiots!*" Leon screamed over the radio. "*The Messenger knew you were coming!*"

"*They're not here for us!*" Virgil shouted back. The tribe had found a different path through the leg farther down, and the Peacekeepers now guided their rover to the other side of the hamada. Most of the bandaged warriors focused their assault on them. "*They want the StormCell!*"

The tribe fanned out in a counterattack, and the battle spread like wildfire. Ion smoke flooded the area in a stifling fog, and Diane couldn't see two feet past her own visor. Plasma shots zipped from every direction. Battle cries grappled with digitized chirps. Diane felt like she was caught in a bloodthirsty hurricane, and terror compelled her to speak.

"What do we do?" she yelled.

"Hang on!" Virgil cried. He swerved off the road, mere seconds before a missile obliterated their would-be path. He forged ahead over unpaved ground, dodging shrapnel and giant machine parts as best he could.

"*Virgil!*" Ishmael radioed. "*Where are you?*"

"*I can't find anybody!*" That was Rok.

Virgil caught sight of a skull-shaped silhouette looming in the battle fog, and he made another call: "*Everyone take cover in the head!*"

He took a sharp turn for the distant cranium. Diane's trailer whipped behind him.

"*Hear me?*" Virgil shouted. "*Get to the head—*"

Another missile exploded nearby. The shock wave spun the trailer at a ninety-degree angle, and while the chain held, the railing snapped off in Diane's hands. The Grave Walker sailed into the air.

"No!" Virgil screamed.

"Virgil—!" Diane landed on the giant's belly. The oxidized metal crumbled beneath her weight, and she dropped into the yawning depths of a buried abdominal cavity, somersaulting out of sight.

Her fall created a ripple effect that shifted the earth between the giant's ribs. The once stable terrain undulated wildly, forcing Virgil to seek more secure ground.

Distance weakened the radio signal from Diane's helmet, silencing her cries for help.

CHAPTER 24

Back when the first missile hit and the vehicles dispersed in a mad dash for self-preservation, Ishmael had caught glimpse of Virgil and Diane seconds before their jeep disappeared into the giant's leg. He had accelerated in pursuit, but the entrance collapsed before he could follow. He had been forced to take the long way around, and by the time he finally circumvented the great battlemech's foot, the hamada was lost in the ever-thickening smoke of combat.

He is gone, the Master jeered. *All was for naught. You have failed.*

"*Virgil!*" Ishmael called into his radio. "*Where are you?*"

"*I can't find anybody!*" Rok piped in.

"*Everyone take cover in the head!*" Virgil barked. "*Hear me? Get to the head—*"

A loud *boom* filled the CB channel, and then Virgil's line went dead.

Frantically, Ishmael surveyed the battlefield for any trace of his employer. The fog offered no clues as to the old junkie's fate, but Ishmael could see the giant head in the distance, crowning just above the haze. If he wanted to find Virgil alive, his best bet was to go there.

Ishmael drove forward.

He ducked and weaved through someone else's fight, passing pockets of conflict that jumped out from the smoke—a reaper hacking off a roadkiller's head, two argonauts smashing each other to bits—only to vanish as quickly as they'd come. Ishmael pushed his motorbike to the limit evading these scenes, and he soon realized he wasn't the only one running the obstacle course. A bluish glow kept pace beside him, moving parallel to the motorbike not three yards away. As the gap between them narrowed, Ishmael realized it was Gage, pushing his enhanced reflexes to their maximum potential. The two junkies shared the briefest of weary glances, but when they looked forward again, they both witnessed something odd rolling into their path.

It was a clunky cylinder of wires, electrodes, flashing yellow lights. At first, Ishmael mistook the device for some kind of bomb. Then Gage screamed the truth:

"EMP!"

The lights on the cylindrical EMP emitter turned red, and a high buzzing filled the air. Ishmael's motorbike died, bucking him forward like a traitorous steed. He landed on a merciful patch of soft earth, battered but unbroken, and he gawked up in time to see Gage tumble into a ditch that, upon closer inspection, Ishmael saw was actually the cupped palm of a great mechanical hand. The cyborg's arms and legs had gone rag doll; Gage's deactivated eyes were dull gray.

Ishmael heard two sets of feet approaching the cyborg.

"Long time no see," a voice slurped, muffled behind leather.

"We've been tracking you for days, junkhead," a woman added, her words bungled from abnormally large teeth.

Gage groaned. "You've got to be shitting me."

The two voices cackled like hyenas.

Pulling himself forward, Ishmael recognized the junkies standing over Gage's blind, paralyzed body. Around Caravan, they were nicknamed Gimp and Dentures.

"We'll get a nice payday off you," Dentures said, then to Gimp: "Watch our backs."

Gimp climbed back out of the ditch and took up the watch, and Ishmael rolled away from their field of view. He considered sneaking off to find Virgil; protecting Gage wasn't his mission, after all, and taking on these two deviants would be more trouble than it was worth.

For once, the Master voiced his support.

The cyborg reeks of sin. Behold its body, a desperate bid to defy the natural order. The cyborg is a bastard child of the Old Ways. The cyborg is damned.

But try as he might, Ishmael couldn't pull himself away as Dentures turned Gage onto his back, arranging his limbs spread-eagle. The cyborg looked like a toy in the hands of a cruel toddler. Something about it made Ishmael feel sick.

"You're crazy," Gage said to his captor.

"No we ain't," Dentures said, rummaging through a toolbox.

"What would you call this then?" Gage asked. "Business as usual?"

Dentures leaned closer to Gage's face. "Justice. Justice for Belle."

Though Gage and Dentures didn't know it, they had just put themselves on trial.

Ishmael had spent many Junkyard nights plotting his imaginary return to the Shallows, planning his revenge on the Master with meticulous detail. He knew so little about Gage's life prior to their meeting, and if Dentures had legitimate reason to exact vengeance, Ishmael wouldn't deny her that justice.

He crouched on the foggy rim of the giant's hand, judging all that he heard.

"I didn't do anything to Belle," Gage swore.

"You stabbed her in the back," Dentures said. "You left her to die."

"No! You don't know what happened! You weren't there!"

"Neither were you."

Dentures raised a laser saw out of the toolbox, and Gage's mouth trembled at the sound of its telltale hiss. Every cyborg's worst nightmare.

"Wait . . ." Gage said.

Dentures didn't wait. The hiss grew louder as the laser saw lowered toward its prey.

"Just wait a second!"

The saw hovered above his right shoulder, over the bionic seam between metal and flesh. Amputation was imminent.

"*It was the Chimera!*" Gage shouted.

The energy tool froze, neither rising nor lowering.

"It wasn't roadkillers," Gage said. "It was the Chimera. It killed Belle. It followed me back to the village and killed all the townies. It would have killed me. I know how it sounds, but I swear. There was nothing I could do. Nothing anybody could've done."

Gage held his breath. Dentures paused to consider the explanation. So did Ishmael.

As detached as he was from Junkyard gossip, even Ishmael had heard of the Chimera. It wasn't like Crybaby or the Pest, Tower or the Babel Virus—Relics that affected the world in tangible and undeniable ways. The Chimera was the scourge of bedtime stories, devourer of all Junkyard settlements that disappeared without explanation. It was a folktale, an impossibility in a world of impossibilities. No surprise that Gage kept his story a secret until now. Who would believe him?

"The Chimera ain't real," Dentures said, and then her saw continued its downward course.

Milliseconds before the laser made contact, Ishmael came to a verdict. He had seen plenty of strange things in his time by the sea; who was he to deny one more monster's existence?

He shot his harpoon at the EMP emitter. It punctured the cylinder, making a mess of its inner workings.

Gage's eyes filled with light. Dentures turned with a start. She frowned at the harpoon head. "What in the—"

Gage ejected his forearm blades and lashed upward. Dentures's artificial teeth went sailing, along with most of her jaw. She fell back, gurgling blood, taking the laser tool down with her.

"¡*Maldita sea*!" Gimp shouted.

As Gimp ran toward Gage, Ishmael opened his fist. The harpoon head withdrew from the EMP emitter, catching and slashing Gimp's leg on its way back to the gauntlet. Gimp toppled over onto their dying crewmate, and the laser saw burned into their belly, through their spine, out their back.

Gage climbed out of the ditch. Ishmael was waiting.

"Don't tell the others about this," the cyborg pleaded. "Okay?"

Ishmael went to leave, but Gage grabbed his arm. "We have to find Diane. I saw her fall off the trailer."

Some trace emotion passed over Ishmael, but he quickly repressed it. "The suit will protect her."

"Maybe," Gage said, "but what if she can't find her way back to us?"

"Maybe she is better off without us." Ishmael pulled away, jogging off toward the head's foggy shadow.

"What's that supposed to mean?" Gage yelled after him.

Ishmael didn't look back.

CHAPTER 25

Though Virgil had been the first crewmember to spot the giant's head, he was the third to reach it. His flight from the seismic disturbance had forced him on a roundabout path, and the surrounding battle only delayed him further. By the time his jeep passed through the skull's grimacing fissure, Rok's tank and Leon's convertible were already parked inside.

Immediately upon entry, Virgil's jeep died. The engine, the dash meters, everything. Even the Volt Caster went dark. He might have panicked then, but the mystery behind the blackout was short-lived: Rok's tank glowed and crackled with static electricity, and Peacekeepers from both factions—the tribe and the Messenger's army—lay deactivated across the ground in a wide radius. Rok must have rigged her tank with an EMP emitter, modified to have a larger area of effect than the portable devices used by most junkies. Nearby, Leon sat awkwardly behind the wheel of his car. In range of the EMP, his fancy Wellington legs couldn't move a robotic muscle.

Virgil hopped out of the useless jeep, and Rok greeted him with frantic rambling. "You're alive! Did you see Gage? I think he ran off in time, I don't know. I don't know—"

Virgil cut her off. "Did Diane make it here?"

Rok saw the trailer, empty and lopsided. Her look of horror answered the question.

"This is unbelievable," Leon bellyached. "If you'd handled those centipedes faster, we could've left Pozo yesterday."

Virgil drew his magnum and headed back for the fissure.

"Where the hell are you going?" Leon asked, bewildered.

"Diane's still out there," Virgil said.

"Who cares?"

The junkie whipped around like a dog whose tail had just been pulled. "I care, *cabrón!*"

Leon raised a brow, more intrigued than intimidated.

Virgil turned again to leave, only to find a tattooed wall named Ishmael standing in his way.

"You are alive," Ishmael said, not with joy or relief. Merely stating a fact.

"Come on," Virgil said. "We're going out for Diane—"

He moved to leave, but Ishmael shoved him back with one firm hand. Virgil stiffened, more confused than angry at first. Rok and Leon both went very quiet.

"What is this?" Virgil said.

"You are staying here," Ishmael replied.

That's when the anger caught up with Virgil. "You forget who's *jefe?*"

Ishmael stayed put. "I have no *jefe.*"

"Like hell you don't." Virgil tried to pass again, and the second shove nearly put him on his ass.

"You hired me to keep you alive," Ishmael said. "If I let you go out there, you will die."

"Let me by!"

Furious, Virgil swung his dead Volt Caster like a club. Ishmael dodged the attack, retaliating only with a forceful palm to Virgil's chest. This time, Virgil tripped over a downed argonaut and joined the Peacekeepers on the ground.

He pointed the magnum at Ishmael's head. "Fish-faced *freak!*"

When Ishmael didn't move, and Virgil's finger didn't leave the trigger, Rok hurried in to de-escalate.

"Diane's in a Grave Walker," she said to Virgil. "You'll die out there before she does."

The gun's aim wavered.

"She'll be okay," Rok promised. "Don't do anything stupid."

Leon's right eye glimmered. "What's the girl to you?"

Virgil didn't respond. He didn't dare. Not with Ms. Violet listening in.

CHAPTER 26

Something clicked inside the Grave Walker's helmet, and Diane drifted back into consciousness. Her visor looked undamaged; the HUD showed all systems operational; the only problem in the suit was her. A throbbing pain squeezed her forehead, and it hurt to think. If she couldn't think, she couldn't move. If she didn't move, she would likely die.

The suit knew this, and it set to work. Osmotic agents pumped through the tubes drilled into Diane's body. Electric currents flowed through specific needles around her head. The pain from the concussion vanished, and Diane was back to her numb, incorporeal self.

She sat up. The giant's abdominal cavity was enormous, roughly the size of the antechamber where she first met Crybaby. Smoky daylight shone through a hole overhead, but that light barely reached the vertebral column. Much was lost in darkness. The suit's night vision would only engage if Diane ventured out of the sun.

"Virgil?" she called. The helmet's radio emitted only static. No signal in the belly of the machine. "Anybody?"

Someone spoke to her then, but not from the radio. The words came from outside. From the dark. "*Grave Walker.*"

Diane yelped. "Who's there?"

Her call echoed off the abdominal walls. No answer came.

"Come out!" she demanded.

Something moved in the shadows, something heavy and fearless. Diane zoomed her visor toward the sound.

A man stepped into the light.

His face was almost perfect. Flawless complexion, symmetrical bone structure, hairless yet ageless—he was beautiful, and it gave him a distinctly inhuman quality that his muscular frame and tranquil smile only served to intensify. Wearing a sleeveless coat and tattered pants, he walked barefoot over glass and metal without shedding a drop of blood. His left arm and hand were wrapped in dirty white bandages, and at the sight of them, Diane realized she had seen this man before. He looked so different without the mask.

"You . . ." she breathed.

"Yes," the Messenger said. "Me."

He came toward her slowly, but with all the unstoppable power of the queen centipede. Debris crunched and scattered at his feet, and he never blinked. Never stopped smiling.

"I can only imagine what you've heard about me," he said. "The Witch behind the Wall, the Old Man, what have they told you?"

Diane scooted backward. The Messenger halted, laughing heartily. "I won't hurt you, Grave Walker. I'm a friend."

"My name's Diane," Diane said, "and they say . . ." Thinking back, she recalled Virgil's pitch to Rok on Caravan. One detail stuck out. "They say you turn people into slaves."

"¡*Hipócritas*!" The Messenger threw back his head and laughed again. He spoke like the passengers on Caravan. "They lie, Diane! I don't want *esclavos*. I never have."

There was such a lightness to him, a charismatic warmth that contradicted all the horrible things Diane thought she knew. His voice was deep and rich, underlined with a subliminal musicality. Maybe her concussion was to blame, but Diane felt her fear beginning to dissipate. She felt brave enough to engage.

"What do you want?" she asked.

His reply was simple, and quick. "Peace."

An ion grenade exploded overhead, raining fresh debris into the abdominal cavity. Diane guarded her visor with one hand, while the Messenger put up no defense. He let the soot fall over his face and body, painting him gray. He seemed not to notice.

"Then why do you keep starting fights?" Diane asked.

"To demand peace, you must first establish authority," the Messenger said. "Authority's in short supply these days. You've seen it. You've been down here long enough."

Diane blinked. Down where? In the giant's belly? In the southern Junkyard?

The Messenger clarified, as if he could read her mind. "How far *Cradle* fell, eh?"

Impossible. Diane could barely speak. "You . . . know about—"

"I know that last week, you lived in a heaven above this wretched planet. You breathed clean air. You felt safe." The Messenger's smile faded. "I know something went wrong. The clouds parted. Your *paraíso* came crashing down, and now you're trapped with people you cannot trust, in a battle you know nothing about, against a foe who never meant you any harm."

He took a knee, and Diane saw that his irises were little more than extensions of his pupils. Totally black.

"Why do you ride with junkies?" he asked. "Why put your life in their greedy hands?"

The Messenger had recounted her plight to the letter, hypnotizing her battered brain into candidness.

"Dr. Isaac," she answered.

"What about him?"

"He can free me."

The Messenger's smile returned. "You want out of the suit?"

"Yes."

"Then we want the same thing."

Diane gasped, but not with joy or relief. She knew this routine, had played the victim in it. *Fool me once . . .*

"Why?" She stood up. "Why would you care about me?"

The Messenger stood as well. His head came to the Grave Walker's chin. "It's easier if I show you."

"No! I am *done* being used!" Diane planted herself in a combat stance. She would not be the cog in a strange man's machinations. Not again.

Still grinning, the Messenger flexed his bandaged arm, and a ring of soldiers materialized from the darkness around them. A ring of missile launchers, plasma rifles, and argonaut arm cannons all pointed at the Grave Walker's helmet, all waiting for the signal to fire.

"Do you believe in destiny, Diane?" the Messenger asked.

Diane tried and failed to count the enemies around her. How many rockets could the Grave Walker take? Had stomping roaches and centipedes prepared her for a real fight, on her own? She didn't know. She just couldn't know.

"I do," he continued. "It speaks to me. Calls to me. Every day."

He put his wrapped hand on Diane's shoulder, and despite the layers of titanium alloy between them, she could feel its heaviness weighing her down. A punch from that hand could do real damage, maybe even to the Grave Walker. The soldiers became the least of her worries, and her remaining courage evaporated on the spot.

"Let me take you to Dr. Isaac," the Messenger coaxed. "Let me show you what we've built together. Then you'll understand why I care about you. And I do care, Diane. I care very much."

His bandaged fingers twitched, and a soldier broke from the circle to place an object in his unwrapped right hand.

"The Old Man will fail. His kind always does. Stay with him, and you'll die in that suit. Come with me, and I'll free you from your shackles. I'll keep you safe."

He secured the object over his face, and Diane recoiled in disgust. The Messenger's persuasion strategy was twofold. With his words, he promised her everything she wanted, but with his mask—that barbaric amalgamation of metal and dead flesh—he issued a threat. To disobey the man was to face the monster. Succumb to his charm, or face the savagery.

The Masked Man walked away, and the soldiers behind Diane marched forward. The implication was clear. Time to follow the leader.

"Destiny brought you this far," the Messenger called back. "Why stop now?"

Much later, Diane would blame the Grave Walker for moving her forward, reacting to a subconscious fear before she could act herself. But in truth, Diane and the Grave Walker were in lockstep, both heeding a survival instinct that knew this was no time to pick a fight.

If she wanted to find Dr. Isaac behind enemy lines, this would be the safest way to do it.

CHAPTER 27

Hours later, the shooting stopped. The engines quieted. Smoke began to thin.

"Diane!"

Virgil bolted from the giant's head, galloping over broken bodies and mangled machines that meant nothing to him because they weren't her. Though his crewmates protested, he paid no mind to his surroundings, to any threats that could be lingering in the haze. His own safety, what his death would mean for the secret community that depended on him, these were distant concerns. All he could think about was finding Diane, making sure she was okay, saying all the things he should've said to apologize to her in Pozo.

A self-loathing shadowed his concern, directed at the fact that he felt concerned at all. So what if he pulled one over on the kid? What's done was done. She had fulfilled her purpose, and he couldn't afford to dwell on it. Yet here was, dwelling up a storm. This wasn't him. He never let a guilty conscience cloud the big picture.

Damn it, how did this happen? Why did Diane have to be so . . . Diane?

At the edge of the sternum-pit, he called her name again. Only his echo responded.

"Oh no," he heard Rok say.

The others had chased him onto the battlefield, and now Rok stood on a huge knuckle mounding from the sand, looking off into the distance. Virgil joined her on the rusty hill. He saw what she saw.

The Messenger's raiding party was driving away on the southbound road. The bandaged soldiers had claimed the rover drone and its precious tier-five cargo, but that wasn't all they'd stolen. Even from a distance, Virgil could spot the Grave Walker sitting beside the giant StormCell, getting smaller and smaller with each passing second.

"Why?" Virgil moaned, then he started screaming. "Why her? Why are they taking her?" He hurried back to the giant's head.

"Don't be stupid," Leon called.

The junkie ignored him, and when Ishmael began to approach, Virgil pointed the now-functioning Volt Caster at his tattooed face.

"You stay the fuck away from me," Virgil said, and the look in his eye told Ishmael not to argue. Not this time.

On bionic feet, Leon quickly caught up. "Stop."

"I'm getting her back," Virgil said, nearing the jeep.

"You're outnumbered. They'll blow you to pieces, and she'll get to watch."

Virgil opened the driver's door but stopped just short of getting in. He was so rarely the one with questions.

"What does he want with her?" Virgil asked. "You've been to the Heap. What is he doing? What does he *want*?"

"All I know for sure is that Diane's alive. She's alive, and she's going to the same place we are. We can get her back, but we have to be smart."

Logic dampened Virgil's bullheaded resolve, and his fire began to extinguish.

"Be *smart*," Leon repeated.

Just as tensions between them were dying down, a sudden force knocked Virgil and Leon off their feet. It was Ishmael, tackling Virgil—and Leon by proximity—seconds before a plasma bolt struck the cranium wall behind them.

"Time to go!" Rok yelled. "Go go go go go!"

She dove into the battle tank. Steam wafted up from beneath its armor, the result of an overheated EMP emitter. Until it cooled, blasting out another EMP pulse was no longer a viable defense.

Outside, the remnants of the Peacekeeper tribe were emerging from cover, digging themselves out of rubble, sprouting from the ground like zombies. Twenty able-bodied argonauts remained, plus the strongman—which unleashed a gut-shaking howl that told the humans exactly what it meant to do. The battle had been lost. Their treasure had been stolen, and someone needed to pay. Their combat protocol demanded a target.

"Yup. Time to go," Virgil confirmed.

Rok blasted a new hole in the giant's head, and the crew fled from the Peacekeepers' wrath. As they neared the limits of the hamada, Gage jumped out from hiding and took his place on the back of Rok's tank.

"Everything sucks!" he shouted. The sentiment was shared by all.

They drove east across the open desert, and the Peacekeepers followed. The tireless argonauts could run fast enough to keep pace, and every bounding stride brought the strongman a step closer to ending the hunt. The vehicles and the Peacekeepers ran on the same Storm-Cells, and the entire race came down to a simple factor: Whose power supply would deplete first? Virgil cast a nervous glance at his dashboard meter. It was down to half, and he imagined Rok's EMP had dropped the tank's power even lower. She and Leon fired plasma shots behind them as best they could, but the argonauts dodged the panic fire easily. They were built for this.

"*We can't keep this up!*" Leon shouted over the radio.

"*Yeah, no shit!*" Rok replied. "*So what do we do?*"

Virgil checked the desert around them. Miles to the northeast, a thin structure barely rose above the horizon. It was too short to be a Conductor, too tall and sturdy to be a post-Finale structure. From this distance, there was no way to know what the building really was, or who it might belong to, but those were the least of their worries right now. One problem at a time.

"*We need to find cover!*" Virgil radioed. "*Follow me!*"

He led the crew in a wide northbound turn. The change in direction only seemed to fuel the Peacekeepers' urgency, and the argonauts somehow accelerated their maximum speeds. The strongman was getting closer all the time.

Many desperate miles later, the crew finally saw their destination in full. The structure Virgil had spotted was the temperature control unit of a concrete dam. Cracked and crescent-shaped, its turbines long dead, the great hydropower facility bridged the walls of a deep canyon where the river had dried up ages ago. A covered traffic tunnel lined the dam's crest, feeding seamlessly into the sunbaked road, and its blast-proof doors hung wide open. Shelter was theirs, if they could live long enough to reach it.

As Virgil led the team forward at full speed, Gage jumped off the tank and threw himself into the jeep's front seat.

"We can't go this way!" Gage cried.

Virgil could barely hear him over the wind, and what he heard didn't make a lot of sense.

"The Chimera!" Gage said. "The Chimera is here!"

"Chimera?" Virgil shouted. "Are you outta your damn mind?"

He slowed a little behind the others, but when he didn't stop, Gage bailed out of the jeep, running away from the dam as fast as his legs would take him. A few argonauts broke off in pursuit, but not enough to justify the desertion.

"*Where's he going?*" Rok asked.

"*No idea!*" Virgil said.

Virgil wondered then if hiring Gage had been a mistake. Twice now the cyborg had abandoned his crew, running toward danger or away from safety. He had figured Ishmael would be the one to watch out for, but this job had been full of surprises. Terrible, pain-in-the-*culo* surprises.

But Virgil had little time to dwell. As the vehicles reached the entrance ramp onto the dam's crest, forcing them in a single-file line, the howling strongman came within pinching range of the jeep's trailer. The strongman lashed out, barely missing it.

"*Detach the trailer!*" Leon called.

Virgil wouldn't. The strongman reached out again, nicking the trailer's edge.

"*It's going to pull you back!*" Leon said. "*Let it go!*"

Virgil couldn't. *Where would Diane sit?*

The strongman took a mighty leap forward . . .

"*Virgil!*"

Rok's tank launched an ion missile at a nearby rock wall. Boulders showered from the blast, pummeling down onto the ramp in a devastating sleet. The crew's vehicles cleared the avalanche just in time, but the strongman did not. A jagged rock struck the Peacekeeper's head, shattering its ocular lens and sending it wailing down into the canyon. More boulders piled onto the ramp in a great pulverulent wall, one that not even the argonauts could pass.

"*Good looking out!*" Virgil yelled to Rok.

"*Yeah, yeah,*" she replied. "*How you've lived this long, I'll never know.*"

Her comment struck Virgil with an unexpected sadness. Back in the sewers of Jericho, Diane had made a similar observation.

The crew raced into the narrow traffic tunnel. After they parked, Virgil and Ishmael rushed to seal the blast doors behind them.

"What about Gage?" Rok said.

Virgil groaned against the door's weight. "He made a call. He's on his own."

The barrier slammed shut, and when its echo faded, the only sounds came from the Peacekeepers outside. The argonauts were firing on the dam's exterior; their plasma shots splattered harmlessly against the concrete.

The crew turned around to observe the small fleet of abandoned vehicles filling the traffic tunnel before them, some marred with dark burn marks but otherwise untouched. Nobody, or bodies, in sight.

"Rok . . ." Virgil began.

"Way ahead of you." Rok pulled out her radar console, watching the white rings carefully. Nothing appeared. "Looks like we're alone."

Virgil leaned back against the entrance gate, his exhaustion finally catching up with him. He sighed heavily as Leon approached.

"When can we move out?" Leon asked.

"When the argonauts tire themselves out," Virgil said.

"We can't afford delays—" Leon shut his eyes, cocking his head at an odd angle. Virgil couldn't hear the sequence of Morse code beeps playing in the company man's ear, but he knew enough about Wellington agents to recognize the sign.

Leon opened his eyes, changing the topic. "I need to radio my Heap contact. If the Messenger's expecting us, security might be a problem."

"You do that," Virgil said.

Leon returned to his convertible. Ishmael went off to secure the tunnel.

"We're gonna be here all night, aren't we?" Rok asked.

Virgil massaged his forehead. Fun fact about Peacekeepers: they didn't tire easily.

CHAPTER 28

Leon's contact confirmed his worry; the Messenger's forces around the Heap were on high alert for any suspicious travelers, and the crew would have better luck entering the city on the following day anyway. Leon bemoaned the notion of losing more time, but Virgil pointed out they couldn't have left any sooner. Outside, the remnants of the Peacekeeper tribe paced along the sealed blast doors, scouring for entry points, firing plasma shots at random. Until the crackling *pops* of those arm cannons died down, the crew would have to stay put.

To pass the time, Ishmael sat cross-legged on the hood of a pickup truck and prodded the gears of his harpoon brace with a screwdriver. The weapon had smacked the ground when he tackled Virgil and something had been knocked awry. A few feet over, Rok busied herself by repairing Virgil's jeep. The vehicle had taken a beating during their escape, and for Virgil's last tobacco pouch, Rok agreed to nurse it back to good health. She went above and beyond replacing the axles, recalibrating the wheels, tuning the energy circuits, scavenging parts from abandoned vehicles around her. The mechanic spent hours under the hood, beneath the chassis, and when she finally came up for air, Ishmael thought she looked calm for the first time since they left Caravan. Virgil and Leon had disappeared into private corners of the dam, and Gage was still missing in action.

"I can fix that for you," Rok said to Ishmael, wiping her hands on her jumpsuit.

The offer confused Ishmael at first until he realized she was looking at the harpoon brace. "I can fix it myself," he said.

Rok came to his side, eyeing the brace with ravenous curiosity. Ishmael doubted she had ever seen anything like it.

"Also noticed your launch speed could be faster," she said. "I could make some tweaks—"

Unclean!

Ishmael jerked backward, lifting the screwdriver like a dagger. "No one touches the harness but me."

Rok took a big step back. "Fine! Whatever, goddamn."

He lowered the tool, and his face burned with white-hot shame. How quickly he had fallen back into his old conditioning. In the Shallows, the harpoon rig was more than a hunting tool. It was a sacred deviation from pre-Finale electronic weaponry, suitable only for the hands of the Enlightened. Though Ishmael had renounced the Deep and all their doctrines, some traditions were difficult to break.

You would let this vile heathen taint our sacred instrument? How far you've fallen, Brother Ishmael.

"We're on the same crew, you know," Rok said, crossing her arms.

Still embarrassed, Ishmael kept his eyes on his work. "I am part of no one's crew. My task is my own."

"Loners tend to die a lot faster in the Junkyard," Rok said. "Statistically."

Ishmael said nothing, and with nothing left to repair, Rok sat against the tunnel wall and treated herself to a Nutribrik dinner. As she ate, her idle hand opened the spiral-bound notebook on her belt and flipped to its most recent drawing—the Grave Walker. Ishmael saw that she had captured the suit's likeness in stunning detail, and yet she appeared dissatisfied. Her gaze kept drifting to the visor as if trying to penetrate its blankness. He guessed what was bothering her moments before she spoke it aloud:

"I've got no clue what she looked like."

Neither of them did. What color were her eyes? What shade was her skin? How had she reacted to Ishmael's confession on the edge of Pozo? Or to Virgil, when he stole her blood?

Rok pressed a finger to the Grave Walker's graphite chest, roughly above the heart. "It's weird. I only knew her for a bit, but . . . I liked her. I really *really* liked her."

She smacked her head back on the wall, so sudden and hard it made Ishmael flinch. Then she knocked the floor twice with her fist, and through grinding teeth, she whispered, "I didn't mean to hurt her, you know?"

Before Ishmael could reply, a voice cut in—

"Damn, gang. The Peacekeepers had better vibes than this." They found Gage lingering in the tunnel entrance, beside the unopened gate.

"How did you get in?" Ishmael demanded.

"I'm just that good," Gage said. "Miss me?"

Ishmael went back to fiddling with his harpoon brace.

"Got any more of those?" Gage pointed to Rok's Nutribrik, and she tossed him another from her backpack. He peeled off the wrapper with ravenous intent.

"Where are the others?" he asked.

"Virgil's up in the lookout," Rok said. "Leon's . . . around."

Gage chomped at the mushy nutrient block, scrutinizing the tunnel around them. He checked inside wrecked cars, under the tanker truck, across every inch of the ceiling.

"Must've moved on," he muttered, just loud enough for Ishmael to hear.

"Why did you bail on us?" Rok asked.

Gage sat down beside her. "Don't worry about it."

"I'm pretty worried about it."

"I don't want to talk."

"That'd be a first."

Gage took a long time to finish his Nutribrik, but Rok had nowhere to be. She waited for him to swallow the last bite, watched him closely as he shut his artificial eyes. Ishmael listened from his perch on the truck.

"If you cross this dam," Gage said, "follow the road on the other side, you'll get to a village. Or what's left of it. The townies used this tunnel as a trade route. Quickest way to the Heap."

He tossed the Nutribrik wrapper aside. "But then they lost a supply truck, and then they lost the truck sent to find that truck. They figured roadkillers had staked out the dam, so they sent out an SOS. Mercenaries didn't pick up, but they got ahold of a junkie named Belle. They hired her to clear out the dam, and she hired me and a few others to help. I was happy to do it. We were going to do some real good, you know?"

Ishmael knew all too well. It wasn't fashionable among junkies to look beyond self-preservation, but there were those who secretly fantasized about changing the Junkyard for the better. He had been one of those people, during the early days of his junkie career. And he suspected it was a big reason mechanics like Rok loved their job. They got to fix things.

"Pretty soon after we showed up," Gage said, "we knew roadkillers weren't the problem. The trucks hadn't been looted, just abandoned. We split up to look around, like idiots, and by the time I found out what was really going on . . . I was the only one left."

"What was it?" Rok said, on the edge of her seat.

Gage hesitated, and Dentures's last words replayed in Ishmael's head. *The Chimera ain't real.*

Considering how much shit Gage talked on a daily basis, it hadn't surprised Ishmael when Gimp and Dentures thought he was full of it. Just a greedy cyborg spinning a tall tale to hide his failure. Gage had done it before. But the thing about lies: they were meant to be told. Their usefulness relied entirely on external validation. Gage might have conjured a more believable lie to explain his scandal, but instead, he had landed on this outlandish tale of a dubious Relic. And in direct opposition of a lie's purpose, he kept the tale to himself. He had only told Dentures when his life was on the line, and from the sound of things, he wasn't going to tell Rok at all.

"Doesn't matter." Gage stood up and started pacing, leaving Rok with a cliffhanger. "All people care about is that I ran. When the others fought, I ran."

Though Ishmael detached himself from the social scenes on Caravan, he wasn't blind to them. He had seen Gage and Rok together. Rok had mended countless wounds, Gage had shared countless jokes, and the two of them had passed more than a few lonely nights getting drunk and messing around in her tank. Gage cared about Rok, and it seemed he would sooner hide his story from her than risk losing her to the same skepticism that took Dentures. Gage knew that his truth was unbelievable. If Ishmael had allowed himself a heart, it would've broken for the cyborg. He too had witnessed things that no one in the Junkyard would ever believe. *Unbelievable* was a lonely place.

"But you survived," Rok said. "That's all that matters."

"Wrong," Gage said. "When people think I'm weak, they just see me for my arms, and my legs, and my eyes. They just see the parts. I'm a payday. I'm junk."

"You took on a queen centipede. Word gets around."

"Technically, Diane did that," Gage said.

Diane. The mention of that name seemed to sting everyone in the tunnel.

Ishmael reexamined the Grave Walker sketch in Rok's open notebook. The machine was so durable, literally designed for durability, but it was still a machine. Machines could break. Machines could fail.

"I'm so scared for her," Rok said.

Gage continued pacing. "I'll get her back. I'll cut the Messenger's head off, spring Diane, and everything will be good. I don't care how big and bad he's supposed to be. I've seen worse. Way, way worse."

While Gage jabbered on, Ishmael rose and slipped off into the dam proper. The Master's voice had returned; there was too much noise.

You could have searched for the girl.

"Leave me alone," Ishmael whispered.

You abandoned her. Like you abandoned us.

"Be quiet."

She is dead. And you are to blame.

Stumbling through the dark, Ishmael could now see the skeletons of mutant fish dangling in the air, grinning down at him with far too many teeth.

"Please don't."

The industrial turbines and concrete corridor melted around Ishmael, and he was now running between the pews of an old timber church. The fish skeletons hung facedown from the rafters. A thick mold festered on the stained-glass windows, coloring the nave like a Battery capsule gone bad.

The Master stood waiting behind the altar.

Were we not enough? Must you cause harm to every soul that enters your cursed life?

"Leave me alone," Ishmael sobbed. He now held a bottle of gasoline in one hand, with a flaming cloth stuffed down its neck. Just like the night he ran away from home.

The world would be so much better without you.

"Go away!" Ishmael tossed the bottle, and blue fire consumed the altar—

"Look who it is."

Ishmael blinked.

In his delirium, he had wandered up the switchback stairs of the temperature control structure, and he found himself looming in the doorway with a horrified look on his face. Virgil didn't seem to notice. He sat in a weathered office chair by one of the room's many broken windows, puffing on a sticky ground herb wrapped in a paper joint. Ishmael had never smelled anything like it.

"Come take a look at this," Virgil said, mellow and groggy.

Ishmael went to the window. Light acid rain now drizzled over the desert, and a constellation of red lights drifted in the sulfurous haze. A few stuck close to the dam, but most were wandering off in different directions, fading gradually.

"They're losing focus," Virgil said. "Could be running low on Storm-Cell, or they just forgot what they're looking for. We should be outta here by morning."

Ishmael nodded, only half listening. He couldn't understand why his subconscious had led him here of all places. His own mind was foreign to him.

Virgil held up the paper joint. "Wanna hit?"

Ishmael shook his head.

"You sure? It's rare shit. Makes everything funny. Perfect cure for a bad day."

Ishmael took a seat on the floor. "Drugs and drink do not agree with me."

Virgil brought the joint back to his lips. "Suit yourself."

They lingered quietly for a while, listening to the rain pelt and sizzle off the roof. After a few more hits of herb, Virgil sunk deeper into his chair.

"I feel really bad about the kid, man," he groaned. "She wasn't supposed to get pulled into this. Hell, *I* wasn't supposed to get pulled into this."

Virgil looked to the southwest. *Somewhere*, Ishmael thought, *behind all that night, Diane was alone with a danger no one in the crew fully understood.*

"*Chamaca* really grew on me," Virgil continued.

"Will you search for her when we get to the Heap?" Ishmael asked.

Virgil puffed his joint. "I have to. I gotta make this right."

"Even if it means fighting the Messenger?"

The old junkie coughed in surprise, hacking up smoke, wheezing with laughter. It was a good thirty seconds before he got the air to speak again. "Have you seen the *size* of that guy? I'd get crushed!"

Coward, the Master spat. For once, Ishmael agreed.

"We'll let Gage do the fighting," Virgil said. "If he's still alive."

"He returned not long ago," Ishmael confirmed.

"Good for him."

"But . . ." Ishmael chose his words carefully, ". . . he struggles . . . under a great mental burden."

Virgil took one last all-or-nothing hit from his joint, letting the ember consume the rolled-up parchment all the way down to his lips. When he exhaled, there was no paper left. Only smoke and ash.

He smiled caustically. "Don't we all?"

CHAPTER 29

The Messenger and nightfall came to the Heap hand in hand.

He had pushed the rover drone to its highest speed on the drive south, leaving the raiding party to scramble after his dust trail, forcing Diane to cling to the edge of her seat. The tier-five StormCell left minimal room for the Grave Walker on board, and every pothole threatened to buck her into oblivion. She was so sick of falling off vehicles.

Defying the drone's autonavigator at every turn, the Messenger had taken sharp detours and dangerous shortcuts without hesitation, even before the sun had begun to set. Diane had the feeling it wasn't the night he was racing against. It was as though he had finally obtained the missing piece in some grand design, and his excitement could not be contained. If he didn't put the pieces in place soon, Diane imagined, he would burst.

This was not Diane's first exposure to the Heap. She had seen the Junkyard capital through Leon's eyecam footage, but those had been fragments—chaotic and subjective. Now, as one of the rover's sharp turns gave Diane a full view of what lay ahead, she beheld the Heap in full. She saw the old industrial factory towering at the city center, working overtime as Battery producer, Conductor plant, and mighty fortress; its workshops and silos flared in the night with the smoky lights of production. Moving out beyond the citadel's reinforced circular wall, the shabby concrete structures of the Inner Ring glowed dimly by the grace of the city's power grid. The lights grew fainter as Diane's eye moved toward the Ring's edge, and then just beyond another barrier, the slums of the Outer Rim were lit only with fires and glowsticks. A center, within a circle, within a forsaken circle.

There was no formal beginning to the Heap's Outer Rim. They passed a couple of stray tents, then a few more, then many more, and soon they were weaving through a shantytown of primitive shelters that seemed to jostle and elbow each other for real estate. Facing backward, Diane could only glimpse the townies here after they had retreated from the speeding drone, frightened eyes watching through parted tent flaps.

The barricade around the Inner Ring was no Wall of Jericho, merely a crumbling cinder-block structure lit with torches, but it was heavily guarded. Gruff-looking mercenaries patrolled the wall with flame-throwers, grenade launchers, and other weapons designed to make their enemies combust. They wore no bandages around their heads, but they stood aside without question when the Messenger approached. As they drove by, Diane saw patches of shiny pink skin on many of their faces and hands. A mercenary clan defined by its burn scars.

"Before I came here," the Messenger told Diane as they entered the Inner Ring, "the Heap was all greed and violence. A city racked with desperation. Now, the people here have a purpose. They are desperate no more."

The environment changed dramatically as they crossed into the Inner Ring. The roads were now paved. The buildings were stable enough to hold two or even three stories. Some establishments even had buzzing neon signs to market their wares. But Diane suspected this sense of order came at a price; there were soldiers patrolling everywhere.

The rover passed a long line of townies entering a building empty-handed, exiting with halved Nutribriks or low-grade Battery capsules. More mercenaries watched over them, also without bandages, even stranger than the ones at the outer barricade. They were all cyborgs, but their augments looked grungy and ill-fitting, as if built by amateurs.

"They know where their next meal is coming from," the Messenger went on, "how they'll pay for their Battery. All they have to do is fulfill their purpose."

Diane zoomed in on the townies as they drove by. Looks of glum resignation gave way to unease when they saw the rover and its passengers, and something told her it wasn't the Grave Walker that disturbed them.

"They're afraid," she said.

The Messenger drove on. "Change is always frightening."

They came to a second wall, but this one was metal. Blast-proof. They drove to the northern entrance, where electronic gates swung open as they approached, closing after they had passed. The road ramped up suddenly, and Diane had to work hard to keep from falling off the rover. For someone who claimed to *care very much*, the Messenger did a poor job of looking after his cargo. For the billionth time that drive, Diane wondered if she had made a mistake.

When the rover finally parked, they had arrived at the industrial citadel she recognized from Leon's eyecam video. The fortress was even bigger in person, made taller by smokestacks and a Conductor spire, but that was not the sight that captured Diane's curiosity. That honor went to the orange glow flickering on the southern horizon, stretching as far as eye or visor could see: a brilliant sunset at the wrong place and time.

"What is that?" she asked.

The Messenger disembarked from the rover. "Firelands."

Diane remembered the sea of flame on Rok's Junkyard map. Its breadth had not been exaggerated.

"It grows little by little each year," the Messenger said. "Sometimes only a few feet. Sometimes half a mile. It never retreats, and it only grows hotter."

"How far away is it now?"

"Almost two hundred miles. Not a threat in our lifetime." An explosion of yellow spewed from the orange, like a solar flare. "Does that distance comfort you?" he asked.

Diane tried to find solace in the distance, but nothing could shake her fixation on the inevitability. If what the Messenger said was true, the Firelands would consume the whole world, eventually. Not in their lifetime, but someone's lifetime would be cut short.

"No," she answered.

"Then you are wiser than most," the Messenger said.

The soldiers guarding the fortress were of bandaged stock, roadkillers and Peacekeepers marching to the same drum. A small group worked together to unload the tier-five StormCell from the rover, while others followed Diane closely as their leader guided her into the fortress. The Messenger did not summon these soldiers or deliver orders. They appeared when needed, and they fulfilled their function with unquestioning loyalty. His was a well-oiled war machine.

The Messenger took Diane through narrow halls of pipe and steam, filled with exhausted townies lugging tools and building materials in every direction. More soldiers lorded over the workers, shouting commands, kicking stragglers. Regardless of station, all froze when the Messenger passed by. All paid respect to the Man in the Mask.

They emerged into a wide-open concrete yard at the center of the fortress. All the factory buildings, the smokestacks, and the Conductor spire were arranged in a perfect square around this empty space, and there was nothing directly over their heads but the Junkyard sky. A scattered collection of freight crates implied that the space had once been used as a loading dock, but all vehicles had been cleared away, and the yard was now dedicated to something else entirely. For a moment, Diane forgot how afraid she felt. Whatever she expected to find in the Messenger's domain, it definitely wasn't this.

The yard was dominated by some kind of vessel, thirty feet high and almost two hundred feet long. Caged in scaffolding, it was surrounded by hundreds of workers who drilled, hammered, insulated, programmed, rigged, welded, and wired the structure on shifts around the clock, day and night. The vessel was long, like the barrel of a gun, and flat on top. Huge propulsion jets protruded out from the stern, and the plating on the hull was a collage of scrap metal gathered from anywhere and everywhere, specked with white sensor nodes, netted with pulsing blue cables.

It was the grimy execution of a brilliant design. A *Mona Lisa* painted by cavemen.

Diane couldn't look away. "What is it?"

"Something the world hasn't seen in hundreds of years," the Messenger said. "Something that will unite the Junkyard in ways no one ever dared to dream."

They were a long way from the nearest body of water, so Diane made an educated guess. "Is it some kind of aircraft?"

The Messenger removed his mask and tucked it into the pocket of his coat. He smiled warmly. "We've been constructing it for nearly a year, in separate pieces hidden across the Junkyard. When it came time to bring everything together, we needed a secure location. And resources. Things only the Heap could provide."

Lighting flashed over their heads. The townies atop the scaffolds reacted, and the human soldiers ordered them to get back to work. The Peacekeepers chirped angrily.

"What about the storm?" Diane asked. "I thought nothing could fly because of the storm."

"That's why we need you," the Messenger replied.

Before Diane could follow up, a familiar face appeared in the crowd of workers, pushing and jostling toward her. She couldn't quite place him at first, but when she saw his white lab coat streaked in filth, recognition struck. Ms. Violet had pointed this man out in Leon's eyecam footage, zooming to identify him in the jumble of battle: Dr. Isaac. This was the moment Diane had been fighting for, the promised meeting that kept her from shutting down a long time ago. This was the man who could get her out of the Grave Walker. This was the man who could make her human again.

"It's *beautiful*," Dr. Isaac jubilated.

The scientist didn't linger for any kind of introduction. He drank in Diane's suit, hands running over the armor without actually touching it.

"I can't believe I'm seeing a Grave Walker in the flesh," he said. "Er, in the steel. Tungsten alloy, actually." He addressed the visor. "Do you realize how rare you are?"

"In more ways than one," the Messenger said.

The sound of the Messenger's voice knocked Dr. Isaac out of his wonder-daze, and he seemed to remember something dire.

"How many Wellington operatives were there?" he asked. "Did you handle them?"

The Messenger shook his head. "I found her alone."

"They're still coming, then," Dr. Isaac said. "We must be careful."

"The Jericho puppets are no threat to us."

"Do not underestimate Ms. Violet—"

"*Wait*," Diane interjected. Her confusion emboldened her. Dr. Isaac spoke to the Messenger like they were equals, and he referred to Ms. Violet's rescue team as if they were some kind of threat. As if they weren't his ticket home.

"Do you not . . ." she tried to put her question delicately, but there was only one way to ask it: "Are you not a prisoner?"

The Messenger looked amused. "Is that what the Witch told you?"

Dr. Isaac straightened his posture, trying to reshape his bookish physique into some kind of militant pride. "I'm no prisoner. I resigned from Wellington, and I designed this airship, of my own free will."

"But why?" Diane asked, unable to help herself.

"The Messenger and I want the same thing."

"Will you be able to free her?" the Messenger asked.

Diane held her breath as Isaac mulled over the Grave Walker again, circling it, seeming to notice details from the outside that most wouldn't have seen with the suit torn open and laid bare. From what she'd heard, he was among Jericho's top minds, the smartest man in the Junkyard by a landslide. If he couldn't help her, no one could.

"It will be a difficult procedure," he said, "and I'll need to run diagnostics first to make sure, but . . . yes. I think I can."

Diane exhaled. "Thank you. Thank you so much."

Isaac reacted strangely to her gratitude, an uncomfortable mix of pride and equivocal pain. Then he turned to the Messenger. "First, though, um . . . Our guest is here."

All warmth vanished from the Messenger's face. "When did he arrive?"

"This morning. He's up on the deck now."

The Messenger set off toward the airship, donning his mask again as he marched. Dr. Isaac hurried after him, and Diane's guard detail pushed her to keep up.

"I gave him the tour," Isaac said. "He seemed . . . To be honest, I can't really read the man."

"Has Brutus returned?" the Messenger asked.

"Not yet. God, I hope he didn't get caught out in the night—"

"He's fine," the Messenger said, both confident and irked. "Just late."

They rode an elevating platform up to the airship's deck, which lay open to the sky, surrounded by an outline of support beams that would eventually hold walls and a roof. Diane immediately noticed the laser cannons standing at each corner of the deck and noted how they were among the only "finished" aspects of the ship's exterior. The Messenger certainly had priorities.

"Santiago!" he called out.

Three otherworldly figures emerged from the crowd of workers.

Two young acolytes—both in chain mail, both armed with harpoon rigs identical to Ishmael's—escorted a wizened old priest as he answered the Messenger's call. The priest's straggly beard fell nearly to the hem of his silk indigo robe, and the severity of his veiny gaze implied a great madness and even greater intelligence. Like his guards, like Ishmael, he was covered head to toe in strange aquatic tattoos.

"You are to address the Master as *Father* Santiago," one of the acolytes said.

Diane half expected the Messenger to rip out the acolyte's tongue, but he remained cool.

"Apologies for the delay, *Father*."

"I was beginning to think the night had taken you," Father Santiago replied. His voice was soft, yet acrid, like it had a way of worming into people's heads.

"Not a chance," the Messenger said.

The Messenger reached out for a handshake with his bandaged left arm. Father Santiago's acolytes aimed their harpoons at the Messenger, whose own troops drew their weapons in response.

"That is close enough," Father Santiago warned. "I know your tricks."

The standoff came from nowhere, and Diane couldn't begin to understand how a handshake was worth instigating a shoot-out. Thankfully, when the Messenger lowered his hand, the weapons lowered also.

"Dr. Isaac gave you a tour of our operation?" the Messenger asked, putting the moment behind them.

"He did," Santiago replied.

"And?"

"I saw much . . ." He took a passing glance at the labor around them, regarding the massive construction with glowering disinterest. ". . . but I see no reason to give you access to the Shallows."

Behind his mask, Diane heard the Messenger's breathing quicken. Things were not going as planned, and this wasn't a problem that could be killed or intimidated. He needed Father Santiago alive for some reason, and Santiago knew it. The old man had only brought two guards.

"Have you forgotten our deal?" the Messenger asked.

"I recall your *petition* perfectly," Father Santiago said. "You wish to occupy my village. To use it as a checkpoint in your voyage across the ocean, and as port when you return home."

Diane remembered what Virgil had said about the Grand Finale screwing up ecosystems, how places near water got it the worst. She could piece together why the Messenger would want to fly over the ocean instead of sailing across it, but why brave the ocean at all? A flying machine offered limitless potential in the Junkyard. What more could an army need?

Father Santiago wandered around the deck, apparently unimpressed at everything the Messenger had worked so hard to build.

"And in exchange for our hospitality," he continued, "and our blind eye to your hubris against the Deep, you give the Order of the Shallows authority in your impending dominion." He reached into his cloak and pulled out, of all things, a Battery inhaler. He huffed the smoke, then let it billow from his mouth as he spoke without coughing. "I see no promise of dominion here."

"Have you tried looking under your feet?" the Messenger snapped. Father Santiago's guards stepped in front of their master, sensing a fight in the warlord's tone.

"Your scientist tells me the airship cannot be piloted," Santiago said. "And it cannot fly."

The look Isaac received from the Messenger could have stopped a queen centipede dead. Rage. Pure, barely contained rage.

"*Yet*," Dr. Isaac clarified. "I said the ship can't fly *yet*."

"Suppose it never flies," Santiago said. "Suppose I let your troops into my home, and your plan fails. You will become desperate, groping for any strand of power within reach. Your peaceful occupation will become a hostile takeover."

"You realize how paranoid that sounds," the Messenger said.

Father Santiago waved off the accusation with a long, boney hand. "You may be strong, *Messenger*, but you are new to Junkyard politics. I am not. I have seen what the strong do when their ship sinks. I will not be pulled down with you—"

The buzz of the elevating platform cut Santiago off, and its passenger stole everyone's attention. It was the hulking cyborg from Violet's holoscreen video, the one branded *9-T-9*. The tanned skin over the cyborg's breathing apparatus was cracked and graying. His limbs were scuffed with plasma burns. Up close, Diane saw that his cheek rash was comprised of countless curving lines, red, irritated, the residue of a demon's touch.

"I'm back," he rasped.

The Messenger all but jumped for joy. "Father, this is Brutus 9-T-9! My chief lieutenant."

"The bastards didn't make it easy," Brutus 9-T-9 said, "but we got through to 'em."

The cyborg lifted a diplomat Peacekeeper's head for all to see. The mask of flesh and metal was still attached.

Upon recognizing that horrible face, Diane's first thoughts were of

Sacred Chapel—the gunsmith village where Virgil had sold the head for much-needed StormCells. A simpler time with simpler problems. To what lengths had Brutus gone to retrieve this mechanical prize? In the dizziness of the moment, Diane allowed herself to believe that Brutus could have traded for it, or used intimidation to pry it from some townie's still-living hands. She could not yet bring herself to consider the grisly alternative: that Brutus might have slaughtered an entire village to claim his prize. Not with the cyborg responsible standing right in front of her.

As the shock passed, it occurred to Diane that Brutus had known exactly where to find the diplomat's head. He had probably been tracking it, and her, all along.

The Messenger accepted the Peacekeeper's disembodied head, slapped Brutus's back in a gesture of praise, then handed the head off to Dr. Isaac.

"Don't fail me," he warned the scientist.

Isaac connected the head to a cable then hustled to a computer console across the deck, semicontained in a half-built command bridge.

"The airship's navigation systems are extremely complex," he lectured, trying to keep his own panic at bay. "More so than I, uh, initially predicted. The Junkyard lacks the resources to build an adequate . . . um . . . piloting program, so we need to repurpose a program that already exists." He plugged the head into a rounded housing port on the console. "One we can trust."

A switch flipped, and the diplomat's ocular lens kindled red. The computer hummed, booting up.

Isaac addressed the head. "Sixty-Seven, can you hear me?"

A digitized voice replied from tiny speakers. "I am online."

"What is your function?"

"I am . . . a generation twenty-five, diplomat-class—"

Isaac typed on the console. The diplomat's voice warped, screamed, rose and fell to impossible pitches, then leveled off in a one-note slur. "I . . . ammm . . . navigation."

Dr. Isaac was visibly relieved. "Reprogram successful. Navigation systems online. Sir."

"But the airship still cannot fly," Santiago said.

The Messenger put a friendly hand on the Grave Walker's shoulder. Friendly, but still heavy enough to weigh her down.

"This suit contains *Cradle*'s sole survivor," he said. "Thanks to her, it will fly."

Diane could feel Father Santiago's perplexed glare without even looking. She was just as confused herself, and she feared the Messenger had mistaken her for some kind of expert on space travel. That training had been reserved for the Block Fours. She was out of her element, and these didn't seem like good people to disappoint.

The Messenger's claim also reiterated to Diane that she was the last of her kind. She was here now because the Messenger wanted a space colonist, and she was the only one still breathing. He had probably combed the entire crash site to no avail. Whatever he wanted from her, he could not find anywhere else.

"Follow me," the Messenger said.

Everyone obeyed, and he guided them to a flight of stairs near the command bridge. Diane, Brutus, and Dr. Isaac followed the Messenger down into the airship's interior, while Santiago and his acolytes waited on the topmost step, watching on from a safe distance.

The stairs led to an open chamber belowdecks, where the stolen tier-five StormCell was being added to an engine system that already contained two others. In the room's center, all the glowing cables around the hull converged at a triangular pedestal made of spotless chromium. An orb hovered just above it, an orb of rare minerals and ethereal light, spinning slowly, glistening like a diamond in the sun. Two golden rings surrounded it, hanging motionless in the air, awaiting activation.

"The Gravity Core," Diane whispered.

The sight of the orb stirred something inside her. They were kindred spirits, alien artifacts wrapped in ugly shells on an uglier planet. Powered by subconscious attraction, the Grave Walker moved slowly toward the heart of *Cradle*. The bandaged soldiers tried to follow, but the Messenger held them back.

"How . . . ?" was all Diane could say.

"We salvaged it from the wreck," the Messenger said.

"It wasn't easy finding schematics on Armstrong's design," Dr. Isaac piped in. "So little information survived the Grand Finale, but . . . we were persistent."

He turned to Father Santiago, who watched on from the top of the stairs.

"I believe we arranged the Newtonian conduits correctly," Isaac said. "The gravity field should elevate the vessel and protect it from lightning strikes. Thrusters control momentum, and boom. Airship."

Father Santiago stroked his beard, curious but not yet sold.

"We're only missing one thing," the Messenger said. He was at Diane's side now, and he guided her eye from the Gravity Core to the pedestal that housed it. A computer from the Gravity Control Room had been salvaged as well—the only device capable of mastering the Core. Hooked to the pedestal, it displayed a request on-screen that no amount of hacking, rebooting, or punching could satisfy.

DENIED: GRAVITY INSTALLATION REQUEST.
PROVIDE BIOMETRIC SECURITY CREDENTIALS TO OVERRIDE.
CLEARANCE LEVEL: BLOCK THREE OR ABOVE.

Below that screen, Diane found something more familiar to her than even the Gravity Core. A device she never thought she would see again.

A glass palm scanner. Undamaged, waiting to feel a *Cradle* resident's warm, living touch.

"You need my hand," Diane realized.

The Messenger leaned closer to the Grave Walker's helmet. "We'll free you from the suit, give you the autonomy to walk on your own, no kill switches. And in exchange, you will unlock the power to usher a new era of prosperity into the Junkyard. No more senseless violence. No more roadkillers and junkies and Jericho influence. There will be order. There will be *peace*."

At first glance, Diane had no qualms with the bargain. The Junkyard could use a little authority, someone to unite the villages and police the open roads. Someone to end all the fighting and explosions. Junkies like Virgil wouldn't take kindly to the intrusion, but tough luck. Their bloodsucking days were numbered. An alliance with the Messenger would free her from solitary confinement, and it could make the world safer. For her. For everyone.

Despite these qualifiers, a voice in Diane's head wouldn't stop nagging.

Read the room, it whispered. *Read the room.*

"You've seen what the world has become," the Messenger said. "Help me fix it."

Read the room. The room was built around the Gravity Core. So what?

Read the room.

No, that wasn't accurate. The entire ship had been designed around the Gravity Core. It was a crucial component. The key ingredient.

Read the room.

Without the Core, the ship was nothing.

"Help me fly," the Messenger said.

Without Cradle, *the ship would never have flown.*

Diane felt sick. She charged for the stairwell, a move so fast and sudden that her guards could only dive aside to keep from getting squashed. The stairs rattled violently as Diane clambered back up to the airship's deck, and Father Santiago's acolytes made no effort to stop her. Between Diane's grief and the Grave Walker's size, any such effort would've been futile.

When the Messenger, Dr. Isaac, and Brutus 9-T-9 reached the deck, they found Diane peering over the edge, trying to measure the fall.

"What are you doing?" the Messenger asked.

Diane whirled to face him. "A year!"

No one had the faintest idea what she was talking about.

"You said you've been working on this ship for a year!"

"So what?" the Messenger said.

"*Cradle* hasn't even been down here a month!"

The Messenger was unreadable behind his mask, but Dr. Isaac's reaction told Diane she was on track to a horrible truth.

"How did you know the Gravity Core was coming?" she asked. "It's the only one of its kind. I know it is. They drilled that into our heads up there."

The Messenger took a step forward. "Diane—"

The Grave Walker stepped back, closer to the edge. "How'd you know we would crash?"

"Calm down."

"You knew *Cradle* was coming! You knew . . ." She looked to Dr. Isaac—the scientist, the brains, the smartest man in the Junkyard. ". . . because you brought it here."

Dr. Isaac averted his gaze, but not before Diane saw the tears welling in his eyes.

"Now you're the one being paranoid," the Messenger said.

"Do you know what you've done?" Diane screamed. "Do you know how many people you killed?"

Isaac's shoulders trembled. Diane pushed harder. "Five hundred colonists! A hundred children! Babies, dead! Dead because of you!"

"We just wanted it to *land*!" Isaac cried out. "We didn't know it was going to crash—!"

The Messenger backhanded Isaac, knocking him to the floor. Bruised and blubbering, the scientist made no effort to stand back up.

"There it is," Diane said.

Finally, she had an explanation for the tragedy that destroyed her world, and nothing anyone said would convince her otherwise. The Messenger must have known this, because he made no attempts to apologize.

"Peace demands sacrifice," he said simply.

"*Sacrifice?*" Diane shrieked.

Nearby, a team of workers hung around a semi-installed laser cannon, unsure whether to proceed amid the commotion. Diane pictured the cannon's muzzle aiming down at one of the Junkyard villages, striking the children from Gatetown or the old woman from Sacred Chapel who had offered her a bottle of water. Then she realized that old woman was probably dead already, her entire gunsmith community reduced to a smoldering boneyard. The idea of Brutus taking the diplomat's head back from them peacefully now felt absurd. In the Messenger's hands, policing the Junkyard sounded like the worst idea imaginable, and it frightened Diane that she had ever believed otherwise.

"What happens to the people who don't want your type of peace?" she asked. "Will you sacrifice them too?" The Grave Walker clenched its fists. The bandaged troops readied their weapons. "This world is sick," she said, "and I don't know what it needs to get better. But it's not you. People like you only make things worse."

"Do you want out of the suit, or not?" the Messenger threatened.

The price of rebellion was not lost on Diane. Her one wish would slip through her fingers, through fingers that were hers yet not hers, and she might never get a chance to escape the Grave Walker again. She might never feel a breeze on her cheek. Never hold hands with someone she cared about. Never taste a Nutribrik. Never share a kiss.

If the Messenger had issued this ultimatum a week ago, or three days ago even, she might have buckled to his will. But that Diane was a different person. That Diane had not suffered an endless barrage of danger, needles, and vampiric betrayal. But now, forced to meet the architect of her own private apocalypse, something snapped. The floodgates opened within her psyche, and a great dogmatic anger was unleashed. Perhaps it was newborn, or maybe it had been there all along, but it filled her mind with a single, all-consuming idea. A crazy idea. An idea reserved for the gifted and the damned.

If the Messenger was right, and destiny did exist, it had chosen *her*. Diane had lived while hundreds had perished so that she could be the one standing here, now, placed in the Grave Walker's lofty shoes, hand-selected to confront this oil slick on the universe and say—

"No. Not if it means helping you."

She watched the words sink in. Then, without warning, the Messenger ripped a support beam out of the deck floor. He threw it at Diane with all his might.

The force knocked her over the edge, sent her free-falling three stories to the concrete yard below. The Grave Walker landed on its back, knocking the wind out of its occupant. Through a spasming HUD,

Diane watched the Messenger step off the deck above her, fearless in his fury. He fell, landing on the suit's belly, and pinned the support beam down across her neck.

He dug his fingers into the seams of the Grave Walker's chest plates, and then he began to pull. A loud creaking filled the suit. Diane's visor went ballistic. *WARNING! ARMOR COMPROMISED! BREACH IMMINENT!* Veins bulged in the Messenger's neck as he pulled with more strength than a human being should possess. Behind the mask, his black irises all but devoured his eyeballs.

"Stop!" Dr. Isaac leaped off the elevating platform. "You'll kill her! This isn't how it's done!"

"*¡El barco vuela esta noche!*" the Messenger snarled.

He kept pulling, and the visor HUD flashed red. Another two seconds, and the chest would rip open. Another second after that, and Diane would be dead.

"*Look at her wrist!*" Isaac cried.

Something in his voice made the Messenger stop pulling.

"It's a transfusion rig!" Isaac said, inspecting the little black box. "Virgil must have had it installed. That explains why he kept her around."

"So what?" the Messenger grunted.

"We can access her blood! And if my theory about the Arm's genetic replicator is correct . . ."

The Messenger's irises contracted to their original size. Still kneeling on the Grave Walker's chest, he unwrapped the bandages from his hand.

What Diane saw next made no sense. It was impossible, yet she had a front-row seat to the entire thing.

The Messenger's hand looked like it was made of jellyfish tentacles, some bioluminescent fiber tangled together in the shape of fingers, knuckles, a palm. Diane felt a sharp prick in her arm again as Dr. Isaac pulled the transfusion tube out of the black box. He passed it to the Messenger as it filled with blood, but the Masked Man made no effort to inject the needle into a vein. The Messenger simply held the tube over his glowing appendage and squeezed. Diane's blood poured over the fibrous hand, filling it, and its shape slowly transmuted in response.

What was once the hand of a large brute became smaller and more delicate. A feminine hand. Diane's hand.

A ring of bandaged soldiers appeared around them.

"If she moves," the Messenger said, "kill her."

Dr. Isaac went to shut off the transfusion rig, but the Messenger grabbed his collar and hauled him back toward the airship before he got the chance.

Bleeding out, Diane gazed up at the bellicose clouds forever locked in civil war, striking each other with volleys of lightning, shouting threats in the form of thunder. A sudden feeling of weightlessness came right before she passed out, and an unseen force levitated the steel beam pinning her neck. Through a power Diane could not understand, the Messenger had unlocked the Gravity Core's palm scanner. The secrets of *Cradle* were now his to exploit. He didn't need her anymore.

The gravity field's too wide, she thought when she saw her own blood floating into the air. *They'll . . . have to work . . . on that . . . .*

Everything went dark.

CHAPTER 30

"*We're here.*"

Leon announced the crew's arrival into his CB radio. They were parked on a ridge just outside the Heap, watching the occupied city from on high, and it pained Virgil to see the heart of the Junkyard in such a state.

Virgil had fond memories of his previous visit to the Heap. Beginning at the city's unmarked borders, the shanty Outer Rim had been a madhouse of buyers and sellers, a feeding ground for hungry merchants and young junkies starving to make their mark. True order had begun at the outer barricade, a weak but well-guarded checkpoint that formed a perfect circle around the Inner Ring. Things beyond that wall were more civilized: the shops here had policies; gamblers and sex workers operated behind closed doors; the Junkyard's Big Four mercenary clans made their headquarters here, protecting their respective blocks pro bono. And then, safe behind the reinforced wall at the Inner Ring's center, green smoke had billowed from chimneys on the Aardwolf fortress—a visual confirmation that fresh Battery was in production. The wheels of industry were turning. Everything was as it should be.

Today, there were no junkies or merchants bringing goods into the Outer Rim, and all the pop-up shops were closed. Cut off from their usual supply chains, the starving townies here hungered only for Nutribriks, which bandaged soldiers lobbed at them from behind the crumbling outer barricade. The Inner Ring was silent, more prison camp than center of commerce. The smokestacks were dead. Only the Conductor spire on the fortress was running correctly, but with the Messenger in charge, Virgil would bet all the seeds in his possession that the energy it harnessed traveled solely to those in the new regime's favor. It all felt so wrong.

Standing by the convertible, Leon listened to his Heap contact through an auxiliary cord hooked to a jack behind his ear. He nodded in response to words only he could detect.

"*Copy. Standing by.*" Leon unplugged himself from the radio.

"What's up with the FireFighters?" Virgil asked.

The mercenaries atop the outer barricade kept their flamethrowers aimed at the hungry townies below, singeing the brows off anyone who ventured too close. Clad in turnout gear, displaying their burn scars like badges of honor, the FireFighters took no prisoners and gave no warnings. As a drastic misinterpretation of pre-Finale rescue services, they believed the best solution to any problem was to cook it alive.

"Only townies chosen to work get to live inside the Inner Ring," Leon said. "Everyone else rots out here."

Virgil glanced at Rok, mourning the sad state of the Outer Rim. Ishmael watched on without expression. Gage paced in a loop around the cars, antsier than normal.

"How come we're just sitting around?" Gage said. "I wanna kill this three-faced son of a bitch!" He was the only crew member with any desire to face the Messenger, and the others balked at his death wish.

"We're waiting for the signal," Leon said.

"What signal?" Gage asked.

A loud horn pulled everyone's focus back to the city below. Their attention was drawn to the Outer Rim, where a trio of semitrucks parted the crowd. The mercenaries standing atop the cargo beds held the deadliest rifles in the Junkyard, and their battle armor could stop a plasma shot at point-blank range. Stripes of blue paint adorned their faces.

"Are those Oxen?" Rok asked. Virgil guessed she had only come to the Heap a handful of times, when Caravan made its annual visit.

"The Messenger has them on supply runs," Leon confirmed.

"Makes sense," Virgil said. "Only clan who wouldn't skim any supplies off the top."

A mob gathered around the trucks, desperate townies demanding more food, water, and medicine. The Oxen troops ordered them back, but they didn't fire their rifles. Oxen wouldn't kill civilians.

The FireFighters, on the other hand, had no problem killing anyone. They unloaded dragon's breath on the mob, setting a few townies ablaze, driving the rest back. Virgil and his crew watched the human torches flailing from afar, and not even Ishmael was unaffected. This wasn't the senseless mayhem they knew from the road. This was organized oppression, on a scale the Junkyard hadn't seen in a very long time.

"Oh my god . . ." was all Rok managed to say.

"How the hell's your contact going to get us in?" Virgil asked Leon.

"Just wait for the signal."

"Holy shit!" Gage yelled. "What signal?"

Just then, an ion grenade exploded to the east. Townies fled to their tents, and all but a few FireFighters converged on the disturbance.

Suddenly, the stretch of barricade nearest the crew was totally unguarded.

"Move," Leon said.

Everyone shuffled down the ridge, leaving their vehicles under sheets of earth-colored tarp. They moved in a tight pack through the Outer Rim, where the air seemed hotter and clammier than Virgil remembered. Sounds of sickness rose weakly from many of the tents, as did the heavy stench of vomit. Virgil knew the signs; this district was overrun with the Junkyard Blues. It was a much slower death for people still on low- and medium-grade Battery, but *slower* didn't always mean *better*.

Still, there were plenty of able bodies left to create the Outer Rim's usual pandemonium, giving the crew ample cover as they navigated their way through the district. Seeing their haste, numbers, and general fuck-off energy, all the usual hasslers and cutthroats kept out of their way.

The crew slipped through an old breach in the outer barricade, one of many such cracks undermining the cinder-block wall's entire purpose.

Now in the Inner Ring, they ran up a narrow alleyway toward a street paved in recycled plastic.

Leon signaled for them to stop and hide. Seconds later, a band of cyborg mercenaries marched up the road. When they passed the crew's hiding place, Virgil could see the fetid puss caked around their bionic seams, the rusted metal under their skin.

"Who let the Modified out of their cages?" Gage gagged. Back when the Aardwolves were in charge, the Modified had rarely walked the streets before nightfall.

"They supervise the workers," Leon said.

Gage squirmed. "Sucks to be the workers, then."

Once the Modified passed, Virgil and his crew followed Leon across the street, up another alley, and into a city square. A work shift transition was underway, and they used the commotion to walk among the townies undetected. To the Modified goons on duty, they were just five more fish in the river. A squad of bandaged Peacekeepers rounded the corner up ahead, and Virgil's heart stopped. Thankfully, the troops weren't here for them. The argonauts grabbed a scrawny yet able-bodied teenager out from the herd, dragging him off toward the fortress.

"What are they doing to him?" Rok asked.

"Recruiting," Leon said.

The boy cried out for someone named Annette as the Peacekeepers took him away, and Virgil recognized the name. He couldn't understand at first what his favorite Gatetown merchant was doing in the Heap, but then he remembered what her brother Al had said. When none of the mercenaries would answer Gatetown's call, Annette had set out to find out why.

Took her boy Andy with her . . .

Bad timing, Virgil thought. He skimmed the crowd for Annette, but if she was present, she had already been lost in the dismal horde. If she was crying out, she was one voice of many.

"That kid's not a soldier," Virgil said, watching sadly as Andy was ripped from sight.

"He will be," Leon promised.

At a fork in the road, Leon directed the crew to a two-story building no different from so many others filling the Inner Ring. Its foundations were crooked, its faces webbed in cracks, and the worst of its damages covered by little more than sheets of tin. Its one distinguishing feature was the red neon sign hanging unlit above the doorway. *Batty's!* it read in big, lifeless letters.

Leon knocked on the door five times at varying speeds, indicating some sort of code. A seven-year-old girl, frail and haunted beyond her years, answered the summons.

"Are your parents home?" Gage asked with a laugh.

Silent, the child ushered the crew into an empty cantina, barring the door behind them. Virgil noted the empty liquor shelves, the toppled stools, the heavy layer of dust coating every surface. It looked like this place hadn't seen action in a long time.

The girl walked purposefully to the other end of the room, where she lifted a framed portrait of a prewar musician—dressed in purple, sitting on a motorcycle, surrounded by fog—off the wall. A hidden lever waited behind the frame, and when she pulled it, a trapdoor beside the bar fell open. *Whap!* Everybody except Leon jumped with surprise.

"Down here," Leon said.

Gage scowled. Leon mounted the ladder and slid down into the hidden basement. The other crewmates followed.

One by one, they met Leon's contacts in the Heap.

"Damn," Rok murmured.

The bunker below the bar was packed with Aardwolf soldiers; Virgil recognized some of them from the battle footage in Ms. Violet's office. Under their rule, the Heap had survived for years in a state of pure cutthroat capitalism, and the Aardwolves had lived large off the taxes they collected. Now, the city was under new dictatorial management, forcing the old guard to retreat underground. These Aardwolf soldiers sat around tending to fresh wounds, gathered in packs to hear each other above the rabble. A team of cybersmiths, pudgy biomechanics, was dutifully hacking off Aardwolf legs and replacing them with cybernetic prosthetics. Half the soldiers waited for their turn on the operating table; the rest were applying epoxy gel to their bionic seams—fresh divides where human thigh ended and robotic leg began. Painkillers were passed around like candy. Nervous systems had just been rewired, and they hurt like nothing else. The bunker reeked of blood and Battery.

"The Aardwolves got safe houses all over the Inner Ring," Leon explained as he guided the group through the bunker. "They've been hiding out since they lost the fortress."

"How did so many get out alive?" Virgil asked. Having seen Leon's eyecam video, he knew the Messenger's invasion left little room for escape.

"They didn't," Leon said. "Only half the Aardwolves were at the fortress when the Messenger attacked. The rest were out in the Junkyard, doing mercenary work."

"These Wellington parts?" Virgil asked. He recognized the high quality of the legs, in material and design. Too rich for the Junkyard's blood.

"Ms. Violet's bankrolling the resistance effort," Leon said. "An Aardwolf victory is in our best interests."

They came to a heavily guarded steel door, and Leon raised his hand to the other crewmates. "Virgil and I will go in. Rest of you wait out here."

Rok didn't need to be told twice. She wandered off to watch the cybersmiths at work. Gage crossed his arms and leaned against the bunker wall, looking put off. Ishmael stayed by the door, unwilling to let Virgil out of his sight.

"I'll be fine," Virgil promised, and despite Ishmael's protests, followed Leon into the next room without his bodyguard.

The cramped office contained a chewed-up wooden desk, two plastic lawn chairs, and a man-child no older than eighteen, dressed in a faded officer's uniform that wouldn't fit him properly for another twenty pounds. An antique Luger pistol hung from his belt—a family heirloom, no doubt. He was standing over a basin, drawing murky water into a cracked ceramic mug. Like the Heap's energy production, running water came from the fortress. The Messenger was holding all the utilities hostage.

"Took you long enough," the boy captain complained, sitting behind his desk.

"This is Virgil Ceres, Wellington's Junkyard consultant," Leon told the young officer. Then to Virgil, he said: "This is Jeremiah Aardwolf, new patriarch of the Aardwolf clan."

Virgil bowed his head in respect. "Shame about your dad. He always did right by us junkies."

"I don't get why he's here," Jeremiah said to Leon, ignoring the condolence.

Leon regurgitated his employer's phrasing. "Ms. Violet believes he can lend . . . perspective."

"What do we need perspective for?" Jeremiah complained. "We got the augments! Tomorrow, we scale the fortress wall and push those bastards back into the Junkyard!"

Virgil gawped at the boy-king. "That's your strategy? Just run in, guns a-blazin'?"

"Got a problem with it?" Jeremiah said.

"What about the other mercenary clans?" Virgil asked. "They're on the Messenger's payroll. What happens when they come to his rescue?"

"We can take them."

"Ha!" Virgil plopped down in one of the plastic lawn chairs. He was beginning to understand why Violet wanted him here. "No, even with your fancy new limbs—which, by the way, *garbage* idea to let Wellington plug your boys with kill switches—"

"No kill switches," Leon cut in. "You have Ms. Violet's word."

Virgil squinted doubtfully. "Uh-huh."

Jeremiah hit Leon with an accusatory glare, and Virgil decided that while stirring the pot was fun, it didn't exactly serve him in this moment. He got back on track.

"Even with the augments, you're half the army you used to be. You're outnumbered. You're screwed."

Jeremiah's childish bravado faded before Virgil's eyes. Virgil appreciated his predicament. The boy was the inheritor of a crippled dynasty, facing more hardship than his father had ever known. And to top it off, he needed to prove to his failing army that he was a leader by more than birthright.

"So we buy back the other clans," Jeremiah suggested. "Get them on our side."

"With what?" Virgil asked. "All your assets were in the fortress. You're broke."

"Can't Wellington pay them?" Jeremiah asked.

"You think I didn't try that already?" Leon chided.

Virgil couldn't help but laugh. "They probably didn't even let you in the door."

Poor Jeremiah was lost, Virgil realized. He leveled with him: "Not everyone's as desperate as you, Junior. The mercs don't trust Wellington, and they've got a good thing going with the Messenger. Why spoil it?"

"So what do we do?" Jeremiah asked.

The older men said nothing.

"*What do we do*?" Jeremiah whined.

The hell if Virgil knew. The mercenary clans were the Messenger's ultimate defense, and their combined might would be unstoppable. It still amazed Virgil that they were all playing on the same team. Put an Ox and a FireFighter in the same room, and you had yourself a powder keg. A ticking time bomb. A bloodbath waiting to happen.

Chaos is an instrument, Virgil. And you play it beautifully.

As Virgil recalled Ms. Violet's commendation, the pieces of a plan clicked into place.

He perked up. "What do the mercenary clans hate most in the world? More than Wellington, even?" He didn't wait for an answer. "Each other! They've been kicking each other's asses since the dawn of time. We'll never get them to stand with us, but we can make damn sure they don't stand together."

Virgil leaned forward over the desk. Intrigued, Jeremiah met him in the middle.

"Tell me if I got this straight," Virgil said. "The FireFighters guard the Inner Ring, the Oxen do supply runs, the Modified police the workers . . . Where are the Keres?"

"We think they're spying on the other clans," Jeremiah said. "Making sure everyone stays in line."

No surprise there. The Keres were a sneaky lot, a synchronized squad of assassin Peacekeepers with enough brains and communication skills to trade their services for StormCells. Few people had actually seen these mechanical mercenaries work; their phased-array optic cloaking devices made sure of it. Heartless and invisible, they were the perfect spies.

"And the Messenger's troops are all at the fortress?" Virgil asked.

Jeremiah nodded. "Yeah. Their numbers equal the size of the Modified clan, just about. But they're running thin. Too many dangerous missions in the Junkyard."

"Where's this going?" Leon wanted to know.

"All the clans have their feuds," Virgil said, "but the Oxen and the FireFighters hate each other the most. That's fact."

He traced an invisible map on the desktop. A center, within a circle, within a larger circle.

"If we can start some rumors, get the Oxen pissed at the FireFighters, their battle would consume the outer barricade. They'd be too busy with each other to worry about the Aardwolves attacking the fortress." Virgil looked back at Leon. "And if the Messenger tries to sneak Dr. Isaac out the back during the Aardwolf assault, he'll get hit with a ring of gunfire. We got him locked in."

Leon was skeptical. "You think you can get the Oxen to launch a full-scale assault on the FireFighters? Over a rumor?"

"Yes," Virgil said. "Yes, I do."

"What about the Modified?" Jeremiah asked.

Virgil smiled; Junior was paying attention. "We don't need to buy their loyalty. We just need them to . . . do nothing. Sit around and watch the fireworks."

"I can negotiate that," Leon said.

Now it was Virgil's turn to be skeptical. "They don't want to talk to you, *servidor.*"

"They're cyberaddicts," Leon pushed back. "Violet can work that better than anyone."

He had a point, and Virgil was in no mood to argue. Time was of the essence.

"Fine," Virgil said. "And I don't know what to do about the Keres, but there aren't many of them, anyway. *Es lo que es.*"

He took a hit from his inhaler. This medium-grade Battery felt so much smoother.

"We pull this off, and the Messenger's got no help and nowhere to run," Virgil assured Jeremiah. Then to Leon, he said, "And during the hubbub, we can swoop in and grab Isaac, no problem. Aardwolves get their fortress, Ms. Violet gets her scientist, and you get to go home. Everybody wins!"

And I'll get to find Diane. But Virgil kept that detail to himself.

Jeremiah whooped in excitement, beaming at Virgil like he was the best thing since vodka. "I get why you hired him, now!"

Leon's response was less optimistic. "What if this doesn't work?"

"It'll work," Virgil said.

The manipulation would be the easy part. It was the battle itself that Virgil dreaded, where so much could go wrong. A stray missile could ruin even the best-laid plans, and casualties were inevitable. No matter how careful they were, dumb luck would have the final say in who lived and who died. No matter what Virgil did, he could only control so much.

"Come on, boys," he said, burying his worries deep. "Let's go stir the pot."

CHAPTER 31

Once again, Diane was immobile.

They had removed the Grave Walker's StormCell and rigged the suit with external power cables, providing just enough energy to keep her heart and lungs in motion. She sat on the floor of a cluttered bric-a-brac laboratory, cable running out of her back like a misplaced umbilical cord, unable to lift a finger. Trapped in a state of limited voltage, Diane was too exhausted to even feel moved by the broken Nurse droid lying beside her. The orb of damaged glass, which must have been salvaged from *Cradle*'s remains, was now plugged into a data mining program. It was a piece of home Diane never thought she would see again. If only she had the energy to care.

Nearby, Dr. Isaac moved between dusty computer screens as they downloaded Nurse's contents, never idling for a second. He wouldn't speak to Diane. Wouldn't even look at her.

Diane didn't want much to do with Isaac anyway, but her rage could no longer distract her from her situation. She had served her purpose, and the Messenger had thrown her into a corner and forgotten about her. Even if he didn't get around to killing her himself, no one was looking after the suit. No one was feeding it food or water. Neglect was a death sentence on its own, and Diane didn't want to die. Not here. Not now.

Swallowing her pride, mustering all the energy she had left, Diane called out to Dr. Isaac. "What are you going to do with me?"

"The Messenger hasn't decided yet," he said, still facing the screens.

Diane was afraid of that. "You could still let me go. I gave you what you wanted."

"He'd kill me," Isaac said.

"We could leave together. I can take you back to Jericho—"

"*Never.*" He smacked his keyboard, filling the screen with gibberish text. Diane had poked a sore spot. "I'm never going back," Isaac whispered.

The scientist returned to his work, leaving Diane to wonder, *What would Virgil do in a situation like this?*

Well first, he would attempt to cut a deal. Diane had tried that, but she was fresh out of bargaining chips. That wouldn't stop Virgil, though. He'd find a hole in Dr. Isaac's armor, some weakness that could be leveraged. The hook, as Rok had called it. How could Diane get Isaac on the hook?

She knew the answer as soon as she asked the question. Dr. Isaac had already revealed his weakness on the airship.

"So you won't be satisfied until everyone from *Cradle* is dead?" Diane asked.

Dr. Isaac stopped working. He faced Diane for the first time that day.

"It was never my intention to wreck *Cradle*," he said. "You have to believe me."

"But you did," Diane said. "And even if you didn't, the Junkyard would've eaten us alive. You should've left us alone."

Isaac wrung his hands together, probably wishing that he could just turn away and bury himself in his work. But Diane knew that he couldn't. Dr. Isaac was like her in that way. When a problem entered his brain, he would find no peace until he made the solution known.

"Civilization can't go on the way it has," he tried to explain. "Jericho and the Junkyard both, they're not sustainable. The Messenger understands this—"

"I don't want to hear your excuses," Diane said with scorn.

Isaac rushed across the lab and grabbed her by the helmet. Diane lacked the motor functions to look away.

"You must," he said. "You must understand what really happened. I need you to understand."

Diane didn't want or need an explanation; what's done was done. But the more he told her, the more ammo she would have against him. So she let Isaac say his piece.

"When he asked me to build a flying machine, I knew the Armstrong Gravity Core was the only solution. It's a legend in Jericho. The most important invention in the history of mankind; a device that could have given the Grand Finale an actual winner, and Armstrong threw it into space. Refused to make another. Everything could've been different if the Gravity Core stayed on Earth. Everything."

He paused, dragging himself from the brink of a rant. If blaming a dead man for the state of the world was his motivation for killing hundreds, Diane was not impressed.

"I found the biggest satellite dish in the Junkyard," he said, getting back on track. "I bounced my signal around for weeks, pinging from satellite to satellite, until I finally made contact with *Cradle*. Then I hacked your system, initiated the landing protocol—"

Diane finished the tale herself, "And you messed it up, and *Cradle* crashed."

"No!" Isaac said. "Everything was perfect on my end—"

"You're blaming *Cradle* for crashing itself?"

"Listen to me!" He ran back to his keyboard. "The satellites! I linked with *Cradle* by satellite, and when I finished uploading the landing command, I got this response . . ."

He typed something, and a black rectangle appeared on every computer screen. They all contained the same lines of green code, repeated over and over and over again:

```
c={state:function()]error}cmd=recall.TOWER(if cmd=recall
{override})_error = override invalid (cmd=recall.TOWER)
[override]error(cmd=recall.TOWER)[override]error
```

For Diane, it was like reuniting with a ghost. She had only seen those lines on *Cradle*—and in her nightmares.

"Has anyone told you about the AI?" Dr. Isaac asked. "The Hive Mind?"

Diane forgot all about her manipulation, now hungry for the truth behind those dreadful lines of code. "The one that controlled the Peace-keepers?"

The scientist nodded grimly. "Tower. Its name was Tower. Symbol of providence and triumph, built to end the war, attempted to end all wars by pacifying the human race. It's alive. It's not Junkyard superstition. Tower *lives*."

As Virgil had told her that first night, *nobody wants to make that reintroduction.*

Diane zoomed on the computer screen, on the lines of code, on the single word:

TOWER.

She didn't know what to think. It was all too big. A threat too immense to comprehend.

"When I connected to *Cradle*," Isaac said, "Tower must have used the connection to access your system. It turned my landing code into a crash."

"Why?" Diane asked.

"Who knows? But it's out there, somewhere, and who is going to stop it when it decides to make a move? Wellington? They use satellites all the time. Jericho is doomed."

Isaac went back to the Grave Walker, filling its visor with desperation.

"There are evils in this world, Diane. Scarier than Crybaby. More dangerous than any roadkiller. The Junkyard needs a guardian."

"A guardian," Diane repeated, "like the Messenger?"

"Exactly!" Dr. Isaac exhaled with relief.

"If you think the Messenger's guardian material," Diane said, "you're sicker than I thought."

Her rejection confounded Isaac, and she didn't stop there. "Tower or no Tower, you made the connection. *Cradle*'s blood is still on your hands."

More arguments and justifications spewed from Isaac's mouth, but this time, Diane did not engage. She sat silently, ignoring him until he gave up and went back to work. But she knew the argument was still racing around his mind even then. He wasn't a blind fanatic like the Messenger; his actions needed logical explanations. By challenging that logic, Diane had thrown his entire worldview into question.

In other words, Dr. Isaac was on the hook.

CHAPTER 32

Virgil waited outside the sturdiest building in the Inner Ring, the only one with surveillance cameras, barbed wire, automatic plasma turrets, and other hallmarks of an actual security system. He didn't have to worry about the Messenger's troops finding him here; even they knew better than to encroach on the Oxen headquarters.

He had a hell of a time convincing Ishmael to let him go out alone. Virgil stressed repeatedly that he and the Oxen were on good terms; showing up with a bodyguard from the Shallows would have sent the wrong signals. Plus, Leon needed Ishmael's intimidation factor way more than Virgil did. The Modified were on good terms with no one. Ishmael had gone on and on about his mission to protect Virgil, his disassociation from the rest of the crew. It had taken a bag of tomato seeds for him to get with the program. Spooky bastard was relentless.

An electric buzz sounded from the door. "*State your business.*"

Virgil pressed a button on the door's intercom box. "Tell Hudson that Virgil's in town."

The door swung open almost immediately, and a brawny merc invited him inside.

The Oxen were the closest thing the Junkyard had to a shoe-shined, buzz-cut military force, and their barracks owned it. No soldier was idle. If they weren't running drills, they were briefing their next mission.

If they weren't shooting targets, they were cleaning rifle parts. A very specific generation of Grand Finale propaganda decorated the walls, hand-drawn posters from the war's final stretch when Tower reigned and Peacekeepers were the enemy. A few older artworks infiltrated the mix. Photocopied and optimistic, they featured a blue-armored battalion escorting a giant battlemech dressed in lumberjack clothes. *Bunyan and the Blue Ox Unit—Protecting Your Nation in a BIG Way!*

"Major Bishop!" Virgil hollered.

His escort delivered him to a heavyset woman wearing StormCell-powered ballistics armor. On sight, she slapped Virgil's palm and fist-bumped him, smiling wide.

"How the hell'd you get past the FireFighters, you crazy son of a bitch?" Major Bishop asked.

Virgil shrugged his shoulders. "Just walked right in."

"I seriously doubt that," Bishop said. "Come on. Colonel's upstairs."

She led them to a quarter-turn stairwell, passing a squad that was running laps up and down the steps. They reminded Virgil of the argonauts outside the dam, going through the only motions they knew.

"So you're a private army now," Virgil said. "How's that been?"

Bishop kept a straight face. "It's been . . . an adjustment. But we trust Hudson's call. Colonel's never steered us wrong before."

She was good at hiding her resentment, but not good enough. Virgil could feel her straining to stay positive. Time to add some pressure.

"What's it like working with Peacekeepers?" he asked.

Bishop tensed. "We don't work with Peacekeepers."

"Didn't recognize them under the bandages?" Virgil joked.

The Ox didn't find it funny. She stopped them on the stairs, poking a finger into Virgil's chest.

"We're not part of the Messenger's ranks," Bishop said. "We're on a contract, and everything we earn goes right back into purging Peacekeepers out in the wild."

The squad in training passed by again. Bishop lowered her voice. "The Messenger's got his bots house-trained, so we tolerate. But the second one steps out of line, we'll bring it down."

"Bring it down, huh?" Virgil said. He had removed all snark and challenge from his tone, and now there was only sympathy. He was a concerned friend, nothing more. "The longer you wait, the harder that'll be."

Bishop stepped back, calming gradually. It wasn't Virgil who angered her. He was merely digging up fears that weren't buried deep enough.

"We're all a little on edge," she admitted.

"Colonel's never steered you wrong before," Virgil said. Somehow, he managed to sound reassuring and foreboding all at once.

They left it at that.

When Bishop led them into Colonel Hudson's office, the Oxen commander was looking out a window at the Inner Ring, facing away from the door. Virgil caught only a glimpse of the colonel's back before Bishop announced their arrival, but it was enough to spot something out of place. Something that did not belong.

A bizarre rash festered on the back of Hudson's neck, shaped like a fingerprint.

As Virgil was processing his discovery, the red-faced colonel spun around.

"Long time no see, junkie!" he said.

Virgil had never needed to mask a reaction faster in his life.

"How's it going, Colonel?" he asked, shaking the Oxen commander's hand.

"Client's got us running all over hell and back," Hudson lamented. "But it's safer than our usual work, and it pays well."

"Then you can afford my merchandise," Virgil said.

Colonel Hudson smirked. "Your food does boost morale. Let's see what you got."

Virgil laid out six leather pouches in a line across Hudson's desk. The colonel checked through each, already recognizing the crops. He was an old customer.

"Inventory's a little light," Virgil said. "I had to bribe some Fire-Fighters to let me into the Heap."

"They give you trouble?" Hudson asked, pinching a pumpkin seed to check the texture.

"Eh, pushed me around a little. Not the brightest flames, are they?"

Hudson grunted a confirmation. "Degenerates. No better than road-killers."

The Oxen hated the Peacekeepers on a professional level, like an exterminator hates ants, but their loathing for the FireFighters ran personal.

"Boastful lot too," Virgil pretended to recall. "Just bragging their heads off, nonstop. Brag, brag, brag."

The colonel huffed. "Brag? What do those burn victims have to brag about?"

"Kept saying how it was their time," Virgil said. "How they're finally gonna make bank."

Hudson shook his head while scrutinizing the quality of some strawberry seeds. "They won't make shit standing around a brick wall."

"No, like . . ." Virgil strained to remember the details of his fictional encounter, ". . . they kept talking about how much extra junk they'd earn when the Messenger sent them on supply runs."

A startled look passed between the colonel and Major Bishop.

"How they'd spend it on booze," Virgil went on. "Brothels, bonfires. They sure love burning things, huh?"

"Why would *they* get put on supply runs?" Hudson shouted. "That doesn't make any goddamn sense!"

A few passing Oxen hesitated outside the office. Bishop stepped out to shoo them away.

It was exactly the reaction Virgil had hoped for. The Messenger didn't need two clans running out for supplies, so why would he promise that work to the FireFighters? Was he putting the Oxen on something different? Was he pushing them out? What did this *mean*? So many questions. So many reasons for the Oxen to distrust the FireFighters more than ever.

Virgil feigned innocence. "Hey, man, I just got into town. I don't know what the hell's going on."

Hudson bought the act. He cleared his throat, embarrassed by his own outburst, and tried to use business to play it off. "Carrots, grapes, pumpkin seeds," he said.

Virgil gathered up the reject pouches. "*Great* choices, Colonel."

Virgil left the barracks carrying garbage bags stuffed with Battery. The Oxen had a fun habit of mixing chemical stimulants into their medicine, and the capsules were red instead of green. Though everything had gone according to plan, Virgil suffered a vague sense of unease. He'd been afraid to ask Bishop about the rash on the colonel's neck. Maybe it was just a coincidence? Wishful thinking at its finest. He hurried back toward Batty's, lost in his thoughts, and he almost missed the barely visible light distortion on a rooftop overhead. He did a double take, but the refraction had vanished.

Just a trick of the light? Virgil hoped.

More wishful thinking.

CHAPTER 33

Ishmael scrutinized the oblique rooftops over the alleyway, hunting for spies that might be watching from above. He found none, but that did little to ease his mind. The Heap was packed with enemies, and as a former religious fanatic, he knew a thing or two about believing in the unseen. He remained on high alert.

While Ishmael, Rok, and Gage kept watch, Leon knocked on a nondescript door in the Heap's darkest alley. Rusty and crooked, invisible to the untrained eye, the entrance to the Modified headquarters could only be found if you knew where to look.

And if you were looking . . . god help you.

A magnified eyeball appeared in the door's peephole, splotched red from a burst blood vessel or two.

"Go away," a voice croaked.

"I need to speak with Pipes," Leon said.

"We already told you to get lost, company man."

"He'll want to hear—"

"¡*Vete*!"

Something slammed behind the door, and the peephole went black.

"Maybe we should leave a note?" Gage mocked.

Though he showed no signs of it, Ishmael found Leon's blunder amusing. All his strength, all his shiny Jericho connections, and he couldn't open a scrappy little door. To add insult to injury, Rok pushed Leon aside and knocked on the door again. She knocked fast and loud, refusing to let up until the eye reappeared.

"What?" the eye asked.

"You need a mechanic?" Rok asked.

The eyeball hesitated. "We take care of our own."

"Yeah, I've seen the pus. You're doing a real bang-up job in there."

The croaky voice spoke to someone farther away, and after a brief argument, it came back within earshot.

"We can't hire outside help. It's against the Lifestyle."

"I'll work for free," Rok said. "You just gotta hear the company man out."

More arguing behind the door.

Rok shouted into the peephole. "I'm the best mechanic on Caravan, and I sure as shit won't be coming this way again! If you need something fixed, now's the time to open up!"

The door creaked open. There was no one on the other side, just a flight of spiral stairs going down. Leon gave Rok a somber nod, then he marched down the stairs.

Rok and Gage mimicked the nod to each other, then they went down after him. Ishmael followed, watching their backs.

The smell hit them first, a rancid stench of iron and rot that made the Aardwolf bunker seem like a rose garden by comparison. There were barely any lights in the basement, and the few neons present revealed scenes of DIY cybersurgery that made Ishmael want to retch. Sweaty, washed-out mercenaries cut into their own flesh with dull scalpels, swapping pieces of their bodies for avant-garde cybernetics they'd cobbled together themselves: a hand with heated blades for fingers, a miniature laser cannon in place of an eyeball. They huffed stimulant-infused Battery to keep from passing out, and the fanatical pleasure on their faces reminded Ishmael of his former brothers and sisters back home. These mercenaries believed in something. They were adhering to the Lifestyle. They were the Modified.

Their commander wasn't hard to find. He sat upright on a hospital-bed throne, big as a beached whale, his every major organ rigged to some machine that kept it running long past its expiration date. Steel pipes invaded his neck and mouth, and for whatever hellish reason, he had no eyelids. An attendant stood by him at all times, tweaking the machines and applying eyedrops when requested.

"Pipes!" Leon greeted. He had to shout. The basement was filled with blaring industrial rock music.

Pipes looked to Rok. Gagging on his namesake, he said, "It's against the Lifestyle to let an outsider touch our modifications, but . . ." He inhaled, and the mechanical ventilator behind his bed made a loud rattling sound. ". . . this noise is driving me up the fucking wall."

Rok went over to the faulty machine and got to work. Gage stayed close to her, keeping a nervous eye on all the Modified who were leering at Gage's own augments. Leon remained at the foot of the hospital bed, where he could make his sales pitch in clear view.

Pipes noticed Ishmael waiting back by the stairs. "You Shallows types are coming out of the woodwork," he gurgled.

The remark confused Ishmael. "What do you mean?"

"You're not with the tattooed group that came into town yesterday?" Pipes asked.

We are coming for you, Brother Ishmael.

The question implied something that disturbed Ishmael to his core. He approached the hospital bed with a passion so frantic it made the nearest Modified reach for their guns.

"Was there an old man with them?" Ishmael asked.

"Doesn't matter," Leon said quickly. He moved between Ishmael and Pipes, forcing the discussion back on track. "We're here because Wellington has a proposition for you."

"Save your breath, *servidor*," Pipes replied. "It's a precious thing, and we want nothing you have to offer—"

Rok dropped her electric screwdriver in midturn. "Do you want this fixed?"

Pipes made a gurgling sound in his throat.

"Then *escuchas*," Rok insisted.

Bitter, Pipes gave Leon the floor.

"Parts," Leon said. "We can give you parts."

"We have parts," Pipes said.

"Not the kind I'm talking about."

Leon propped his foot on the bed and pulled his pant leg up to the knee, revealing a bionic limb of unparalleled craftsmanship. The CA-2020 Sprinter, manufactured by Wellington Incorporated, designed by one Dr. Malcolm Isaac. No one in the room could resist a look at this apex of cybernetic technology. Even Ishmael took pause.

"I'm talking new, top-of-the-line, Jericho parts," Leon said.

"Rigged with kill switches, no doubt," Pipes said.

Leon lowered his pant leg. "You can do the install yourself. No cybersmith included, just the parts. Use them. Sell them. Stick them up your ass, whatever. They're yours."

"For what price?" Pipes asked.

"There's going to be some fireworks," Leon said. "Sit back, enjoy the show. Don't get involved."

Rok came away from the ventilator, and when Pipes breathed again, the machine made only the softest sigh.

"The Messenger has been good for us," Pipes said. "We make more for doing less." His lidless eyes went back to Leon's leg. "But Wellington would give us the most for doing nothing at all . . ."

The ventilator sighed. The crewmates held their breaths.

"It's gonna be a tall order," Pipes said.

"We can fill it," Leon promised.

After negotiations were complete, the crew returned to the sunlight in high spirits. Gage sang Rok's praises for getting them through the door, and after some intense goading, pushed Leon to admit his gratitude as well. It was about as begrudging as a thank-you could get, but Gage called it a sign of growth for the company man. "Baby steps," he said.

Only Ishmael remained dour, pondering the tattooed group Pipes had mentioned. He barely registered the humanoid light distortion waiting just outside the crooked black door, and by the time he turned to get a better look, it was gone.

CHAPTER 34

The Messenger stood alone on the fortress balcony, where the Heap was an endless jigsaw puzzle laid out beneath him.

Back in the war room, Father Santiago sat perched on a leather chair usually reserved for Aardwolf patriarchs. Brutus 9-T-9 kneeled on the floor, scrubbing at fresh plasma burns on his bionic shoulder and legs. The Messenger knew that his lieutenant's encounter with the Sacred Chapel gunsmiths couldn't have been easy, but Brutus had handled that brush with death like all the battles previous. He moved on. Win, clean up, and win again. This strategy had kept Brutus alive during his years trapped in the Reno blood sports, and now, it made him the perfect soldier.

In a gesture of trust, the three men conversed without their entourages present. All soldiers and acolytes had been told to wait elsewhere.

"The Junkyard will fight you," Father Santiago said. "They will fight tooth and nail to keep their freedom."

"Not after the voyage," Brutus replied. "When we come back with the gifts, everyone will join us. They won't have a choice." The Messenger could hear his lieutenant scrubbing harder, wiping at stains that refused to fade. Some traumas never did. "No more cybersmiths," Brutus said. "No more Reno. We'll build *paraíso*."

"Unity is inevitable," the Messenger called back.

Father Santiago joined his host on the balcony. The Messenger held the Shallows archpriest in high regard. What the Masked Man had accomplished here through brute force and deception, Santiago had done with belief back home. Armed with his words—words and nothing more—he had all but deified himself in the eyes of his people, harnessing raw fear to build an army of his own. He would make a powerful ally in the coming days, if all went according to plan. Or a costly enemy, if they did not.

"You already have a gift of your own," Santiago said, "and a ship that can sail the skies. Is your voyage so essential?"

The Messenger looked down at his rebandaged hand, tapping its fingers on the balcony rail. "My grip is strong, but my reach is limited. I need to make more like me."

"Then I have one final condition," Santiago said, "if you wish to dock in the Shallows. One more request."

"Name it," the Messenger said.

Before he could, two transparent beings dropped onto the balcony.

Cloaking devices powered down; the refractions solidified into Ker assassins—sexless charcoal mannequins, bodies of alloy, faces of glass. They were built with speech processors, but they spoke in the digitized chirps of their Peacekeeper kind. The Messenger understood every word.

Brutus ran onto the balcony. "What happened?"

"Jericho agents are in the city," the Messenger translated. "I believe they're trying to unite the human mercenaries against me."

"Fucking greedy mercs!" Brutus said. "You pay them more than they deserve!"

The Keres leaped away, reactivating their cloaking devices in midair. The Messenger couldn't say where they landed.

"Material goods won't be enough anymore," he reflected. "I've pushed the order of things too far. Retaliation was inevitable."

Commotion rose from the streets, drawing all three of the men's gazes downward. Not far beyond the fortress wall, a townie had stolen a plasma rifle from one of the Modified, and she used it to open fire on a pack of bandaged soldiers. She was calling for someone named Andy, and it was the last thing she said before an argonaut shot her in the back.

The Messenger watched on. "I must inspire loyalty. True loyalty. I must show them what I am."

"That will be risky," Santiago warned.

It was a risk the Messenger wanted to take.

He had grown tired of working in the shadows. Tired of sharing his name and reputation with his lesser lieutenants. These methods had been necessary in the early stages of his campaign, but things were different now. Had he not forced the Heap under his rule? Had he not constructed a device thought to be scientifically impossible? Yes, he had done the impossible, and the time for subtlety was behind him. He would show these mercenary scum and Jericho rats what power they were up against. Not just power; *righteous* power. The Messenger was convinced that if he called on the loyalty of his people, they would answer. He truly believed that he was in the right, and only a fool would disagree.

He would suffer fools no longer.

"Escort Santiago back home," the Messenger ordered Brutus.

"I should stay and fight!" the cyborg protested.

"If fighting does break out," the Messenger said, "and Santiago's caught in the crossfire, our line to the Shallows will be cut forever."

Brutus wouldn't hear it. "Our numbers are low enough as it is. If the mercenaries rebel, you'll need me here—"

The Messenger rested his bandaged hand on Brutus's shoulder, and he flexed.

"You're the only one strong enough guarantee his safety across the Junkyard. You're the only one I trust."

The rash on Brutus's cheek darkened, lines squirming. The fingerprint came to life, and all resistance in the cyborg faded like a bad dream.

"*Hasta pronto*, my friend," the Messenger said.

Brutus returned to the war room, motioning for Father Santiago to follow. The tattooed elder made sure to keep a safe distance between himself and the Messenger as he passed.

"Whatever your final condition is, Father," the Masked Man promised quickly, "I'll see it done."

"I will hold you to that when you arrive at the Shallows," Santiago said, then he followed Brutus out.

Now alone, the Messenger could hear the whispers in his head with perfect clarity. How sweet they sounded as they encouraged, persuaded, and influenced him. Their messages defined him, and soon, they would redefine the Junkyard entirely.

The future is coming, they said, *and it belongs to you.*

CHAPTER 35

Things moved quickly in the Junkyard.

The day after Virgil had paid his visit to the Oxen clan, the leaders of the Aardwolf resistance gathered on Batty's roof, where a makeshift patio bathed in the ominous shadow of the fortress a hundred yards away. Jeremiah Aardwolf, Leon of Wellington, Rok of Caravan, Gage 4-D-5, and Ishmael the Heretic all sat around Virgil Ceres as he laid out his plan for the coming invasion. They all listened closely.

"You hit the Oxen with a grenade or something at sundown," Virgil was saying. "Something combustible. They'll think it was the FireFighters, get crazy pissed, and launch a counterattack."

"And that's when we go for the fortress?" Jeremiah asked.

"Exactly," Virgil faced out to the rest of the group. "Then Gage will take Rok over the wall so she can hack the gates—"

Gage slipped his hand under the mechanic and lifted her a couple inches off the floor. She responded by slapping him in the face.

"—then we'll split up in teams to look for Dr. Isaac. Ishmael sticks with me; Leon can rendezvous with Gage and Rok."

In truth, Virgil wanted Leon away so that he could focus on finding Diane. He only hoped that he would reach her before the battle did.

"So your plan," Rok said, "is to make two armies fight to the death. Over nothing. That doesn't feel screwed up to you?"

Virgil shrugged. "They're mercenaries, Rok. It's what they do." He turned to Leon, moving right along. "You sure the Modified will stand down?"

"Everything's set," the company man said. "You sure the Oxen will connect the dots you want them to?"

Virgil gestured to the enhanced, Wellington-issued CB radio set up in a corner of the patio. Leon had provided it to the Aardwolves so they could communicate through the Heap's radio blackout, and Virgil had just been using it to keep tabs on the Oxen's private channel.

"Without a doubt," he said. "They're just waiting for the last straw—"

Thud . . . Thud . . . Thud.

"What was that?"

Thud . . . Thud . . . Thud.

Around them, at street level, hundreds of feet stomped in unison, keeping a steady tempo. The beat captured the crew's attention, as it captured the attention of every townie, Oxen, FireFighter, and Modified mercenary in the Heap. Thousands looked to the fortress, where Virgil could see bandaged warriors standing along the wall and in the streets around the wall, stomping in rhythm, stomping until every eye in the city was looking to them.

They needed no cue to end the demonstration. They had begun as one, and they stopped as one.

Silence fell over the Heap. Even the storm kept quiet.

Virgil spotted someone tall and muscular taking their place above the southern gate, and he knew that it must be the Messenger. His presence was daunting even from hundreds of yards away, across a sea of townies, and his voice boomed loud enough to be heard by all.

"I've asked so much of you," the Messenger called to the Heap. "I've upset the balance of your lives, and for what? For what purpose? Why am I here?"

Quiet commentary spread across the patio. "The hell is he doing?" Jeremiah asked.

Virgil went to Leon. "He ever call a town meeting before?"

"No," Leon replied. "No speeches."

"I am the Messenger," the Masked Man said, "but I haven't given you my message. I thought it could wait, but now, as the forces of Jericho conspire against us . . ."

Townies and mercenaries alike cast wary glances around their city. Up on the roof, the resistance leaders felt a communal chill.

". . . there's no time to waste. We must unite against a common enemy. You must be told."

"He thinks we're turning the mercs against him," Virgil realized. "He's trying to rally the troops."

Gage clicked his tongue. "With a speech? Damn, the ego on this guy . . . He's out in the open . . . I could finish him now—"

Gage moved to the patio's edge, but Leon grabbed him by the arm.

"Don't be an idiot," the Wellington man said. "You'll blow everything."

Gage's optic implants narrowed to dangerous slits. "Don't touch me, *servidor*."

Rok stepped in. "Gage, relax . . ."

While the group bickered, Virgil detected another sound that most of his crewmates did not. A van was weaving down the plastic streets away from the fortress, using the Messenger's speech as cover. Its windows had been ripped away long ago, and Virgil could easily see its passengers. A bandaged soldier drove, Brutus 9-T-9 took up much of the back seat, and two tattooed acolytes sat in the middle. Sandwiched between them: an old man with a long, sickly beard and the scariest eyes Virgil had ever seen.

When his memory caught up with him and he recognized the tattoos on the soldiers for what they were, Virgil checked on Ishmael. The Shallows refugee was watching the van as well, his face mirroring the look of horror Virgil had seen when Ishmael first climbed the stairs into the dam's temperature control room. Virgil hadn't thought much of it at the time—Ishmael was always making weird faces—but now he wondered what it was that had made his bodyguard so afraid.

"You good?" Virgil asked.

Ishmael said nothing.

"Forget them. Remember the mission. We're almost home free."

Virgil turned back to the Messenger's speech. The Masked Man paced along the wall, playing the crowd like a seasoned performer.

"In a past life, I was a junkie. Sick, hopeless, a slave to the Battery life. I know what it is to be desperate, my friends. So desperate to live that you forget your reasons for living."

Virgil shushed his scuffling crewmates. He was listening now, really listening. The Messenger, a junkie? Bugshit.

"I grew so desperate . . . that I began taking junk dives on the coast, by the sea. At night."

A primal aversion shook the audience. They all knew the dangers of that place, at that time.

"I think I did it because I wanted to die. I wanted something to come out of the water and free me. To end the pain."

Virgil understood. Wrapped up in the horrors of the Junkyard, every junkie felt the urge to call it quits every now and again. Some were better at ignoring the urge than others, and if Virgil didn't have the unique responsibility of a home that needed him, maybe he would have taken his own walk on the beach a long time ago.

"One night, I almost got my wish," the Messenger said. "A tentacle came out of the water and caught my arm. I escaped, but the arm was ripped clean off."

He lifted his bandaged arm. "I wandered up the shore, bleeding, attracting every predator for miles. I really thought I was going to die."

A loose thread dangled from the Messenger's elbow. He grabbed it, pulled it back, and began to unravel the bandages.

"Until I saw a light."

It was hypnotic to watch, the strands unwinding one by one. The Messenger was a mystery, and he was untangling that mystery for all to see.

"The light came from a battleship marooned on the beach. I crawled inside, and I found something I'd never seen before."

Rays of color-shifting light seeped out from between the final bandages. No one in the Heap understood what was happening. No one could look away.

"It had no shape at first, but as I got closer, it became the one thing I needed most. It reached out to me . . ."

The last bandage fell.

". . . and I embraced it."

In structure, the Arm was normal—a proportionally muscular arm on a large, muscular man—but all normalcy ended there. From fingertips to armpit, the hand and Arm were a translucent tangle of organic strings writhing around each other, defying gravity to maintain their collective shape. An electrified luciferin coursed within the fibers, glittering so technicolor bright that some onlookers had to shield their eyes. Virgil figured everyone in the Inner Ring could see it, and those confined to the Outer Rim would hear plenty about it later. It was an alien thing, not of the Junkyard, an anomaly in a world of anomalies. No one, not even Virgil, had seen anything like it.

"It gave me strength," the Messenger said, flexing the fingers as if they were his own. "It cured me of the Blues. It sculpted my body into something powerful."

Virgil was just as captivated as the rest of the audience, and Leon's voice next to him took him by surprise.

"Look at them. They're hanging on every word."

Virgil followed his eyeline, confused. "Who?"

"The Peacekeepers."

It was true. The argonauts in the Messenger's army were all staring at their leader, engaged and attentive. Reactive, even. They were listening. They understood.

"Dr. Isaac's work? Did he hack them?" Virgil asked.

Leon shook his head. "I don't think so."

From then on, Virgil was keenly aware of an irregular quality in the Messenger's voice. He wasn't just loud; there was something layered under his words, a subliminal timbre running at a nearly imperceptible frequency. Imperceptible to human ears, maybe, but not to Peacekeepers. Virgil imagined they could hear him loud and clear.

Whatever that Arm really was, it let the Messenger speak to Peacekeepers.

"It's a gift," the Messenger announced to human and machine alike, "but not one of a kind. There are others. They call to me from distant shores, waiting to bestow their power onto others. Waiting to make *you* like *me*."

Something rumbled deep inside the fortress, too loud to be stomping feet.

"If only we could reach them."

As the heart of the Junkyard watched in awe, the airship rose suddenly from the industrial yard of the fortress. It was still missing pieces of cabin and hull, still bound to its dock by long tethers, but it could fly. It floated up until it was just beneath the clouds, and when lightning struck, the bolts deflected off a sphere of invisible energy.

"This just keeps getting better," Virgil murmured.

The sight caused most of the audience to forget all about the Messenger's Arm. Here was a miracle they understood. An airship could change everything. It could conquer the world.

"I am the Messenger!" the Masked Man called. "And my message is a power that can bring the Junkyard to its knees!"

He made a fist. The Arm turned lime green, and his troops chanted and stomped in a booming display of military might.

While others were ogling at the airship, Virgil had never taken his eyes off the Arm, and he saw that the fist and the chanting began in unison. Even the three soldiers on the street outside Batty's—two argonauts and a human—hit the cue with micro-perfect timing. These weren't trained soldiers following a cue. These were puppets, obeying the pull of an invisible string.

"Join me, and receive my gift!"

A terrible thought came to Virgil, insane at a glance, but the evidence was undeniable. He ran downstairs, ignoring the confusion from his crewmates.

"Accept the gift, and our union will make us invincible!"

Virgil dashed across the empty cantina, threw open the door, and waved his Volt Caster at the three soldiers on the other side of the street. A wave of energy knocked the two Peacekeepers out, and before the human soldier could react, Virgil punched him with his metal fist. He fell unconscious.

"Our foes will die screaming!" he heard the Messenger say.

Virgil tore away the soldier's bandages, and he found exactly what he had feared. A fingerprint, dark and inflamed, writhing like a swarm of maggots on the soldier's chin. It was the same mark he had seen on the cyborg Brutus 9-T-9 and on Colonel Hudson of the Oxen. The mark he would likely find on all the bandaged human soldiers, and anyone else who had let the Messenger get too close.

Esclavos.

"The Wall of Jericho will crumble at our feet!"

Jeremiah was the first one to follow Virgil down the stairs, and when he emerged from the cantina, Virgil grabbed him by the collar of his uniform.

"Get your troops ready," he said.

Jeremiah looked lost. "I thought we were waiting until sundown—"

"How do you feel right now?" Virgil asked. "Everything you just saw, how did it make you feel?"

"Confused . . ." Jeremiah stuttered, ". . . and scared."

"The other clans all feel the same way," Virgil said. "We can't give them time to realize it. We need them angry, not scared."

He released Jeremiah, who flew down the secret hatch and could be heard belting orders from the bunker. Virgil went back to the roof, pushing past Leon and the others as he made his way to the Wellington CB radio.

"What's going on?" Leon asked.

From the wall, the Messenger's speech came to a manic crescendo. "We will claim authority over anarchy! We will demand peace!"

Virgil's radio connected to the Oxen headquarters. "*This is Virgil for Major Bishop! I need to talk to Bishop!*"

Bishop's voice sounded distant but clear. "*Virgil?*"

Colonel Hudson interrupted. "*How'd you get on this channel?*"

Virgil's grip tightened on the radio mic. Hudson couldn't be trusted. He had the Messenger's mark.

"*Bishop, listen to me!*" Virgil said. "*The speech, it's a . . . it's a* signal! *For the FireFighters! They're going to hit you any minute!*"

"*Hit us?*" Bishop sounded confused. "*What are you—*"

"*The Messenger owns them, and he thinks you're a threat! He wants them to clear you out of the Heap! This speech is the signal!*"

"We will save the Junkyard from itself!" the Messenger continued.

Hudson cut in again. "*These are dangerous accusations—*"

"*I see them gathering now!*" Virgil cried.

On the outer barricade, the FireFighters were assembling for a clearer view of the Messenger, straining to see what all the commotion was about. They were clueless, babes in the woods. But from a distance, they could easily be mistaken for a raiding party waiting to get underway.

"*I knew something like this would happen!*" Major Bishop said. "*I told you, Colonel!*"

"*Bishop, you have to hit them first!*" Virgil said.

"*I'm in command here, junkie!*" Colonel Hudson shouted.

"*So give the order to attack!*" Bishop demanded.

"*Now hang on*," Hudson said. "*We've got no reason to believe him—*"

"*He's got no reason to lie!*"

Virgil knew he only had seconds, so he made them count. "*Hudson won't stop them, Bishop! You know he won't! He can't!*"

"The future is coming, my friends!" the Messenger bellowed.

"*They'll kill you all, Bishop!*"

"And it belongs to us!"

"*Do something!*" Virgil shouted.

The line went dead. Virgil dropped the mic as the chanting around them grew louder.

"What have you done?" Leon shouted.

Virgil took out his inhaler, meeting Leon's anger with a sheepish repose. "Well . . . I've either screwed our entire plan, or I've triggered a coup."

As he took a hit of Battery, something exploded by the outer barricade. Everyone on the roof ducked down. The Messenger's troops quit chanting. The Heap's undivided gaze turned outward, away from the Masked Man.

Virgil coughed. "That's a fucking relief."

CHAPTER 36

Things moved *very* quickly in the Junkyard.

From his stage, the Messenger saw a battalion of Oxen attacking the outer barricade with everything they had. Rockets filled the air with bricks and body parts. Laser beams ended lives before they even realized they were in danger. The FireFighters seemed totally caught off guard, unprepared for an assault from their own city, but they were quick to take up their flamethrowers and grenade launchers in retaliation.

As the battle consumed the border between the Outer Rim and the Inner Ring, the Messenger could only watch in bewilderment at the circle of fire closing around him. This was not the unified strike he had set out to prevent. This had nothing to do with him. This was chaos.

A laser hit the fortress wall, mere inches from his feet. The Messenger looked back to the immediate city beneath him.

"Ah," he said. "There it is."

The Aardwolves poured out of random buildings across the Inner Ring, howling their battle cry, dripping blood from the raw seams of their new bionic legs. They ran at full speed for the inner wall, and the townies scattered to avoid the crossfire.

Some of the Modified mercenaries joined the Messenger's soldiers in retaliation. They ejected hidden blades from their gangrenous fingers, powered up electric canons rigged to their nervous systems, and they lashed and shot at the Aardwolves until their fingers bled and their nerve endings fried. They were a formidable force, but they were ultimately a minority in their clan; someone must have paid the Modified to stand down in the event of an attack. The Messenger's promise of power had swayed a few of them to ignore the bribe, but not enough. The Aardwolf charge was merely slowed. They would reach the fortress. It was inevitable.

The glow in that fibrous Arm shifted red, and half the soldiers on the wall followed the Messenger back inside. The rest stayed behind to fend off the invaders.

CHAPTER 37

From the patio on Batty's cantina, Gage saw that the Messenger, his ticket to glory, was getting away. He jumped off the roof.

"Gage, wait!" Virgil protested, but the cyborg ducked into a crowd of fleeing townies and was gone.

"Now what do I do?" Rok said.

With no other choice, Virgil reworked his plan as fast as he could.

"Go back to the cars," he told her. "Move slow; don't cross the outer barricade until you have the perfect opening. Keep the vehicles safe. Your tank's got the firepower."

Rok turned to leave, but Virgil caught her arm.

"Don't leave without us," he said. "You stick around, and your debt's paid. You're off the hook."

Before the weight of his promise could crush her flat, Rok pulled away and fled down the stairs.

Virgil found Leon sitting on the patio floor, eyes closed, a hand covering one ear.

"You get hit?" Virgil asked.

Leon opened his eyes; the right iris was ablaze in violet. "She wants the Arm," he said. "Dr. Isaac is secondary. Optional. Wellington wants the Arm."

Virgil had been afraid of that, but he didn't argue. The situation had changed again, and he would need to play this one smart. Very smart.

"Okay, let's—" Virgil realized they were the only two left on the patio. "Where the hell's Ishmael?"

CHAPTER 38

Ishmael raced over the tented rooftops of the Outer Rim, chasing after the van.

He had narrowly cleared the FireFighters' checkpoint before the Oxen attacked, and the Inner Ring was now a volcano erupting behind him. He barely noticed. His mind was fixated on that face he had seen beyond the van's broken window. He knew it well. He saw it every time he closed his eyes.

Father Santiago. High Priest of the Order of the Shallows.

The Master.

Poor Ishmael. Lazy. Weak. Lost at sea.

If you find me, what will you do?

You are no threat. Merely an angry child.

What will you do, Brother Ishmael?

What can you do?

The waves crashed in Ishmael's mind, and he was everywhere at once. Running on the rooftops. Kneeling on the beach. Screaming in the church. He was there, and the Master was there too. He would never leave Ishmael alone. Not while he lived to spread his poison.

Not while he lived.

Ishmael caught up to the van as it slogged over a mess of rubble jamming the streets, slowing the escape considerably. Just when the vehicle had cleared its obstacle, and the edge of the Outer Rim was in sight, Ishmael jumped onto the flat roof.

"The fuck was that?" the driver inquired.

Ishmael shot his harpoon downward, splitting the driver's skull wide open, then reeled it back in. Dead weight pushed the gas pedal to the floor, and the van careened off the road, bulldozing any shelters in its path. Ishmael laid flat on his stomach; he wasn't going anywhere.

One of the acolytes in the back seat jumped up and shoved the driver's body aside. He hit the brakes and struggled to regain control of the steering wheel. The van finally stopped in an empty cul-de-sac, all scuffed and steaming from the calamitous detour. Ishmael rolled off the van, taking cover on the cul-de-sac's edge.

"That was one of our weapons," he heard Father Santiago say.

Brutus kicked open the trunk door. "Wait here."

Ishmael watched as Brutus stomped around the van, searching for any sign of the assailant. The cul-de-sac was a patch of quiet in the chaos until the driver's-side door creaked open. The acolyte joined Brutus outside.

"I told you to wait," Brutus said.

Whatever the acolyte's reply would have been, it was cut short when Ishmael fired his harpoon. The spearhead pierced the back of the acolyte's neck.

When Ishmael opened his hand and the chained harpoon retracted to the brace on his wrist, the acolyte keeled back and fell dead on the ground. His fall cleared the eyeline between Ishmael and Brutus 9-T-9, putting them face-to-face for the first time.

"Stand aside," Ishmael told the cyborg. "I am not here for you."

Brutus 9-T-9 stepped between Ishmael and the van. "My orders are to get this man home alive."

"That is no man," Ishmael said. "You are in league with a monster."

Ishmael looked to that very monster sitting in the center of the van. His face contorted when he and Father Santiago made eye contact, and all the tattoos on his body began to sting, as if they were being carved all over again, carved by the Master's hand.

Father Santiago spoke his next words in a low whisper, but Ishmael could read them on his lips. He had heard them so many times before.

"The Heretic."

"Leave me alone!" Ishmael screamed.

Ishmael launched his harpoon at the windshield. Brutus threw out his hand—an augment as fast as it was strong—and metal crashed and rang as he slapped the spearhead off course.

Instead of recalling the chain, Ishmael swung the tethered harpoon like an iron whip, lashing at Brutus in an effort to drive him away. But the Reno fugitive was undeterred, and he charged at the tattooed junkie while swatting the spearhead each time it came close. Ishmael dove out of Brutus's path at the last possible second, retracting the harpoon in midroll. He landed on his back and launched it again. This time his aim was perfect, set to rip the skin from the cyborg's sickly face, but Brutus caught the harpoon with one robotic hand. Before Ishmael could react, the cyborg's hand began to spin three hundred sixty degrees atop its wrist, like a power drill.

The chain twisted around Brutus's knuckles, dragging Ishmael closer and closer. The pulley rig on Ishmael's back creaked in protest, but there was no resisting the cyborg's strength. Ishmael dug his heels into the dirt as he tore at the straps on his harpoon brace, desperate to free himself. He had to get away before—

Brutus punched Ishmael in the chest. Ishmael felt something crack, and something else tear. All the oxygen rushed out of his lungs, and he couldn't get any of it back.

When Ishmael hit the ground, Brutus stomped on the harpoon brace. He shattered the chain, the harpoon-launching mechanism, and the bones in Ishmael's arm. Ishmael wheezed in absolute agony. He prepared to become another tick in the cyborg's endless body count, but then Santiago called out from the van:

"Leave him be."

The Master crossed the cul-de-sac and knelt by Ishmael's side, laying a boney hand on his forehead. The Heretic tried to squirm away, but every movement felt like knives in his chest. He was a child again, laying broken on a desolate beach, beaten for disobeying. His brain was on fire.

"Do you seek forgiveness, Brother Ishmael?" Santiago asked.

Seek forgiveness?

Forgiveness?

Ishmael shook his head. Tears poured down his face.

"Then your pilgrimage is not yet complete."

Not yet complete.

Not yet.

The Master was no longer an old man to Ishmael. His tattoos had eaten the human parts of his face, leaving only the visage of a beast—a terrible kraken with burning eyes. It leaned down and kissed Ishmael on the forehead.

"*Never forget the way back.*"

Feeling those lips on his skin, Ishmael had two options: black out or go insane.

His brain chose the former.

CHAPTER 39

Back across town, Virgil saw that the invasion of the fortress was in full swing. The Aardwolves were using the magnetic soles of their new bionic feet to scale the fortress wall, shooting at their bandaged opponents all the while. A righteous bloodlust propelled them forward. They were swifter than ever before, and just as pissed off. This was their city. They were taking it back. A demolition squad set about rigging the fortress door with ion bombs, attracting fire from all bandaged troops in the immediate area.

Amid the distraction, Leon vaulted from a shanty rooftop onto the fortress wall, then down to the other side. Virgil clung to his back for the entire maneuver, and when Leon's bionic feet touched the ground, the men separated in a flash.

"*No le digas a nadie,*" Virgil warned.

"It's embarrassing for me too, asshole," Leon said.

While confirming that no enemies had spotted them, Virgil caught sight of Gage for the first time since the cyborg had abandoned their crew. The cyborg was flailing atop the wall, punching the air, as if battling a swarm of ghosts. Something unseen sliced Gage's artificial cheek. The cut was shallow, but long. Painless, but alarming. Virgil squinted to see the unseeable. Who hit Gage? *What* hit him?

The cyborg lashed the blades out from his forearms, puncturing the veil of refracted light, revealing a Ker assassin with an energy dagger sizzling from its wrist. The Peacekeeper struck at Gage again, as fast as the cyborg was, if not faster, and it looked to Virgil like it was taking every ounce of Gage's concentration to keep the death machine at bay. When he tried to retreat, another invisible blade sparked at his foot, keeping him in place. There were two Keres on Gage now. Maybe more.

Virgil took a step forward, but Leon called him back. "No time. Gage can take care of himself."

It pained Virgil to admit it, but he knew the company man was right. Gage had chosen to go it alone. His life was in his own hands.

There was no need to wait for the demolition team at the door. Leon had scouted the fortress from top to bottom in the days before his rendezvous with Virgil, and he knew things about the building that even the Aardwolves did not. For instance, he knew where to find a defunct storm drain that led directly under the fortress. The drain's cover was rusted shut, but fortunately, Virgil's heated knife could cut metal like butter. And it did just that.

Jumping down, the interlopers landed with a *splash* in a setting Virgil was all too familiar with: a sewage tunnel. Knee-high blackwater, abominable stench—they could've been on their way to Jericho. Grated ceilings gave a porous view of the industrial halls above, allowing the faintest of lights to trickle down to the depths. The sewers under the fortress were a dark, slimy, putrid hellhole, but Virgil had seen worse. At least nothing down here was trying to eat them.

They slunk through the tunnels, bickering over their aimless and repugnant route, until a clanging sound overhead caught their attention. The sewer filled with darting shadows, and they looked up to see a team of soldiers passing the grate above them. As Leon rushed to follow the soldiers from below, Virgil slowed a few steps behind him. He knew that the Wellington agent would want to take on the Messenger right away, but he had other plans.

Virgil made a move to turn down a different tunnel. Leon caught him in the act.

"The Messenger's this way!" Leon said.

"You go," Virgil insisted. "I'll look for Dr. Isaac."

"Dr. Isaac's no longer the priority."

"I was hired to find Isaac, I'm finding Isaac."

"That doesn't make any—"

Leon stopped midsentence. His organic eye twitched, and Virgil knew the jig was up.

"You're looking for the kid, aren't you?" Leon accused.

Virgil's face must have said it all. The truth cracked Leon's cold comportment, and he came undone in that snowballing way that only a company man could manage. "This is why I don't work with junkies," he said. "You're not professionals. You're crazy. All of you. You're a bunch of drugged-up, deep-fried lunatics! And your *priorities* are *fucked*!"

Virgil tried not to laugh. "'Deep-fried,' huh?"

"That kid is not the job!" Leon scolded. "You're under contract! You don't break a Wellington contract!"

"Priorities change," Virgil said.

Before Leon could argue, Virgil slapped Leon's bionic leg with the Volt Caster. The limb went temporarily stiff, and Leon could only shout after the old junkie as he disappeared down the wrong tunnel.

"Ms. Violet won't forget this!" Leon shrieked. "You hear me? *She'll have your fucking head!*"

Leon's threats followed Virgil deep into the sewers, a rambling tirade that went on until the man was out of earshot. The hate in Leon's voice sounded personal, downright resentful, and Virgil could guess why. It wasn't abandonment that enraged the company man. It was Virgil's ability to abandon. He was not bound to Ms. Violet by the omnipresent threat of a kill switch. He could come and go as he pleased. His legs were his own.

Virgil allowed himself a moment to catch his breath. The stun effect on that bionic limb would have passed by now, but he knew that Leon couldn't chase him. Ms. Violet would order Leon to prioritize finding the Messenger, and despite all his vengeful promises, he would obey. Leon always obeyed.

As Virgil plodded off down the tunnel, he reflected on his new enemy. If he and Leon ever crossed paths again, it wouldn't be pretty.

CHAPTER 40

Silent. Numb. The world reduced to a grain of sand.

After Dr. Isaac unplugged the Grave Walker's power cable, Diane hovered in the dead place, unmade and slowly suffocating. It was peaceful in a morbid way. If something happened outside, if a rocket struck the laboratory and killed Dr. Isaac, there wasn't a thing she could do about it. In this powered-down state, she had no responsibilities. Everything was beyond her control.

Was this what it felt like to be dead?

All too soon, Isaac pushed a tier-two StormCell into place, and life came crashing back. Diane's lungs inflated. Her visor filled with renewed vision, and she could hear Isaac in mid-rant.

"—for nothing! I told him the speech was a bad idea! He showed our hand—"

Not far away, an explosion ripped the fortress doors off their hinges, and the whole building trembled. Dr. Isaac fell to his knees, weeping in terror for the second time that day. The first time had been when he saw the Aardwolves scaling the fortress wall, and Diane had seized that moment to dig her metaphorical hook deeper than ever. She redirected Isaac's fear to unravel his faith in the Messenger's army, adding that if he left her immobilized when the battle reached the fortress, his genocide against *Cradle* would be complete. Isaac had agreed to free her from the shackling power cable then and there. Virgil would have been proud.

"Just calm down," Diane said, now fully functional. "I'm going to get you out of here."

The scientist wailed, "And go where? The whole city's a war zone! The Aardwolves will kill me for helping the Messenger, and the Messenger will kill me for trying to leave!"

"We'll get out of the city," Diane said. "We'll find Caravan. You'll be safe . . . but you have to keep your promise."

Isaac grabbed the Grave Walker's leg, groveling at her feet. It was a bad look. "Get me to safety, and I'll get you out of the suit. I promise. I swear—"

Sparks burst from the autodoor sealing the laboratory, followed by black smoke. Isaac hid behind the Grave Walker.

A contest raged between the door's electronic locks and a surge of intrusive energy, and the locks inevitably lost. The door zipped open, but there were no Aardwolves on the other side. Diane was shocked to see Virgil step out of the smoke, his magnum drawn and his Volt Caster sparking. Diane's reaction was a complex hybrid of joy, anger, and relief. Meanwhile, Dr. Isaac moaned in horror.

"Get away from her!" Virgil yelled, aiming the gun at Isaac's head.

Diane moved between them. "Wait! It's okay!"

Virgil's arm went limp. "You're okay?" The sight of her had pacified him instantly, conjuring a gentleness that Diane had never seen in Virgil before now.

He wasn't there to find Dr. Isaac. He was there to save her.

"I'm okay," Diane confirmed.

"Did they hurt you?"

"No. Well . . . Isaac didn't."

Virgil darkened again, chewing on the implication. "Excuse me a sec," he said.

Before Diane could stop him, Virgil dashed around her and threw Dr. Isaac onto his back, pushing the gun muzzle into his forehead.

"What is it?" Virgil asked.

Isaac was baffled. "What's what?"

"The Arm! How does it work?"

An eerie euphoria came over the scientist. "You could never understand. It's a gift—"

Virgil bashed the magnum barrel across Isaac's nose. Cartilage snapped, and blood squirted across the laboratory floor.

"Don't!" Diane cried.

"Try that again," Virgil said, reuniting gun with forehead. "Less creepy this time."

Isaac gagged on the blood pouring into his sinuses. "It's . . . ugh . . . an artificial symbiotic life-form."

"Meaning what?"

"It was made, not born, but it's a living thing. And it needs to bond with another living organism to survive." Despite his pain, the look of wonder came back to Isaac. "The life-form can edit DNA to make the host stronger. I've never seen anything like it."

Virgil eased the pressure from his gun. "So *you* didn't make it? He really found that thing on a beach?"

Isaac spat more blood onto the floor. "I've only studied it. It's . . . it's old. Very old. I think it was meant to be the next phase in the Peace-keeper program. Tower could control the machines, but the Arm can influence machines *and* humans. Directly."

"That what the fingerprints do?" Virgil asked.

Dr. Isaac nodded. "The hand secretes an enzyme that makes the human brain susceptible, um, to certain frequencies."

This was all news to Diane. She thought she had grasped the full extent of the Messenger's wickedness, but she wasn't surprised to learn that he was infinitely worse. *Fingerprints.* Plural. That meant there were more victims out there other than just Brutus 9-T-9. A whole army of them.

While Diane reeled, Virgil continued his interrogation. "He said there were more life-forms on distant shores. How can he know?"

"The Arm connects the Messenger's mind to a kind of . . ." Isaac struggled to explain, ". . . It's so hard to put in laymen's terms—"

Virgil poked Isaac's broken nose with the magnum, making the scientist's eyes water with pain.

"You're a smart guy," Virgil said.

"It's like . . . an organic radio signal. There really are other life-forms calling to him, in a manner of speaking. They want transportation to the mainland. They want hosts."

Virgil began to laugh. Not his good-humored laugh, nor the punchy laugh from surviving a deadly close call. To Diane, it sounded like Virgil was losing his mind.

"Fuck, he's just another slave!" Virgil said. "You're all slaves to a stupid glowing Arm!"

"No!" Isaac protested. "He's in control. His personality's intact—"

"How would you know? You only met him a year ago!" Virgil grabbed Isaac's head and twisted it around, inspecting every patch of bare skin. The scientist whimpered, confused and hurting.

"Don't see any fingerprints on you, *cabrón*," Virgil accused.

Isaac tried to put on a brave face. "I believe in what the Messenger's doing. The Junkyard needs unity."

"Thought you were supposed to be smart." Virgil stood up. "He doesn't want unity. He wants war. He wants to drop those parasites all over the Junkyard, turn us into *esclavos*, and then he wants to take on Jericho."

"Maybe it's time someone took on Jericho," Isaac countered.

"We can't survive another war, Doc!" Virgil said. "The last one almost wiped us out. If the Messenger gets his way, he and Wellington will finish what the Grand Finale started. There won't be anything left."

Dr. Isaac smirked hatefully through his blood. "So you'll take the Arm to Ms. Violet? You think that'll make things better?"

"No," Virgil dismayed. "That'd be worse. So much worse."

He punched Isaac again in the nose, then left the scientist to wallow in his own blinding pain. The good doctor wasn't going anywhere. Diane watched Virgil as he went to the laboratory computer. He began to type, faster and more skillfully than she would have expected. He had never seemed like a computer guy.

"What're you going to do?" she asked.

Virgil stared at the computer screens, tracking the big picture. "The Arm can't go to either side. Any side. It needs to be taken off the playing field."

There was a challenge in his words. A threat. Diane didn't like it.

"I've seen the Messenger up close," she said. "I've seen what he is. He'll kill you."

Virgil kept working as if he hadn't heard.

"What about getting a StormCell for your greenhouses?" Diane asked. "What about your home?"

"There's no escaping war, kid," Virgil said. "It spreads everywhere, leaves nothing alive. A tier-five StormCell's worth jack if we're all dead."

He pressed the Enter key, and the phrase *UPLOAD READY* appeared on the screens. "And even if war didn't reach the mountain, my home can't survive without the Junkyard. We're parasites too, in a way."

He unplugged the cord from the broken Nurse droid Isaac had been data mining, and a quivering light in its glass body died for good.

"I've been the worst kind of parasite," Virgil told Diane. "I wasn't straight with you, and I took without asking. That was fucked. I'm sorry. I really am."

Diane had never heard him say the word *sorry* before. Not once.

"I just—" Diane felt herself choking up. She was still angry with him. Glad he was alive, afraid that he wouldn't be alive much longer, and majorly pissed off at him all at once. "I really let myself trust you, you know?"

"Problem is," Virgil said, "I never trusted you. I've never trusted anybody in this dump; that's how I survived so long. But I forgot you're not from this dump. You're not even from this planet."

He reached out for the black box on the Grave Walker's wrist. Diane flinched backward.

"It's okay," Virgil said softly. "It's more than a blood rig."

Diane couldn't bring herself to move toward him. She was still afraid of the needle, and the Grave Walker wouldn't budge.

"Please trust me," Virgil said.

With no little effort, Diane lifted her wrist to him. He plugged the data cord into a hidden slot on the box, then went back to the computer.

"I'm gonna do right by you," he said, "if it's the last thing I ever do."

He pressed the Enter key again. A torrent of ones and zeros poured out from the computer, through the cord, and when they entered the Grave Walker, they took the shape of a topographical map in Diane's visor. A marked route led north, deep into a mountain range at the end of the Junkyard, along a winding pass hidden among the rocks. The route ended at a peak marked with a low-res image, but even through the muddled resolution, Diane could make out a river, pine trees, children in homemade tunics playing with furry four-legged animals. *Dogs? Dear god, they really had dogs.*

Diane blinked, and the map shrank to a corner of her HUD.

"That's how you get home," Virgil said. "It's a long trip, and dangerous, but you'll manage."

"Virgil . . ."

"Tell them I sent you. Take Isaac, so he can pull you out of the Grave Walker when you get there. And tell them . . . tell them they should start prepping a new courier. Sooner the better."

And just like that, Diane was off the hook. It was a new feeling, and it made her feel stranded, like a tether had broken. She was free-falling.

"I can't make it there without you," she said.

"Yes you can," Virgil promised. "And when you're settled, you do me one more favor. Find a woman named Úna. My age, red hair, got a smile bright enough to melt your face off."

Now Virgil was getting misty eyed, but he didn't try to conceal it. He had given Diane his last secret, and there was nothing left to hide.

"You tell her I love her," he said. "I love her so goddamn much, and I did what I did to keep her safe."

He unplugged the cord from Diane's wrist, then he snapped his Volt Caster at the laboratory computer. The screens exploded. The console went up in flames. There were only two maps to the mountain pass now. One in the Grave Walker's head, the other in Virgil's.

After giving Dr. Isaac one final death glare, Virgil went back for the door.

"Please don't do this," Diane said.

Virgil took out his inhaler; it was loaded with capsules that glowed red instead of green. He took a hit, and a ruby mushroom cloud billowed from his green-stained mouth. His pupils dilated with chemical-induced mania.

"Someone's gotta," he said. Then he was gone.

CHAPTER 41

As the airship lowered back into its dock, Virgil snuck quietly into the industrial yard. Virgil felt sharper and deadlier than he had in years, but also just as reckless. It took all his willpower not to run at the airship guns blazing.

From behind a stack of shipping crates, he watched bandaged soldiers pour into the open arena, weapons aimed at the doors from which they'd come, ready to defend their leader until the very end. The Messenger stood among them, now armed with his bladed battle staff, arranging his troops into tactical formations. Virgil could guess where his head was at. The Messenger didn't need the Heap anymore, and even in this incomplete state, the airship seemed completely flyable. A team of engineers scurried across the ship's deck, no doubt making some last-minute calibrations. The Messenger just needed to hold off the Aardwolves long enough for his engineers to complete their work, and then he could leave the Junkyard for grander shores. When he returned . . . god help them.

But the situation wasn't quite so simple. Virgil spotted Leon perched above the airship on a girder, the sights of his Deckard plasma pistols aimed at the Messenger's head. He was clearly tired of playing this mission the Junkyard way, all bombastic and guns a-blazing. He could do this the Jericho way. He could kill from a distance.

Virgil held his breath, waiting for the assassin to take his shot . . .

but then a sudden weight landed on the girder, throwing Leon off-balance.

Leon realized what had happened just a millisecond too late, when a Ker's invisible dagger slashed at his arm. The blow sent him tumbling off the girder, and though he landed on his feet, the impact was loud. Everyone in the yard looked to him, the Messenger included. Virgil swore under his breath.

"I thought there'd be more of you," the Messenger said.

Virgil stopped himself from running to the company man's aid. Leon and Ms. Violet were no longer his allies, and if his enemies wanted to duke it out, he'd rather not get in their way. Then, in the span of one-point-five seconds, several things happened nearly at once:

Leon took aim at the Messenger.

The luciferin in the Messenger's Arm went red.

Leon fired his pistol.

The nearest human soldier leaped in front of the Messenger and took Leon's plasma shot to the chest.

The soldier died. The Messenger lived.

The Arm made a fist, and all nearby troops began to run at Leon. The ones with guns and arm cannons opened fire. The ones with clubs and machetes swung wildly.

On Wellington legs, Leon ran forward in a Z formation, evading plasma shots while firing off some of his own. He blocked the first swinging club with his left foot, then broke the owner's neck with his right. Other warriors fell upon Leon, fifteen combatants against one, but not a single machete touched him, and no plasma shot grazed him. He was a deadly danseur in a ballet of dodging and execution, no movement wasted, every shot hitting its mark. Additional soldiers joined the fray, but none could hurt the company man.

Virgil was ready to call the fight in Leon's favor when something cracked—

Suddenly, Leon could no longer move his right foot. He found the Messenger's battle staff impaled through his ankle, pinning him to the ground.

Virgil cringed; Leon hadn't seen it coming.

The Messenger caught the Wellington agent with an overhead blow from the Arm, splitting his brow and instantly blackening his human eye. Then he grabbed Leon off the ground and punched him again, and again. Over and over, beating the cyborg's face to a pulp. Leon floundered to get away, but the staff held him tight. He was a fly caught in a web, and the spider was draining him one crushing blow at a time.

Finally, when the Messenger delivered a brutal uppercut, Leon's bionic ankle tore free, and Leon went sliding across the concrete floor. He staggered upright, shooting wildly to keep the soldiers away as he limped off down the yard, his right foot dangling beneath him.

The Messenger ripped his staff out of the ground and held it up like a spear. He took aim—

Suddenly, Leon stopped. The cyborg's legs went rigid, sending his upper body flailing before his back snapped upright, stiff as rigor mortis. His arms froze, and when his head turned to look over his right shoulder, his purple eye burned brighter than ever. When the cyborg's mouth opened, a woman's cordial voice addressed the Messenger instead.

"I think it's time you and I had a chat."

The Messenger lowered his staff. Virgil knew that voice instantly, and though the Masked Man had probably never heard it before, he seemed to recognize it all the same.

"The Witch behind the Wall," he said.

"'Ms. Violet' will do fine," the voice said through Leon. "Is there an actual name I can call you? 'The Messenger' is so melodramatic."

The Messenger parted his soldiers, giving him a clear view of the Wellington puppet. "It's the name you'll beg for mercy, right before I rip out your tongue—"

"Please," Ms. Violet said, "don't waste my time." She kept a pleasant, unaffected tone. "I've heard it all before. You think you're something new? That you can change things? The Junkyard squeezes someone like you from its bowels every couple years, and it always swallows you back. You're a temporary inconvenience, at best."

The Messenger walked toward Leon, who tried and failed to will himself away. Virgil wondered if this paralysis was a new trick up Violet's sleeve or an old trick being revealed for the first time.

"What would you know about the Junkyard?" the Messenger asked. "You hide behind your wall, sending puppets to do your bidding. You fear the Junkyard because you can't control it. You never will."

"Neither will you," Ms. Violet said. "You think you have power, but your little speech told me you have no idea what power is. You're not a ruler. You're a mascot."

The Messenger readied his staff for a killing blow. Sweat poured down Leon's forehead.

Violet didn't sound concerned. "I'm offering you a lifeline. If you want any longevity, Wellington is your only option. We're the future."

"¡*Mentiras*!" the Messenger shouted. "Who mastered the will of man and machine? Who conquered the sky? I have reprogrammed the natural order, and *I* am the future!"

Ms. Violet laughed. "You are entertaining, I'll give you that. But the future? You won't even last the night."

Shivering with rage, the Messenger lowered his staff.

"You'll be a part of my future, soon," he said. "You and all of Jericho."

The light filling his index finger turned to a dark merlot, and he lifted it slowly toward the cyborg's beaten face. Ms. Violet would see how little her kill switch meant to one of the Messenger's followers. If touched by that hand, Leon would forget the kill switch was even there.

"You won't have a choice—"

The crackle of plasma fire cut him off, immediately followed by the galvanic groan of dying Peacekeepers.

The Messenger turned to the rising sound of disordered footsteps. They rumbled within the fortress, sprinting, jumbled with countless whoops and battle cries.

Moments later, the Aardwolves reached the industrial yard.

They poured in from every entrance, unloading plasma shots with reckless abandon. The bandaged troops fought back with equal fervor, and while the commotion distracted the Messenger only for a moment, it was enough time for Ms. Violet to release her grip on Leon. Virgil watched as the *servidor* limped past the invaders, putting as many bodies between himself and the Masked Man as possible. The Aardwolves must have recognized Leon as an ally because they made no effort to impede his escape.

Virgil pitied Leon, then. He was leaving the battle with no pride, no autonomy, no Arm, and no Dr. Isaac. He had only his life, and the chilling knowledge that his life was not his own. Leon was truly Wellington property, and Wellington must have decided that his presence in the Heap was no longer required. The cyborg limped back into the fortress, heading for the Inner Ring beyond, and Virgil assumed that he wouldn't be coming back.

The Aardwolves, by contrast, seemed to have everything under control.

They were faster than their enemies, craftier and more passionate than the argonauts, and they were many. If the Messenger had anticipated Aardwolf reinforcements, his ace in the hole would have been the loyalty of the mercenary clans. But the clans had failed him, and now his army was outnumbered and slowly dwindling. Things were looking bleak.

But none of this seemed to faze the Messenger. Not for a second. If Leon had been a danseur, then the Masked Man was a tornado. He spun his battle staff at supersonic speed, ricocheting plasma shots back to the Aardwolf enemy, decapitating and disemboweling anyone who got too close.

When he was deep in the heart of battle, a squad of hatchet-wielding Aardwolves tried to take him on at once, coming at him from all sides. They were the bravest of their kind to rely on melee weapons, and they were all nearly as quick as Leon had been. To the average soldier, the Aardwolves were elite. To the Messenger, they were playthings. He parried the first volley of chops, then he lodged one end of his staff into one of their chests and left it there for safekeeping. He caught the wrist of another charging soldier, ripped away their hatchet, and used it to cleave their skull wide open. The Messenger proceeded to fight off each member of the squad with their own weapon of choice, hacking them down one by one, using the freshly dead as human shields. By the time he chucked the hatchet and reclaimed his battle staff, the remaining Aardwolves had formed a wide circle around him.

The Messenger scanned the mob around him until his sights landed on the youngest soldier in the pack. The weakest and most terrified. The Messenger pointed his alien finger at the frightened teen, and the message was clear. *You're next.*

Virgil had seen enough. He took one last hit of red Battery, waited for the stimulants to kill his lingering fear, and then he went to work.

Taking advantage of the chaos, Virgil maneuvered across the industrial yard as the young Aardwolf turned heel and ran for his life. The Messenger gave chase, laughing with cruel amusement, and the pursuit brought him right into Virgil's path.

The junkie leaped out from the blur of combat, grabbing the Messenger's battle staff with his Volt Caster. The Messenger suddenly found a weathered old face glaring at him with dilated pupils, green lips curled into a half smile. The Volt Caster began to glow, and Virgil shot an ungodly voltage into the madman's staff. When the Messenger released his grip, the electric charge sent him flying backward across the yard. He landed at the foot of an elevating platform beside the airship, singed and smoking, but somehow still alive.

Struggling to his feet, Virgil threw the battle staff aside and stalked forward toward the Messenger, still flying high on military-grade stimulants. Flying high and out for blood.

The Messenger climbed onto the elevating platform, and to Virgil, it looked like an act of retreat. He gave chase, thinking the Masked Man wasn't as tough as everyone had made him out to be. But once Virgil had climbed to his level, the Messenger smacked a control panel and sent the platform rising high above the concrete yard. The junkie realized his mistake too late. When the lift settled, the battlefield was a distant memory below them. They were on level with the airship's deck, but the workers must have moved the platform while they were prepping for takeoff, and it was now an island in the empty air. He and the Messenger were alone at last. *Mano a mano.* Two men enter; one man leaves.

"Aw, hell," Virgil mumbled.

He snapped the Volt Caster. The Messenger held out the Arm, and when the energy bolt made contact, its membrane actually absorbed the lightning, feeding it to the fibers. The previous electric charge must have made contact with the Messenger's real hand, and that clearly wasn't going to happen again. Shock attacks were off the table.

Reluctantly, Virgil drew his knife and pressed the button on the handle. The blade heated to a piping orange. Behind his mask, the Messenger greeted the challenge with a lunatic's grin. Virgil could see it in his eyes.

In the fleeting moments when they weren't fighting for their lives, many Aardwolves looked up to catch a glimpse of the second war raging over their heads. It was a close fight, a duel between raw strength and seasoned experience. In theory, Virgil should've had the upper hand. He had a weapon, and the Messenger did not. But the Messenger was faster than him. Much faster. The stimulants helped, but Virgil's heightened perception could only do so much with his limited reflexes. He was only human, and the Messenger was so much more.

When the Messenger dodged a knife swing or Virgil ducked a punch, it was always by the skin of their teeth. When a blow connected, it seared flesh, drew blood. The Messenger's Arm could block the knife without succumbing to heat or pain, and those twisty fingers—made from a thousand tiny tendrils—would reach out for Virgil's face every chance they got. One touch, one gentle caress, and the fight would be over. Meanwhile, Virgil's head throbbed after taking his first punch, and the second made him see stars. He couldn't keep up this routine much longer. A third punch would be the end of him.

The Messenger must have grown tired of the fight as well, because the next time the knife came at his face, he grabbed the blade with his bioluminescent hand and squeezed. Steam hissed between his fingers. The knife crumpled in his grip. Virgil released the handle and staggered back, helpless to save the first weapon he had ever scavenged from the Junkyard.

Rest in peace, ol' buddy.

As the Messenger dropped the ruined blade, his Arm pulsed red. Far below, an argonaut received the message. It retrieved the Messenger's battle staff and tossed it upward with a Peacekeeper's strength. The

Messenger caught the staff and spun the blades in front of him, slowly moving forward.

Robbed of his knife and electricity, faced with a coming propeller that could deflect bullets and plasma shots alike, Virgil was left with one final strategy. It was a bad plan, probably the worst plan he'd concocted in years, but it was all he had left. Peace demanded sacrifice.

"Bright sun," Virgil whispered. "Bubbling brook, crystal clear . . ."

The blades drew closer, pushing Virgil to the edge of the platform.

"Úna's tears when she makes me promise to come back in one piece."

The Messenger was nearly upon him.

"Green grass. Green trees. Green everywhere. *Green*."

Virgil ran at the blades, blocking them temporarily with his Volt Caster. His parry left an opening, and he used it to wrap his gloved fingers around the Messenger's throat.

This too left an opening, and the Messenger used it to plunge his blade into Virgil's belly.

The junkie screamed as jagged steel pierced his armor and ripped into his stomach, pouring digestive acids onto the platform. He coughed blood, turning his beard from gray to dark red.

The Messenger peered into Virgil's watering eyes. "I expected more—"

But something clicked. Looking down, the Messenger found a magnum handgun digging into his armpit, right above that seamless divide where his skin met the artificial symbiotic life-form.

Virgil unloaded his rounds. All six of them.

They tore through skin, muscle, and bone, and by the time the cylinder was empty, the Arm was dangling off the Messenger's shoulder by a measly bit of sinew. With a light tug from Virgil, that too snapped away. The junkie pulled himself off the Messenger's blade, taking the Arm with him. He fell back onto the platform, while the Messenger remained standing, stumbling in a daze, trying to make sense of the gory stump that had once held his greatest asset.

He didn't notice how close he had wandered to the platform's edge. Not until he stepped right over it.

As the Messenger fell, Virgil lay on the platform in the fetal position, clutching the Arm to his chest. It was warm, slippery, yet a kind of static kept it clinging to his clothes. The fingers jerked on their own, but he didn't have the strength to notice. His world was going dark and blurry. His insides had turned ice cold.

At some point, he felt the vague sense of being lifted by two mechanical hands, and he saw the faintest glimpse of a blue visor looking down at his paling face.

Then, to no one's surprise, Virgil slipped into hypovolemic shock.

CHAPTER 42

Diane allowed herself the tiniest sigh of relief; the edge of the Heap was in sight.

Gage led the escape, jogging as fast as he could while carrying a battered Ishmael over his shoulder. They had found him lying half dead in a cul-de-sac, not long after Diane found Gage running aimlessly through the Inner Ring, covered in flesh wounds and fleeing unseen enemies. Lost in a paranoid trance, he hadn't responded to her call right away, looking at Diane like she was some hulking stranger. But then he saw Virgil dangling in her arms. The old junkie was unconscious, hugging something shiny and colorful, and his coat was drenched with blood. The image had snapped Gage right out of his stupor, and he brought Diane back to the hidden gap in the Heap's outer barricade. They continued their escape across the Outer Rim side by side, picking up Ishmael along the way.

As they cleared the vague border between the Outer Rim and the Junkyard, Diane chanced a peek at the Heap behind them. The battle had expanded outward like ripples in water, consuming the city in screaming chaos. The factions weren't clear to Diane. The Aardwolves and the Messenger's soldiers were clearly at odds, but whose side were the Modified on? Why were the Oxen and the FireFighters duking it out? And amid all of this, what would become of the townies?

Yet again, her burning questions would have to wait. She saw that

Gage was leading them over a dirt ridge, but the crew's vehicles were nowhere in sight.

"Are you sure the vehicles are parked here?" she asked.

"Positive," Gage panted.

"And you know how to drive?"

Gage responded with a mien of revelatory panic, but it was short-lived. When they came to the top of the ridge, the earth at their feet magically folded upward, revealing several soiled tarps that had formed a camouflaged tent over the vehicles.

Rok was waiting underneath. "Holy shit!" she exclaimed. "I was *this* close to bailing, you guys."

She lifted the tarp higher, and her crewmates joined her under the tent. Gage laid Ishmael down on the jeep's trailer, propping his broken arm as best he could.

Rok couldn't get to Diane fast enough. "What happened—?"

"Do something," Diane panted.

She set Virgil on the trailer, putting the Messenger's severed Arm on full display.

"*Holy shit*!" Rok said again.

The lights flashed between all the colors of the rainbow, and then some. The hand wouldn't stop squirming.

"You took his fucking Arm?" Rok was fixating on the wrong detail, so Diane rolled the base of its humerus to the side.

"Oh . . ." Rok looked like she might puke. "Oh my god . . ."

Virgil's stomach wound was a sanguineous chasm, a low-pressure fountain of bubbling gore. Rok moved away in disgust.

"You have to help him!" Diane said.

Rok wouldn't budge. "I'm a mechanic! I don't do . . . this!"

Diane could've laughed. Virgil had enlisted the best technician on Caravan, but he hadn't hired a single crewmate with medical expertise. A junkie's priorities.

"Please!" Diane begged. "He's dying!"

Mortified, Rok forced herself back to the trailer. When she pulled a staple gun off her tool belt, both Diane and Gage averted their eyes.

Neither of them could bear to watch what came next, but the series of clicks, snaps, and squelches painted a grisly picture in their minds.

"I hate this," Rok said more than once during the procedure. "I hate this so much."

When Diane finally looked back, she found that Virgil's armor had been removed, and a line of zinc-plated staples now snaked up his belly. It was a sad, probably damaging excuse for surgery, but at least it slowed the bleeding a little. In times like these, Diane figured it was best to count their blessings.

Rok pressed her fingers under Virgil's jaw, feeling his pulse. "He's lost so much blood . . ."

Diane held up her right arm. "Give him some of mine."

Rok looked startled, almost offended. Her breathing quickened, like she was on the verge of an anxiety attack. Like it was her blood on the line, not Diane's.

"You don't have to give him any more," she said. "You've already given so much."

She blames herself for what Virgil did to me, Diane realized. She felt the sudden urge to embrace Rok, to hold her tight and tell her that she was forgiven, that what happened in Pozo wasn't her fault. If only there weren't so much alloy between them, and that lingering sense of betrayal. If only things had played out differently.

"Just do it," Diane insisted.

Head shaking, Rok pulled the needle and tube from the Grave Walker's transfusion rig. While she set up the procedure, Gage started walking circles around the jeep, grumbling to himself. No one else could hear what he was saying, until he kicked one of the headlights in a paroxysm of anger.

"I didn't even get *close*!"

The shattering glass made Rok jump, but lucky for Virgil, the needle was already inserted. Diane's blood was making its journey through the plastic tube; it all felt eerily routine by this point.

With Virgil's treatment underway, Rok shifted her concern to Ishmael. He was a battered thing lying motionless on his back, staring glass-eyed at the tarps above. Add a couple centuries of dirt, and he would look nearly identical to that half-buried giant the crew had passed on the way over, give or take sixty thousand inches.

"What happened to you?" Rok asked.

"I failed," Ishmael said. He began to tremble, whispering the phrase repeatedly. "I failed . . . I failed . . . I failed . . ."

Rok went back to Diane—the only one who seemed to have her wits about her.

"What happened to Leon?" Rok asked.

Diane shook her head. She had no idea. None of them did except for Virgil.

As Rok counted their dwindled numbers, something else seemed to dawn on her. "Wait . . . What about the scientist? Oh, Diane, your suit—"

Diane cut the consolation off. She couldn't think about Isaac now and what leaving him in the laboratory had cost her. She had her reasons for going after Virgil, but they didn't make the loss any easier to bear.

"We were wrong about Dr. Isaac," she said. "He wasn't a prisoner, and he didn't give the Messenger his power."

Everyone watched the pulsing life-form clutched in Virgil's arms, groping at the edges of his coat.

"It was always the Arm," Diane said.

Rok went into solutions mode. "So we can still get paid. We can sell this to Jericho—"

"No!" Diane screamed. Her outburst sounded dire enough to stop Gage in his feverish tracks. "We can't give the Arm to Violet. It's too dangerous."

Rok tried to make sense of their situation. "So . . . what the hell was all this for?"

"I don't know who put the kid in charge," Gage butted in, "but right now, the only thing we *can't* do is stick around here. I say we haul ass to Caravan. We'll get everybody patched up, and then we can figure out what to do with Virgil's phantom limb—"

Another explosion rose from the Heap, followed by a rumbling vibrato. Those who were physically able stuck their heads out from under the tarps. They all looked toward the sound.

Back at the Heap, the airship was taking flight.

Weightless and untethered, it floated up from the fortress in a perfectly straight line, stopping just below the clouds. The ship's gravity field hit the smokestacks as it passed, and when the chimneys crumbled, the barrage of rubble wreaked havoc on the fortress below. Lightning couldn't touch the airship, nor could the plasma shots assaulting it from below. Whoever was attacking the vessel was fighting a hopeless battle, and the ship's laser cannons made quick work of letting them know it.

"Think they're retreating?" Gage asked hopefully.

Diane did not, and the airship soon proved her correct. Thrusters blazing, it sailed to the city's northern edge, turned right, then proceeded to fly in a perfect circle around the perimeter of the outer barricade. The ship made no effort to participate in the chaotic battle below, and Diane was the first to understand why.

"It's looking for us," she whispered.

A terrible uneasiness seized the crew. They were being hunted, tracked by a physics-defying sentinel that could see farther and move faster than anything the Junkyard had ever known. Diane figured that Isaac must have taken charge. Behind all the crying and cowering, he was just as ruthless as the Messenger had been; maybe more. He didn't care what happened to the Heap. What Virgil had stolen was infinitely more valuable, and now Isaac had the power to take it back.

The crewmates dove back under cover when the airship got close, and no one spoke until its baleful shadow had passed them by.

"We'll never outrun that thing," said Gage, of all people.

"Then we'll wait," Rok said, trying hard to sound calm, "and first chance we get, we're out of here."

She removed the tube from Virgil's arm, which retracted back into the Grave Walker. She sat down in the dirt, resting her back against the tank. Diane took a seat as well, and after a few more laps of futile pacing, Gage joined them. There was nothing else to be done. Outgunned in every sense, all the crew could do was wait.

Diane couldn't tell how long they sat there, listening to the battle, holding their breath whenever the airship darkened their claustrophobic hideout. In this stretch of inactive tension, Diane found herself fixating on the redness pooling around Virgil's body, seeping between the staples. She felt irritated with the bleeding, annoyed that after all the trouble she'd gone through to give Virgil her blood, he was just letting it spill. It underlined the futility of their situation, and this grievance was but a single rock in the avalanche Virgil had triggered. Diane was angry at his deception. Angry at him for roping her into this perfect disaster. But underneath all that anger, her old fear for the junkie's life was alive and well. Staring at his washed-out face, she realized the dynamic he had fabricated between them was finally real. Virgil was on his last legs, and Diane was the only one keeping him safe. The only person who seemed to care if he lived or died.

Despite everything he had put her through, Diane believed that Virgil was on the right side of this whole mess. Both he and the Messenger had used her, but where the Messenger had chained her up and left her to die, Virgil had set her free. He had spent what could have been his final words apologizing. That didn't make him a saint, and it didn't earn him Diane's forgiveness by a long shot . . . but it was something. A sliver of hope in all this hopelessness.

These were Diane's final thoughts before idleness and blood loss put her to sleep.

In the dream, everything was on fire.

Flickering yellow and orange, it burned on roads and blackened stop signs, houses, and charred school buses, clinging to surfaces like algae on a sunken ship. Things that had no business burning burned bright, and though Diane had never seen this place before, she knew exactly where she was. This could only be the Firelands.

Free from the Grave Walker, she stood at the center of a suburban roundabout. All *Cradle*'s passengers were gathered around her, burning like human candles, staring at the planet Earth hanging inexplicably in the black sky. A member of the crowd approached Diane, and the flames on his body extinguished. It was Ben Five-Zero-Nine.

"This will be everything, one day," he said. "Many orbits from now, everything you know and everything you've never known will burn."

Diane felt tears coming, but they evaporated in the heat.

"No," she cried. "We can't let everything burn."

New flames covered Ben's entire being, and when they disappeared, the Caretaker stood in his place. The bullet hole in his forehead was still fresh. "You can't fight it. Fire will take everything in the end. The living are the doomed."

Diane wouldn't hear it. "We have to stop it. We have to try."

In a final eruption, the Caretaker gave way to Virgil, free of his stomach wound, smiling his green-lipped smile. "And why's that, kid? Why should the doomed fight back?"

Voices, muffled and angry, rose up from everywhere and nowhere. Diane barely noticed. She was too busy remembering the last thing Virgil had said to her in the fortress.

"Someone's gotta," she repeated.

A single voice broke the sound barrier: "*Leave him alone!*"

Diane woke to find Ishmael swatting at Gage and Rok with his good arm, while the broken limb hung uselessly in a sling of torn cloth. The setting sun dimmed the world under their tarps, making the scene difficult to see and even harder to understand.

"Come on, man," Gage whispered urgently. "We don't got a choice."

"Stay away!" Ishmael barked.

Diane shook the grogginess from her head. "Guys, what's happening?"

She looked at Virgil, and the Grave Walker could barely repress her gag reflex. The Arm was no longer an arm. The luminescent strings had unwoven across Virgil's body, and while some ran up into his nose and mouth, most had wormed their way into his stomach wound. Rok's staples lay bloody and scattered around the trailer.

"What's it *doing*?" Diane retched.

"We don't know," Rok said.

"Yes we do," Ishmael objected.

Diane crawled to the trailer, intent on ripping the life-form off its prey, but when she got closer, she saw that Virgil wasn't prey at all. Far from it.

"The bleeding stopped," she gasped.

In a manner of speaking, Diane was correct. The blood from Virgil's wound ran up the glowing fibers, through the life-form's amorphous body, then back into the stomach. Virgil's breathing was also steadier, and though Diane knew it was impossible, she could have sworn the wound itself had shrunk.

The life-form wasn't preying. It was healing.

"Diane," Rok said, "we've been talking—"

"No!" Ishmael cut in, squeezing the trailer's edge with his good hand. "I will not let this happen!" He tried to pull himself upright, but the pain from his broken ribs kept him down.

"What's he talking about?" Diane asked. No one replied. "What happened while I was asleep?"

"We can't stay here," Rok said gently. "The battle's expanding, and now there are freaks in bandages driving around the Outer Rim. They're going to find us. Just a matter of time."

Diane could hear the grumble of motorcycles prowling outside the tent. They had to be close, because the explosive sounds of combat had reached new cacophonous heights. More bombs, more battle cries and wailing death. Underneath it all: the hum of that tireless airship, still making its rounds. It knew they were close, and it would not give up until they were found.

"So we need a plan," Diane said.

"We have a plan . . ." Gage began, but when it came time to elaborate, he looked to Rok to deliver the news.

"We're giving the Arm back," she told Diane.

"You cannot!" Ishmael yelled.

"We don't have a choice," Gage said.

"It is the only thing keeping *jefe* alive!" Ishmael pulled at the trailer's edge again, and this time, he brought himself upright so that he could see Diane, so the two of them could lock eyes.

"I failed," he said. "My book fell open, and I failed my only mission. I cannot fail again."

Gage smacked the trailer. "Listen, asshole. We all got screwed out of a payday. Let's not get screwed out of our lives—"

"Why would we give it back?" Diane asked, sounding oddly composed.

"Whoever's piloting that ship doesn't care about us," Rok said. "If we give back the Arm, they'll leave us alone."

"We do not know that," Ishmael said.

"It's the best chance we got," Gage argued.

More debating ensued, but Diane paid little attention. Her mind was already made up. Where Virgil couldn't drop his investments empty-handed, and the Messenger couldn't fathom that he might be in the wrong, Diane could not let the monsters of the world have their way. That was her particular brand of crazy.

"What about your blood pact?" she asked Rok.

The mechanic flinched. "What about it?"

"You owe Virgil," Diane said.

"I don't owe him *shit*." Rok was shaking now. "Five years, he's been holding it over my head. Working me to the bone for scraps. Making me build things I would *never* build." Her eyes darted to the black box on the Grave Walker's wrist. "I'm done. I'm not going to let him own me anymore."

"What was your hook?" Diane asked. "What did Virgil hold over your head?"

"That's not—" Rok bit her lip, cutting off her own refusal. "You know what? No. You should hear this. You need to know who it is you're protecting."

She sat back in the dirt, already exhausted from the tale she had yet tell.

"I'm from an auto repair village, east of Reno. I lived there with my family. When business was good, we lived like Wellingtons. When business was bad . . ."

Images of famine played in Diane's head. Parents and children splitting a single Nutribrik. Battery doses taken only at the last possible moment. Disturbed, she pushed the images aside.

"One day, a man came to our garage," Rok continued. "He said he'd give me a hundred Nutribriks if I hooked a bomb to a certain junkie's car. Guess they were chasing the same contract."

Diane could see where the story was headed. All the road signs were clear. "You didn't . . ."

"We were starving." Rok kept her head down. "Virgil drove a pickup back then. He came in that afternoon, just like the man said he would. And every night after Virgil left, I'd have these horrible nightmares. I'd see my bomb ripping the truck apart. Over and over. I felt like I was going crazy.

"But two days later, Virgil came back. He was pretty messed up, but he was alive."

She forced herself to look at Virgil, still clinging to life in his trailer.

"He made me a deal. I wasn't too good with bombs, but I was damn good with cars. If I agreed to be his personal mechanic, leave my family, and set up shop on Caravan, he wouldn't tell the Junkyard that my village made their customers explode. It would've ruined us."

Blackmail, Diane realized. *Sounds like Virgil.*

"I deserved to be punished," Rok said, "but not my family. He would've made them all starve just to keep me on the hook. That's the kind of guy he is."

Diane knew exactly what kind of guy Virgil was. To Rok, to her, and to probably so many others. She was one of the few people who understood his motivations, but the ends did not always justify the means.

Nevertheless, Diane stood her ground. "The Arm can't go back."

Gage moved toward Virgil. "It has to—"

The Grave Walker stepped in Gage's way, bowing its head under the tarps. "It won't."

"You think Virgil would take a stand for you?" Rok asked.

Diane didn't answer, watching Gage for any sudden moves.

"He lied to you," Rok said. "Stole your blood. Didn't deliver on any of his promises. Why are you defending him?"

"I'm not," Diane insisted.

It still hurt to think about what she had given up, abandoning Dr. Isaac to go after Virgil, but now was the time to articulate her reasons. She had no mind control powers to win her crewmates over, no perfect bargaining chip that would fulfill their hearts' desires. She had only her reasons.

"This isn't about Virgil," she said. "If we give the Arm back, they'll make a new Messenger, or something worse, and all of this will have been for nothing."

"What do you even care?" Gage asked. "You've got no skin in the Heap."

"They don't want the Heap. They want everything."

"It's not your fight!" Gage made a move to dash around the Grave Walker, to get at Virgil and rip the life-form away, but Diane's reflexes were too quick. She caught Gage by the chest and shoved him back, knocking him to the ground.

"They destroyed my home!" Diane screamed. "They murdered everyone I ever knew, and now they're trying to do it all over again! *You'd better goddamn believe it's my fight!*"

Gage shuffled back across the dirt. "You said you were from—"

"I lied!" Diane said. "I'm from fucking *space*!"

Rok pursed her lips. "Knew it."

The Grave Walker shook with rage. "I'm sick of letting bad men hurt me. And I'm done pretending there's nothing I can do about it."

She spun to Rok, panting and fervent, keenly aware that she had everyone's attention. For the first time since her accident on *Cradle*, people were listening.

"They will own you," Diane said. "They'll make you build weapons for their war, and you'll do it for less than scraps. You'll do it just to survive. And if you try to get out, or get even, they'll kill you."

She pointed at Virgil lying in the trailer. "Don't fight for him. Fight so you never have to do anything for people like him ever again!"

"Whoa whoa, *fight*?" Gage rose to his knees. "Who said anything about a fight?"

"We don't have the firepower," Rok said, shaking off the charm of Diane's invocation.

"You have a tank," Diane countered.

"If lightning can't hit that thing in the air, my cannons are useless."

Diane consulted all her knowledge on the Gravity Core, every firsthand observation, every detail overheard, hoping to unearth some crucial weakness. Something she would have feared while living on *Cradle.*

That's when she noticed the spiral notebook dangling from Rok's belt.

"Then we bring it down another way," Diane said.

She ripped the notebook away, ignoring Rok's protests while flipping clumsily through the pages. When she found the right sketch, she threw the open notebook onto the ground.

"This."

Everyone else rubbernecked at the blueprint for Rok's Conductor-turned-EMP device, and Rok was the first to speak. "You're kidding."

Diane was dead serious. "The station's gravity field was never full-proof against solar flares. They were enough to shut the Core down for a while, and those came all the way from the sun. A close-range EMP burst would definitely take out the airship, at least temporarily."

Rok considered the idea. "I mean, I have the EMP emitter in my tank. I could probably— No, the design's completely untested. And we'd need a Conductor."

"Closest one's in the fortress," Gage said. "So that's out."

"Why is that out?" Diane challenged.

Gage laughed. "Do I really have to spell it out for you? The second we peel out of here, the ship will spot us. It'll blow us off the map before we ever get close."

"So we split up," Diane said, thinking fast, unwilling to abandon her plan so easily. "The vehicles distract the airship while one of us goes for the Conductor."

"You haven't seen the emitter in that tank," Gage said. "It's huge. You can't just pick it up and carry it around."

"I can," Diane said, then she looked to Rok. "Can't I?"

Rok smiled. The longer she studied her own blueprint, the more confident she seemed.

"Yes, you can."

"Hold up." Gage waved his hands at Rok as if trying to free her from a spell. "You're not actually considering this."

Diane knew she was. Rok was a mechanic. She liked to fix things.

"We helped make that mess out there," Rok said, nodding toward the sounds of war. "And we're the only ones who can clean it up."

"We don't even know if your thing will work!" Gage shouted.

"If Rok designed it," Diane said, "it'll work."

"You're *adorable*." Gage sat down, turning his back on the others. "You guys want to commit suicide? Have a blast. I'm out."

Rok and Diane were primed with an abundance of arguments, insults, and pleas that might persuade Gage, but they never got the chance to unleash them. Ishmael beat them to the punch.

"I watched you run at a queen centipede head-on, with no regard for your own safety."

His voice startled the others yet again—Gage most of all.

"You are many things, Gage 4-D-5," Ishmael said, "but you are not a coward."

Gage peeled back a corner of a tarp, stealing a look outside at the omnipresent airship circling above. The lightning storm was hitting the gravity field with everything it had, but the invisible sphere would not be breached. The vessel was untouchable.

"The centipede couldn't fly," Gage said.

"Could the Chimera?" Ishmael asked.

While Diane and Rok hung awkwardly out of the loop, something profound passed between the cyborg and the Heretic.

"No," Gage whispered.

"Then this would be the deadliest foe you have ever encountered," Ishmael said. "But you must face it. If you run, your fear will chase you to the ends of the Earth, hurting everyone in your path, and the fault will be your own. You made a mistake when you led the Chimera to that village by the dam. You did the right thing outside Pozo. Do the right thing now."

The cyborg made a whimpering sound, one that might accompany tears if his eyes had any tear ducts.

"What is he—" Rok gasped at Gage, comprehension dawning. "You saw . . . You didn't say anything about—"

"Would you have believed it?" Gage asked doubtfully.

Rok thought for a moment, then knelt beside Gage. "If it was you telling me . . . Yeah. I would have."

Ishmael sat up straight to face the crew, no longer clinging to the trailer for support. "If we run, they will kill us. If we surrender, they will enslave us. And if we do not fight this together, all of us, we will fail."

"You didn't want anything to do with us before now," Gage accused.

Wincing, Ishmael gestured to his mangled arm. "In the Heap, we all got separated, and . . . you see the consequences. Against the centipedes, we stood together, and we won."

Gage lowered the tarp corner as the airship passed overhead. With sunlight failing, its shadow plunged their hideaway into a total blackout. Then a spotlight washed over them, burning away the darkness, giving everyone a half-second heart attack. The moment quickly passed, but the fear did not.

"I didn't sign up for this last-stand shit," Gage moaned, burying his face in his hands.

Rok squeezed Gage's shoulder. "None of us did."

"But here we are," Diane said.

The crewmates listened to their enemy sailing across the evening sky, defying the laws of nature just to hunt them down. Diane figured they all had their selfish reasons for agreeing to face the night, but she also felt there was a revelation—universal and unspoken—that they were engaged in something much bigger than themselves. It would be a new feeling for some, a long-forgotten feeling for others, and now they all labored under its weight. A combined load of importance and uncertainty.

The future was coming, but who it belonged to was anyone's guess.

CHAPTER 43

Ishmael cast away the tarps, and the wind pulled them flapping and twisting into the moonless Junkyard night. Exposed, the crew gazed out at the Heap as it flashed, popped, and burned with a battle that traced the city's edges in combat—a twinkling chandelier of mayhem. The airship drifted around the northern border, searchlights probing the bomb and battle smoke tirelessly.

It would find them soon. They were counting on it.

Ishmael took the wheel of Virgil's jeep, unable to ride his bike with one arm, while Virgil and his parasite were stuffed into the passenger's seat. Gage occupied Diane's usual place in the trailer, tapping his fingers impatiently. They were waiting on Rok. She had disconnected the tank's EMP and fitted the power socket with a StormCell's outer halo, making the device compatible with any Conductor charging port. The bulky invention was tied to Diane's back with some towing cable, and Rok was now wrapping the Grave Walker's limbs and chest with electromagnetic-shielding fabric.

"This should help deflect the EMP blast," she told Diane. "If the suit goes down, don't panic. The more you struggle, the quicker you'll suffocate."

When she began stapling the seams a second time, Gage shouted, "It looks fine! We gotta move!"

Rok forced herself to lower the staple gun. "You know what to do?"

Diane nodded. "Seems easy enough."

"We'll keep the airship distracted," Rok said, climbing up onto the tank. "Be careful. Be quick."

"I don't blame you," Diane called.

Rok froze halfway down the cupola hatch.

"I know how Virgil can be, and this"—Diane raised the black box on the Grave Walker's right arm—"this wasn't your call."

The mechanic looked away from Diane, turning her face toward the jeep, and Ishmael could now see the tears running down her cheeks.

"If you die on me," Rok said, "I'm gonna be really pissed."

"Same goes for you," Diane replied.

The Grave Walker left then, marching north for the outer barricade, passing through a ribbon of fire like it was nothing. Ishmael watched Diane go until the smoke swallowed her from view.

"She will be okay," Ishmael called to Rok. "I know she will."

The mechanic gave him a thankful nod, wiped her eyes, then ducked down and closed the cupola hatch above her.

"*Ready to make some noise?*" she radioed.

Gage leaned into the jeep and grabbed the CB mic. "*Whose side should we take?*"

Rok thought for a moment, then said, "*I always liked the Oxen.*"

"*Oxen it is,*" Gage said. He hung up the radio, winked at Virgil's unconscious body, then took his position back in the trailer.

Ishmael led the drive into the Outer Rim, and it didn't take him long to find some action. The skirmish between the Oxen and Fire-Fighters had spilled over the wall, expanding messily in all directions. The Oxen had better artillery, but only a small percentage of their ranks had joined Major Bishop's coup. The FireFighters had superior numbers, and guerrilla battles like this were their specialty. Meanwhile, the local townies hunkered down in their tents and shanty huts, praying the madness would steer clear of their streets. They prayed to whatever idiot god controlled their fates, and they held their families close.

As the crew weaved up a road blighted with tiny wildfires, Ishmael pointed out a trio of FireFighters standing atop a fuel tanker, their flame-throwers hooked to the truck by custom hoses, pinning an Oxen squad behind cover with an endless stream of heat.

"*Stay clear!*" Rok lobbed a plasma blast at the tanker, and a dazzling explosion ripped the truck and its occupants to burning pieces. They never knew what hit them. Confused, the Oxen troops ventured out from behind cover. A small FireFighter mob was engaged in random acts of arson on some nearby tents, but at the sight of their opponents, they gathered their weapons and charged.

Gage leaped off the trailer and met the FireFighters with forearm blades drawn. His skin grafts were fireproof, so there was nothing to stop him from cutting the nearest mercenaries down at lightning speed. One of the FireFighters had the foresight to lob an ion grenade, only to watch the cyborg catch it in midair and toss it back. The last of the arsonists died a fiery death, and the Oxen squad barely had to lift a finger.

"When people ask," Ishmael heard Gage shout to the bewildered Oxen, "Gage 4-D-5 saved your life, and he looked damn good doing it!"

While Gage was busy on the ground, Rok and Ishmael drove on. They barreled down nearby avenues, causing as much damage against the FireFighters as they could muster. In the jeep's front seat, Virgil's head shook and swayed with every bump in the road, as if he were laughing hysterically at the havoc he had indirectly caused.

It wasn't long before the rumbling of motors announced two pick-ups and a motorcycle on their tail. Looking back, Ishmael could see that their pursuers all wore bloody bandages around their heads. Each pickup carried two gunmen, one in the truck bed and another in the front seat, both armed with semiauto plasma rifles. The soldier riding pillion on the motorcycle brandished an ion rocket launcher

"*Split up!*" Rok ordered over the radio.

Ishmael veered right down a narrow road, while Rok kept going forward. While the motorcycle pursued the tank, easily dodging Rok's cannon fire, the two pickup trucks set their sights on the jeep. Ishmael bobbed and weaved through smoky streets, taking about as much plasma fire as he dodged. Whenever he shook one pickup off his tail, the other was waiting to test the jeep's armor, denting the vehicle with heavy blasts of concentrated energy.

When it became clear that escape was impossible, Ishmael focused on keeping the trucks behind him or to his left. No matter what happened, he couldn't let them hit Virgil in the front seat. That was the job. No matter what, he had to keep this manipulative, half-dead *jefe* alive.

As the chase skimmed the edge of the outer barricade, a bandaged argonaut leaped down from one of the sentry posts. Its ocular lens strobed as it flailed its arms, making the worst shrieking noise Ishmael had ever heard. Something was very wrong with this Peacekeeper, a fact made even clearer when it ran at one of the pickup trucks at full speed. The front bumper made scrap metal of the argonaut's head, but the impact shattered an axle, forcing the pickup to slow.

Gage was on them instantly.

Through his rearview mirror, Ishmael watched the cyborg dash up to the enemy truck's passenger window, slice off a shooter's arm, and then catch the falling rifle in midair. All of this happened in the span of two seconds, with enough time left for Gage to pop the driver with a well-aimed plasma shot. The pickup crashed into the outer barricade, and the second gunman tumbled off the bed, breaking his back upon landing. Dead, dead, and dead.

Now armed and twice as dangerous, Gage jumped back into the jeep's trailer, kneeled, and fired at the other truck. The driver took a shot to the face. He crashed his team into a cluster of burning tents. The flames devoured them instantly.

From a few streets over, Ishmael could see that Rok wasn't getting so lucky. A rocket had made contact with her tank's storage compartment, and now the junk she had scavenged from the underground shelter was up in flames, trickling a burned plastic smell into the air. Ishmael mashed the jeep's pedal to the floor, but he would never reach Rok in time. The motorcycle was right behind her. The bandaged soldier riding pillion had a perfect shot at the tank's tires; a light pull of the trigger was all it would take to end the chase then and there.

Ishmael held his breath, waiting for Rok's horrible end—when the tank heaved to a sudden halt.

The motorcycle was too close to break or swerve in time; the driver could only scream as he smacked headfirst into his target. His face left a macabre smear on the tank's armor, and the bike flipped upward in sequence of dizzying flips. The other soldier catapulted over the tank, landing on the road a foot or so ahead of it.

Rok hit the accelerator, and the tank made a blood-and-guts pulp out of the soldier's torso. *Splat.*

The motorcycle crashed down by the outer barricade, mauled and useless. Rok's tank was scuffed, smoking, but otherwise the victor.

Gage cheered at the top of his lungs. "Rok, you absolute *freak*!"

Even Ishmael cracked a smile. He hadn't smiled in at least a decade.

"*Come on,*" Rok radioed. "*Let's keep—*"

Without warning, a laser struck the Outer Rim.

It came from the sky, and it was so dense and powerful that it seared a block of huts off the face of the Earth. A yard to the left, and it would've hit the jeep.

"Well, shit," Gage moaned.

All eyes looked up, and they were met with a blinding spotlight. The airship had arrived.

CHAPTER 44

Diane passed through a slender gap in the outer barrier, making sure not to bang the EMP on her back against the jagged concrete edges. On her way through the Outer Rim, she had hoped that all the fighting there meant the battle was moving outward and the leg of her journey through the Inner Ring would be easier. Unfortunately, the battle hadn't moved an inch. It had merely *grown*, and the levels of violence in the two districts were now indistinguishable.

At the very least, the conflict in the Outer Rim had been clear to Diane. Oxen versus FireFighters. The soldiers in blue armor versus the freaks with flamethrowers. The battle out there was organized into a neat us-against-them package, and if nothing else, it made it easy for a bystander to know where everyone stood.

But deeper within the Heap, she quickly discovered a different scene. In a disturbing reversal from the norm, the Inner Ring was in complete and utter turmoil.

The Aardwolves had retaken the city center, but their grip was flimsy at best. Bandaged soldiers under the Arm's lingering influence still fought tooth and nail to push the enemy out, while the Modified mercenaries who had taken the Messenger's side were now infected with notions of grandeur. Why couldn't they be in charge of the Heap? Why couldn't the future belong to them? The result was a nebulous skirmish between Aardwolf and the

Bandaged, Aardwolf and the Modified, the Bandaged and the Modified, the Modified and the loyal Modified out to punish the traitors in their ranks.

It was a free-for-all.

Then there were the Peacekeepers. Something terrible had happened when Virgil disconnected the Messenger from the Arm. The harmonious signal that united the bandaged argonauts and reapers—giving them a sense of purpose they hadn't known since the Grand Finale—had gone silent, and now they were all alone again. Shrieking, they ran through the streets, firing and slashing at anyone who crossed their paths—even each other. Diane wondered if Peacekeepers went berserk because they wanted to be shot down. Maybe this was the closest their programming allowed to an act of suicide.

On the bright side, this absolute chaos presented the ideal setting for a Grave Walker to sneak through the city unnoticed, and that's exactly what Diane did.

Running as fast as the device on her back would allow, ducking and weaving past countless fights to the death, Diane understood Virgil's fear of war better than ever. She could not have asked for a better re-creation of the Grand Finale's horror. All around her, humans, machines, and everything in between annihilated each other for reasons very few of them truly understood. And where were the townies? The lucky ones were hiding in fear, hoping their flimsy shelters wouldn't collapse on top of them. Diane could hear them speaking as she passed the ramshackle buildings—sharp cries and hushed tones, amplified in the Grave Walker's helmet:

"Why is this happening?"

"Let me go! She's still out there!"

"Oh my god . . . Oh my god . . ."

"Don't let them in, Daddy. Please don't let them get me."

"Wake up. No, no, don't do this. Don't leave me alone."

The lucky ones lived in fear. The unlucky were dead in the streets.

This was war. The Messenger had brought it back to life. Diane would see it killed again.

She made it to the fortress, or what was left of it. The collapsed smokestacks had destroyed large portions of the structure, but the Conductor spire remained standing. That was all Diane needed to move forward.

She passed through a freshly torn gap in the inner wall, only to find the fortress entryway congested with gunfire. The Grave Walker might have survived that route, but the EMP device would be wrecked for sure. Stifling panic, Diane jogged around the fortress in search of another way inside.

Her pleas were answered when she found a large storm drain with the cover sliced open. Great chunks of rubble blocked the passageway, but the Grave Walker pushed them aside with ease.

As soon as she did this, Diane found two Deckard plasma pistols aimed at her visor.

It was Leon, free at last from the cave-in. Swollen bruises covered his face; his bionic right foot hung uselessly by a few strands of wire. He looked shocked to see Diane, who was just as startled by the sight of him. For a few seconds, neither of them moved or spoke. Neither was quite sure what to make of the other.

Finally, Diane nodded at the pistols. "I don't think those can hurt me."

"You'd be surprised," Leon said. He began to limp around the Grave Walker, keeping his pistols trained on her head. Diane shifted to face him, but she made no effort to prevent the escape. She had no reason to.

"What's that for?" Leon asked, noticing the EMP device.

"I'm taking down the airship," Diane said.

"For Virgil?" Leon spat blood onto the tunnel floor.

"For me," Diane replied.

The company man stopped moving, and he stared at Diane for what felt like ages. Then he smirked, twirling his pistols once before dropping them into their holsters.

"Good for you—"

He began to leave, but then his whole body went stiff. His fingers contorted. His mouth dropped open, and the voice of a certain corporate mogul came crackling out.

"I just love your initiative!" Ms. Violet exclaimed. "Glad *someone* is putting my Grave Walker to good use."

Diane stepped back, startled by the puppet routine. She could see pain in Leon's human eye. This was hurting him.

"I can't wait for us to work together," Ms. Violet said.

"I don't think that'd be a good idea," Diane replied.

The voice from Jericho chuckled lightly. "Darling, I didn't ask."

Leon gasped as his body became his own again. He looked to Diane like he had something to say, something important, but he didn't speak another word. He limped out of the tunnel and vanished in the haze of smoke, leaving Diane to wonder if she would ever see him again. She hoped not, for both their sakes.

The sewers beneath the fortress were a crumbling mess, and it wasn't long before Diane found a hole in the ceiling big enough to climb through. Struggling to her feet, wobbling to keep her balance with the EMP's added weight, she found herself in the middle of some kind of factory floor. Townies lined the conveyor belts, loading burlap sacks with capsules of fresh Battery. Looters, hard at work.

"Excuse me?" Diane called.

The townies froze, caught in the act.

"Which way to the Conductor?"

Relieved, all fingers pointed to a nearby stairwell. Diane followed their collective guidance, climbing the stairs, sprinting through a maze of industrial halls until she came to a jagged opening where a door should have been. She passed through into a large, dome-shaped room: the Conductor plant.

A previously unseen fraction of the spire ran from ceiling to floor, haloed by some cross between a nuclear reactor and a hadron collider. The spire's base was pocked with circular charging ports, many of which were occupied. Tier-one, tier-two, and even a few tier-three StormCells lay dull in their slots, waiting for a surge.

Diane pulled the EMP emitter off her back, popped the modified plug into one of the open ports, stood back, and braced for the next bolt of lightning. When it came, the gloomy shadows of the forgotten dome gave way to electric blue. Sparks filled the air, and the EMP emitter flickered, whined . . . then died.

There was nothing more.

CHAPTER 45

"Something's wrong!" Gage shouted.

Ishmael had been watching the Conductor spire when lightning struck, along with the whole crew, but nothing had changed. Enemy vehicles were still pouring into town, their engines and weapons firing at full capacity. The airship was still hovering overhead, raining lasers with ever-increasing accuracy. The crew was outnumbered and outgunned in every respect.

"*We cannot keep this up!*" Ishmael radioed, ramming a four-wheeler off the road.

"*Diane needs more time!*" Rok replied, dropping flares that burned the tires chasing her down.

"*Time?*" Gage hollered back from the trailer. "*Tell her we're fresh out!*"

Something strange pulled Ishmael's attention to the rearview mirror. Gage's plasma rifle had launched abruptly out of his hand, as if the weapon had a mind of its own. The cyborg immediately drew his forearm blades and swiped outward with an X formation. A cloaking device warbled away, revealing a Ker perched on the trailer's edge. Ishmael knew all about the Heap's mechanized mercenary clan. Unlike the argonauts and reapers, this Peacekeeper would have the intelligence to understand what had happened to the Arm and the ambition to predict what would happen if it got the Arm back.

Gage moaned. "Great."

With his one good hand on the steering wheel, Ishmael could only aid Gage by keeping the trailer steady. The assassin droid struck out with its energy dagger, and the old waltz of death began anew. With Gage fighting for his life, there was no one to lay suppressing fire on the soldiers in pursuit. They shot at the jeep unhindered, and eventually, one of those shots hit Gage square in the knee. He collapsed into the trailer bed.

"No!" Ishmael cried.

The Ker ignored him, reeled back for a killing strike—

"Stop," a voice called.

The Ker obeyed, and when it looked to its new master, a sequence of Volt Caster snaps blew its head away.

Gage and Ishmael turned to find Virgil leaning over the jeep's front seat. The life-form wrapped around his belly was shining brightly, and his irises had turned jet black.

"We can't go back to him," Virgil said, voice layered with something else's. "He corrupts the message. His way is not ours."

Virgil grabbed the radio mic from Ishmael, who was too awestruck to notice. "*Shoot when they do*," Virgil said, pointing toward the airship.

"*Virgil?*" Rok's voice crackled back. "*How are you—?*"

"*They have to open the gravity shield before they can fire,*" Virgil said. "*Shoot when they do.*"

"*How do you know that?*" Rok asked.

"*Shoot first!*" Virgil yelled, sounding more like himself. "*Questions later!*"

The airship was right above them now, its laser cannon aimed straight down. Every cell in Ishmael's being wanted them to drive away, to get out of the blast zone while they still could.

Radiation swirled around the cannon's muzzle. The laser was getting ready to fire.

Rok aimed her own ion cannon upward. A red light twinkled on the airship deck.

Rok fired an ion cluster. The projectile passed through an invisible hole in the invisible shield and struck the laser cannon, backfiring all that pent-up radiation, blowing a decent chunk out of the airship's deck. Everyone on the ground watched the debris swirling in the gravity field, unable to escape its grasp.

"Great *shot!*" Virgil hollered.

Relief and triumph permeated the crew. The airship had a weakness, and if it tried to fire on them again, they'd be able to dish the pain right back.

The problem was, the airship didn't fire again.

As the nodes on the hull blinked in a seizure-inducing light show, the smaller vehicles below—the motorbikes and the four-wheelers—lifted off the ground. Their drivers tried to jump away, but jumping only sent them floating higher. The speed of their ascent quickened, and soon, anyone not anchored down was flying up toward the airship. Virgil's jeep and Rok's tank were caught next, and no amount of horsepower would free them from the Core's invisible grip. Even lightning got caught in the phenomenon, outlining a transparent globe that spun out of control around the stationary airship.

The ship was the eye of a gravity storm, one that would not cease until it had ripped its enemies apart.

"This is worse!" Gage yelled to Virgil. He was hanging on to the jeep's back windshield. The trailer, along with most nearby tents, had been sucked into the gravity storm's pull. "This is so much worse!"

Virgil shouted to the drivers. "*Get the hell away from it!*"

The jeep's back wheels lifted off the road, and though Rok's tank was still too heavy to rise, she could not move forward. There was no escaping gravity.

CHAPTER 46

Diane stared at the EMP emitter sitting dark in the charging port, and she truly knew what it meant to feel helpless. She could not check the device interior; the Grave Walker's hands were not built for such fine motor skills. She stood there alone, surrounded by destruction and failure, and she wished for death. She wished that *Cradle* had taken her life along with everyone else's; then she wouldn't have lived to bring her new crewmates to their doom. Her power meter was still halfway full, so she would have a long time to think on her defeat. Plenty of time to dwell on how she came to a place like the Junkyard and somehow made everything worse.

Another lightning strike hit, but Diane wasn't focused on the emitter this time. She let her visor wander the dome, *reading the room*, and that's how she noticed the smoke leaking out from behind a dented wall panel. When the sparks from the energy intake died, the smoke died with it.

Diane ripped the lead panel away, revealing an insulated wire cut into sparking halves. Considering all the destruction around her, it was amazing that a broken cord was the only substantial piece of damage.

Thunder boomed overhead. A third lightning strike might be on its way.

Diane got another dumb idea, one that made her plan to jump off a hill seem levelheaded by comparison. She checked the dome around her one last time, searching for any possible alternatives. She found none.

"Peace demands sacrifice," Diane whispered, and she grabbed both ends of the broken wire. She held them together in her hands, mending the severed cable as long as she held on tight.

Lightning struck again. Electricity shot through the wire and made its way to the charging port, but it also passed through the Grave Walker along the way.

Could she call it pain? Did that word even begin to describe the affliction boiling her brain cells, reducing every nerve to cinders? The HUD went red with exploding pixels, and Diane saw things that could not be. She became one with her image of the Firelands, she and all the dead space colonists, all five hundred and one. Ben Five-Zero-Nine. Jessica Three-Three-Two. The Caretaker. Diane herself. They stood together in fiery solidarity, burning eternally for what the world did to them, for what they did to the world.

Everything, inside Diane and out, was on fire.

Then the EMP emitter filled the dome with light, and all pain stopped. Everything stopped.

And from deep in the sunken darkness of her suit, Diane heard something massive crashing back to Earth.

CHAPTER 47

Virgil wobbled to his feet, hunched over like he had the worst bellyache imaginable. The bioluminescent life-form, now dimmed to a pale yellow, still clung to his body. Nearby, Rok kicked open the cupola hatch and crawled out from the tank, which laid tottering on its side. Scraped and bleeding, she pulled herself across the road to Gage's limp body—deactivated except for his mouth.

"Your EMP thing worked," Gage said, coughing.

"I guess so," Rok said.

They were on a narrow street going nowhere. The southbound route was blocked with rubble from the airship's crash, as well as the airship itself. The way north went straight to the outer barricade, and all the alleys were dead ends. Ishmael sat propped against the upside-down jeep, his sling missing and broken arm dangling. The bandaged soldiers around them were all dead, or close to it.

"Everyone okay?" Virgil called.

The crewmates groaned as one. *Okay* was pushing it, but at least they were still alive.

Unfortunately, they weren't the only ones.

Everyone heard a body sliding off the airship's canted deck. They heard feet hit the road, followed by the *tink* of a blade striking asphalt.

"By the glory of the Deep," Ishmael whispered.

"Oh my god," Rok said.

"What?" Gage asked, his eyes powered off. "What is it?"

Virgil was speechless.

Diane had been wrong to assume that Dr. Isaac had taken control of the Messenger's army. She had overestimated the zeal of one man and greatly underestimated the tenacity of another.

The Messenger limped toward the crew, alive but no better for it. The pectoral and deltoid muscles on his left side had begun to atrophy, shriveling back to their original mass. His arm stump had been cauterized, and the battle staff had been repurposed as a walking stick. He was a shadow of his former self, but that shadow was long. The bulk of his body still rippled with muscles. Among the wounded, the Messenger was as dangerous as ever.

"Give . . . it . . . *back!*" the Messenger shouted.

"Oh," Gage said, "this guy again."

"It's mine!" the Messenger said, never breaking stride. "*Mine!*"

Ishmael reached for the Messenger's leg as he passed, but a cold-blooded kick to the head knocked the tattooed junkie right out of commission.

Virgil considered his options. His knife was gone, he was out of magnum rounds, and his Volt Caster—shut off by the EMP blast—was little more than a bludgeon. Also, the whispers in his head were begging him to keep away.

Keep away! Don't let him take us back!

It was hard to think with all that noise. Virgil decided he could do without it.

He grabbed the life-form's tangled mass and pulled. The strings didn't fight. They slipped out of his stomach, leaving behind a wound that was now mostly scar tissue, and Virgil's eyes faded back to normal.

He tossed the life-form to Rok, who shrieked as it landed in her arms. She tried to let it drop, but its tendrils clung to her jumpsuit.

"Get it out of here!" Virgil said.

Rok stared back at him, stricken dumb with fear.

"*Go!*" Virgil cried.

With that, Virgil ran at the Messenger, Volt Caster swinging. He knocked the Messenger's battle staff away, but as the weight of his glove made Virgil stagger, the Masked Man grabbed the back of his neck and slammed Virgil's forehead into a rising knee. Blood poured into Virgil's eyes, and he could barely see his opponent as the Messenger grabbed his throat and held their faces close.

"The future . . . belongs . . . to me," the Messenger panted.

"*Chinga tu madre*," Virgil spat back.

The Messenger slammed his masked face into Virgil's face. The tanned human skin ripped away, leaving the argonaut faceplate to knock the junkie's brain against his skull. The Messenger released his grip, and Virgil crumpled to the ground.

Rok had darted past the men during their skirmish, and she was now trying to rip the planks off a hut window. Seeing double, Virgil watched two Roks struggle with the boards as two Messengers approached.

"You can't steal my destiny," the Messenger called.

Rok pulled harder at the planks, to no avail.

"It calls to me," he said. "Not you. *Me*."

Virgil noticed the electrodes on his Volt Caster sparkling back to life. If only he possessed the cognitive clarity to snap his fingers.

Rok pulled and pulled, but she wasn't making progress. The Messenger was only getting closer.

Virgil's breath caught in his throat. *Not like this. It can't end like this.*

"Give it back to me—!" the Messenger began to shout, but then something large and metallic groaned behind them. Those who could still move their heads looked north.

The Grave Walker sprang over the outer barricade.

With a queen centipede's fury, it ran at the Messenger with one objective. As it closed the distance, the Messenger held up his hand in feeble defense, but it did nothing to stop the charge. He was powerless to stop Diane from bringing her fist down onto his collarbone.

Virgil heard a gut-wrenching *crack* as the Messenger collapsed, neck broken, staring up at the suit's merciless visor.

"*Leave us alone*!" Diane shrieked.

Howling mad, she punched the Messenger in the face. Then she punched him again, and again, over and over, beating flesh, metal, and bone into a pulpy soup. Then she kept punching. If left unchecked, Virgil imagined that she would punch the Messenger one time for every space colonist who had perished on *Cradle*. From Block One to Six, a punch for every death, and an extra punch for herself.

"Diane, stop!" Virgil shouted, rising onto his elbows.

The Grave Walker did not stop. It was running on pure hate, and Diane had so many punches to go.

"Diane, he's done!"

Punch. Scream. Punch. Scream. Punch—

"*It's over!*"

Diane stopped in midswing, and she finally saw the mess she had made. Or lack of a mess, rather. There was nothing left of the Messenger's head. No mask, no skin, not even teeth. Just blood and empty space.

The suit trembled, and Diane fell onto her back. Virgil crawled over to her as fast as he could, but he found nothing wrong with the Grave Walker itself. Its collapse was just another manifestation of the user's subconscious.

Right now, that user was sobbing her eyes out.

"It's okay," Virgil cooed. "It's over. It's done. Breathe, kid. Just breathe."

CHAPTER 48

Eventually, the junkie's words and the suit's cardiac regulator mellowed Diane.

She lay there whimpering, Virgil on one side, the Messenger's headless and armless remains on the other. She couldn't see much beyond all the smoke and dust, but she looked to the sky anyway. She looked east, and she imagined seeing the last trace of unimpeded sky from *Cradle's* descent. She saw the last trickle of starlight, and then storm clouds finally converged, sealing the heavens away forever.

What's done was done, and there would be no going back.

CHAPTER 49

For the first time in recent memory, ancient memory, or anyone's memory, Caravan came to an unscheduled stop.

The mighty treads grated as they ceased rotation. The coupling bridge compressed as the rear cart bumped into the front. Diane imagined a cacophony of mugs flying off counters, billiard balls tumbling off pool tables, passengers slipping off their feet or out of their seats. The surrounding escort vehicles halted as well, and the drivers aimed their rifles at the strange new obstacle in Caravan's path. Nervous shouts passed between them, frantic calls for orders, for answers: *What do we do? What the hell is that thing?*

The airship hovered above the road, just ahead of where Caravan ground to a stop, all bashed and beaten, but still flying. Virgil leaned over the gunwale, flapping a tattered cloth in a gesture of truce. Diane assumed this was the only reason Caravan hadn't fired at them on sight.

"Will they be angry at us for making them stop?" she asked.

Virgil dropped his makeshift flag. "Do we care?"

Diane shrugged. Point taken.

Eventually, a hatch on Caravan's front cart swung open, and a squad of high-ranking guards emerged to investigate the disturbance. Duke stumbled after them, never one to be kept out of the loop.

"Virgil!" he called up. "What'n the hell's going on?"

Rok pressed a button on the ship's navigation console; an automatic gangway slid down to the road. Virgil wrapped Ishmael's good arm around his neck, and together they staggered off to greet Caravan's representatives. The tattooed junkie leaned on the elder for support, his face telegraphing the pain of every movement. Bruised and bloody, Virgil only looked better off by a slim margin.

"Get this man fixed up," Virgil called to the guards, "and two months' lodging. Bill it to J-Five-Eight-Zero."

Hearing that magical account number, the guards went to Ishmael's side.

"The deal was one month," Ishmael said, confused.

Virgil winked with his unblackened eye. "You earned a second."

The guards shifted Ishmael's weight onto their shoulders.

"Thank you," he said.

"Better days," Virgil replied.

While the guards took the Heretic inside, Duke reunited with his oldest client. "What . . . the . . . fuck?"

"What?" Virgil said. "I'm a generous guy."

"Not him." Duke pointed at the airship. "*That.*"

From on high, Diane watched Virgil drink in the sight of his unexpected prize. Once the EMP wore off, the crew had learned that the airship was still flyable, and the diplomat head serving as pilot no longer recognized allegiances. Good thing, because the gravity storm had wrecked all of their vehicles, and no one felt much like walking. Nor did they want to contend with any vengeful mercenaries. The Oxen would have questions for Virgil when they realized the Fire-Fighters had not conspired against them. Best to get out while the getting was good.

"Yeah, things got a little wild," Virgil said, "but everything worked out. Everything always does."

"You delivering this to Violet?" Duke asked.

Between defeating the Messenger and everything else, Diane had almost forgotten about Ms. Violet. She wouldn't be happy with Virgil's choice to abandon Leon, withhold the Arm, and render their contract moot. The bridge between them was officially burned, and Virgil could kiss the idea of peddling his wares on the streets of Jericho goodbye.

But he didn't seem too broken up about it.

"I'm off the Wellington gigs," Virgil decided. "Indefinitely."

Duke popped a downer from the pill bottle in his breast pocket. "She'll make a dangerous enemy, man."

"She can get in line," Virgil said.

"Where's that line start?" Gage stomped down the gangway, looking as angry as he could manage. "We had a deal, asshole."

"I gave you the lima beans," Virgil protested.

"Screw your shitty beans!" Gage said. "You told me I could take on the Messenger! I never even got close!"

"Says who?" Diane cut in. She chucked the Messenger's battle staff down to Gage, impaling the asphalt at his feet. The diplomat's creepy mask was tied to one of the blades.

"Tell people whatever you want," she said. "They're your trophies. Your street cred."

The cyborg was almost at a loss for words. *Almost.* He pointed the staff at Diane, grinning ear to bionic ear. "I like you."

Then Gage lifted the battle staff and swung the blade toward Virgil, forcing him to step away. "Don't know about you," he said, then he pointed back to Diane, "but I definitely like *you.*"

Gage skipped off toward Caravan, twirling the staff like a baton. "Break out the vodka!"

From the airship deck, Diane and Rok watched on with matching amusement. "You have *no* idea what you've done," Rok said.

Diane giggled, and Rok set off down the gangway with the headless Ker droid from their battle slung over one shoulder.

"Sorry about your tank," Virgil said as she came by.

"Eh, I'll get someone to tow it," Rok said without stopping. "I can do a lot once I cash in this Ker cloaking device." She looked back over her shoulder. "We're even?"

"Square," Virgil confirmed.

Rok left it at that, and when she caught up with Gage at the Caravan entrance, the cyborg flipped the dead Ker his middle finger. "Invisible prick," he sneered.

Shaking his head, Virgil walked back up the gangway. "Keep an eye on the market," he told Duke. "When the Heap settles, things should get back to normal."

"You out already?" Duke asked.

"Yessir," Virgil said. "Got places to be."

Duke allowed himself one last ogle at the airship. "See you around, I guess."

Virgil tossed him a thumbs-up. He passed Diane on his way to the navigation console.

"This thing's gonna cut our travel time down to nothin'," he sang.

Diane lingered by the gangway. "Um, Virgil—?"

"And we got not one, not two, but *three* juiced-up tier-five Storm-Cells! They'll heat the greenhouses for a decade."

Diane couldn't believe it. Even after all the detours their trip had taken, Virgil had gotten exactly what he wanted all along. Everyone on the crew had. Everyone except her.

"That's amazing," she said, and she meant it.

While inputting the coordinates home, Virgil cast a brief but noticeable glance at the deck floor. He had wrapped the artificial symbiotic life-form in a blanket, then wrapped the blanket in barbed wire, but he and Diane could still see the technicolor light pulsing under the fabric.

There had been some initial debate about what to do with the Arm. The crew had unanimously called for its destruction, but the creature proved more durable than anyone expected. Fire, plasma, even ion blasts failed to make a dent. There were talks of burying the life-form or tossing it in the ocean, but these all left a risk of rediscovery. Any poor soul could stumble on the life-form by accident, and then the Junkyard would have another Messenger on its hands. Eventually, Virgil had *volunteered* to take the Arm someplace beyond the Junkyard's borders, where no wandering junkie could ever find it. The others hadn't been quick to trust him with such a task, but after he divided his entire remaining collection of seeds between them, they ultimately let it go.

Now, Virgil toed the life-form with his boot, pushing it out of sight. Diane suspected that he wouldn't talk about his experience bonding with the creature, no matter how often she asked.

"Our gene jockeys back on the mountain are gonna have a ball looking at this thing," he said, straining to sound casual. "It's got healing properties. We can use that."

Diane didn't move from the gangway. "Virgil . . ."

"Get off the ramp thingy. I gotta pull it up—"

"I'm not going with you."

Virgil's fingers turned to stone on the keyboard.

"I'm staying on Caravan," Diane said. "At least for now."

Virgil couldn't seem to wrap his head around it. Choosing the Junkyard over the mountain? A foreign concept, spoken in a foreign language. "What are you . . . What?"

Diane stared at her feet. "I've been talking to Rok. She connected with a cybersmith back in the Heap. She's gonna get some training."

Virgil looked to Caravan, where he found Rok and Duke both hanging by the door. Duke was waiting to wave goodbye. Rok was waiting to show Diane inside.

"And if she keeps studying the Grave Walker," Diane said, "she might be able to get me out. With Dr. Isaac missing, Rok's my best bet now."

Diane knew her decision wouldn't be easy for Virgil to swallow. Opening the Grave Walker had been his first promise, and it was now the one thing he couldn't provide. After escaping the Heap, whenever their crewmates were out of earshot, Virgil had talked incessantly about the mountain. All the wonderful things he would show Diane. How happy she would be living among his people. These promises were his last opportunity to make things right between them. All of his lies, all the grief he had caused her, all would be made right if he delivered Diane to the safest place on Earth. He seemed to need that closure more than she did. It was a new dynamic, and Virgil clearly wasn't a fan.

"I can take you away from all this," he said, almost pleading. "No more shooting. No explosions. I can take you home."

Diane shook the Grave Walker's head. "It's your home. All I've ever done is go where people tell me to go. I want to find my own way. I want to choose who I'm with, and if I make a home . . . I want to be able to feel it." When she looked up, her visor was bright with passion. Her journey wasn't over. "I want to feel things again."

Virgil returned to Diane's side of the ship. The sun was on its way up, stretching shadows, lighting the polluted sky in a way that reminded them both of the Firelands. Diane was no stranger to losing the people she cared about, but all her losses up to now had been sudden, jarring, and immediate. She was new to formal goodbyes, and she wondered if they all stung as bad as this one.

"What you gave up to help me," Virgil said, "and to help the people I care about . . . I can't thank you enough."

Diane smiled inside her helmet. "I guess you owe me one."

Virgil cackled. "Guess I do."

It wasn't easy for Diane to go down the gangway. Virgil's scarred and shadowy mug was the first one she had ever seen on Earth, and though her life had been a mess from the moment she escaped the pod, it was Virgil who had freed her to begin with. She was alive now because of him, and she decided that meant something. It always would.

As Diane walked the long walk back to Caravan, Virgil leaned precariously over the gunwale again. He had gone from melancholy to manic in his usual breakneck way, and he shouted at Duke with laughter in his voice. "She's on my tab! Good kid! Look out for her!"

Duke waved in confirmation, and Virgil screamed his last order of business to Diane.

"And if you change your mind," he said, "or you want to swing by, you know the way! ¡*Mi casa es tu casa*!"

Virgil's map was still minimized at the edge of Diane's HUD. A constant reminder that whatever happened next, however things developed with Rok and the Grave Walker, Diane had a place to go. If she wanted safety, she could have it.

The gangway slid up and out of sight, and the airship took to the sky. The CB radio on deck blasted Junkie FM at full volume, treating the storm clouds to a psychedelic rock song. Thrusters blazing, the airship sailed north, and no one on the ground had the slightest clue where it was going.

No one, except Diane.

ACKNOWLEDGMENTS

The path to publication is a long and difficult one, but we do not travel it alone. There are guides along the road—a network of helping hands willing to point lost travelers in the right direction. These guides often go unacknowledged, so it feels all the more important that we recognize their contributions here and now. This book would not exist without them.

Our road began with Keyshawn Garraway, a friend and fellow writer who helped us gain an audience with the right people simply because he could. In this instance, "right people" came in the form of Emily Teera, a passionate creative who went beyond our wildest hopes and forwarded our work to the best talent agency in the world. Arian Akbar met us at the door; were it not for his vote of confidence, we never would've connected with our agent, Abigail Walters. Abby's a goddamn superhero. We didn't know if we could write a book, and we definitely weren't sure if it would be worth publishing. Abby's support gave us the bravery we needed to take a chance on ourselves. For that, we can never thank her enough.

We also want to thank Daniel Ehrenhaft and the amazing team at Blackstone Publishing for championing our vision and using their un-rivaled expertise to help make it stronger; Thomas Lang for gracing our earliest draft with thoughtful feedback and enthusiasm; Lisa VanDyke Brown for her invaluable help with the Spanish; and Erin Walsh for her much-needed encouragement, and for commissioning the world's first *Battery Life*–themed cake.

Additional thanks to Gregory's mother, Doris, and Brennan's parents, Mike and Kelly, for supporting our creative endeavors long before they made any sense. We love you deeply.